Praise for *Tidewater Murder*

In C. Hope Clark's novel, TIDEWATER MURDER, Carolina Slade establishes herself as a new genre superstar, taking her place beside Dave Robicheux and Harry Bosch. Well-written and informative about a little-known arm of law enforcement, Clark has written a story that carries the reader along as surely as the tides of the lowcountry. Don't miss this one!
—*Carl T. Smith, Author of* A Season For Killing *and* Lowcountry Boil

Riveting. A first-rate mystery and a real education. C. Hope Clark continues her series following Carolina Slade, an agriculture investigator, in Tidewater Murder. All I can say is if all government employees had Slade's get-the-job-done tenacity, I wouldn't mind paying taxes.
—*Donnell Ann Bell, Bestselling Author of* The Past Came Hunting *and* Deadly Recall

Terrific. Smart, knowing, clever…and completely original. A taut, high-tension page-turned—in a unique and fascinating setting. An absolute winner!
—*Hank Phillippi Ryan, Agatha, Anthony and Macavity winning author*

High tension in the Lowcountry. Feds, farmers and foreigners collide in this coastal crime novel with as many twists and turns as a tidal estuary.
—*Janna McMahan, national bestselling author of* Anonymity *and* Calling Home

I want Carolina Slade to be my new best friend. Smart, loyal, tough but compassionate, she's the kind of person I want on my side if I'm in trouble. In her second outing, a missing tomato crop, dead bodies, and Gullah voodoo lead Slade into the dark heart of the new south, where the 21st century collides with the past and the outcome can be deadly. As a native South Carolinian, I thoroughly enjoyed revisiting my home state in this engrossing and unusual mystery, and I look forward to seeing more of Hope Clark's refreshing heroine.
—*Sandra Parshall, award-winning author of the* Rachel Goddard *mysteries*
http://www.sandraparshall.com

Other Bell Bridge Books Titles from C. Hope Clark

Lowcountry Bribe

Tidewater Murder

by

C. Hope Clark

Bell Bridge Books

Bell Bridge Books
PO BOX 300921
Memphis, TN 38130
Print ISBN: 978-1-61194-257-6

Bell Bridge Books is an Imprint of BelleBooks, Inc.

We at BelleBooks enjoy hearing from readers.
Visit our websites - www.BelleBooks.com and www.BellBridgeBooks.com.

10 9 8 7 6 5 4 3 2 1

Cover design: Debra Dixon
Interior design: Hank Smith
Photo credits:
Lighthouse photo (maniuplated) - © Pavelgr | Dreamstime.com

:Lmty:01:

Dedication

To my Uncompensated Executive Personal Assistant

Chapter 1

SAVANNAH CONROY was one of the sharpest rural loan managers the Department of Agriculture had: she slung attitude like paint on a canvas, wore sweaters like a Hollywood starlet, and managed an office like Steve Jobs. They'd built the Beaufort, South Carolina, office around her to harness that charisma, and then added two more counties to keep her busy.

Sitting in my soon-to-be-ex-apartment, I glared at the new permanent marker stain on my carpet as this Beaufort wonder now shrieked in my ear. My breakfast, a bowl of instant grits with no butter, sat like a rock in my gut. My empty twenty-two-foot rental truck sat outside my apartment, awaiting boxes I'd been packing for a week. Thunder rumbled. It started to rain.

Days didn't come any more thrilling than this.

I pulled the phone further from my ear. "Savvy," I said. "Chill. What's wrong with you?"

"Monroe's ransacking my files, Slade. He won't answer my questions when I ask what he's snooping for." She exhaled hard. "He's not listening to me."

"Dammit," I grumbled, sitting on the floor and dabbing at the marker stain with a paper towel. "Maybe you need to ask nice."

"Bite me," she replied.

The sky roiled with angry, gunmetal gray clouds. Trees arched. Wind whistled as it whipped around the building, warning me that Mother Nature ruled my moving day.

After our decade-old friendship, casual banter came easy between Savvy and me. We shared a camaraderie that never failed us, but when Savvy lost her cool, it was watch out world. "Aren't you being a tad bitchier than normal?" I asked. "What's Monroe there for anyway?"

"He *says* a routine audit."

"Okay, so it's an audit. You sail through those things. Plus, you drew Monroe, the nicest guy in the bunch."

"With the sharpest eye," she said. "That has to mean something."

I quit worrying about the carpet stain and stood, hand on a hip. "Hey, are you all right?"

"No. Want me to show *more bitchy* to convince you things aren't right?"

Monroe Prevatte was a loan director operating from an office down the hall from mine. He was one of headquarters' gurus when it came to audits, and another dear friend. I'd been on leave for my move, or I would've known about his mission.

"I *hate* tight-lipped people," Savvy said. "Hell, they audited me only six months ago."

This wasn't the Savvy I knew. Between loan season, my recent promotion, and the subsequent move to Columbia, we'd lost touch of late. Thanks to a calamity at my last duty station in Charleston, I'd demonstrated an ability to solve problems, to include nailing my boss, his boss, and a few scattered players in between. Thus, the promotion to headquarters. My frequent calls to Savvy had petered out over that time. Still, all it took was a regional meeting and we fell back in sync. Savvy, tall with her close-cropped curls and Cherokee cheekbones, and me, in my J.C. Penney coordinates. We'd reconnoitre at the nearest bar after some meeting let out to solve the world's dilemmas. And we thought we were damn good at it.

"Savvy, just be patient, and he'll be gone by Friday, when he'll brief you on all he found . . . or didn't find. You're over-thinking this. Might be a stupid hotline call, and you know those things are usually frivolous. Let him do his job and get out of your hair."

"He's a butt—"

"I'm hanging up now," I said.

"This sucks," she fumed.

"Goodbye." I disconnected. She'd settle down and call me later in a better mood, or I'd make a mental note to call her back after Monroe left and remind her how sour she'd been over nothing.

Lightning flashed a bright ghostly hue across the kitchen. My shoulders hunched up around my neck, and I instinctively covered my head. Thunder crackled, building a snap at a time until a sonic boom shook the windows. The lights flickered, then went out, leaving me in gray shadows.

My cell rang again. Heart still pounding, I scowled, expecting to hear more craziness from Savvy. "Is this the Wicked Witch of Beaufort?"

"Ms. Slade? This is Margaret Bellingham from St. Andrews Presbyterian Church. There's been an incident involving Zack."

Thunder rumbled again. The line spit static. "Hello? Hello?" My pulse raced as I switched the cell phone to my other ear. "Can you hear me? What kind of incident?"

"He's fine, Ms. Slade. He's just bruised, but he beat up our Jesus pretty good."

I stood, no longer interested in boxes and a carpet stain. "Excuse me?"

It was the last week in July, the hottest and wettest time of the year in South Carolina. I'd enrolled my preteen, ready-to-be-twenty daughter and

2

seven-year-old son in Vacation Bible School while I packed for our move from a temporary apartment to our newly built house.

The church administrator sighed, which I read as a sign I was too heathen to understand what she was talking about. Sure, I didn't attend services regularly. Okay, never. "So what happened?" I asked.

"During a skit," she continued. "Zack argued with the lead boy playing Jesus. Before we could reach them, they'd exchanged punches. We're sending both boys home. Zack will be in the front office waiting for you. May I tell him you'll be coming soon to pick him up?"

Wonderful. Bible school was supposed to simplify this move, not complicate it. Maybe God didn't like babysitting. Or maybe He was telling me to deal with my son, who'd not been the most model child for several months now. I knew that Zack had festered inside for months about all the changes that had taken place in his life, but he still refused to open up to me.

I hung up and shuffled through my keys. After locking the apartment, I ran to my car, got in, backed out of my parking space, and drove southeast on Lake Drive. Then I took a left on St. Andrews Road, heading toward the church.

As I pulled in front of the church office, fat drops of rain splatted on the pavement, warning of more to come. The wind almost growled as it wrapped around the vehicle. As I reached for the door handle, the rain fell as if someone stuck a knife in a gorged cloud and let it rip.

With the engine off, the windows began to fog, but I wasn't about to venture out yet. Anxiously, I waited for an opportune moment. Across the annex that contained the church offices and classrooms, anxious faces peered out of windows, watching the coming storm. Ten minutes later, the noise decreased to a drone, most of the faces gone. I reached to the backseat floor for my umbrella. Darn it. Ivy had taken it with her.

I snagged my purse, opened the door, and ran, splashing in inch-deep water that was still trying to run off and dissipate into the grass. Snatching open one of the double doors, I rushed inside. As I huffed and attempted to wipe rain out of my face with wet hands, a sixtyish lady with a gray pageboy haircut and powder-blue elastic pants exited the first door to my right. She handed me paper towels.

"Ms. Slade, right?" she asked.

"Yes, thanks," I said, soaking the towels in two swipes across my face and neck. "Are you Ms. Bellingham?"

She nodded and waved toward the door. "Your young man is right in here."

Zack sat at the far end of a floral sofa, probably designed more for visiting deacons than prophet beaters. I started to sit, and Ms. Bellingham sucked in a breath, most likely worried I'd ruin the sofa. So I stooped over, speaking only for Zack's ears. "Care to talk about it?"

His gaze darted toward the other woman, then returned. "Can I just go home?"

I stood and wiggled my fingers, telling Zack to stand and follow.

"Thanks for calling me," I told Ms. Bellingham. Then I remembered tomorrow was the last full day of Bible school, with only a half day on Friday. "Is he supposed to come back in the morning? Or is he—"

"Expelled?" she added with raised brows. "We don't do that here. But if he doesn't want to be here, we perfectly understand. I mean, we are concerned about him and only care about his best interest."

"We'll discuss it tonight and be in touch," I said, not sure of the problem, much less a solution.

Zack came with me peaceably, his stoic expression reflected in the passenger window. Red welts decorated his left cheek and ran down his neck. "Jesus" had a mean temper and a scrappy way of showing it. My daughter was already scheduled to come home with a neighbor, thank goodness, giving me time alone with my son.

"What's the deal, kid?" I asked as we left the parking lot, clueless how to bridge the chasm between us.

"Brandon's an idiot," he said, scrunching his body tight.

"Idiot enough to deserve your fist?"

"Oh yeah, easy."

Okay, wrong question. "Who hit first, Zack?"

He mumbled.

"Didn't hear you."

"I did. He called me a bastard."

"Whoa," I said. "Why would he call you that?"

"He said it was because I didn't have a dad."

I hoped the other kid sported a shiner as big as a baseball. "Sweetie, that's not the definition of bastard."

"Told you he's an idiot."

"Your daddy's death doesn't make you . . . Maybe Brandon isn't the brightest young man, but that doesn't mean you start swinging. When you get mad, he wins."

His facial expression softened. "I need a cool dad."

"Yes, you do," I said, unsure what else to say, aching for him, my instinct still advising me to keep secret about how ugly his father had been to us all. Knowledge of his father's deed would only upset Zack worse.

"Mr. Wayne's a secret agent. He'd be a good dad, don't you think?"

I coughed at the name of my semi-boyfriend in Atlanta and checked the clock for a reason to change the subject. "We've got to get back to packing, kid," I said, anxious to refocus. With the contractor's blessing and a virgin set of keys in my purse, I yearned to settle into my home with its view of Lake Murray and its peaceful environment. My children needed a fresh sense of home after the death of their father. It was a luxury afforded me by his life insurance policy.

I snorted to myself. *Life insurance.* Zack missed his father, but what he didn't know was dear old dad had nearly killed me in Charleston, to collect *my* life insurance. A fateful twist of events cost him his life at the hands of one of my farmers. I shivered at the memory that still crept in at night—since I'd held the shotgun that killed the farmer.

A gust almost blew my Taurus off the road. I quit daydreaming and gripped the steering wheel, telling Zack to make sure his seatbelt fit snug. Pine limbs were strewn across the road. Traffic lights swayed and bobbed overhead on tenuous cables. My front tires hit a puddle, and the car slid a few feet before righting itself. By the time I reached the turn to our apartment complex, my shoulders, arms, and hands ached. Finally, the rain stopped.

I relaxed until I saw a Jet Ski perched atop my rental truck.

"Cool," Zack exclaimed, as he jumped out of the car and headed toward the chaos filling our apartment complex.

The apartment manager wandered around in a wet T-shirt and jeans, stepping around glass, tree limbs, and trash. Before he disappeared to another block of buildings, I cornered him.

"What—What happened? Everything was fine when I left . . ."

"A goddamn tornado touched down," he said. He lifted a limb off a parked motorcycle. "I'll be two weeks cleaning this place up."

I shouted at Zack to come take my keys and go inside. "Anyone hurt?" I asked the manager, instinctively glancing at my apartment, grateful to see the windows intact. It seemed as though every person in the complex stood outside, analyzing damage, checking on neighbors.

"No, thank God," he said, turning to leave. "Gotta go, though. Still have to inspect six more buildings."

My phone rang. This time I checked caller ID and recognized Savvy's number. I put it to voice mail and waved at my banged-up moving truck. "Surely this buys me another couple of days."

"Only two," the manager said, holding up fingers as he trotted off. "Got a tenant waiting."

I lifted a branch, tossing it on a pile. Pine sap stuck to my hands, and I caught myself before wiping them on my favorite jeans. The air was thick with the heady Christmas scent; green needles sprinkled every surface. A huge bough too heavy for me to lift lay in my parking space, and I sensed a weird serendipity. Zack belting Jesus possibly saved my car.

A crowd had gathered around my rental truck, pointing, laughing at the watercraft on top.

"At least it wasn't a pontoon boat," I said, which solicited another round of guffaws.

As I reached for my cell and pondered whether to call my insurance agent, the rental truck company, or Savvy, my Clemson ringtone rang. A University of South Carolina fan heard the rival tune and hollered, "Go Gamecocks!" Most of my neighbors were born about the time I took driver's ed.

I walked away from the neighbors' looping chatter about what happened and what could have happened to answer the call.

"Hey, Slade. It's Monroe. You sitting down?"

I rubbed my face, flinching as I felt the pine sap stick to my cheek. "Just tell me what's up, Monroe. I don't have the patience for a dramatic lead-in. I take it this is about Savvy?" The silence made me wonder if I'd dropped the call. "Monroe?"

"What did she tell you?"

His tone made me raise a hand to my throat. "Just that you were being secretive. Why?"

"Listen, I'm calling you officially, okay?"

"Okay." I sat on the wet curb, not worried about the water soaking through to my underwear. "Go ahead."

"I looked at the file of a client named Heyward and found falsified documents."

"Look harder, Monroe. That's Savvy's county." A young couple came over to get in their car. I stood and moved. "Better make sure before you jump to any conclusions. She'd peel the skin off your bones if you stir up stink that isn't there. I might even help her." I'd experienced bureaucracy coming after me in the past. It was not enjoyable.

He cleared his throat, making me think of the summer cold beginning to tickle the back of mine. "Can you be open-minded about this?" he asked with mild frustration.

I blew out slowly. "Sorry. Of course I can. Go ahead."

"Signatures in the file don't match. Someone other than me might call it fraud. If y'all weren't such good friends, I'd have called the boss first." He paused. "Tell me I did right calling you, Slade."

I slumped onto my car bumper. Savannah Conroy was a first-class smart-ass, but she was honest. She practically dared people to find problems with her work.

"You did right," I said, leaning my back against the radiator grill. I rummaged through my purse for a notepad and flipped past my pending grocery list. Not finding a pen, I realized that I didn't need to record this information. The thought of my best friend under scrutiny for a financial crime already bored a permanent hole in my brain.

I glanced up, my instinct telling me to pinpoint Zack. Unable to find him, I stepped into the parking lot, scouting the area.

"She's also nervous," Monroe said. "She's—"

"Just a minute." Holding my hand over the phone, I shouted, "Zack! I told you to come get my keys and go inside. Where are you?"

"I'm not doing anything, Momma." My son was balancing on a pile of debris, teetering left and right on a branch.

"Inside, Zack!"

He ran over, and I threw him the keys. I returned my attention to Monroe. "Sorry, go on."

"Like I said," he continued, "she's anxious, uncooperative, almost nasty. There's serious problems in this file, and probably money missing." He relayed point by point what he'd found.

I stopped cold when he used the words *fraud* and *$300,000*. This couldn't be true. Savannah and I had been the first two female managers in the state, a formidable team. I knew this woman better than a sister.

"You still there?" he asked.

"Yeah. I'll meet you down there at Hardee's on Boundary Street at nine thirty a.m. Let me handle the boss."

"I called you first, didn't I?"

Bless his heart. He did do that, but I still suspected an error. "I really appreciate this, Monroe."

"Yeah, well you owe me dinner."

I hung up and dialed the office, my household move no longer the most urgent matter at hand.

"Thought you were on leave, Ms. Slade." Barely twenty, Whitney was the headquarters clerk who handled my messages and calendar. Her biggest flaw was making me feel old. Biologically, I could be her mother, in a Loretta Lynn kind of way.

"Something's come up. Put me on active duty for tomorrow and Friday. I just got called to the field."

"I'm sorry, but there isn't a government car available tomorrow," she said. "And Ms. Dubose is out until late this afternoon. Want me to take a message?"

Good question. The car deal was fine. I preferred driving my own anyway. Fewer eyes on who I was and what I was doing. How to word the message was the problem. No point asking for permission and risking a refusal.

"That's all right, Whitney. I'll call back."

The original plan was to pack for the move in peace, enjoy family, and find time to christen my new back porch with a cold beer, all of which seemed trivial now after God, Mother Nature, and Monroe had intervened.

My brain refused to wrap around the concept that Savvy fell into murky waters. How often had the two of us scoffed at others who'd found themselves transferred, demoted, even fired over self-serving, stupid decisions?

I moved inside. My phone stuck warm and sweaty in my hand, practically grafted to my skin from the day's activity, sticky as my wet hair. Zack watched warily from my recliner between moves on his electronic game as I paced the length of the apartment, walking up and down the fifteen-foot hall on matted, cheap carpet sucked lifeless by shampooers. I paused to smile at Zack, worried about him and Savvy both.

I'd have postponed and argued that my personal life came first, but this was Savannah. She'd indoctrinated me as a young hire, teaching me how to be a woman banker amidst the testosterone-driven boys of agriculture. She'd put my shattered pieces back together after an attempted rape. She jumped when I needed her and taught me to laugh when I wanted to cry. I had to go. But, my boss, State Director Dubose, might envision this as investigating my best friend behind her back, a view not too far from the truth.

The Office of the Inspector General served as the federal agents for most agencies, including the Department of Agriculture. Our OIG, ever read to jump in at Dubose's request, considered my job as Special Projects Representative a milk-toast version of a real agent, often times not taking me seriously. Six weeks' training and a badge stated I possessed the authority to snoop only until the stink turned pungently criminal. Folks like me solved the minor cases and ran interference for political bosses, advising them when to request the gun-totin' agents for the more critical crap . . . or how to dodge that crap when it hit the fan. My best friend was about to test my ability to make that judgment call.

Chapter 2

AS EXPECTED, when I called Daddy, he agreed Zack needed a man's influence after hearing about the Bible school boxing exhibition. I'd learned the absence of even a bad father left a hole in a boy's life. Add Zack's behavior to my twelve-year-old daughter's hormonal spikes, and no way in hell would I leave him and Ivy overnight with someone I didn't know as well as my underwear drawer. Beaufort beckoned ASAP. That meant only the firm, guiding hand of a grandparent for a babysitter would do, even if he had to drive 120 miles to get here.

By nightfall, Daddy walked in the door like he'd cruised over from the next block. I loved that man. I fed him and the kids fried chicken from the mom-and-pop restaurant a mile up the road and butterbeans and cornbread from my own kitchen to put a homemade spin on it.

Bellies full, Daddy took Zack outside for guy talk. Ivy disappeared into her room to pack boxes. I stood at the window and watched Daddy and Zack until they rounded the corner toward the pool, out of my sight. A deep sigh escaped me. Seeing that sweet baby boy acting so contrary to everyone in his path tugged at my heart.

I turned away from the window and retreated to the bathroom to take advantage of the moment . . . to call Savvy.

Her voice dragged as if she'd worked a fourteen-hour day. "Hey, girl. What's up?"

My smile waned in the mirror's reflection. "Not much. How're you doing? Feeling better? You worried me today."

She responded like I'd opened floodgates. Her words tripped then ran, splashing feelings at me. "I'm so glad you called. Monroe's acting stranger than when we talked earlier, and he won't tell me why. He's super tense. Will you talk to him and see what he's up to? I can't deal with his paranoia."

She sounded like a wreck. She sounded like someone in fear of someone else finding the truth.

I wiped at soap spots on the faucet. "How about I come down there? I'll talk to him then. Want to catch lunch while I'm in town?"

She paused. "He called you, didn't he?"

I gazed into the mirror, fighting not to let my friend hear concern. "Hey, we can talk when I get there around ten."

"Fine, but I'm wringing his goddamn neck for not being frank with me." Her rancor rang firm enough, but faded into a tired breath she probably thought I didn't hear. My friend didn't do *fade*.

"Wait until I get there," I said. "You might change your mind about ol' Monroe." I ached at the distance and time we'd allowed to lapse. "He could've easily called Dubose."

"The Director? What the hell's going on, Slade?"

Crap. I was making it worse. "I'm sure this is nothing, hon."

"Nothing, my ass. Two of headquarters' managers in my office at the same time? Like that doesn't scream *shit* with a capital *S*."

Fifteen years ago, Savannah Conroy had sashayed across a conference room full of government hacks and thrown an arm around me, a loan assistant fresh out of college. I'd withdrawn, but she'd used one hand to tether me and the other to direct a grizzled, middle-aged man to give up the seat beside her. Throughout the staff meeting, some eyes had rolled when she asked questions, while others ogled the 38 Ds under her pastel silk blouse.

After the meeting, she hooked her arm through mine and led me to the Sandlapper Bar. We were the only two women in the state on Agriculture's managerial payroll. A beach band in Hawaiian shirts crooned too loud into a cheap sound system, and I leaned across the Formica table to hear her.

"Carolina, right?" she yelled.

I admired her carriage and saucy outfit. A woman so sure of herself. "I go by Slade," I hollered. "Just Slade."

"Cool." Under the pink neon glare of bar lights, she shoved a margarita in my hand. "Listen to me, Slade. Farmers don't often appreciate bankers with bras." She licked salt off her glass. "So some days you just don't wear one. Makes everybody happy."

I recall laughing so hard I'd sloshed margarita on the table, staining my favorite skirt.

THE NEXT morning, as my tires ate up interstate highway a hundred miles outside Columbia, my thoughts retraced the day I'd met Savvy. I sped past a real estate billboard that read "Invest in Value" and smiled. She'd schooled me how to deal with the public, restructure a loan, bail out a client on the brink of bankruptcy, and how to mess with a man's mind when he attempted to mess with mine. Many a time she'd stabbed at me, often with a toothpick remnant from a happy hour hors d'oeuvre, to emphasize a point she thought I didn't understand. A birthday didn't pass without a card and a gift from her. Sometimes we called when the other was picking up the phone.

Much of my success I owed to her. Now, behind the wheel of my year-old Taurus, I headed to investigate a girlfriend who'd be terribly hurt if I didn't handle this personally—but devastated if I opened a case.

I lifted my foot off the gas again, lowering my speed from the four-point, two-hundred-dollar-ticket range. Traffic ran steady on I-26, which split South Carolina in half, but once I turned south on 95, cars zoomed past. On this freeway, Yankees and Canadians drove their kiddies to Florida, and drug dealers hauled their product north to south and back again.

Thinking of kiddies, I almost dialed Daddy to remind him one more time about Zack's presentation tomorrow. I didn't care if my son and Jesus couldn't see eye to eye; Zack didn't need to let the whole cast down. Hopefully, Beaufort was a false alarm, and I'd be home tonight. I didn't want to be the stereotypical parent who couldn't make her kid's play.

Again, I eased my foot off the gas. To my left, a deep green sprawl of soybeans on the Kendrick farm undulated, the silver undersides of the leaves waving in the hot summer breeze. Savvy kept that farmer afloat, and he swore by her. A dozen other farms dotted my route, whose owners embraced her like their own. She was the Beaufort County Manager, and I pledged to a passing field of cotton to keep it that way.

The miles flew by like the years of our friendship. Before I knew it, I'd reached the exit to Point South, which would take me through Garden's Corner to Beaufort.

My phone rang.

"Hi, what're you up to?" I answered, marveling at his timing.

"Just checking on you," Wayne said. "How's the packing going?"

"Boring, slow. Horrible weather."

"Yeah," he said. "Saw something about tornadoes on the weather report."

Senior Special Agent Wayne Largo and I had dated about once a month since the death of my ex. A long-distance relationship between his home in Atlanta and mine in Columbia. The kids, however, had met him and fallen in love. He worked for Agriculture's Office of the Inspector General, the same outfit that issued my badge. He was the guy who swooped in when cases were over my head. I hadn't had to use him yet in my new role.

Now was not the time to share news of Savvy, not until I knew what I was up against. One, Wayne would take issue with my involvement. Two, he might feel obligated to participate.

"Still got packing to do?" he asked.

"Plenty."

A year ago, when I naively functioned in a small world, making loans, oblivious to other ways of man, I'd have told you that operating by the rules, i.e., telling the truth, was the only way to go. When all those rules almost cost Wayne his job and me my life, I quickly learned to adapt . . . in a good way.

"You sticking around the apartment all day?" he asked.

"Probably. Daddy's coming to help."

He paused. "Sure you're not driving to Beaufort?"

"Damn," I whispered. "Yes, I just turned off I-95. Where are you?"

He chuckled. "Standing in your apartment parking lot, wondering why you loaded a Jet Ski on top of your moving truck. Just had coffee with your dad."

Of course he did.

I grinned into the phone. "You're something else."

"I try to be. You're pretty far-fetched yourself."

Outside of the kids, Wayne was the light of my life. Our dates weren't frequent, but they'd rekindled a fierce attraction we'd denied in our Charleston introduction. His professional duties started where mine stopped. We often disagreed on where that line appeared in the shifting sand of our relationship, but outside that small rub, we got along well. Damn well. I'd envisioned him in my king-sized bed more nights than not. It just hadn't happened, thanks to certain young eyes. Wayne cared deeply, a beautiful yet scary thought to me, a girl unsure she was ready for a full-time man so soon.

The lawman took his job as seriously as I took mine, which I highly respected. But he would have a problem with my current mission. Conflict of interest almost got both of us canned in the past, so he'd be overly sensitive to that potential in my dealings with Savvy.

"So why are you in Columbia?" I asked, hoping to center attention on him.

"Nice try," he said. "Actually I'm here to help you move. Guess the surprise is on me, huh?"

I didn't know how to answer.

"So what's in Beaufort?" he asked.

"A farmer," I said, taking the right at Garden's Corner.

"Tell me about your farmer. Maybe I can help."

"Nothing you need to worry about."

"Who says I'm worried?" he asked. "Were you worried I'd be worried?"

"What does that mean?"

"It means you've never gone to your girlfriend's office before on official business. At least not to my knowledge."

I slowed behind a truck hauling building supplies. "That's because she's so good at her job." The truck slowed to turn, and I mashed the gas and passed it. "Just let me do *my* job, lawman. I'll call you if I need you." Hardee's was about four miles ahead.

"Ever hear of conflict of interest?" he asked.

"Ever hear of mind your own business?"

"Okay," he said, dragging the syllables. "You're worried. I get that. But you're still kind of green at this, remember."

"I'm sorry," I said, rubbing a temple. I wasn't handling this well. "It's the move . . . and Zack."

"And your best friend," he added.

He gave me the opportunity to address the case again, but I didn't.

"Call me when you leave there, so we can coordinate getting you packed up. Just watch yourself, CI," he said, using the *Cooperating Individual* nickname from our past. "We both know what I'm talking about. Be careful."

He hung up. I waited at a light, the Hardee's where I was supposed to meet Monroe only two blocks away. Unfortunately, the lawman had made a valid point. Only months into my job, and here I faced a situation in which I should clearly recuse myself.

But this was Savvy.

Right at nine thirty a.m., I parked in the near-empty Hardee's lot next to a government-issue, light-blue Taurus matching my personally owned twin of white.

Bacon and coffee odors assaulted me as I opened the glass door. I returned a smile to two grinning senior gents, probably at their daily morning ritual, as I walked past to a back corner booth where Monroe Prevatte waited, coffee in hand. If he led with an apology for dragging me down here for nothing, I'd hug his neck.

He stood as I approached. A perpetual bachelor in his mid-forties, Monroe carried a trim runner's physique and stood a respectable five foot ten in his tasseled, burgundy loafers—taller if you counted the thick, prematurely white hair that craved a woman's fingers. His khakis held a fresh crease, his baby-blue dress shirt rolled up at the sleeves. Growing up in the rural town of Aynor with a church upbringing had taught him conventional manners with a country air. He smiled in greeting, but the lines around his mouth indicated he still meant business.

"So, what've you found?" I asked. "I promised Savvy I'd meet her at ten."

Puzzlement stole his boyish grin. "The state director doesn't have a problem with you checking out your buddy?"

"She doesn't know."

He handed me my steaming cup and shook his head. "Aw, Slade, that's not real smart."

"Until I know it's not an administrative oversight, I'm not calling in the Inspector General, which is what would happen, and you know it." I pointed my coffee stirrer at him. "Savvy doesn't need that kind of mark on her personnel record."

"And . . . ?"

A fry cook scurried by, and we stopped talking. I rapped the table softly with a fingernail in bad need of a buff. "I can do more good without someone breathing down my neck."

"Or make it go away?" he said, eyeing me over his cup as he took another sip.

Monroe and I were professional buddies, like Savvy and me, only without the tampon talk. We understood each other, and when we held a doubt, we gave the other the benefit of it. He held doors open for me and escorted me to my car after work. We shared frustrations at staff meetings when directors circled wagons around one pissant change or another. Our peers couldn't understand how such a friendship existed without the after-hour benefits of a bed.

I shook my head. "I won't stray, but I won't let her get burned unnecessarily, either. I learned in Charleston not to jump too soon in asking for the upper echelon to get involved."

He bowed his head. "I'll settle for that. Just don't get sucked into anything."

Luckily both of us ranked high enough on the bureaucratic food chain to slide by with such last minute junkets, and headquarters considered us management enough to decide when to draw in the big boss. I teetered on a razorblade with this one.

Monroe laid out some papers. "The farmer in question is Daniel Franklin Heyward. Age fifty," he said. "Been farming for twenty years. Sold real estate before that, but he cut his teeth on his daddy's farm. Has a college degree in business."

I reached for the sweetener, shook two yellow packets, and ripped them open. "Not many dirt farmers with degrees. What else?"

"Heyward came to us two years ago—"

"For a disaster loan after the last big drought." I stirred and tapped the plastic straw against the cup. "Like a zillion other people."

Monroe nodded. "His signatures don't match on documents, though. They aren't all his, assuming any of them are. He paid on time the first year, but he hasn't paid a dime in the second."

The signatures alone meant fraud. The parties involved could be the farmer, any secondary players from his world, or one or more of our agency's employees—including Savvy. I considered how much personal chat to allow her before asking the hard questions. Her temper matched her feisty, kaleidoscopic personality, and she'd turn it on full blast.

Monroe lowered his head to look up into my eyes. "So what're you gonna do, Ms. Investigator?"

"Does Heyward have a wife? Partner? Co-farmer?" I asked.

He laughed. "Co-farmer? You might call him that. Purdue Heyward. A cousin. He didn't sign the loan, though."

I frowned.

"Yeah, I know."

Our farmer operated alongside a partner with no legal connections to the enterprise. We normally placed a lien on the farm and obligated all partners, making them financially accountable for situations just like this. Too many red flags. "Let's go," I said, grabbing my purse. "Wait . . . give me a half hour. I don't want us coming in together like we're double-teaming her."

"Be careful," he said. "Miss Savannah's kind of mouthy these days."

"I can handle her. Still, no leak to Ms. Dubose without checking with me first. I'll take the heat if the boss boils over." I wanted the information spoon-fed to our state director. Too much too quick, and she'd yank me home.

"You know me better than to ask," he said. "Go on. See you in thirty minutes." Monroe always covered my back.

I slammed my car door and cranked the engine. *Damn, Savvy. You'd have skinned me for being this loose when I was making loans. What the hell is up with you?*

Chapter 3

PARKED AT THE Palmetto Building, home of Beaufort's U.S. Department of Agriculture offices, I exited the car and smoothed the wrinkles out of my brown linen slacks and straightened the matching cropped jacket.

A clerk glanced up as I entered the lobby. "May I help you?"

I flashed my credentials as required, my third time since assuming the job. Always felt like overkill to me. "Is Ms. Conroy available?"

The young blonde gawked at the badge. I fought a grin. The first time an agent flashed an ID in my face, I'd been scared witless, too. With its restricted purpose, my badge's bark held no bite, but to the average government employee, I was Miss Sit-Up-and-Act-Right.

She scooted to her boss's door.

A saucy Southern drawl filtered down the hall. "Honey child, come on back here." Before I took two steps, Savannah pranced out, threw a hug around my neck, and scrunched me against those 38 Ds. The expression on the clerk's face made for a cool Kodak moment of confusion. In a second, Savvy's would, too.

She waved toward the desk. "This is my clerk, Raye. She married a Marine stationed at Parris Island. She saved my fanny when Melanie left us."

I held out a hand. The clerk timidly brushed my palm with her cold one. I glanced at her nameplate. Raye H. Tankersley. Raye, with an *e*.

Savvy escorted me to her office, shut the door, and disposed of the smile. "Why lead with the friggin' badge, Slade? The girl's barely three months on the job."

My friend seemed pale. Her Cherokee heritage blessed her with skin that remained golden in February. Her tan should've been dead-on gorgeous now in July. Her tight-cropped head of curls flaunted a hot frost job, but she had lost weight.

A chair rested against the wall, and I repositioned it in front of her desk. "I'm here about Dan Heyward, Savvy." I caught the whiff of foreign cologne, Chanel perhaps. She'd worn jasmine as long as I'd known her. The watch was silver. She only wore gold. So many changes.

Savvy cocked her head. Dropping my purse and briefcase to the carpet, I sat straight-backed like a customer, allowing her the security of her managerial desk and a moment to collect her thoughts. I tried to compartmentalize my presence as investigator. Awkward.

"The guy's behind on payments," she said. "I'd expect Monroe to write it up in the loan audit, but not rat me out to you." One hand clenched, and I noted the French manicure, a luxury we'd once condemned as hoity-toity. "You're making this sound too damn formal, Slade. Should I be worried?"

"Not sure yet." I reached in my briefcase. "I hate to do this, but I have to take notes."

Her eyes went cool as midnight water at the sight of my pad. I eased out a pen. "The three mismatched signatures in the loan documents," I said. "They're a problem."

Savvy stiffened, her expression one of sincere amazement. "Mismatched?" She rose, leaning on her desk with one hand.

"Please, go get the file," I said. "Let's go over it together."

She threw back her shoulders then left the room. I jotted her words verbatim, leaving nothing for recall. She returned with the file and stood beside me. I spread it out on the desk.

"Glance at the initial application," I said, gently shifting it in front of her. We studied it, and I placed a sticky note on that page, next to the tight, slanted handwriting of Daniel F. Heyward. "Now, what about the loan approval form?" Like Monroe said, the name was scrolled bolder, larger, with less angle—similar, but not the same. I stuck another note on that page. "And the loan closing," I concluded. The capital letters looped more, the pressure on the paper less, obvious enough to notice. Monroe's eye for detail amazed me.

Savvy yanked a chair from under a table and sat beside me, sending a whiff of the cologne in my direction. I didn't like it.

"Holy cow shit," she said.

"Which one did you witness?" I asked.

She turned to the approval paper. "This one. Evan took the application, like he normally does. Melanie would've closed it."

"Are we sure Heyward received the money?"

She inhaled and narrowed her eyes, wary. I could tell she didn't know, since she wasn't at the closing when checks were written from the loan funds.

"What happened to this year's crop income?" I asked.

Noting the number in the file, she dragged her phone over and dialed. I hit the disconnect button. "What're you doing?"

She yanked the phone back. "I want to know what the hell happened. I'm calling Heyward."

"Let's do it strategically, without tipping our hand." I relaxed my posture, hoping she'd follow suit. "You're saying you don't know about this?"

She whipped a hand in the air. "Hell no. What the devil did you think?"

My pulse spiked at her reaction as I approached enemy status. "Go ahead then," I said. "Call. However, ask *calmly* if Dan can come in. Say it's a loan miscalculation that could save him a few dollars or something. I'll ask him the real questions face-to-face. Not you."

Her glare smoldered, but her voice flowed like warm honey when someone answered her call. She covered the mouthpiece and whispered *"Purdue Heyward"* at me. She tried to leave a message for Dan, and Purdue obviously wasn't happy.

"Well, I'm sorry, Mr. Heyward," she said. "You may be farming with him, but I don't see your name on the documents. When he gets back from his trip tonight, could you tell him I called? I'd really appreciate it." She hung up.

"The cousin?"

"Yeah," she said, sitting rigid. "Never met him."

"For all you know, you've met Purdue playing Dan instead," I said. "But neither has paid you this year."

Savvy shoved the folder away and flopped back in her chair. "I don't understand."

"What's not to understand?"

She shook her head. "Heyward made a decent crop. We should have received payments by now. Teddy drives by there, visiting his insurance clients. He told me the crop seemed great."

"Teddy? As in your ex-husband?" I snatched the file, licked my finger, and shuffled papers. The log said Savvy inspected the tomatoes, vouched for the crop's existence, even stated the yield appeared healthy with payment likely.

Her pink lips tightened, but I wasn't cutting her any slack on this gross error. "As in the cocaine-breathing idiot who nearly bankrupted you five years ago? The asshole who screwed every band groupie across ten states while you brought in the bacon?" I snapped an annoyed scowl back at her. "You ought to be whipped, Savannah. Within a damn inch of your life."

Savvy glowered, as if studying what to say.

She'd hated Teddy Dawson for years; now she trusted him with her work responsibilities? What else didn't I see about the girlfriend I used to know so well? "You used Teddy as the poster child for what not to marry."

"That's got nothing to do with these signatures." Challenge hung in her voice.

"But you lied," I said softly. "You didn't see a crop. You don't know what's going on with this farmer. Do you realize what this appears like to someone who doesn't know you?"

Her fingers played with an amber and silver necklace that fell long between her breasts, the chain twisting, untwisting between those floozy nails. Her voice quivered, and I fought the urge to squirm. She'd always been my rock and a grand adversary in many an argument. "I've experienced some problems lately," she said, looking away.

In a typical investigative interview, even as a newbie on the job, I'd recognize this point as a coup—a declaration teetering on the edge. All I needed was to tap it a little to make it fall. The moment froze between us. She waited for me to ask the next question. My pulse accelerated as I recognized the loaded potential of where we stood. My poor friend.

I eased forward and leaned my forearms on her desk. "What is it, hon?" I asked, wondering if I really wanted the answer. The last thing I needed to hear about was collusion between Savvy and a crooked client. Knowing about Teddy was bad enough.

She rubbed her forehead with the heel of her palm. "I can't think straight anymore."

I melted, dropping the investigator shell. I rushed around and embraced her shoulder, taking her under my wing much as she'd taken me under hers way back when. I laid a soft kiss on the top of her head, her cologne irritating my nose. Regardless, my cheek pressed to her hair; my gut squeezed into a knot, pleading to the heavens she wasn't leading to a confession.

The air conditioner whooshed on and loose papers waved then settled on her desk. "You can talk to me," I said, hugging my friend. My words rang sincere, but Savvy was shrewd enough to know I could use her words against her. That reality hovered around us like a suffocating fog.

She leaned her head on me. "Just more headaches."

Monroe knocked on the doorframe. "Sorry I was slow getting here. Had calls to make."

Savvy turned away and snatched a tissue from the box behind her on a credenza.

I returned from around the desk and stretched out a hand. "Nothing like showing up late," I said, playing the game we'd planned.

His face flushed, a reaction I'd ordinarily label cute as I feigned irritation with him. "Um," he said, "I said I was occupied." He peered at Savannah, uncertain. "Everything all right?"

I motioned to a chair. "Have a seat."

"Yes," Savvy said, rubbing her nose once. "Thanks for the warning, Monroe. Fuck you."

I jerked around toward Savvy. "Stop it. We're trying to help."

Monroe froze, as if wondering whether to leave. I thrust a chair in front of him. "For Pete's sake, sit. We already studied the file."

He eased into the chair. "Then I hope y'all have an answer for the falsified signatures. I'd love to hear it and go home."

His harshness cut like a harrow blade. I could only imagine what it did to Savvy.

However, confidence filled her eyes. I leaned back, relieved at the flash of her old self.

Savvy's cool stare underscored her words. "My assistant, Evan, accepted the application and confirmed the crop loss for a disaster loan. Heyward got stuck with a hundred acres of sun-scorched tomatoes year before last. The package seemed complete, so I called the guy in for loan approval."

She handled herself well, her posture strong and forward, her stare daring Monroe to toss her any crap. She also used it at staff meetings when directors peppered the county managers with queries about loan production. They learned quickly she'd take over the floor and run *their* show.

Monroe didn't cower under her stare though. He recognized her tactics.

I diverted attention to the security listed in the file, the collateral for the loan. "Real estate, equipment . . . we took a lien on a shrimp boat?" I asked.

She shrugged. "Hey, whatever he owned, I mortgaged it. Glad I did now, seeing he hasn't paid."

Monroe stopped scribbling on his pad. "Can you describe Dan?" He shoved back his chair to give his long legs more room in front of her desk.

"Dan is fiftyish, six foot, broad shouldered, a little heavy but not overweight. Bright red hair. But as Slade pointed out, no telling whether it was Dan or the cousin, or some bum off the street, for that matter."

"Where's Evan?" Monroe glanced around like the assistant should walk in the door. "Let's get him to describe the guy who signed in his presence."

Savvy twisted toward Monroe. "He's in the field. If I'd known what you were up to, I would've called him here."

I almost grinned at her touché. "Who else handled this loan closing?"

"Melanie, who got married and moved to someplace in Georgia."

The intercom buzzed, and Raye broke in. "Ms. Slade has a phone call from Columbia."

Savvy pointed toward the door, then rubbed her temple.

"You okay?" I asked.

She blinked hard then returned to normal. "Yeah. Take the call at

Monroe's desk in the other room."

Monroe rose. They understood, as I did, that Columbia meant headquarters. We left her office, and as he made room on his desk, I seized his shoulder. "Don't question her anymore."

He frowned. "Maybe I shouldn't have called you down here."

"Let me take this first." I punched the button and lifted the receiver. "Carolina Slade."

"Hold for the state director," said the secretary.

I closed my eyes and prepared for Margaret Dubose to rip a chunk of flesh out of me. She'd caught up with me much sooner than expected.

"Ms. Slade, might I inquire why the sudden trip to Beaufort?"

Dubose's manner commanded attention in a steady, low-spoken way. Her words came across just soft enough to make you strain to hear them, a trait I suspected as strategically intentional.

Phone tight to my ear, I tried to explain with assurance in my tone. "I wanted to clarify the parameters of this dilemma before I met with you."

"Protecting an old friend?"

I stood to pace, but the phone cord reined me in. "This case has potential criminal merit, but I wanted to rule out administrative error first."

Her voice remained a hard, steady alto. "And why would Mr. Prevatte call someone on vacation instead of me?"

"Monroe's not trained in investigations, and he knows my background. He found falsified signatures on a six-figure loan." Monroe turned at the mention of his name. I shook my head, scowling. He grimaced, recognizing an unpleasant conversation. "Not a case to put off until later, ma'am," I said, facing a window, putting my back to him. "Thought I'd check it out today and spend next week digging deeper." A drawn out silence worried me. "Ms. Dubose?"

"I take it you found something?"

"Doesn't appear administrative."

"Return tomorrow in time to brief me before close of business. Understood?"

"Yes, ma'am. Appreciate it."

"And don't step on anyone's toes. I'm too fresh in this job to put my neck on anyone's chopping block." She paused, and I tensed. "Ms. Slade?"

"Yes?"

"Don't backdoor me again."

I sucked in air between my teeth, relieved of the distance between us. "Yes, ma'am."

"Now put Mr. Prevatte on for me."

I handed Monroe the receiver and retreated to Savvy's office. He embarrassed easier than I did.

Agriculture had its own style of illegal activity and misfits like any other branch of the federal government. My boss understood that what I didn't handle went straight to the inspector general, Wayne's outfit, tossing any control Dubose could have out her tenth-story window. I could handle this chewing-out session if it put her at ease and bought us, and therefore Savvy, some time.

In the meantime, the drop-dead date on my lease drew nigh. Chicken spit.

Savvy glanced up when I tapped on her door. "We're going out," I said. "Get your bag. You're driving." While she shut off her computer, I returned to Monroe, who was rifling through audit files. "Thanks, dude," I whispered, assuaging his predicament, all done on my behalf.

"Bring me back a chicken sandwich," he mumbled.

"I said I'm sorry. You want fries with that?"

He scoffed. "You ought to buy me a steak dinner."

Savvy appeared, and I led the way to the door. I intended to have a long lunch with a friend—while she still was one.

Chapter 4

SAVVY DROVE away from the office like my grandmother, ten miles under the speed limit.

"What's wrong?" I asked from the passenger seat. "You've never poked along like this before."

The car accelerated with a lurch, jolting me back in the seat. "What did Dubose want?" she asked. "My head on a platter?"

"No, Savvy."

She focused on the road, navigating streets like she owned them. "How're the kids?" she asked through clenched teeth. "They managing okay?"

Fine. She could stay pissed. Obviously she didn't know how to deal with being the subject of an investigation. "Zack's giving me fits," I said. "Ivy's turning into a teenager, something that scares the begeezus out of me."

She remained silent as she sped past charming, white-columned homes and historic clapboard churches. We reached Bellamy's Curve, at the juncture of Boundary and Carteret, and parked under a moss-laden oak. Its gnarled gray roots pushed through the cracked asphalt, resembling the crust of fresh-baked bread. We ducked under a wisteria arbor and into the quaint establishment of Magnolia's Bakery Café, the soft smell of yeast rolls greeting us at the threshold.

The young brunette hostess led us past racks of quilted purses, sachets, and hand-woven baskets to a table overlooking the saltwater river. Seated, I picked up my wrapped silverware and tapped her with it. "Quit with the silent treatment. Now, what are these headaches about?"

She picked at her white paper napkin. "Teddy already made me go to the doctor."

Teddy again. I unrolled my napkin. "Why didn't you call me? You've never kept your distance like this."

"You could've called, too, girlfriend. Besides, I didn't want to create a fuss. You were juggling your promotion, new house, the kids."

"You know I'd have driven straight down here. Margaritas and hot chips in hand." My humor fell cold between us. No sign of her smart-aleck grin. Her eyes didn't sparkle. I swear, illness just wasn't part of her constitution. "Is it . . . serious?"

She rubbed the back of one hand. "I'll tell you when I know more. It's not like I'm dropping dead tomorrow."

I winced. "Jesus, Savvy."

She stilled and rested elbows on the table, leaning across her placemat. "You could've called and warned me about this Heyward issue. What's with that? And what did the state director want? I feel like you're sneaking around."

"I was sneaking," I said. "Dubose just romped on me for coming down here."

Savvy's eyes bugged. "You came without telling her?"

"You can thank Monroe for that. He was trying to do me a favor and protect your fanny at the same time."

Her surprise flipped to a scowl. "I remember you not liking the role of suspect, either."

"No, I didn't. And this isn't easy. I never signed up for this job expecting to investigate you." I playfully hit her with the back of my hand. "Help me help you, so I can smooth everything with the boss."

She sat back in her chair. "Sorry, hon, but I'm dumbfounded. Totally. I've been conned."

I removed the lemon wedge from my tea and set it on the saucer. "If we have to call in the IG, it'll be out of our control."

She nodded. "So be it. I shouldn't have taken Teddy's word for Heyward's crop."

There was that vulnerability again . . . and the giving up. I was hell-bent to find its source. "It's not so much Teddy's report as the signatures."

The waitress appeared with my crab cakes and Savvy's Dijon chicken salad. I took a huge bite of my order and sighed. A lone doughnut had served as breakfast over six hours ago. "Teddy turn you on to that perfume?" I wrinkled my nose.

She toyed with her salad. "Yes, he did, and I like it."

"How did he slip back into the picture?"

"Drop it, Slade." She sliced through a big piece of lettuce and set down her knife, lowering her voice. "No real story to tell."

An elderly woman glanced over.

I leaned in to remind my girlfriend of what we both knew. "That's bullshit, Savvy. You spent a year deciding to leave him and another year getting over him, the whole time telling me what a mistake he was. Last I recall, you wouldn't walk on the same side of the street. So spill it."

"One damn mistake in a file, and you're dissecting my life? Get over yourself, Slade."

I gave her a frown she'd recognize. "Stop it. It's not like that, and you know it. I'm worried about you."

Her lapse in judgment didn't bode well with me and wouldn't carry much credibility when *real* agents marched in. I would credit her illness for the signature oversight if I knew what the hell it was, but this loan took place two years ago, back when her logic sliced BS like an oar through water. This wasn't my old friend.

I ducked down a bit, peering up into her eyes. "He still snorting? Drinking? Chasing any skirt that crosses his path?"

She dropped her fork on the plate. "Shut up, Slade. I can say those things. You can't."

Maybe I sounded rude, but long ago, Teddy'd been Savvy's fix, and cocaine his. She'd endured silent torture, allowing him to devour her from the inside out. That is, until he disappeared for a week and returned with a tattooed, scantily-clad twenty-one-year-old. Savvy moved into a friend's spare bedroom, then promptly called the utilities and shut down Teddy's modern conveniences. The groupie bailed, leaving him alone and strung out. Savvy filed for divorce the next day. We'd bashed Teddy a thousand times since.

We ate until I could take the standoff no longer, my deadline from Dubose tapping my brain. "Are you really back with him?"

Her hand rose quickly and tipped my glass, sending ice and drink across the table. My chair toppled backward as I jumped to avoid taking the full wash in my lap. My shoes took the brunt of the tea.

The waitress rushed over with two towels. I stepped aside to give her room, and then out of my shoes to dry the tea from my leather flats. Thank goodness they fit snug, or I'd have been wading in the sticky stuff.

Spill cleaned up, we returned to our seats, and Savvy changed gears. "Sorry about that," she said. "But you make me nervous. Either you're my friend or an investigator. I'm not sure I can handle both. You're flip-flopping." She smoothed a fresh napkin in her lap. "Like a stinkin' reporter. I can't be sure what's off the record."

I clenched my teeth. "Savannah, I'm trying to help. The more I know, the more I can troubleshoot."

She wiped her mouth. "You're reading too much into Teddy. I also think you'll report to Columbia whatever you hear. That includes my social life and all my shortcomings. My cologne, for all I know."

I peered at her, not sure what to say next. She had a point.

The waitress arrived. "Food all right?" she asked. "You ladies haven't eaten much."

"I'll take that," I said, reaching for the check.

"Two checks," Savvy said. We faced off across our half-eaten lunches.

Our server shifted anxiously beside us. "I'll just lay it right here and let you ladies figure it out." She scurried off like a mouse.

"Do what you want." Savvy stood and slapped a ten on the table. "I'll meet you at the car."

I paid the bill and tucked the ten in my pocket to return once her tantrum blew over. When I stepped outside into the July heat, I heard the car running. The ride would be cool, even if Savvy wasn't.

Monroe's observations were spot on, and Dubose's deadline wouldn't grant me near enough time to find a fix. Savvy sounded mildly guilty, even to me.

She sat stoic in the car and stared out the windshield, not speaking, revving the engine. The hot seatbelt burned my palm as I clicked it in place. At the sound, Savvy sped out of the restaurant parking lot, not stopping to check both ways, leaving me gripping the dash.

She drove along side streets she'd known since birth, back to the office. As she shifted down at a stoplight, I couldn't miss the elderly black gentleman on the street corner spouting animated lessons from the top of a plastic milk crate. I eased my window down.

The man was neat, casual in his loose linen pants, sandals, and chromatic, jungle-print shirt, but dignified and formal in his posture and presentation. His hair expressed age around the edges, the white contrasting against dark chocolate skin. Passersby ignored him; a few obvious tourists snapped his picture. I found him striking.

He spoke in English, then in another dialect. He didn't rant, but talked firmly, in a deep, accented voice. "If you don't know where you are going, you should know where you came from." The words that followed, however, made no sense.

"He's repeating it in Gullah," Savvy said, still in a pout.

The man waved his arms and chanted loudly, "Muka wee! Muka wee!"

"What's he going on about?" I asked, relieved to have her talking.

Savvy drove away from the light. "That's Kamba and his apocalyptic warnings. Couple times a week he stands there giving his just-say-no lecture. He's one of the few Gullah wise men who still try to maintain a praise house."

I watched him disappear behind us in the side mirror.

"A praise house is where their wise men deal with local transgressions. Keeps dirty laundry close to home," she said, driving easier now. "Something we could all learn from."

I let the comment fly out the window as I rolled it back up.

"I thought most of the Gullah descendants were on St. Helena," I said. The tight-knit community was directly descended from the Sea Island slaves imported from Sierra Leone. Any coastal South Carolina kid knew that. The next generation might not. The Gullah heritage had died slowly as its children grew up and left the island.

Savvy turned onto Bluffton Road, toward the agriculture building. "He claims white men are feeding drugs to their young people. *Muka wee* means 'get away.' He's telling kids to resist temptation and remember their roots. He's just part of the local color, I guess."

The salty river rolled past with warm breezes fondling palmetto fronds and marsh grass. The sun flickered on water tips, gulls riding the roller coaster ripples. "God this place is gorgeous," I said, eager to keep a conversation going. "Nobody has to remind you of your roots."

Her face softened. "I do love it here. That's why I like my work. I help the rural residents stay afloat and maintain some of the heritage, in spite of the development."

"I know you do."

She slowed the car and turned left into the parking lot.

Monroe's vehicle joggled my forgotten promise. "Aw, shoot."

"What?" Savannah switched off the engine and reached for her purse.

"Forgot Monroe's lunch." I gently touched her wrist, hoping the chat had broken the ice wall between us. "Are we okay now?"

The defensive starch dropped from her shoulders, and she peered at me. "You might be too close, you know? You might cut me too much slack . . . or overplay your hand. Either way hurts us both. Just call in the big boys."

She exited the car and walked toward the glass door. She was either giving up or didn't want me on the case. My objectivity danced in and out of my grasp. The IG wouldn't cut her any slack, that's for sure, headaches or no headaches. Unless I figured this out fast, I'd be the culprit on record who recommended they send in their agent.

Raye's demure smile greeted us as we entered the office. Monroe sat at his desk, bored over audits.

I motioned toward the front door. "Let's go, Monroe. Your turn."

"It would be nice to eat first," Monroe replied. "A guy gets—"

"Sorry I forgot your sandwich. I'll make it up to you. Bring the Heyward file."

Over half the day was shot. I needed to leave by this time tomorrow to update Dubose. I peered into Savvy's office. She was already on the phone. "Hey," I said, planning my words carefully.

She hung up without a goodbye. "More questions? If not, I've got work to do. Evan still hasn't come in, and I might have to take an application from one of his appointments."

I held up my palms in peace. "No more questions. We're leaving for the day. Dubose put me on a short leash. One or both of us will be back tomorrow. We're taking the file."

"Fine." She picked up the phone again. When I hesitated to leave, she dropped it back in its cradle. "If you're wanting touchy feely right now, you're out of luck. Do your job. God knows I better do mine with two monitors in the office."

I sighed for her to hear. "We're going to make sure there's a crop out there. Someone will ask, and you haven't seen it."

"Whatever."

I waved at Monroe to hurry as I walked past Raye into the lobby. Outside, Monroe trotted up as I reached my vehicle. "Okay, spill it. The air hung thick as cane syrup in there."

"She's nervous, fussy about a lot of things, mainly because I asked about her ex." I unlocked the door and fingered my keys. "Wait. You have the G-car. Let's take yours. We'll come back for mine later."

"Where we going exactly?" he asked, dumping his car keys in my outstretched hand.

I walked around my car to the driver's side of his. "Let's see these crops for ourselves. No way am I trusting the reports in that file now. She can't vouch for the farmer, the signatures, or the tomatoes. For all we know, she handed a check to someone to buy dope. Let's find Dan Heyward and get his side." I unlocked the doors. "I aim to save her butt, whether she likes it or not."

THE TAURUS bounced as I hit the exit dip too fast. In a spike of frustration, I outraced an oncoming Honda Civic. Monroe's hands braced on the dashboard. "Maybe I should drive."

"Just point me to Heyward's farm on St. Helena."

He unbuckled his seatbelt and retrieved the spilled beige folder from the floorboard. "Drive like a sane woman, and I will." He opened a map. "Stay on Highway 21."

Now I sounded like Savvy. "Sorry, dude. This case is tougher than I thought. Just kick me when I turn bitchy, okay?"

"You'll be black-and-blue." He settled in his seat. "You think she's dirty?"

I hesitated, not caring to answer what might be.

"Never mind," he said.

We reached the main field of Heyward Farms, thirty acres give or take, bounded by thick woods on three sides. Dark-skinned, straw-hatted workers bent over long, even rows of staked, four-foot tomato plants. At least there was a crop, and a healthy one at that. Two loaded flatbed trucks sat at the end of the field, large wooden crates weighing them low with the green fruit. Lean bodies toiled in the summer heat, trudging up and down rows, toting twenty-five-pound buckets for a hard-earned forty cents each. The same tomatoes would sell for over ten dollars. A Heyward ought to be somewhere around, eager to haul the cash crop to the packing shed.

Shielding my eyes from the intense afternoon sun, I sought the man in charge. A Caucasian, red-headed guy like Heyward ought to stand out like a ripe strawberry in that sea of green.

Monroe squinted. "Hard to tell who's in charge with all the hats and long sleeves."

I eased onto the dirt road. "If we can't find the man in charge, let's talk to anyone. Hired hands often know more than their bosses anyway."

The straw boss stood straight, watching, easily distinguished from the twenty or so stooped pickers. He turned as we approached, then strode to meet us. Good. It would save me climbing over the rows in damp shoes. I parked, threw on my sunglasses, and stepped out of the car. Monroe followed close behind. The acid scent of rotted and sunburned tomatoes told me not to brush up against the sticky plants.

"You pick bad day for visitin'," Straw Boss said to Monroe with a Caribbean accent I'd heard only in the movies. His shirt flapped open, buttons gone, his faded, stained T-shirt already soaked with perspiration. He wielded a roughhewn four-foot walking stick in one hand. "Busy time, mon."

Monroe explained who we were. "We need to ask Mr. Heyward some questions." He swatted away a fly and held out his other hand. "My name's Monroe Prevatte. And yours is—?"

"Boss-mon not here. You go. I have to run da farm."

"It's pretty important," I said.

The foreman cut a hard glance at me.

"It's about the tomatoes, and the farm's future."

"Go!" he yelled, his lanky body lurching as he shooed at us, swinging his stick, like herding stray cattle. He spun his back to us and marched to the field, hollering to two young men thirty yards away, as if they were at fault for our being there.

I turned to Monroe. "You handled that well."

He shrugged. "I'll bet most of these guys are illegals. Can't expect them to tell us much."

My scan stopped at a pretty, sweat-slick girl lugging a bucket on her hip, her movements weighted and slow. She glanced at me then snatched her gaze away. I snagged Monroe's shirtsleeve. "I'm talking to that macho foreman whether he likes it or not."

"Oh come on—"

"Hey," I shouted at the straw boss. "Wait a minute."

The man turned, a rancid scowl on his face.

Carefully parting tomato plants, I marched over rows and shoved my investigator credentials under his nose, for some reason riled at this semblance of slavery. Didn't know if he could read or write English, but badges spoke a universal language. His eyes widened, flashing white in contrast to his cocoa-colored skin. There was the reaction I wanted.

"I'm here to speak to Mr. Heyward. Where's his house?"

He pointed up the road, his expression one of bitter defeat.

"Thanks," I said, brow raised.

He scowled.

Backing away through the plants, I waved for Monroe to get back in the car. We got in and eased the vehicle into drive, slowly bouncing past the man.

"Aren't you big and bad," said Monroe.

"You do what you gotta do," I said, eyeing smudged young girls in rags gently separating fruit from plants. Just bone-tired sacks of humanity in clothing layered with stale sweat. Something about their predicament tainted my opinion of Mr. Heyward even more.

Chapter 5

DAN HEYWARD'S house sat a quarter mile down the road beyond the field, tucked behind the jungle of oaks, sawtooth palmetto, and vines thick as a man's thigh. This climate had caused slavery to mushroom back in the day of indigo and rice plantations, when owners realized imported African workers knew more than European whites about growing the crop in this semi-tropical climate.

Monroe and I came upon a two story, white Tidewater-style beauty with a wrap-around porch, sheltered by a broad, charcoal gray hip roof. A small, dirt road continued farther into the dense woods. I pictured a Fourth of July gathering on this massive porch, with every rocking chair occupied by generations of adults, while barefooted youngsters hopped up and down the steps and across the yard throwing firecrackers.

A burly black man toting a rifle interrupted my picturesque vision as he strode across the drive, through the backyard and into the trees. Appeared someone might have trouble with wild dogs or coyotes.

I parked in the empty driveway, wondering why the straw boss was so defensive. At the door, a short, ample Mexican woman answered our knocks, her lavender, floral smock hanging almost to the floor over cheap sneakers.

"Is Mr. Heyward home?" I asked through the screen.

Her gaze wandered from me to Monroe and back. "*No entiendo.*"

I handed her a business card and emphasized short syllables. "Give to Mr. Heyward. Okay?"

She grinned quickly, the smile of a subservient woman. "Okay."

We returned to the car. Monroe slid in and twisted the vent toward his face, his white hair dancing in the blast of air. "She'll probably fold your card and use it to balance a chair leg."

I studied the grounds. "Does the map show anything farther down this road?"

Monroe flipped papers. "Outbuildings, maybe a mobile home. Probably some tenant stuff. They've got to be sleeping somewhere." He fixed a narrow-eyed gaze on me. "But should we meddle around someone's place?"

"It's what you do in an investigation. Why?"

"The guy with the gun, for starters."

I kept forgetting Monroe crunched numbers for a living.

The woods encroached and squeezed the road to one car width as we slowly made our way past the vegetation. Then it widened into a clearing beaten bare by foot traffic. A shed and a dozen portable metal buildings with fiberglass roofs, like those at construction sites, stood in opposite rows with dirt paths between them. A crude wooden sign reading *Store* hung on two nails on one shed. A padlock encircled the door handle and hasp. One other structure appeared secured as well.

Sour air hit my nose as the wind shifted. I scanned the compound until I found the source—an old-fashioned three-by-four-foot outhouse at the end of the row. A hose rested on a rusted garden hook nailed to gray planks of the john. The well tank that drew their water stood stark and unprotected only twenty feet behind the outhouse. That meant water I wouldn't want to taste. Tenant housing at its finest. I'd thought these days of forced labor and sub-human living conditions were gone.

"What you need?"

I jumped in my seat. The man with the shotgun appeared in my blind spot. Monroe moved around the Taurus to my side. The elephant of a man dwarfed Monroe by eight inches, and Monroe was already four inches taller than me.

"We're from the Department of Agriculture," Monroe said. "We'd like to talk to Mr. Heyward. Could you please take us to him?"

I would've laughed at Monroe's take-me-to-your-leader speech except for the giant's weapon resting on an immense bicep in the crook of his arm, muzzle pointing down. He peered through a lazy left eye, and his bent nose had parried a few knuckles in its lifetime. "He ain't back here. This area's off-limits. Go on." He waved at us with his free hand, like we were gnats.

Not a soul wanted us to find the boss. I stepped out of the car and extracted another business card as the beast stepped back. "Then would you give this to him?" As I reached out, a thump echoed from the locked trailer. I turned.

"Inventory," said the giant. "Y'all go on." An order short on conversation and without options.

"Come on, Slade." Monroe yanked me toward the car by my shirt as he spoke to the guard. "Please let Mr. Heyward know we came by."

I shrugged from his grasp. "Don't forget the card. It's urgent we speak to him." Monroe tapped my shoulder like a woodpecker. I ignored him. "Will your boss be back today to pay workers?"

"Payday's Friday."

"Thanks." Tomorrow was Friday. I slid behind the wheel, and once Monroe got inside, locked the doors. After I cranked the engine and turned the car around, I braked for a moment. As I pondered my authority and studied my rearview mirror, formulating an excuse to ask more questions, two more men appeared from behind the portables. One a blond, wiry Anglo in camouflage fatigues and a week's growth of beard. The other was Hispanic-dark in loose-fitting jeans, a brown T-shirt, and a hunting vest. Both sported rifles.

"Think I can get information out of them?" I asked Monroe, who stared back at the rowdy trio. I reached for my badge again.

The Three Musketeers marched faster up the road toward us, one of them pointing in our direction. The Hispanic guy raised his rifle and pretended to shoot us, sending the others into rolls of laughter.

"Dang it, Slade, let's go," Monroe yelled.

I stomped the gas pedal.

Monroe peered over his shoulder until we turned out of their sight. "They don't give a rip about a business card, Slade. You shouldn't fool around with those types without a posse."

The big guy and his buddies had shoved my heart into my windpipe, too. How the hell did Evan handle farm inspections at this place? The least he could've done is highlight some comment in the file about overseers with guns. "Are migrant help that dangerous, or are armed guards typical around here?" I asked.

"Maybe they're growing weed."

"Add that to your list of prizes to hunt for," I replied, turning back toward the field. "If I lived here, I'd float it in on the water, though, not grow it."

"Don't tell me how you know that."

Monroe's comment raised a thought. Smugglers loved coastal towns. Heyward owned a boat.

As we hustled toward the highway, the same young female picker straightened up and watched. Her hand raised a little, half hidden by her skirt. My foot eased on the pedal, and I waved, wondering if she wanted to speak. The straw boss yelled, and she bent double again, her attention on her tomato bucket. Poor sweet girl. Where was her mother?

I reached the asphalt state road and headed toward town. We passed a couple of block houses. A gang of ragtag urchins ran between them, chasing a blonde, wire-haired dog. "Notice something?"

"What?" Monroe asked.

"No kids on the farm. Most migrants travel with their children. A lot of them pick alongside their parents. What's with that?"

"Maybe Heyward doesn't allow kids on the place. I could see where they'd be in the way."

From my experiences in Charleston, I recalled that seasonal migrant farming meant families, not single twenty-year-olds. I assumed the same here. Three generations picked together—seniors to grade school kids, helping each other. Sure, young men often created after-hours disturbances and some women sold themselves for extra money, but these workers usually came in family clusters.

Monroe tipped his head toward the field behind us. "Kinda bold of you back there with that goon. You're not Wonder Woman, you know."

I slammed on the brake, stopping on the sandy side of the road, my fisted hand with a tight index finger thrust before his nose. "Don't ever call me that again. Ever!"

His face washed blank. "What? Wonder Woman? It's a cartoon character."

A chill rippled down my spine at hearing the words again. My ex used that nickname in a sarcastic moment, right before his partner in crime blew him to bits. I enlightened Monroe about some of the details of the past that hadn't made the grapevine, which included two attempts to have me raped then two to have me murdered. Both men involved called me Wonder Woman.

Monroe blanched at the story. "Oh my God, Slade."

I gripped the steering wheel to hide a mild tremor. The past still gave me nightmares. Sleeping pills hid tucked away in my nightstand for the worst of them.

"I'm sorry," Monroe said as he touched my shoulder.

"Well, now you know." I inhaled for composure and turned toward him. "Keep going? We don't have a lot of time."

He nodded ever so slightly.

Back onto the asphalt, we visited the other fields. Our inspection revealed picked-over tomato plants, but from their appearance, the harvest should've been respectable. The next logical place to scout for the elusive Dan Heyward was where he dumped off the tomatoes and collected his checks.

I glanced at Monroe. "Does the file say which packing house Heyward uses?"

"Triple R."

The car's digital clock showed the day wasting. Time constraints didn't allow for the social etiquette of an appointment. "Let's give them a shot."

Five miles farther, we parked against a chain-link fence and trudged across the silt lot toward an open-sided metal building large enough to hold a rodeo. The packing shed teemed with day labor, their dusty cars ringing the property. The manager's office wasn't hard to find as it was the cooled section of the place. A tanned, sandy-headed guy in his early twenties answered our knock.

Only a few minutes and a limp handshake later, we left. The kid assured us Dan Heyward no longer used Triple R, didn't know why he'd switched, and held no idea where Dan delivered his crop now. His eyes never made contact with mine. Expensive tomato crops ripened fast and laborers packed them quickly. I guesstimated a low-six figures in revenue. The loan's security drifted elsewhere or discreetly found its way north on Triple R trucks disguised as somebody else's crop. But rural folk knew where each farmer carted his business. It was just common knowledge.

Back on the highway, I figured the boy lied from beginning to end. Any other shed meant hauling tons of aging fruit in summer heat further down the road, each mile an unnecessary expense in terms of labor and gas.

"We've got to find that crop or Savvy's in deeper trouble, Monroe. Even if she isn't directly involved with the illegal disposition of security, she's party to the way that loan played out. Letting Teddy account for the crop wasn't the brightest move on her part." My throat scratched worse than yesterday, and I turned my vent away. Maybe it was allergies—not a cold? "God, this whole thing stinks." I debated the notion someone would claim Savvy hid money and tomatoes from the record for some reason. That meant jail time.

Monroe spoke up. "Maybe Heyward didn't make much of a crop this year."

"Come on. You saw that crew of migrants out there working their butts off. Sure he made a crop." I cocked my head and rocked it back and forth, mocking. "Even Teddy said so, remember?"

"Do I get to kick you now? While you're driving? You said if you acted—"

"Oh hush, Monroe." I halted at the stop sign to Highway 21, analyzing the facts, none of them helpful to Savvy. An older Chevy pickup cruised by, heading onto the island. "I've seen that guy before," I said, my gaze following the truck. The back end of the vehicle disappeared in a stream of cars. "He was kinda cool, Monroe. Real other-worldish. He preaches on a street corner in town doing this Gullah drug prevention spiel."

"Sounds good, but I'm starved."

I recalled he'd missed lunch and sped up. As we traveled due west back toward the city, the evening sun peered just over the horizon, blinding shards of sunlight flitting through trees and over rooftops. "What else can we do today? I've got to leave by noon tomorrow."

"It's almost six, Slade. Everything's closed, unless you want to invite Savannah to dinner and pick her brain."

I shook my head. Monroe gave me an I-thought-not grin. He turned to watch the marsh roll by. Tiny birds and crabs frantically scavenged, feasting in pluff mud glistening with the orange glow of sunset, using up the minutes until the tide rolled back in and covered up their food supply.

I understood their frustration.

LATER, MONROE and I sat in a back corner of Steamer's Restaurant with an aluminum metal bucket sunk into a hole in the middle of a thick timber table. We'd half-filled it with our shrimp peelings. I kept telling myself boiled shrimp wasn't fattening, no matter how many you ate.

I drew a smiley face in the condensation on my iced tea glass, and then erased it. "Savvy might be ignorant about the crop and the signatures."

"No more than we are." He shoved his plate back. "So many clues I don't know where to start."

I threw an uneaten shrimp back on the plate. "This isn't just about this year's crop disappearing."

"Enlighten me, Sherlock," he said, tossing his paper napkin in the bucket.

"Falsified papers could mean anything, even a shill farming operation, which tells me our loan money funded something other than tomatoes. We need to find Heyward."

"So you keep saying." Monroe drained his cup. "You ready? I booked you at the Hawkins Motel, a room across the hall from mine. You want to go get your car or leave it at the office?"

We retrieved my overnight bag, left my vehicle where it was, then checked in at the motel about three miles away. The lobby was a dated potpourri of heavy gold and olive green upholstery in need of a retread, but the sheets in the room smelled clean. No water bugs or stains on the ceiling.

My overnight bag slid across the dresser as my butt sank on the end of the too-soft bed. The travel clock read a quarter to eight. I flicked on the cable news channel as a long-lashed, red-lipped blonde drawled out a special report on corporate embezzlement, showing slick CEOs walking into federal courthouses. I switched off the set and stepped across the hall to Monroe's room.

He answered in a Clemson T-shirt, jeans, and socked feet. "What you need?"

"I'm going stir-crazy over here. You want to review the file again?"

He invited me in. For the next hour, we scoured documents, studying each page in the two-inch-deep binder to analyze signatures, facts, and dates. I studied another section of the eight-position file, telling Monroe dates from when Dan Heyward first walked in until the moment I arrived, and every action in between. Briefly, I wondered what other fraudulent files might exist, then dashed the nasty idea.

Monroe tossed his hand-drawn timeline on the bed and cracked his knuckles. "So what's the agenda for tomorrow?"

"Find Heyward. Call other tomato sheds." I snapped my fingers. "Could use Savvy for that to save time. I also left a note on Evan's desk to stand still long enough for us to catch up to him."

After another hour, my eyes saw double. "Stick a fork in me. I'm done." I stood and stretched my arms over my head. "Need to call home anyway."

"I'll meet you in the lobby at eight," he said, walking me across the hall.

"Better make it seven thirty." I swiped the keycard and stopped. "Monroe?"

"Yeah?"

"Sorry for dragging you into all of this."

He grinned. "I dragged you, remember?"

"Not really. We could both be back in Columbia right now if we'd reported—"

He waved me off, turned, and went to his room.

Door locked and double-locked, I called to check on my bad baby boy, hoping Daddy talked some sense into him about his recent rebellion.

Zack's problem wasn't new. His teachers had let him off the hook in May, attributing his misbehavior to end-of-school-year agitation. Truth was, his father's death and my relocation to Columbia had served to undermine his sweet disposition. I held no clue how to deal with that. He'd always seen the good in his dad.

Zack answered the phone. "Yo."

"Try that again, this time with manners."

"Hello?"

"That's better. Hey, kid. How's it going?"

"I'm beat," he whined.

I asked the question, knowing the answer. "Why's that?"

"Grandpa made me pack boxes. He's old, Momma. He's not supposed to work this hard."

I stifled a laugh. "He can be a stringent taskmaster."

"A what?"

"He can work you to death."

He sighed as if he'd put in a migrant's day. "Yeah."

"So are you behaving for him?"

Wayne's voice sounded in the background.

"Gotta go, Momma. Love you."

Wayne picked up the phone. "Slade?"

His use of my name wrapped me in a comforting, long-armed, Southern embrace. "What're you still doing at my place?" I asked.

"Your dad invited me over for hotdogs and moving exercise."

Ha, more like my father helping smooth the road between his daughter and her beau. Daddy and Wayne shared two things in common—me and guns. I probably came in second to a freshly oiled Springfield or a Limited Edition Colt. Two men with like minds for sure, but in reality their strongest connection was adoration for me.

The male attention, heavy-handed or not, would prove good for Zack. My son envisioned Wayne as more of a CIA spook than an agriculture agent.

"How's Savannah?" Wayne asked.

"No details. Not now, Cowboy." Not before I collected my facts straight. "Seriously, I'm tired. Long day."

In the background, I heard the sliding glass door open and shut. Tree frogs echoed in the distance as Wayne's footsteps clunked on the wooden porch. I wasn't sure which noise was louder, the frogs outside or the kids inside. He cleared his throat. "I'm sorry I leaned on you yesterday," he said.

A warm wave of longing rolled through me. "Well, I . . . next time don't . . ." I bit my lip. Again, we headed down the only path that created friction between us—how to handle investigations.

"Don't what?"

"Nothing." I didn't want a squabble. "I'm worried. My work here won't scratch the surface."

"Is she in trouble?"

"She isn't herself."

"Follow the money trail . . . the crop, the loan expenditures, whatever you're dealing with. You know what to do." He breathed long and slow. "Nobody's giving you trouble, are they?"

I snorted. "Can't find anyone to give me trouble. Can't find a crop, can't find Savvy's assistant, can't find money or the farmer."

He went silent for too long, wildlife in the background my only company. "Got a weapon?" he asked with hesitation.

"Don't I always?"

Wayne had taken a while to accept the fact that Daddy had taught me to shoot, and that my .38 went most places with me. I possessed a concealed weapon permit, even though the federal government frowned on it. So I never told anyone whether I had it on me or not.

This time I'd left my personal .38 in the car parked at the agriculture office, since I wasn't authorized to carry in Monroe's government car.

A call beeped in on my line. Monroe. He could wait. Heck, I'd just left his room. "Thanks for helping my daddy."

"Glad to, CI. I've missed you."

"I've missed you, too. A month's a long time."

His voice lowered, becoming enticing. "Yeah, it is. And you ran off."

"I'll be back tomorrow," I answered low in return. "Surely we can find a moment or two without a herd of people in the room."

Both of us hushed, Wayne probably thinking like me about the *what if* and how to get together alone.

A polite knock sounded on my door. "Slade?"

"Who's that?" Wayne asked.

I squinted through the peephole in the door. "It's Monroe. He and I have been working together on this case. Guess I need to go."

"Darn. I was getting ready to talk dirty to you," Wayne said.

"And I hate missing it, too. See you tomorrow."

"Goodnight, CI." He hesitated a second as if about to say something else. "Well, goodnight."

I rested against the door for a moment. Damn I wish I was home.

Knuckles sounded again. I slid open the chain lock. "Thought we were done," I said.

Monroe stood with file in hand and no shoes. "Here," he said, flipping papers. At the back, a property lien document lay anchored between other pages. "Didn't Savvy say she mortgaged the boat?"

"Yeah, why?"

He pointed to the paper. "She didn't record the lien. This is the original, unrecorded document." Typed and prepared properly, the legal paper lay filed and hidden, unexecuted.

"Chicken spit," I said. Monroe didn't cuss, but his frown indicated agreement. "We probably just lost over fifty thousand dollars in collateral." I glanced up. "What the hell is wrong with her, Monroe?"

Chapter 6

I DREAMED in color. Lots and lots of green. Lost in plants towering over my head, I hollered for Wayne. He called my name, searching, but he sounded muffled in the thickness of tomato plants as large as trees, so I couldn't tell where he was either. Jungle drums pounded.

"Slade, wake up."

Climbing back to consciousness, I sifted through stimuli until I recognized the motel room. I threw off the covers and shuffled to the noise, wearing only a nightshirt covered in cartoon cats. Through the peephole, Monroe rocked in the hall, freshly dressed, and way too anxious for this early in the morning. I opened the door. "What do you—"

He bolted into the room. "You've got to see this."

"Dang, what time did you get up?" I glanced at the nightstand clock. "It's only six thirty."

"When I went to get a Danish in the lobby, I grabbed a newspaper."

My fingers tried to comb my hair. "Can you give me a moment?"

He thrust the morning paper in my face. "Read this."

Pushing the paper away to arm's length, I blinked and focused. *"Local man missing in shrimp boat explosion."* I rubbed the corners of my eyes. "Okay."

He pointed repeatedly at the paper. "Read the first paragraph."

I held up the page and, flipping it to the bottom half, read aloud. "The owner of the *Southern Lady* is missing, along with two crew members, after a local farm worker found remnants of the boat late Thursday evening. A local farmer and shrimper, fifty-two-year-old Dan Heyward was assumed to be on the boat. He grew up in Beaufort County and operated an enterprise on St. Helena Island."

I slumped to the bed. "You've got to be kidding."

Monroe remained in the middle of the room, rereading the article. "Purdue Heyward is listed as his cousin, residing at the same address."

No wonder Purdue was out of touch. I shoved Monroe toward the door. "Meet me in the lobby in fifteen minutes."

As I dressed and clasped my watch, I realized my hair held little importance in the scheme of death, fraud, and Savvy's future. I snatched the curling iron plug from the wall, brushed hair from my face, threw a clip in it, and left. In twenty minutes, we headed to Savvy's house. Monroe drove.

The sun rose in a panoramic sky of pinks and blues. The slow yawn of day. Our energies, however, delivered us tout suite to Savvy's driveway just after seven. I ran to the door, opened the screen, and rapped energetically on the window.

Teddy's bare chest and feet, along with facial stubble, sapped the urgency right out of me. "Ah, the slick and clever Slade," he said. "Haven't seen you in forever, babe. Where's the damn fire?"

"Where's Savvy? It's important."

"Come on in," he said, holding the door for me like he owned the place, the other hand scratching his chest. "I'll get her for you."

I sidled past, trying not to touch his six-foot frame and paunchy belly, the major dividend of his beer investments. He carried a slighter frame than Wayne and had wavy blond hair. His face held a rosy dark tan from hours spent nursing Jack Daniels and Budweisers on his fishing boat. Old habits didn't die with Teddy, they embedded more deeply into his character.

My twitching hand clutched the newspaper.

Savvy's house wasn't huge, maybe eighteen hundred square feet, but strategically placed antique mirrors exaggerated its size. Savvy lived loud and hard, but her residence gave her another world to retire to and decompress. Few people could guess she flaunted doilies on mahogany end tables and a collection of china thimbles in a shadow box on the wall. Lace adorned her windows, and a few times we'd downed tequila shots in Victorian teacups.

Raised voices went back and forth before Savvy strutted up the hall, fully dressed, her mouth tight. She smelled shower clean. Coffee brewed. Domestic as holy hell.

"Here," I said, shoving the newspaper at her. "Read the story on the bottom of the front page." My foot tapped double-time on the braided rug.

Her hand covered her mouth as her eyes widened. "That explosion was Dan Heyward's boat? Are they sure?" She read on then yelled, "Teddy!"

I gripped her wrist. "You ought to keep your mouth shut until we know what the hell's going on. He can't help."

"The heck he can't," she said. "He has the insurance on the house, the equipment, the crop, and the boat. His agency insures Heyward Farm and most of the farms in this county." She glowered at me and shook off my hold. "Whether you like it or not, he's already involved."

Bad had just gravitated to worse. I snatched the paper back. "Meet me at the office. Maybe you can explain how you didn't record the lien document giving us the mortgage to *that* boat." I gripped the doorknob and nodded toward the hallway. "I'm not discussing this with him around."

She appeared genuinely puzzled. "That's not true. I ordered the boat mortgaged like everything else."

My disappointment brewed a deeper, darker anger in me. "Not here. I'm taking Monroe to get something to eat, then we're meeting you at your office. Don't keep me waiting. Dubose wants a report this afternoon."

Savvy flopped in a recliner and rubbed her right temple. Heaven help me, but for a split second, I questioned whether or not she was performing. I stepped across the threshold. "I'll see you in an hour."

I returned to the car. Monroe waited, leaning an elbow out the passenger window, his brow knitted tight. "Not good, huh?"

I got in the car. "Let's get some coffee. I don't care where. If it wasn't so early, I'd spike it."

He fired up the engine, but left the car in park. He remained still, staring.

"Go, Monroe."

He pointed under the carport. "Get a load of that." In my excitement, I'd rushed to the door without taking in the sights. Under the carport sat a brand new convertible. The personalized tag read *SAVVY*.

Monroe and I sat, staring agape at the car. And not any new car: Savvy's much dreamed about Mercedes convertible. I'd heard her joke about buying one the minute she could lay hands on her retirement savings without a penalty, or win the lottery. I hung my head. Why on earth buy it now of all times? And how?

Monroe nodded toward the machine. "Real smart. So what're you going to do?"

"Not a whole lot I can do, except ask why she decided to pick up a luxury car about the time we start an internal investigation. She didn't have that at work. And I have no idea how she can afford it."

He sighed. "Sorry, Slade, but I'm not so convinced she's on the level. Not anymore."

I turned toward him, amazed I believed him. "I'll just flat out ask her the hard questions," I said, trying to tell myself more than anyone else what I needed to do. "I can tell if she's lying. I just don't see a motive."

"These days she wears her temper like cologne, Slade. She'll eat you up."

I almost smelled Savvy's Chanel. "She can try." I can try.

Monroe tapped the steering wheel with one finger, then two, playing some tempo I didn't know. His stomach growled.

I hooked my seat belt. "Guess you're starving. Let's grab a fast bite and then meet with Evan and Savvy."

We rolled through a drive-in at a local place called Bailey's Biscuit Bistro and parked long enough to fix our coffees and unwrap food.

The missing farmer may have pulled some stunt faking his death, maybe because he couldn't pay. I needed to check on whether Dan was indeed the body lying in pieces in the morgue. Without him we had nobody to squeeze for information, unless cousin Purdue knew something. If Dan had really died, all this fell on Savvy, assuming the loan went belly-up, which appeared almost inevitable now. I replayed Savvy's conversations from yesterday over in my head, trying to determine what she hadn't said.

Monroe's words sifted through sausage biscuit as he started the car and drove off. "What did she say in the house?"

I swallowed a mouthful of egg-and-cheese biscuit and gave him the highlights. I preferred to shut out the vision of Teddy's hairy torso amidst Victorian lace.

I licked a glop of cheese off a knuckle. "I've been thinking."

"God help us."

"Just listen," I said, wagging my finger. "If we find where they sold the crop, we could wrangle money from that packing shed. They bought mortgaged property, so we've got them on that count. Might tone down the heat on Savvy if we *collected* the loan." I scorched my tongue on the coffee, licked my lips, and blew across the top. "And maybe we wouldn't have to bring up Teddy and the crop inspections."

"Assuming she wasn't involved up front," he said.

"I'm not ready to go there yet."

He balled up his empty biscuit wrapper and lobbed it into the trash bag. "Well, you find out where they sold the crop, and I'll run by real quick and pick up the money."

"Just go with me here."

He cut me his serious grin. "You ready to tackle Savvy?"

"I guess so." I hated the idea of *tackling* my best friend.

ARRIVING AT THE office, I slung my purse over my shoulder, stepped past my dew-covered Taurus over to Savvy's Mercedes, and admired her toy.

"What is that?" Monroe asked.

I grinned. The guy didn't know much about cars. "It's a CLK, a Cabriolet. I'd just buy a Supercrew F-150 with the King Ranch package. Always wanted a truck, and what I want costs less than this little piece of chrome."

"No, no, I'm talking about this."

He lightly touched a miniature, yellow silk bag hung on the antenna of my Taurus, tied with a hemp rope string. Judging from the dew, the bag must have sat there part of the night.

I yanked it free and opened the drawstring. The sour smell made me turn my head and close it. "Bet Savvy knows how this hoodoo stuff works. This area is full of this kind of history."

We caught her at Raye's desk, sunglasses still on. Dressed in a straight khaki skirt and short-sleeved cotton sweater that hugged her, Savvy stood cocked on one hip like the stuff she was. The sunglasses hid a lot, but not all, of her attitude as represented by a taut jaw.

I glanced at Raye. "You ever seen one of these?"

Raye shook her head, tucking her chin like she wanted to duck.

"It's a conjure bag," Savvy said, taking it from me. She poured out the contents on a piece of typing paper. Yellow dirt mixed with two pennies. "Someone's put a hex on you."

Monroe and I gawked at each other, wide-eyed.

Savvy folded the paper, funneled the mixture back into the bag, and tried to hand it past me to Monroe. I intercepted it. My thumb rubbed the soft silk. "So am I supposed to quake in my shoes? I know your grandmother taught you about this stuff."

"These bags are usually made by a witchdoctor on the islands," she said, "but lots of frauds sell mojo to tourists all the time. The dirt's supposed to be graveyard dirt. A silver dime is left on the plot as payment. Could be good, could be bad, depending on the grave it came from."

She sauntered into her office. Her stiff-necked posture was more than defensive, it was downright rude. I marched after her with Monroe hard on my heels. "What's bad about it?" I asked. "Give us a voodoo lesson."

She sat and pivoted in her chair, removing her glasses. "If the dirt came from the grave of someone evil, or someone who died in a bad way, then the bag is putting a spell on you. The copper pennies relate to the police. The dirt contains sulfur, so any cop involved is hexed. The stinky smell adds to the aura. Some go all out and add powdered snakes, bugs, or snails. Poppy seeds are for confusion and oregano is to repel the law." She grinned. "Someone's given you the whole shebang, sweetheart."

I mentally reviewed the list of people who knew we were hunting for the Heywards. "Have any idea who?"

"Nope," she said too quickly.

Monroe motioned. "I'm going back to my desk. Holler if you need me."

I turned to Savvy. "Be back in a second."

She booted her computer. "I'll try not to escape."

I followed Monroe and leaned on the desk, staring down at the conjure bag.

"She sure is peeved at you," he said.

I tossed the hexed sack. He instinctively caught it, then let it fall to the floor.

"Dirt and pennies in a scrap of cloth doesn't mean squat," I said. "My money's on that sorry ex-husband of hers. He's from here, too. It'd be just like him to pull such a stunt."

"People are funny down here," Monroe said, stooping over to pick up the bag. "But didn't you say Teddy did coke?"

"He did. Who knows *what* he's doing now . . . except spending his evenings at her place." Assuming he wasn't living there. The average person would be curious why Savvy hung around with the infamous Teddy Dawson.

Here I was attempting, for reasons becoming ever more vague to me, to protect the woman. But she didn't seem to care about the borderline walk of ethics I traveled for her. "I ought to check on that dead body, make sure it's Dan," I said, changing the subject.

"Slade." Monroe stretched out my name in warning, peering at me like some school principal. "Listen to yourself. You don't *check on bodies*. You investigate fraud, and not much of that. You're straying off the reservation."

"It impacts the case, Monroe. I've been trying to interview him. I ought to at least confirm whether the man's breathing or not."

"Yeah, well you never saw him, did you? So how would you know who he is?" He pointed to Savvy's office. "Why don't you finish here first? Let me call the sheriff's office. Then I'll try to find Evan."

He was right. I'd done everything but pursue the questionable party—Savvy. My girlfriend and I founded our twelve-year friendship upon blatant honesty. No sense in changing what worked. I took the hex token, marched into Savvy's office, and closed the door. The silk bag dangled from my finger. "I already asked, but I'll try again. Know who planted this?"

Her mouth tightened. "No."

"Not many people know why I'm here. Who have you told about the case besides Raye and Teddy?"

"Nobody."

"So you did tell Teddy why I'm here. Who's he telling?"

Her face reddened.

"Never mind." No point in pursuing this line of questioning. Besides, I'd handed out my card a few times. No surprise I was in town.

She touched her forehead. I stepped closer, wondering if the fresh headache was an excuse to dodge my questions.

"I'm not under any orders to keep quiet," she said. "You'd confide in your boyfriend if you were in my place."

No conceivable comparison existed between Teddy and Wayne, but arguing that fact was pointless. "Count your lucky stars it's me here and not someone else trying to fry your fanny for a gold star in their file and a removal action in yours."

Her mouth opened then snapped shut, her inhale loud and forceful. "I think you're letting Teddy's past taint your professionalism," she said.

I snorted and rested both hands on my hips. "That boat explosion probably got rid of the one person who might've known the truth, therefore clearing you. It doesn't look good, Savvy."

She spoke tight, oozing the words between her teeth. "You'd believe me if Teddy wasn't in the picture. Somebody else did whatever this is, Miss High-and-Mighty. Not me."

We faced off across her desk, our eyes playing chicken, daring each other to think beyond the obvious. Hearing her say the words made me realize more than ever that someone could be setting her up, or at least redirecting our interest from some other phony-baloney.

If we'd been discussing our love lives or politics, we'd have agreed to disagree by now. But this was a crime that couldn't be laughingly negotiated over margaritas.

Chapter 7

I SAT BACK down in my chair to regain composure. Savvy watched me intently from behind her desk, as if expecting me to reach around and draw a gun.

"Listen," I said. "Let's chat like it doesn't involve you."

She didn't move, but her gaze held fast. "And talk about what? You've sort of stripped the air of friendship."

"Breathe, Savvy. Just take a breath."

She did. And I did. And I gave her a moment. When I saw her neck soften a bit, I dared a question. "Did you even suspect Dan of fraud?"

"No," she said. "Met him a couple of times, but he wasn't more than a middle-aged good-ol-boy. Didn't once try to hit on me."

My laughter lifted a weight off my shoulders, and Savvy relaxed. "That's your measuring scale?" I asked. "Whether they hit on you?"

A smile crept in with a playful shrug. "Works most of the time."

"Okay," I said, glancing out the window where I couldn't miss the car. "Where'd the Benz come from?"

The grin disappeared. "Did you just try to soften me up?"

Crap. "No. The car just caught my eye and popped into my head. Let's start over."

"Friend or foe, Slade? My career is on the line, and I'm not sure whether you'll help or hinder my chances." She shoved papers in frustration. "I've had enough of this."

Leaning in, I tried to recover ground I'd lost. "I know you, and I'm having trouble believing you let a farmer get away with this. We can't find a crop financed with government money, and you let God-knows-who sign the promissory notes and run off with federal dollars. You're all over the place in your talk, your actions, even your appearance." I fought getting angry with her. "And what *is* with the friggin' Mercedes? You know what *that* looks like?"

"I don't *know* why those signatures are different," she said. "And no, I haven't searched for the tomato crop, but it's too soon to panic. Some sheds haven't paid yet. And . . ." she sighed, "Teddy thought the Benz would help with my stress."

Yeah, sure he did. "Why didn't you drive it yesterday?"

"He only brought it over last night."

"What's he want in return for that sweet new machine?"

Her eyes tightened to slits. "It's a damn generous move on his part. He's grown up, wants to make amends. He leased the Benz. Wanted me to ride in style and enjoy the feel of leather and the wind blowing through my hair . . . in case I lost it with treatments or something."

My blood froze. "Treatments?"

"The tests aren't back yet. He said that . . . just in case . . . doesn't matter. It was a sweet gesture."

I pinched the bridge of my nose and longed to tell her everything would turn out fine, personally and professionally. She was itching for someone to say it. I bet that's how Teddy crawled back into her life. God, she was stronger than this. She taught *me* to be stronger than this.

Her voice cracked. Tears welled in her eyes. "You think I'd bring the car to work and flaunt it to *investigators* if I had crap to hide?"

She glanced away. I did, too.

Surely she knew I cared; I needed her to know I cared. Teddy was born rotten. At one time she recognized that all too well. He shouldn't be the one holding her hand through the bumps in her life. I should.

I held up my palms. "Let's stop this."

"Please," she said and cleared her throat.

"I need your help with something."

"What?" she asked, sounding tired.

"Where would Heyward, either Dan or Purdue, sell the tomatoes?"

She identified the packing sheds between Charleston and Beaufort. No other facility outside that range would accept the crop, and distance would tear into profits. If Purdue or Dan Heyward sold the crop in their own names, we'd know once Monroe made the calls. Selling in their names, however, was the catch. I'd bet a paycheck they used an alias or two.

I closed the file. She watched as I placed it in my briefcase.

"We aren't the enemy," I said, still peering down.

Her hands rested on the desk. I sensed a quiver in her voice as she spoke way too soft for the warrior she was. "Someone has framed me, Slade. You do see that, don't you?"

"Honey, yes, I see it." At least I hoped I did. "But I've got to make the world see it and find the culprits."

"And the most likely candidate is supposedly dead," she said.

"It's pointing that way."

She shrugged. "What if it was a con on Dan's part, and his death is a disappearing ploy since we're hunting him?"

That idea was already on my short list. I stood.

"Y'all go do your thing," she said abruptly, and spun her chair around toward the computer. "I have business to tend to in case I get yanked away. Plan for the worst, you know."

My head hung at the sound of concession. "Savannah, don't go overboard with this."

She refused to make eye contact.

"Listen . . ." I started.

Her tanned face went milky white. She lurched to the side and vomited in her trash can.

I shouted, "Monroe!"

Quick movements and a thud sounded in the next room. He appeared in the doorway.

"Hurry," I ordered. "Get me a cold wet rag or something." Turning to Savvy, I said, "Hold on, hon."

I reached out to cradle her head. Instead, her body went limp and tipped out of her chair and into me as she fainted. Unable to grip her shoulders and stop her fall, I wrapped myself around her and let her dead weight collapse on top of me.

I rolled her over and held her in one arm. Snatching the phone by the cord, I dialed 9-1-1. Receiver on my shoulder, I relayed the address.

Savvy's eyes fluttered open. "Shit," she said.

I smiled back at her to hide my worry. A hundred illnesses raced through my thoughts, all with horrible endings. And the stress of my being here sure as hell didn't help.

Raye ran into the office and halted, eyes wide, hands clenched against her chest.

"EMS will be here in a minute," I said. "Go wait for them outside."

She didn't move.

"Now," I shouted.

She turned and collided with Monroe, knocking his head against the doorjamb. They scrambled around each other. He handed me a wad of paper towels. "These are all I could find."

I took the wet towels from him and noticed a half-inch gash on his forehead. "Get one of these for yourself, fella. You're bleeding."

Savvy tried to sit up, but I made her stay down, wiping her face. "Don't give up on me, Slade," she said.

Teddy rushed in. "What the hell's going on?" The bum grabbed my arm. "Get out of the way. I'll take it from here."

I jerked away. "Don't touch me, Teddy."

Savvy tried to sit up again. "Teddy?"

"Don't sit up," I told her.

She pushed my hand away. "I just skipped breakfast and forgot to eat last night. Y'all don't fight. I'm all right, Teddy."

I turned the towels to their clean sides and tried to wipe up her sweater, putting me between her and Teddy. "We're just concerned about you."

Teddy leaned over and gripped my wrist. "Get up," he said.

My hand twisted and rolled over his wrist to torque it downward. He yelped with pain. "Ow! You bitch!"

"I warned you to keep your hands off me." I released him.

Savvy's eyes took on a pained expression. "Don't, Slade."

Teddy reached for me again.

Monroe grabbed his shoulders. "Back off, man."

"Or what?" Teddy said, shrugging off Monroe, nursing his wrist.

Monroe's assertiveness astounded me, and my puzzlement caught his attention, drawing a slight grin. Two medics hurried through the door and ordered everyone out. Monroe kept watch on Teddy as they headed into the hall.

I briefed the medics quickly on what little I could of Savvy's recent mention of vague health issues, and then joined the boys. Teddy tried to shove past me back into the office, but I stood in his path. "What do you know about Heyward Farms?"

Fists on hips, he braced me. His goldenrod-colored dress shirt was rolled up at the sleeves, his sockless feet in deck shoes. His gut hung like a water balloon over his web belt. "You want their zodiac signs or what?"

He stood taller than Monroe, but Monroe's jogger physique gave Teddy a Pillsbury Doughboy appearance. Hard to tell whether the sun or bourbon had a bigger hand in his coloring.

His nonchalance only ticked me off. "What's your involvement with Dan or Purdue? The crop's missing, and you *apparently* were the last person to see it." I withheld facts about the signatures and the unsecured shrimp boat like cops do when they keep a pertinent piece of the puzzle secret to gauge the truth.

"So, I saw the crop. It was growing. It made little green fruit. We call 'em tomatoes 'round here."

"Just answer the questions, man," Monroe said.

Teddy eyed Monroe up and down. "I need to be with Savannah."

I stepped in closer, determined to keep him away from an already stressed-out Savvy. "Let the medics do their job. How well do you know the Heywards?"

"My company underwrites all the crop insurance policies in Beaufort and most of Jasper County. We know everyone who farms. Plus Dan went to high school with my older brother. So yes, I know . . . knew, Dan Heyward. And I didn't sign someone else's name, so get off my back."

He knew about the signatures. I was disappointed at Savvy but not surprised.

The medics wheeled Savvy past on a gurney. "I'm telling you, there's nothing wrong. This is embarrassing," she complained.

I offered to go with her, concern niggling me, adrenaline making me crave action of some kind. However, she chose the dolt instead, and Teddy took her hand. Pink already crept back into her cheeks. "Help me, Slade."

I nodded, knowing she wasn't talking about her health. "I'll keep digging, don't worry. You call me the minute you learn something from the doctors."

Teddy moved between us. "Don't you think you've done enough damage?"

Savvy's glance caught mine, and I smiled in assurance.

We followed her out and watched the ambulance drive off, Teddy following in his car. Monroe placed his arm around my shoulder. "This must be eating you up," he said.

"Gets my goat she's seeing that moron," I said, down about not being there for my friend and fearful I'd caused this to happen. I slid from under Monroe's hug and walked back to go inside.

"Sweet move you did breaking that wrist hold in there," he said behind me. "Wayne teach you that?"

I snickered. "Yeah. I laughed at him when he showed me how to do it. Have to admit it felt good testing it on that bastard, though."

"Don't expect Teddy to forget it," Monroe said. He walked past me and held open the front door.

I entered the building, proud I'd just shown everyone I could take care of myself . . . and wishing fixing Savvy's problem was that simple.

WITH SAVVY AT the hospital, Monroe and I handled a couple of her urgent client calls and instructed Raye to cancel appointments. I gave the list of packing sheds to Monroe to see if he could locate our hundred acres of wayward tomatoes.

Evan remained unreachable. I called his cell and got voice mail. It was already lunchtime. Crap. Not enough time to make the boss's meeting and go to Heyward Farm, too. What I wouldn't give for more time to at least talk to Purdue.

I rang Dubose's direct line.

The gravelly, cigarette voice of Harden Harris, the agency's support staff director, came on the line, and I tensed. Harden oversaw engineering, appraisal, and environmental reviews for our agency across the state, but he was on my same managerial level.

"What crap have you stirred up today, Miss Carolina?" he asked.

What an idiot. "Where's the boss, Harden?"

"She's at the governor's office. What's the problem?"

"She coming back this afternoon?"

"Don't know, but I'm filling in for her. Spill it. What's going on down there?"

I wasn't falling for his hogwash. "Down where?"

"I know you're in Beaufort."

"You only think you know where I am. Just leave a note telling the boss I'll see her Monday."

"What if I forget?"

I hung up. "Nut job." I dialed Dubose's secretary, but the call rolled to voice mail. Crap again. I left a brief message about following an important lead in Beaufort and asked her to give the info to Dubose, not Harden.

Harden's connections with real estate entities throughout the state once made him a likely player in the real estate scam I helped dismantle in Charleston last year. The U.S. Attorney stopped short of pinning accomplice on him, writing him off as a minor participant at best. His cohorts, however, went to jail.

As a result, Harden nipped at my heels. He hated Monroe as well, solely for his friendship with me. A misstep by either of us, and we could count on him making a beeline to the director's ear.

Unzipping my purse, I fished for car keys and left Savvy's office.

Monroe hung up his phone as I walked into his office. "The sheriff isn't releasing info on Dan's body yet. Still no definite ID. Also said we needed legal authority to see an autopsy report."

"Man must be related to Harden," I mumbled.

"What?"

"Nothing." I relayed my conversation with the State Office.

"You going back to Columbia now?"

"Dubose only gave me yesterday and half of today, but since she's not in, it gives me this afternoon to find something concrete to justify my trip here. Wish Evan would get back." I glanced at my watch. "Savvy call yet?"

"No, but she'll call you first."

Couldn't help but smile at his remark, but I dug the cell out of my purse and punched her number anyway. The call diverted to voice mail.

"I'll visit the sheriff's office in person," I said, "maybe drop by the

Coast Guard and see what I can dig up on Dan. Then I'll go by the farm again. Thank God the state director doesn't expect me this afternoon."

Monroe shook his head. "Knowing Harden, Dubose could've been in the restroom. You might check in again." His glance down made me do the same.

"What?"

"Where's your briefcase?"

Walking back into Savvy's office, I found it pushed into the corner, probably shoved out of the way during the confusion. I lifted it onto the chair and glanced inside.

My pulse skipped. "You have the Heyward file, Monroe?"

"No, you held it last. Check Savvy's desk."

I did, and then searched the room.

Monroe peered in. "Find it?"

I shook my head. "It's vanished." I canvassed my briefcase, a particular face appearing instantly in my mind. "Teddy stole the dang file."

"You don't know that," Monroe said.

"Like hell I don't." Teddy snatched it during Savvy's fainting spell, as sure as the mole on my butt.

Monroe returned to his desk and lifted a thin stack of papers from a drawer. "My, my, what do we have here?" He waved the papers. "When I found the irregularities, I copied several documents to work from." He smiled mischievously. "What's this worth to you?"

"All of the papers?"

"Note, mortgage, application, and loan approval form. Everything but notes and narrative."

I could almost kiss him. Copies were just as good for what we were doing, and besides, the note was in the safe, the deeds officially recorded with the county. "Aren't you the man? Will supper cover my debt?"

His eyes twinkled. "Just stay obligated to me. You treat me nicer."

If we had to lose one thing, it was the note containing Savvy's white lie about inspecting the crop. As anal as Assistant U.S. Attorneys were about evidence, they wouldn't pursue the issue about the falsified crop inspection without paper to prove it.

Monroe asked Raye to keep her eye open for the originals as I readied to leave.

"I'll search everywhere, Mr. Prevatte," she said in her soft-spoken manner. If she was half as good as she seemed, Savvy should count her blessings. That little lady could be practically running the office until this investigation settled down.

"Thanks, Raye. I'll see you soon. Hold the fort."

She dipped her head in acknowledgment. Blonde, quiet, and sweet. Everything I wasn't.

Monroe touched my elbow. "I'll walk you to your car. Call me if you hear from Savvy. I'll assume no news is good news if you don't." He brushed against me, and the familiar whiff of bay rum cologne eased my anxiety a bit. I glanced at my watch.

I really missed Wayne . . . and I'd miss Zack's play.

Chapter 8

IT TOOK ME fifteen minutes to travel Boundary Street and whip into the drive outside the sheriff's red brick complex, coincidentally close to a street named Heyward. Inside I found the receptionist, her backside molded into her chair so perfectly as to make one wonder if she pried it off each night with a shoehorn.

I scanned her smiling face for clues on making nice. "May I speak to someone about Dan Heyward's status, please?"

"We think he's dead, honey," she said, her coifed head of black hair stiff as she multi-tasked. "What more status do you need?"

From the wall full of certificates, she'd been around a while, playing human shield between the sheriff, the inquisitive, and the unimportant. She'd probably heard every excuse and story on the planet.

I handed her my business card. "That's helpful, but could I see the autopsy report? I'm investigating Mr. Heyward's farming operation. His crop is coming out of the field, and my agency has a mortgage on his place. Any idea when there'll be a death certificate issued? Our money's rotting by the hour," I said.

Her forehead creased beneath lacquered bangs. "Honey, this ain't CSI Miami. The autopsy will take a day or two, lab work more. They only brought in the pieces twelve hours ago."

I winced at the image.

Her coy smile told me she enjoyed my reaction. "But I promise to give your card to the appropriate individual." She placed it in her desk drawer.

"Have they determined if it was murder or an accident?"

"I've got your card."

I peered around. Three uniforms with heavy leather belts on their waists looked away, as if they pitied yet another casualty of Ms. Gatekeeper's vigilance. "Is Purdue Heyward the only family who's been by here?"

She sighed, like I was a pitiful four-year-old begging for candy before dinner. "Someone will be in touch, if they can help you."

The woman slung more useless retorts than a politician's wife. "May I have the name of someone to contact?"

Without missing a beat at her other work, she handed me a card with the sheriff's name and phone number. "Let me guess," I said. "This is *your* phone number?"

She beamed. "You got it, honey."

I slid another card on her desk and placed a third under a huge paperweight with a plastic yellow rose embedded in the middle. "Just in case you lose one . . . *honey*."

The sheriff's mother superior returned to her phone and computer screen, unfazed by my sass. I left, snared a deputy in the parking lot, and begged for assistance, but he pointed me back toward the secretarial sentinel. At least he told me the Coast Guard operated out of Charleston, not Beaufort.

My investigative path led nowhere and everywhere. I wondered where they kept bodies in a small town, and if they'd acquiesce to my flashy credentials.

I'd seen three corpses in my lifetime, all killed within feet of me. Inspecting mangled body parts, or worse, a severed head dangling an esophagus or spinal cord, would scar my dreams for life. Talking to Purdue would provide more answers than Dan's body parts. Skip the Coast Guard. Skip the morgue.

I headed toward the islands for one last attempt at finding the cousin. Only one day in town, and it felt like a week. Once away from city traffic, I pulled up my voice mail on speaker.

One message on my cell. My contractor said he'd finished hanging the extra ceiling fan on the back porch. Maybe it was fatigue, but I couldn't muster a drop of excitement that this beautiful house sat empty waiting for me.

The phone rang in my hand. The jolt of surprise caused me to drop it. One eye on the road, I fumbled for the ringing cell under my feet. I ducked, grabbed the phone, and straightened. Several cars ahead, a driver stopped prematurely to let a landscape truck and trailer cross the stream of traffic. My foot slammed the brake. The Taurus dipped, slid, and mildly rolled off the asphalt to kiss a palmetto tree.

Thank God no airbag went off. Eyes closed, I laid my head on the steering wheel. The phone quit ringing. Stupid, stupid, stupid. How many times had I told Ivy about asinine drivers too busy texting and calling to focus on the road?

Hands shaking mildly, I pulled off the road completely as I should've done and checked caller ID. The missed phone message indicated the State Office.

With a hesitant finger, I checked voicemail. A woman's voice said, "Ms. Slade," and the emphasis on *Ms.* made my stomach sink.

"Margaret Dubose here. My day ends in thirty minutes. You owe me the courtesy of a call."

Rolling up the window for quiet, I hit redial. She answered her own phone. "Dubose."

"Ma'am, my apologies for not catching up with you. Mr. Harris said—"

"He has no business in this case." Her voice clipped each word.

"But he answered your phone, and I asked him—"

"Where are you? I cut short a meeting to be here."

Damn. Monroe was right—Harden had lied. A no-win situation, unless . . . "EMS rushed Savvy to the hospital."

"Is she all right?" No excitement, just a clean, cut-to-the-chase question.

"Yes, ma'am, but I just couldn't get back in time. I left messages."

If I'd been in her office, I'd have seen her fingering a pen, weighing her next comment.

"When did this happen?" she asked.

"Right before lunch."

"Seems like with Ms. Conroy in the hospital, you'd have packed up and kept your appointment with me."

"Ms. Dubose, I promised to keep her office open, and I still need to research a few items on this case. I've known Savvy for quite a long time and—"

"Be here at seven sharp Monday morning. I hope this impromptu trip of yours shows merit, or we have some serious talking to do."

Scorched from my scolding, I exited the vehicle and checked for damage. A mild dent. Nothing worth raising my premium over. I turned on my blinker to reenter the string of cars and eased in front of a commercial van, wondering how the heck I'd function so early on Monday morning. Dubose would eat me alive before I woke up enough to know it. I didn't do mornings well, and this tete-a-tete would test every slow-waking neuron in my brain.

Vehicles crawled through town and across the bridge from Beaufort toward the islands. After the forty-five-minute drive, I found nary a soul in the tomato field so I headed back to town spent and empty-handed.

WAYNE SOUNDED preoccupied when I called. "How long before you get here?" he asked.

"Couple of hours if I don't rush. What's wrong?"

"We have it under control."

I froze. "Have what under control?"

"Nothing urgent. Just get here safe. Drive careful."

Fine. I didn't feel like talking anyway. After reaching voice mail on Savvy's phone again, I called the hospital. "You might try her home," said the nurse. "We released her an hour ago."

I'd try her home, all right. Making a U-turn on Highway 21, I took Ribaut Road toward Port Royal and cruised by Savvy's one-story, white-siding home, her green thumb evident in the giant clusters of pale yellow Lady Banks roses alongside the front porch. Her Mercedes and Teddy's Pontiac were parked cozily side by side. I called Savvy's cell.

Teddy answered. "Hello?"

His voice on her phone threw me. I squeezed the device. How could I have a beer with Savvy and sort details with him around?

"Savvy there?" I asked.

"She's lying down," he said. "You upset her. It's after hours, and she doesn't have to deal with you." He hung up.

I turned around in her driveway. No point talking to her with him in her ear. So I drove toward the interstate and stopped for gas. Tank topped off, I tried to call Monroe. Since he was staying in town, he really needed to track down Evan. The call went to voice mail, and I left a simple don't-forget-to-do-this message.

The whole day boiled down to zero progress.

If not for the kids and my lease expiring, I'd have stayed another night, stalked my elusive farmer, harassed Savvy, and found Evan myself. But motherly instinct and common sense told me to head home, pack boxes, and move.

Time to face facts. No way this case remained at the administrative level. We needed a real agent on the scene.

Thus far evidence painted Savvy in the worst of lights, with a large financial loss for the government—the penalty ranging from demotion to termination. And if she benefited from anything in the mix, she'd do jail time.

Only a weekend to sugarcoat this mess for the state director on Monday. All I could report was what I didn't know, who I hadn't interviewed, and how much wasn't paid on the loan.

I REACHED MY apartment right after seven, with plenty of daylight to spare. A different rental truck sat in front with a ramp extended to the sidewalk. People I didn't know trudged up the platform with lamps, a rolled-up rug, and chairs out of my place.

Wayne stood in khaki shorts, sneakers, and a Federal Law Enforcement Training Center T-shirt. "Hey, CI. You made good time getting here."

"I'm not a CI anymore. You'll have to come up with something different." I planted a kiss on his close-cut, bearded cheek. "What's left in the fridge? I'm starved."

"Sorry. It's cleaned out. I ate the butterbeans myself." He snapped his finger. "There you go."

"What?"

He patted my cheek. "You can be my Butterbean if you hate CI so much."

I rolled my eyes. "Don't think so."

A five foot two, tight-butted brunette carried a box labeled *books*. "Who's that?" I asked.

Wayne hugged me, his damp T-shirt laying sweat on my neck. "Liz," he said. "She and Rob are Richland County deputies. Your dad was going to do this himself, if you can believe that." He smiled. "Surprised?"

"Well, of course. How could I not be?" Finally, a positive to my day. Free labor. I gave him a parting hug. "I'll check on Daddy and be right back."

"Wait. Before you go in, we need to talk."

"Tiger Rag" rang again on my phone. I held up a finger. Caller ID indicated Savvy.

"Hey," she said, her high spirits crystal through the line. "You tried to call?"

If I hadn't seen them haul her away in an ambulance, I'd have expected that buoyant tone to embellish her latest shopping trip or a five-pound loss from some wild organic diet.

"Several times," I said, annoyed at the glee. "What'd the doctor say?"

"Low blood sugar, stress, not eating, a headache from all the above. I'm home now."

"You tell him about your headaches?"

I could almost hear her shrug. "They said for me to go back to my other doctor and finish my tests. They couldn't find the problem."

I thought of Teddy's car in her drive, and the fact she didn't mention he was there. "You feeling okay . . . being alone?"

"Slade."

"Don't Slade me. I drove by before I left Beaufort."

She laughed. "I saw you out the window. Why didn't you stop?"

"Yeah, right. If you're going to spend time with Teddy, how about getting Purdue Heyward's phone number from him? He said he knew every farmer in the area through his insurance company."

She spoke to Teddy, who must've been standing right next to her. "He says he doesn't know him."

"He told me he did."

"Maybe he was mistaken," she said.

"Hard to believe y'all are so ignorant of a county you claim to know inside and out."

She paused. "You think I'm lying?"

Wayne stepped over, trying to listen. I turned my back to him, but my voice probably carried to downtown Columbia. "No, but he is. You think Teddy's as chaste as a choirboy. What about . . . ?"

"What about what?"

I'd almost mentioned the missing file. As much as I hated to admit it, I wanted to see how she'd react in person.

My cherry headboard came out the door in the grips of the Richland deputies and bumped into the truck wall as they trudged up the ramp. "I've got to go. I'll report to Dubose Monday, then do my best to get back down."

"Hey," she said, in what I sensed was a stab at having the last word. "Don't come back down here if it pains you so much. I'd rather have somebody else *investigating* me if all I'll catch is grief about my boyfriend." She hung up.

Now I was pissed. She flashed attitude like a traffic light, green one minute, red the next.

My recliner passed by in the hold of one beefed up, strappy guy. A muted spot on the red fabric stood out, as if damp or stained. "What a minute." Still revved from pummeling Savvy, I strutted to the chair. The mover set it down, huffs and moans accenting the effort. "Where'd that stain come from?"

Wayne motioned for the guy to load it on the truck. "You haven't given me a chance, Slade. There was an accident, and I didn't want you to break your neck getting home."

I bolted into the apartment, angrier than ever at Savvy for drawing me away from my family into her maelstrom, especially with her not recognizing the fact I gave a damn.

My heart hammered as I rushed inside. Zack lay on a yellow blanket in the living room corner, his right arm in an orange cast propped on a throw pillow. I hovered over him, unable to resist kissing his cheek. "Oh my God, baby. Does it hurt?"

He shook his head, his eyes glazed from medication. "Mr. Wayne watched me in my play," he said slurred. "He carried me in the hospital. Cool dad . . ." His eyes closed.

"Oh baby," I whispered as my fingertips ran through his strawberry locks. "I tried to get home."

"He's fine," said Wayne as his hand rubbed my back. "I broke my arm at about his age, and it healed just fine."

I brushed a hand over the fresh gauze. Still kneading his hair, I thought about the play I hadn't even asked about.

An older hand patted my shoulder. "I'm sorry, honey. Guess it was my fault."

I caught sight of the bandage on Daddy's chin and did a double take, rising to my feet. "What happened to you?"

"When we got home from the play, Zack was full of himself." He tucked his chin, glancing over his glasses. "It went well, by the way. No fights." He removed the glasses as if they interfered. "After we got back here, I caught the boy bouncing on the furniture. I tried to make him settle down, and *wham*. His head hit my chin, and he flipped over on the floor. By the time I realized it was my blood instead of his, he threw up on your chair. The doc said broken bones could do that."

I touched his jaw. "So what's your damage?"

"Eight stitches. Boy's definitely got your hard head."

"Oh my gosh, Daddy! I'm so sorry."

A ponytailed Ivy stepped out of Zack's room. With her pout and posture, she already struck a teenage pose at the tender age of twelve. "I'm stuck packing his junk," she said, pointing to her brother. "Figures he'd get out of working."

"I think he has good reason," I said.

"Whatever."

"That's enough, Ivy."

She shrugged. "What did I do?"

Was everybody defying me these days? "I'll tell you what you *will* do, and that's turn around and get back to work."

She withdrew back from me. "What's *your* problem?"

My day's pent-up frustration threatened to flood the room. I turned, went into the bathroom, and shut the door. God, couldn't the kids behave for forty-eight hours without me? Were their behaviors my fault or was I worn out? Our cat Madge scratched the door, and I allowed her in. Picking her up, I closed the toilet lid and sat, hugging her to my chest.

I sucked in air, held it, closed my eyes, and stopped the world.

When silence reverted to bumps and thumps outside, I walked out and changed into jeans to scrub the kitchen in hopes I'd salvage enough security deposit to pay for the rental truck. They say relocation is a high stressor. I'd give my right arm to just be moving.

Chapter 9

SHY OF MIDNIGHT, the crew unloaded my final belongings into our new place, after earlier chugging beer and cola and eating five extra-large pizzas. Wayne and I thanked the movers as they dragged themselves to their cars. We barely threw sheets on the beds before Daddy and the kids fell asleep. Wayne and I collapsed outside on the dock.

I sat between his legs and leaned back against his chest. A cool stir drifted in across the water. Small ripples reflected slivers of undulating moonlight. Aching legs and lower back consumed my bone-weary attention.

Wayne nuzzled my hair, his beard tickling my ear, and I melted into him, dying to stay here, floating, sleeping just like this until dawn. Then he ran slow hands down my chest and back up again, routing fingers between the buttons of my denim shirt. "We could try doing it right here."

I grinned, my eyes remaining shut. "You'd be screwing a corpse." A shiver darted through my shoulders at my choice of words. "I wish you could stay over," I whispered, so tired. "We owe each other by now." My will weakened to wet tissue paper when he brushed across a breast.

He chuckled low after my light gasp.

Relaxed and eyes closed, I recalled what my son said in the apartment. "I didn't have a chance to thank you for attending Zack's play," I said. "He seemed tickled to death you went. Above and beyond the call of duty, lawman. So sweet." I rubbed his legs, oh so cozy now, and oh so in love with his attention to my child.

He wrapped his arms around me. "More than happy to do it, Butterbean. Wish you could've been there, but you sounded like you had your hands full."

I snorted at the icky name. "To say the least."

"You want to tell me about Savannah?"

The weight of the topic crashed across my exhausted shoulders. No denying it anymore. The case demanded fresh eyes. "I need you in Beaufort," I conceded. He listened silently to my update, shrewdly reading that turning her over to him hurt me deeply.

"She done anything?" he asked.

"Guilty until proven innocent, right?"

"It's a simple question, Slade. Try not to think of her as a friend. Do you think she did anything?"

I rose up, a breeze blowing through the space between us. "No, I *don't* think so. And you can't think so either. Promise me. Not until you have solid granite proof."

"So she might *have* done something." He paused, and I suspected what he was about to say. "Distance yourself, CI. If you can't see the facts for the friendship, then back away."

I slid around on the dock and crossed my legs, facing him. "You know her too, lawman."

"But I'm—"

"A professional?"

He placed a hand on my knee. "I'm not as close as you are to Savannah. Give me until Wednesday," he said. "Just stick to the admin stuff until I get there. That's your legal parameter—not the criminal work." He tapped me on the head. "I know you know that."

I did, but I'd snoop where needed. He knew that, too. I brushed his hand away and stood.

Wayne remained seated. He analyzed like an agent instead of a friend. I couldn't decide if that was good or bad and turned, facing the lake.

He stood. "Want me to go back to town?"

"No. It's late. We're way too tired to discuss this. Let's go inside."

Moments later, I dropped on the mattress in my unmarred, freshly painted bedroom, dismayed I'd celebrated my first night in this beautiful place with a disagreement. Wayne crashed on the sofa. As always when I went to sleep overtired, dreams lined up one behind the other.

I hid in a large dark room without windows, the entire scene in a muffled, cotton-batted silence. A cold ghostly presence ran its fingers through my hair from behind me, entangling themselves in the strands, wrapping hair around its fists. I couldn't remember how to scream. The thought of fighting, touching him, scared me, as if his dead flesh would come off in my hands. The slow tugging sensation enticed me to enter his eerie world, an inch at a time. I gripped the mattress edge, pain shooting under my fingernails.

I jerked awake to find Wayne relocated beside me, his arm draped over my belly.

He jumped, reaching for the Glock under his pillow. "Huh? What is it?"

Except for the whirring ceiling fan, hush drifted through the house like December snow. I scratched the goose bumps on my head. "Bad dream."

"Someone chasing you again?" he mumbled. He knew of my frequent nightmares since Charleston.

"Yeah, a ghost."

His eyes still closed, his hand ran slowly under my T-shirt. "Come over here next to me. I'll scare him away."

"Not on your life. Get up before Daddy sees us in here."

We moved to the sofa. I lay against him, hugging until more of our body parts touched than not. My hand reached across his midsection to the top of his elastic gym shorts. His hug encircled me.

That's where we found ourselves at ten a.m., when my doorbell rang. A shrill voice sounded through the door. "Hello? Welcome Wagon."

Wayne rolled off the sofa onto the floor as I scrambled to my feet. He stroked his hair in place, tugged his clothes straight, and almost ran into the bedroom door heading for the bathroom. Daddy stood at the sliding glass door admiring the lake, laughing softly.

I hadn't felt this clumsy since sneaking in drunk from a high school party, pretending to be sick with the flu. The doorbell rang again. I finger-combed my hair, ran to the kitchen to wet a paper towel, and wiped my face before running to answer.

Buddy and Dolly Amick lived across the cove, an older couple in their late sixties. They'd adopted me as my house took shape over the last six months. The five-foot-nothing woman pushed a gray and blonde pin curl away from her temple. "Welcome to the neighborhood."

I took a blueberry cobbler from her hands and gestured for them to come in. "Sorry I don't have any refreshments to offer you other than a soft drink from the cooler."

The short woman scrunched her nose and waved me off. "Didn't come over to drink. I want to see your house."

By the time I'd finished showing her every room but the bath where Wayne showered, I'd settled down a bit. We met up with Daddy and Mr. Amick in the kitchen talking about hunting seasons.

Mr. Amick moved around the island to stand beside his wife. "You didn't meddle, did you, Dolly?"

"You hush, Buddy. Don't embarrass me," she said.

He snickered. "Like that would happen."

Then she turned to me. "Seen Beau yet?"

"Dolly!" warned Mr. Amick.

"Who's Beau?" I asked, entertained at their natural gibe toward each other.

"Beau Wessinger, honey," said Dolly. "The guy who lived here before you."

Granted, my head functioned at half-canter this early, but I'd demolished the vacant ramshackle fishing shack on the property before building my dream house—vacant, as in nobody living there.

Her husband laughed. "She couldn't resist mentioning that sorry haint to you."

I shook my head in slow motion at the word *haint*. "Sorry. Not unless he's hiding behind a box." Why the hell not? Hexed in Beaufort, haunted at home.

Zack ran in on the tail end of the conversation, wielding his new cast. "What's a haint, Momma?"

"Zack, don't run with that arm. A haint's the same as a ghost. Don't let it bother you."

"Wicked!" He ran back to his sister, unbothered. "Ivy, we've got a ghost living here!"

Daddy pointed the Amicks to the porch where they clucked over Zack's injury and explained ghosts. I leaned on the counter, letting my mental faculties catch up with my body. I didn't do morning excitement.

"Baby girl?"

I jumped, even knowing only one person called me that. "Yeah, Daddy?"

"I feel awful bad about Zack."

"Aw, Daddy," I said, stroking his shoulder. "You couldn't help what happened. Zack's been a handful, and you got stuck with one of his moments. God, we've worked you to death. I ought to apologize to you."

"I called your mother, and she made a darn good suggestion."

I hesitated. Mom's ideas could be fabulously grand or imported from another dimension, and she considered her ideas more than suggestions. She delivered them as if already ratified by Congress.

"Why don't I take Zack back with us for a week or two? It's summer. He's over Bible school." A chuckle escaped him at that thought. His hand then rested on mine. "Don't take what I'm about to say the wrong way."

I half-frowned, not wanting to bash his idea before I had a chance to hate it.

"Alan was a sorry father to that boy, but Zack still misses a dad. Let me work with Zack and give you time to settle his home." He squeezed my fingers. "My bet is he'll learn to miss the parent and sister he still has."

His suggestion planted a seed of failure in my head. Wasn't correcting Zack my job? "I don't know, Daddy."

Wayne came in the kitchen, shampooed, combed, and smelling good. He sensed my awkwardness and stopped. "What's wrong?"

"Nothing, I guess," I said. "Daddy thinks Zack would do better if he went to my parents' for a week or so."

"I think it's a great idea," he said. Daddy nodded in return. Of course they agreed.

"Fine," I said, dragging the vowel. Daddy hugged me. I hugged back. What did single mothers do without a support structure as good as this?

RISING EARLY enough to pacify the state director for a seven a.m. powwow sucked.

Disoriented in the house, even after a weekend of organizing, I scrambled to find my mascara . . . then my slip . . . then my iron to get rid of the creases in my suit jacket.

On Sunday, after Daddy had left with Zack, Ivy and I unpacked half the boxes, while Wayne screwed in curtain rods over windows and shifted furniture upon request. Ivy moaned incessantly about Zack dodging work.

This morning I'd left her in bed snoozing with phone numbers for the Amicks and my office written on a notepad in the kitchen in case of emergency. I'd also written a reminder about casserole leftovers in the refrigerator, courtesy of Mrs. Amick. Knowing Ivy, she'd gorge on chips and deli meat instead. Mrs. Amick would be over around nine.

I underestimated the time it took to drive twelve miles further to the federal building in downtown Columbia. Forty minutes later, I flashed credentials to security, then scurried through the metal detector. The elevator deposited me on the tenth floor, headquarters of the state's U.S. Department of Agriculture. I hurried across carpeted floor through the double doors of the director's outer office.

Angela, her secretary, already operated at full throttle. "Ms. Dubose's still in a meeting, Slade, but she should be done shortly."

"At seven in the morning?" The rest of the floor barely stirred, but apparently appointments ran early today. "How's her mood?"

Angela shrugged. The polished wood door opened before I could press her for a better interpretation. Harden Harris exited. Darn it. He'd beaten me to the boss; maybe he'd trip on his way out.

I approached. "Thanks for the blatant lie to the state director Friday."

"Glad to help," he said, staring at my legs. "Nice skirt." He celebrated middle age with cheap cologne, cigarettes, and a coarse sense of what he called humor. He usually celebrated alone.

The secretary waved me in.

Margaret Dubose turned from the window as I walked in. She cocked her head of short, wavy, salt-and-pepper hair and gestured toward a leather chair. Her navy blue suit cost fifteen hundred dollars—minimum. The matching Jimmy Choos were four or five hundred. She entertained guests I only recognized by name, and visited power people in Washington at least once a month. Agriculture and politics crossed paths, especially in states with agrarian economies. Her six-foot frame moved gracefully behind her desk and eased into a chair. I respected this woman—with a dose of caution.

I let her sit first. Pen in hand, I set my pad on the mahogany table that stretched out perpendicular to the front of her desk for staff meetings.

When politics came into play, I always took notes. A locked file cabinet in my office stored my folders. A flash drive went home with me at night. I could cover my butt with the best of them. I dated the page and listed who was present for the meeting—she and I—and prepared for the worst.

"Glad you could make it this time, Ms. Slade. You have fifteen minutes. Brief me."

I'd practiced this opening presentation while dodging cars on the interstate this morning. "The file in question does show discrepancies." I elaborated on the signatures. "Savvy seemed surprised about the inconsistencies."

Her scowl caught me.

"I mean Ms. Conroy," I said, then rolled on. "I already spoke to Agent Largo. He'll be down there Wednesday to dig deeper."

She gave a precise nod. "So how's your relationship with your friend?"

I wiped clotted ink off the end of my pen onto the paper, debating, then assuming she referenced Savvy, not Wayne. "She's not pleased with me at the moment."

The woman measured me, taking stock of my strengths and my flaws, the latter probably planted by Harden.

"Good," she finally said. "Tells me something about you. Mr. Harris doesn't like you for some reason. Know why?"

My back felt the chill of exposure. "Our history goes back to Charleston. He palled around with the previous state director."

"Who went to jail," she added.

"Well, I still don't trust him. I wouldn't even confirm to him I was in Beaufort. You're the only one who can choose to do that." I maintained eye contact.

A diplomatic tip from those eighty-dollar curls gave me my touché. "Fair enough," she said with a slight grin. "Move on to this business with Ms. Conroy."

"I need more time, ma'am. I'm certain she's being set up."

"Is that more of your intuition?"

"No. It's a deduction based on knowledge of the players."

The average employee would've spun a string of excuses, justifications, and arguments to dodge any shift in the executive wind. I didn't want to give her ammunition to come back at me later, so I remained still, avoiding knee-jerk reaction. My actions needed to speak for me, not cheap talk. A case once turned on me like this—the cooperating individual becoming the target. But I wasn't about to let this one mutate into such. Dubose needed to decide who to trust.

"Mr. Largo would like me to go to Beaufort." I sat back, my hands in my lap. "He asked me to locate crop sales and security. We can't rely on the

Beaufort staff until we know more, especially with Savannah feeling ill. I still haven't been able to interview the assistant manager, Evan Canady."

No point in telling her about the missing file, Teddy, or the unsecured shrimp boat. I still held aspirations of convincing Purdue to make the case go away with payment. No need for her to spill unnecessary information to Harden.

She spoke up like she'd read my thoughts. "I heard some colorful history about you and Agent Largo."

"I'm sure."

Sooner or later, Dubose would have to choose between Harden's gossip and my record, and I wasn't begging.

"Harden's asked to go down there and appraise the security," she said.

"How'd he find out I was even in Beaufort, ma'am? I doubt he heard from Monroe or Savannah."

She squinted her eyelids.

"The last thing we need is a herd of employees claiming authority to crawl over the farm, when we haven't convinced the remaining relative to cooperate," I said.

Dubose's head tilted back, her stare on me, her shoulders rigid.

I kept rolling. "There's Savvy's assistant and the farmer's cousin left to interview, the one who's controlling the farm." I hunched forward. "More bodies would bungle the investigation."

The cautious smile on her stone face conveyed she was no fool. "Money missing?"

Always one of the first questions asked when an agency doled out tax dollars with a responsibility to Congress on where it went.

"We don't know yet," I said. "The dead farmer makes it complicated."

She closed the file on her desk. "An accident?" Our little agency didn't get much gore, making her hesitation understandable.

"I don't have details. I came back too soon to get information from the sheriff's office."

"Fraud is in your job description," she said. "But a death is someone else's business."

"A death leads to probate and insurance," I said. "The faster we move on this case, the more collateral we save, and the less loss we incur. This man's demise could satisfy this loan balance and diminish this case's negatives through insurance."

She sat back in her tufted chair. "Do I sense an issue because of your friendship with this manager?"

"We used to be close, ma'am. I haven't seen her in months, but keep in mind, there's not a soul working in this state I don't know by first name. I have fifteen years of service and can tell when an employee's out of sync.

With my history, I can interpret the technical issues as well. That makes me a heck of an asset . . . for you." This time I sat back and pretended my heart didn't skip. "We don't need bad press or rumors in Beaufort. We need this issue to quietly slide out of sight."

She let a grin slip. "Nice argument."

"Just doing my job."

She placed her pen down, parallel to her blotter. "Go back to Beaufort," she said. "But you're watching *my* back, not Ms. Conroy's."

"A given."

"We have constituents and clients who don't need this disruption. Don't disappoint me and don't blindside me. From now on, if you even smell a case, I want to know."

She dismissed me.

Harden's tattling on me embarrassed her for not knowing where her internal investigator was. But how did Harden find out? The green Ms. Dubose was fodder for managers who marshaled agendas of their own. I guess Beaufort was mine.

I'd captured forty-five minutes of her time easing her over to my side. Good. As I stepped toward my office, Harden crossed my path.

"I see she didn't cut your butt too much," he said, eyeing my backside.

"No, she didn't." I turned my fanny away from his view. "And you're not coming to Aiken to check up on me."

"Aiken? Thought you were in Beaufort?"

"Exactly," I said as my door shut in his face.

Chapter 10

STATE DIRECTOR Dubose granted me free roaming, but a short leash. She had reacted both prickly and subtly—defined as indecisive in my book—which meant Harden Harris could continue to undermine me in my absence. Most importantly, she underscored that I reported to her, not Savvy.

I headed home to pack. I was less than two miles out of the parking garage when Monroe rang with an update on tomato sheds. No Heyward sales found, and several shed managers said they thought Dan and Purdue still did business with Triple R.

Raye offered to interrupt Savvy when I called for an update, but I told the clerk not to bother. At least Savvy felt well enough to work.

Two-lane Lexington Road took me home. My house appeared around a curve, and for some reason I slowed. Where would Ivy go while I fought crime in Beaufort? My daughter, a young lady who teetered on the verge of becoming a teenager, and God forbid, womanhood. My parents already had their hands full with Zack. By the time I reached the drive, I'd decided to send Ivy to my sister's. I would meet her halfway between here and her place in Florence, maybe somewhere on I-95—many miles out of my way—then veer south to Beaufort.

The steering wheel created an ache in my clenched fingers. My absences left the kids overnight with someone about once a month, a necessary downside of the job. They always did fine with relatives for a few days. Unfortunately, this case would eat up a week or more. I didn't have this problem when I made loans, or when my parents lived three miles down the road.

I walked in the kitchen door, kicked off my heels, and reached for yet another box, unpacking as my daughter whined. "What do you mean pack for a week? Half my clothes are in boxes, Momma, and I wanted to decorate my room."

One box of winter coats emptied easily, then I groped in the closet for my overnight bag. "Find three outfits. You can wear them twice."

Hands-on-the-hips time. "Wear the same clothes twice? Are you serious?"

"God forbid." I waved across my bed at the three pairs of slacks, three tops, and one jacket, just in case. The president wasn't on my schedule, so shoes meant sneakers and comfortable flats. "Mix and match, kiddo."

"This sucks." Her lower lip jutted out. "You're always going somewhere, ruining *my* plans."

I shot her a stiff-faced glare of disapproval.

She exhaled loud enough to ripple the curtains. "I'll be back in a second."

I finished organizing my bag, figuring she'd pout on the phone with fourteen-year-old Star next door. The doorbell rang, and Ivy's footsteps darted to answer. When I rounded the corner, Mrs. Amick stood in the entry hall in white sandals and red slacks dotted with tiny strawberries. Mr. Amick peered from behind her.

"We came to offer our services as babysitters," the petite woman said.

My glance shifted from the couple to my daughter as I stifled the urge to wring her neck. I invited them in and tossed aside video game wires, boxes, and piles of curtains to make room on the sofa. Dolly pointed for her husband to sit. Ivy perched next to her. They were about the same height.

"Where's your brother, baby?" Funny how Dolly could use the name on Ivy while she threw me fire-studded stares from hell when I coddled her.

Ivy leaned in. "He's at my grandparents', getting his act straightened up." She sat back, nodding her head to accentuate the message.

Buddy spoke up. "Ivy said you needed someone to watch her while you're gone?"

"Good grief, Ivy," I started. "That's not—"

Dolly brushed a hand across mine. "Honey, we kept her before when you dated that fine man of yours a couple of times. What's a few days?"

My words fell out slowly, cloaked in uncertainty. "It could be for the rest of the week."

"Not like we haven't raised young'uns before." Buddy winked at Ivy.

"Our grandchildren live in Salt Lake City, so having Ivy would be a joy," said Dolly.

"Wow, that's like on the other side of the world," said Ivy, wide-eyed. The sparkle in her eye told me the Amicks' offer was a no-brainer. They were good people. We'd eaten on their back porch, fished on their dock, and listened for months to their tales of foxes and raccoons sneaking in their henhouse. They were the country grandparents everyone dreamed about visiting at Thanksgiving.

My daughter thought fast on her feet. Impressive. I gave her a moment of credit as relief washed over me. Babysitters right next door, across the water anyway. Every single mom's wish.

I rose and went to the kitchen for a round of iced teas and observed my backyard, a panoramic view of the lake, and a small flock of mallards. This could work.

Dolly spoke up as I returned with the glasses. "Seen Beau?"

"Only ghost around here was in a nightmare," I said to humor her. "He pulled my hair." I raised my tea for a sip. "But weird nightmares are my forte."

"That's him," said Dolly, pointing a finger. "He held a penchant for girls' hair. He combed mine in high school."

"Oh, yuck," Ivy said, sliding closer to Dolly. "Hope he doesn't like mine."

Dolly pointed to my head with its inherited band of white through brunette. "Probably likes that streak you've got. It's striking."

An ice cube slid into my mouth accidentally. I spat it back into the glass. Ghosts were for movies and slumber parties, not my house. If one crossed my path, I swear, my screams would raise his entire family from the dead, and call mine from Charleston.

NEXT MORNING, after a predawn, zombie departure from Columbia, I made it to Beaufort around ten and worked at a table near Monroe's desk, picking through the Heyward case page by page for the twentieth time. A call to Ivy on her cell got voice mail. She texted five minutes later saying she'd dug up details on Beau.

Since their brush with a kidnapper last year, both children were changed. Zack became moody. Ivy hugged my side for weeks after. Once she settled down, though, she developed a sense of curiosity, as if she would find predicaments before they found her.

I'd uncovered where the kidnapper stashed them, and then delivered them to safety. It was a mom's duty in my eyes, a cool super heroine's exploit in Ivy's. So now she solved mysteries, sleuthing like her momma. Yeah, I was proud. Now if only Zack would come around.

Savvy interviewed a client over the phone. We still missed Evan, but he promised Savvy in a voice mail to come by as soon as possible. He said he was pacifying clients in the field, farmers he'd scheduled to visit for weeks ahead of our arrival. I wasn't too far from driving out and dragging him back by the scruff of the neck.

I'd had no word from Wayne since he'd left the house Saturday evening. Sometimes he worked on weekends. Maybe he was making up for the time he'd taken off to move me or was covering as much ground as possible before he came down to Beaufort. I sort of missed the man, especially knowing he was in the state and not in Atlanta.

I flicked a paperclip at Monroe. "Get up, old man. Let's go back to the farm."

"Forty-six isn't old, and white hair is a babe magnet." He ran his fingers through his locks for demonstration.

I smirked and tapped on Savvy's door before opening it. "We're going to check Heyward's security. Hopefully we'll find his cousin. If you come with us, you might recognize him as the guy you met."

She peered up, her eyes tired. Teddy probably collected payment of sorts last night for delivering her Mercedes, and the stress of my presence didn't help. "No, I need to be here," she said.

She was more approachable, less snappy than she'd been last week—somewhere on the level of tolerable. "What changed her?" I whispered to Monroe as we made our way out of the office.

He gave me one of his know-it-all smiles. "I told her you were having a hard time with work and the move, and suggested she cut you some slack."

"Cut *me* some slack?"

Teddy swept past us in the lobby. The aftershave burned my sinuses. "The busy bee investigator going out to play?" he said.

"Very observant, Teddy. Where'd you pick up such skills?"

Outside, Monroe elbowed me. "Aren't we the bitch?"

"He gives me the creeps."

We reached the parking lot, and my gaze automatically checked the car antenna for conjure bags. The one we'd found last week was still in my purse, forgotten till now. "You drive, Monroe. See if any voodoo winds up on my car again."

Monroe unlocked his Taurus, and we climbed into the sweltering interior. The blast of air conditioning stole my breath, and I lowered the blower. "He's taking her for a ride again."

His right hand cupped on the headrest of my seat as he faced back to reverse the car.

"Don't forget she's still your friend, in spite of that bozo."

"She is and she isn't," I said, mostly for my own need to understand her behavior. My investigator's hat had made her turn on me. I expected a more open mind. But she probably expected the same in return.

Monroe drove to the Tidewater farmhouse. Marsh, scrub oak, and palmettos passed by us, tickled by yards of Spanish moss swaying in the sea breeze.

I wondered if Daddy had made any headway with Zack and started to call, then remembered Ivy's hints about my smothering tendencies.

"Keep an eye out for equipment," I said as Monroe parked. "We'll check them off our security list once we let someone know we're here. We might have to pick this stuff up to sell if Dan really died."

We exited and walked toward the porch. "How's your Spanish?" I asked.

"Nonexistent."

The Mexican housekeeper opened the hardwood door and peered through the screen. My high school Spanish was rusty as a barn hinge. I remembered more about Glenn Jordan in the second row than conjugating verbs.

I stepped up. "*Cómo se llama usted?*"

The plump caramel-colored woman beamed with a smile. "Marie."

"Ah, Marie. *Dónde está el hombre de la casa?*"

She shook her head. "*Él no está aquí.*" When I grimaced, trying to remember what *aquí* meant, she replied, "He no here."

I handed her another business card through the tiny gap of the door. She accepted it with a false politeness. She didn't have a clue who or what I was, just that I'd been there before. I pointed to my eyes then swept my hands across the yard. "We look around. Okay?"

"*Sí.*"

"*Gracias,*" I said with a slight bow.

At the bottom of the steps, I quickly scanned the ten-acre homestead for equipment. When unexpected and unwelcome on someone else's property, I knew to gather information as fast as possible before someone brandished a shotgun. We had a right to inspect items secured on the loan, but shot pellets traveled faster than explanations.

Monroe recognized the drill and followed me to the back of the house. "Impressive."

"Spanish 101," I said, studying a rusted eighteen-foot trailer to find a serial number on the tongue. I brushed off a spider web, raking it off my hand onto my pants leg, and marked the item on my list. A bottom plow and a disk harrow rested on the trailer. I jumped up and rubbed dirt off the imprinted metal plates to confirm their numbers. Every piece we found meant less of a loss if the Heyward farm went under. At least this farmer wasn't around to see me take a tally. I'd inspected other farms with a family watching from behind the kitchen curtains, scared we intended to put them in the street on our way out. The most horrible part of this job was dealing with the honest ones who wanted to pay but couldn't.

Monroe walked through chin-high grass toward a rotary mower and a fertilizer spreader near the trees. I entered an open-sided shed fifty feet behind the barn, blowing gnats out of my face. "What language did you take in school, Monroe?"

"French."

I stooped and noted the serial number under the seat of a small, older-model John Deere tractor. "What the heck did you think you'd do with French?"

Monroe returned and studied another trailer under the carport, then a bush hog mower to the right of it, red paint baking in the sun. "About as much as you're doing with your Spanish." He laughed. "If she'd spoken French, I'd have seized the moment."

"I'll remember that next time we greet a French maid at the door."

"I wish."

Twenty minutes later, sweat trickled down my spine in small rivulets, even though I stood under a shade tree. I marveled that we still rambled around unnoticed. We'd found a third of the equipment. No surprise. The rest was probably scattered in fields or loaned to neighbors. I tilted my head toward the skinny dirt road where we'd met the Three Musketeers. "Want to check out our migrant community back there?"

His face tightened. "Are you kidding?"

As if beckoned, the black overseer quick-stepped toward us from the path, shotgun in hand. Perspiration stained most of his denim shirt. His forehead glistened. "What y'all doin' back here?"

"Still trying to meet your boss," Monroe said, edging toward the Taurus.

I hurried after him and seized the back of his shirt. "Let's ask him to show us where the rest of the equipment is."

He spun around. "Are you crazy?"

Blood throbbed in my ears as I walked up and held a shaking hand to the giant and showed him my list. "Would you know where—?"

A growl rumbled up his throat. "Get yo' scrawny asses outta here," he yelled, then lunged at us, muscled arms stretched out, gun clenched in one hand.

Monroe and I leaped into the car. The Taurus' tires spat gravel as we wasted no time leaving.

Chapter 11

MONROE SLAMMED his foot to the pedal of the Taurus. I groped for my seatbelt. We bounced over the dirt road, my butt leaving the seat in spite of my hand on the dashboard. Timing a downbeat, I finally clicked the belt.

I gawked at the distant gunman in the rearview mirror, thanking the heavens that Monroe drove. Someone didn't want us to see something. My bet was we'd trip over it sooner or later, as long as we hunted equipment, tomatoes, and Dan and Purdue Heyward. But we might not recognize it when we did.

Sweat-drenched Haitian pickers watched from the corners of their eyes as we skedaddled off the tomato farm. My hand jumped off the dash and clenched the arm rest, one foot braced against the floor. Leaning forward in his seat, Monroe turned onto asphalt, drove a mile, and pulled over. For the second time in a week, we'd run like barnyard chickens from a red-tailed hawk.

"My knees don't work, Monroe," I said, watching my legs twitch faster than the pulse in my neck. "That dude gets bigger every time I see him."

He touched his forehead to his hands. "You're going to get me killed, Slade."

"Don't yell at me," I said, trying to contain my own nerves. "He just rattled us. I don't think he'd hurt us."

"You're a lightning rod for disaster, for Pete's sake."

I lifted shaking hands over the vent, AC blowing up my sleeves. "We overreacted."

"Anybody with two brain cells runs from a giant with a gun." He pushed back in his seat, arms straight, hands wringing the wheel.

"Wayne doesn't want me investigating, and now I can't even account for the equipment." I turned the air away from me. "Why hasn't he called?"

"Don't believe he'd like you running from buckshot, either," he said, his face a bit ashen. "And damn, maybe he's busy."

A curse word. Monroe never cursed. "Hey, Monroe, I'm sorry."

He sucked in a deep breath. "I don't know why I'm putting up with you in all this."

"Because it's intriguing. You need answers."

"No, I don't. You're describing yourself." As he put the car in drive, he glanced back for traffic. "So, what next? Go back to the office? Please?"

"Head to the marina," I said. "We need to find out how that boat exploded." Color returned to Monroe's cheeks as I spoke. "Sheriff's office still stonewalling?" I asked.

He shook his head. "Don't think we rank high enough in their 'need to know' pecking order."

I sagged in my seat, scanning the marsh and saltwater inlets for wildlife, hoping to see a dolphin's dorsal fin. "We'll let Wayne deal with them then."

Monroe chuckled. "You're going to sic the G-man on them, huh?"

I sneered playfully. Frankly, I possessed no authority to get a warrant, and cops didn't respect my second-fiddle badge. I didn't care to see Dan Heyward's remains anyway. I merely wanted to confirm the body was his.

Thirty minutes later we parked at the waterfront. Our feet crunched sun-bleached oyster shells as we walked toward the white-sided, blue-roofed marina office. The cold air blasted our bodies when we opened the door, but the saltwater, shellfish aroma slid inside with us.

An elderly gentleman wearing khaki shorts and deck shoes minus socks dipped his head in acknowledgment. His bleached baseball cap bore the Beaufort County logo, a shrimp boat of all things. The compressed squint of his eyes deepened sun-etched wrinkles in his temples. The nametag read Quincy.

Monroe made the introductions. Quincy was affable enough, happy to answer our questions about Heyward and his shrimp boat.

"We have a lien on that boat and need to put the pieces together," I said. "Think you can help us?"

Quincy guffawed, and then spoke in a voice as rough as the surface of his parking lot. "Pieces. That's funny." He draped across his chair like a sheet, leathered arms hanging down, one leg propped on a chair rung. Could a man get more laid back?

"What do you know about the accident?" I asked. "Boats don't sink or blow up every day, do they?"

The man squinted sideways at us, as though one ear heard better than the other. "Boat just never came back." He leaned on the counter and arched a bushy eyebrow. "Savannah Conroy oughta know. Don't she work with you people?"

I forgot everyone in town knew Savvy. I gave the guy a dumb-government-flunky grin. "We're just confirming everything for our files, sir. Did the sheriff's office confirm that the boat was the *Southern Lady*? And that the body was Dan Heyward?"

One eye scrunched more than the other, and I dashed away an image of Popeye before that damn song stuck in my head. "Lady, you never grew up on water, did ya?"

"No, sir. I mean, I grew up near Charleston, but not exactly on the water." Fact was, I wouldn't set foot in the ocean, a lake either. As an impressionable five-year-old, I'd visited Sea World and decided only fools swam with whales that ate fish bigger than my father. Like Santa Claus breaking and entering my house on Christmas Eve, something just didn't seem natural about it. So I limited my breaststrokes to chlorinated settings, where a lizard falling in the water made everyone jump out.

Quincy shook his head. "Afraid there ain't much wreckage when a boat explodes that far out. The tides spread the pieces for miles. Dan Heyward and his crew went out several times a week, never going or coming at the same time. Just saw him when I saw him."

"Who were the guys with him?" I asked.

He shrugged. "They changed. Hank most of the time, but that shrimp boat didn't dock here much anyway, so what I did or didn't see don't mean much." He clicked his tongue. "None of them shrimpers fool with this place."

I followed his gaze and noticed the boat slips filled with sleek Sea Rays, Chris-Craft cabin cruisers, and a few smaller weekend gadabout Bayliners.

Quincy pointed to the left at a distant place across the water. "Most shrimpers unload down at the point. But those who do private business, them who have places to ice their loads, put in all over the coastline. Just depends on what they want to do with their cargo, and who pays the best dollar."

A customer came in, asked for a key to something, and struck up a conversation with Quincy about weather projections. I'd about decided we had wasted our time.

Finally, the visitor noticed our stoic patience and excused himself.

I tried to rehash the problem. "So what you're telling me is no one knows exactly what happened to the boat or Heyward." Made me think even harder about the possibility that Dan wanted us to think he was dead.

Quincy removed his cap. "Try his man, Hank."

Monroe wore the same puzzled expression as me. "You mean he swam back from that accident?"

The old sea dog's vein-riddled hand stroked wisps of white hair, a striking contrast to the freckled, brown scalp beneath. A low chuckle shook his shoulders as he replaced the cap. "Nobody swims that far, fella."

Monroe glanced at me, his eyes telling me to take the ball.

"So what exactly did *Hank* do?" I asked.

Quincy shrugged. "He went out to find Heyward, of course."

"Of course," I repeated.

Quincy's face hardened as he bit on my sarcasm. "He came back with bits of charred bodies."

I softened at my error, trying to keep the old man talking. "Where did Heyward's particular boat dock usually, if not here?"

He opened a ledger and pretended to study it. "Got nothing else to say. Ask the sheriff or Savannah Conroy since you don't like my answers. I got things to do."

Darn my mouth. "I'm sorry. I could ask Ms. Conroy, but she thought you'd know best," I lied.

He gave us a rattled sigh. "Perry and Hancock docks," he said.

I waited for directions. He waited for me to ask.

"Care to point us in the right direction?" I said.

He spat the locations at us, and I ordered my brain to remember. "So you said we should go back on 21 and turn left and go five miles and . . . which way next?"

"Gotta get busy, young lady."

"But—"

He rose and left the room.

Monroe shook his head and turned to leave. "You made a lasting impression."

Armed with the names of two docks on St. Helena known only to locals, Monroe followed me back to the car, frustration on his face. "Now we've got to drive back to the island . . . again."

"How was I supposed to know what boats go to what marina?" I slammed my door. "Feel free to design a better plan."

He jacked up the AC again.

"No wonder you get sinus infections," I said over the noise. "Can't you tolerate sweat?"

"Only when I have to," he said.

Monroe drove back across the water and followed Quincy's directions to the first of two out-of-the-way docks on St. Helena. Urban development petered out as we ventured into areas pocked with tiny square homes of brown brick or concrete block. Saltwater lapped within six feet of the asphalt in some places.

I caught a hind-end view of a young whitetail deer as it darted into dense woods. A black Porsche sped past us, no doubt headed to town from a secluded ritzy beach house. A few minutes later, a seventies-era white Chevy truck rumbled past. Then we saw nothing else for miles.

The dirt roads cloned each other, crushed shells and silt bordered by lush flora, fat from humidity and loamy rich soil. We toyed with heading back, until we found a crude sign entangled with shiny-leafed vines, a faded black arrow directing us to Perry's Dock. Doubt still niggled as we took the turn under the guidance of some dried-up old man who could've played us for fools.

Monroe followed the sandy ruts snaking around oaks and palms to a clearing, which ended at an old, gap-toothed wooden dock. The structure extended, bent and twisted, thirty yards into the water, and a small shrimp boat bellied up to the piers. Afternoon gave the water beyond a dark, flat color. No sign of an office. Two rust-bitten car wrecks were parked in a grass-infested parking area, burs invading the edges. A few feet to their left sat a dark-green Suburban with Georgia plates.

"Stop here," I blurted out, instinct gripping me.

Monroe braked hard. Dust churned around the car. "What's wrong? We found the place, and, miracle of miracles, someone's here."

I pointed toward the pier. "Those guys on the boat."

"Yes, and?"

The Caribbean straw boss scanned the water as the white Rambo dude from the Musketeer trio at Heyward farm stood on the boat, tossing gym bags to the dock. A red-headed man stood next to him, his hands fisted on his waist.

A jolt of alarm ripped through me. "Get us out of here."

Monroe snorted. "You'll ask that big guy about equipment at the farmhouse, but you won't talk to these guys after we spent forever finding this place? What'll it hurt to ask questions?"

"The job entitles us to be on the farm. I don't like being this far out *and* outnumbered." I snagged his sleeve. "I'm serious. These men have already made it obvious they don't love us."

As Monroe eased the car backward, Straw Boss glanced up. Goosebumps erupted all over my body. "Faster would be nice, Monroe."

One of the guys reached in his pocket. Sun glinted off a metallic object in his hand.

"I think I see a gun, Monroe."

He hit the gas. Gravel spat against the car's undercarriage, and the Taurus fishtailed as my partner sought pavement.

"I don't want to die out here," I shouted.

"Let me drive, Slade." Monroe focused hard as we sped up the highway, appearing afraid to glance at his mirror. "How can you be so sure it was a gun?"

"It could've been." I searched the road behind us, in case we had a shadow. It seemed we'd escaped without incident. "They're not behind us.

You can slow down."

Our speed dropped.

"Never seen you move so fast, Monroe."

"Guns do that for me. Thought I told you that at the farm." He eased off the gas and exhaled. "I should dump your butt out right here for scaring the tar out of me twice in one day."

I settled back. "Now who's being dramatic?"

"This is getting out of hand. This is Wayne's territory."

I scowled. "Don't you start. I'm sick of people questioning how I do my job and how Wayne ought to do this, and Wayne ought to do that."

"Your job doesn't involve people pulling guns. What about that don't you understand?" he said.

Monroe represented my last bastion of support. If he doubted my efforts, where did that leave me? Our car tires hummed on the two-lane asphalt. He broke the quiet first. "You run hot and cold more than any woman I know."

"Me? You're the hormonal one. You didn't even recognize those men." I wanted to remain calm, so I put a rein on my mouth. "They were from the farm. The chauvinistic foreman stood there on the dock. I'm almost sure the white guy was the one we caught a glimpse of at that Podville Community Center back at the farm, one of those who pretended to shoot at us."

"And?"

"Hell, riding around with you is like me playing Holmes to your Watson. The friggin' boat supposedly blew up. So if those were our guys, then what were they doing on a shrimp boat unless they have a second one? If so, why don't we have a lien on it? And what would tomato pickers haul on a boat? And why would they hide so far out?" I shifted the air down two notches. "Besides, they outnumbered us, and nobody knows where we are."

"Well, *Ms. Holmes*, we need Purdue. That's it in a nutshell. Our job is to run down collateral for a loan, not play super cop. Wayne'll figure out the crimes. Whether someone goes fishing or not, however ugly they seem, isn't our business."

"That wasn't fish back there."

He sighed. "I don't care if they were bootlegging Tupperware. Not our problem."

"But if we see something, we ought to—"

"Decide if it's any of our business." He tapped the radio clock. "It's after six."

I reviewed a mental list of restaurants Savvy took me to over the years.

"How about 11th Street Dockside for supper?"

"Seafood again?"

"Please tell me you're not one of those who visits the coast then eats a cheeseburger?"

"Aynor is my home and a spit from Myrtle Beach. My first solid food was Calabash shrimp. Left here?"

"Yeah, pretty sure this is it." Thinking of Savvy, I grabbed my cell to extend her an invitation to dinner so we'd appear less adversarial. The call went to voice mail. I hung up with a brief message about where she could find us.

We soon parked and relaxed in plastic chairs overlooking a pier and three docked shrimp boats as we waited for our table. The brackish smell took me back to my childhood in Charleston. My eyes closed as I listened to gulls and the quiet slap of water against pillars, sand, and boats, the subtle sounds of a slow incoming tide.

"This place does a thriving business," Monroe said, sipping on a diet cola. A bourbon-and-ginger rested on the arm of my chair, enveloped in a bar napkin. "How much do you think one of those boats costs?" he asked.

"I don't know. Maybe sixty or seventy thousand for a small one. I imagine the electronics make a difference. Why?"

He sipped his drink and placed the glass down slowly, deliberately. "Just wondering how much money we're short since Savvy didn't perfect that mortgage on Heyward's boat. Far cry from Massey Ferguson tractors and John Deere combines," he said. "I can peg those down real close."

"Listen, Monroe. Maybe we *can* wait for Wayne before we go out again. Didn't mean to upset you today."

"Finally," he said, then drank his drink. A couple drops missed his lip and dribbled on his tie.

I reached over and dried it with my napkin. "Bet a seafood place would have a bib . . . with a big red lobster on it."

He touched my hand. I sensed electricity for a second before he drew it away.

Monroe's admiration for me had been clear for ages, even more so since I'd come to Columbia. But he fit into my life like a favorite sweater or a bracelet that went with everything.

Having jumped from a husband to a quasi-steady boyfriend with no down time in between, I'd never thought of myself as available. The moment fluttered in my chest. Maybe I simply missed Wayne.

I rummaged through my purse, snared my cell phone like a life preserver, and rang Wayne's number. "Where have you been? I've been trying to call you," I said.

"Check your voice mail. I've been shifting gears on cases to squeeze yours in," he said, his business voice on, obviously in front of somebody. He told someone he'd be in touch, said goodbye, then returned. "Okay. I'm back. Update me."

"Dubose is testy. I managed to talk her into sending me back to Beaufort. Monroe and I ran ourselves ragged today." I took a swallow, and ice cubes clanked in the glass.

"You drinking gin or bourbon?"

"If you were here, you'd know."

Monroe glanced over at me.

"When you coming?" I asked. "We keep running into dead ends."

Monroe rolled his eyes.

"Tomorrow evening," Wayne said. "Miss you, you know. Find all the equipment?"

"Oh, we found more than equipment." I turned toward my partner. "Didn't we, Monroe?"

"Oh yeah. Wayne would be proud," he said, his voice flat.

"Hold on a minute," Wayne said. "I said check collateral only. No investigating. What happened?"

"Nothing happened. We just ran into people who didn't like us."

"Mention the guns, Slade," Monroe said loud enough for a tourist to turn. "*Both* of them."

Wayne blew a loud sigh. "Slade."

"We left. We're fine. You'll be here tomorrow?"

"Prevatte, party of two," announced a hostess.

We rose from our seats. "Gotta go, Wayne. Our table's ready."

"Miss you, Butterbean. Please stay safe."

"We'll see you tomorrow," I said, collecting my soppy napkin and empty glass, glad the cell closed on my last word and not Monroe's, avoiding a scolding from Wayne.

We followed the knockout teen hostess with a ponytail and size-two slacks to a table with a view of the panoramic water, the advertised feature of the place. "May I take your drink order?" she asked.

"Yes, bring me another," I said, showing her my glass. "Separate tickets, please."

Monroe ordered dinner and another soft drink. I played with an appetizer, leaving most of it uneaten. Nothing in this investigation fit. I craved finding some of the answers on my own and not relying so heavily on Wayne, maybe because the case involved Savvy. Or maybe I needed to prove something to Wayne, Monroe, Harden, and especially Dubose.

The hired hands disliked us much more than made sense. I saw us as no more than a nuisance. In hindsight, maybe that's all we were to those guys, and intimidation was entertainment for them.

But Savvy wasn't herself. What if she was guilty as sin?

I just didn't know what sin yet.

I ordered my third drink and pushed away the appetizer. "Think you could drive back to our rooms tonight, Monroe?" Thinking sober hadn't worked, maybe bourbon could be my crystal ball tonight.

Monroe shrugged and studied the gulls.

Chapter 12

THE NEXT morning, Savvy called, apologizing for missing dinner with Monroe and me, and asked if she could take me to breakfast. Relief started my day with a fresh, positive outlook with her offer to meet me in the middle.

An hour and a half and a too-heavy Southern breakfast later, Savvy dropped her napkin on the table of the hole-in-the-wall restaurant and glanced at her watch. "It's half past eight. We better go." She paid, and I promised to cover our next outing.

We'd eaten, chatted, and clarified our truce. With a job to do, I convinced her that helping me do it was to her advantage. She intended to see Teddy, and I agreed not to criticize him. Neither of us wanted to throw away twelve years of esprit de corps.

Mentally, however, I'd bash Teddy all day long.

She'd parked her silver Mercedes on narrow Scott Street, off the much busier Bay Street, parallel to the water. The sporty roadster coaxed a grin out of me as I eased onto leather seats and we zipped back to the office.

Savvy smoothly maneuvered her toy into her sweet designated parking spot near the building's sidewalk. It sure beat my urine-perfumed, downtown garage a block from the federal building in Columbia.

"Good," she said. "Evan's here. I'm anxious to hear what he tells you about taking that application from *his* Dan Heyward."

Finally!

The soft closing *whump* of my passenger door gave me an envious craving for sophistication, until I noticed my car several spots over. "Savvy."

"What, hon?"

Another yellow silk conjure bag hung from my antenna. I untied the bag and released the string. The contents were the same as the other, down to the two pennies. "Get a load of this."

Savvy waved a bracelet-bangled wrist. "It's no more than a trinket. Don't let that stuff bother you."

"Oh, I'm not," I lied. It pissed me off.

Monroe stood from behind his desk when we walked in, snickering at the conjure bag dangling from my fingers. "I saw that hoodoo voodoo thing when I came in. Figured you'd want to find it."

"You just didn't want to touch it."

Evan walked out of his office and laughed. "Who's after you?"

"Darned if I know, but the joke's wearing thin. Can you talk or do you need to check your itinerary?"

The five foot ten, thirty-year-old grinned, his straight white teeth enviable. His hair held a slight cowlick on the left so it swept to the right, a dark auburn color, but the sun gave it highlights a woman would pay fifty bucks for. "Come on back. Gotta hit the road in an hour, but I have a minute." He bowed. "Anything for a senior member of the state office echelon."

"Cute. If that were so, you would've been here last Thursday." Actually, he was damn cute, but a few years too young. I tossed my purse on Monroe's desk, retrieved my notepad and the new file Monroe had created. I wanted to be the first person to ask Evan questions, even though Wayne would probably prefer otherwise. The opportunity was too darn good to pass up. This guy proved difficult to track down, plus he might chat more with me as he played the lady's man.

Savvy waited for me to ask her to come, too. I gave her a glance and a mild head shake. Evan would act differently with his boss in the room. I didn't need that.

"So, has Savvy briefed you about Heyward?" I asked, shutting the door. I shed the suit jacket and pushed hair behind my ears.

He cocked himself back in his desk chair like a man about to watch a ballgame. What was that cologne? I sniffed again. Smelled nice.

"Yeah," he said. "Sucks about the farmer getting blown up, but what's the deal with the file?"

"You remember his face? His build?"

"Average, middle-aged guy. Not sure I'd recognize him again. That was two years ago." He squinted ever so slightly, scanning me from the neck down. "It's been ages since I saw you at a district meeting. You're looking good."

I remembered now. Evan could work a room of women like a dog tracked squirrels, relentless until he caught one. "Did your Heyward seem like Savvy's guy who came to the loan approval?"

He hesitated.

"Don't act like you two haven't compared notes," I said. "Do you think they were the same guy?"

He lowered the front legs of his chair with a thump on the carpet. "Honestly? I couldn't tell you one way or the other. In a lot of these cases you make the loan, they pay, and you only remember them as a loan number." He dropped his chin and eyed me. "But then, you know that."

I did, but that standard didn't apply to all clients. The housing people came and went, sending in monthly payments. Farmers, however, were memorable, no two loans alike. Neither were the farming operations. Evan either lied, or he'd been hoodwinked like Savvy and was too embarrassed to admit to it. We rattled on about farming, dealing with clients, while I continually fought to bring the topic back to Heyward.

"You disappoint me," I said. "All this buildup and no substance. You were supposed to be Savvy's salvation."

He snickered. "I'm good, but I'm not God."

Our stares held fast. He retained a slanted grin, as if playing chicken with me.

"I'm serious, Evan."

He rested forward on his desk and lost the smirk. "So am I. You don't think I'd come to Savannah's aid if I could? She's a doll of a boss. I told you what I knew."

"Guess I'll go back to hunting equipment," I said, standing. Then I remembered he'd be out on farms during the day. "Listen, if you get a chance to cross Purdue Heyward's path, how about sending him my way? He's as hard to find as you are."

"Doubt I'll see him. I'm headed away from those islands. Make sure you check for equipment on the other land, not just around the house. He has a pole shed on one tract with a path into the woods where he might stash small pieces out of the sun, and an old barn on the other—or at least he did."

"Funny how you know the details about the farm, but not the farmer," I said.

"What can I say? I'm focused on our collateral." He sounded sincere as he angled his head in warning. "Take Monroe with you. You never know how some of those migrants might behave. An attractive woman doesn't need to be traipsing around that area alone."

"Could've used that advice before yesterday, but thanks." I thought twice, then asked the next question anyway. "Tell me, what do you think of Teddy Dawson?"

He leaned in. "He's a son-of-a-bitch."

"Is he involved in illegal business? Drugs?" Cocaine habits didn't easily disappear.

He tossed hair out of his face. "He's an idiot. That about sums him up. Drugs? Have no idea. Not a part of my world."

"But he insures Heyward Farms, top to bottom, right?"

"His company insures everything. Doesn't make him crooked and doesn't make him smart." The slight creases between his eyes deepened. "You think he did something?"

"No. Guess I'm reaching, trying to make sure your boss doesn't go down for something she didn't do."

"I'm on your side there. Teddy's a piece of shit."

Yeah. A bad taste in everyone's mouth but Savannah's. I reached out to shake Evan's hand.

As his firm grip released, his thumb caressed mine. "Take care out there," he said. "I'll be on Hilton Head today and tomorrow, or I'd go with you."

I slid out of his grip. His dimples were indeed beguiling. "What do you know about conjure bags?" I asked.

"Tourist junk. Don't worry about it. Probably Teddy's idea of a joke."

Probably. "By the way, don't dodge Special Agent Wayne Largo when he arrives," I said. "I wouldn't be as evasive with him as you were with me."

He held up three fingers. "Boy Scout's honor."

"I'm just saying," I warned again.

He winked.

EVAN WAS RIGHT. Monroe and I found additional equipment in the places he told me about, without the worry of Straw Boss, the Black Hulk, or the white hired hand Hank.

I pointed to the woods. "There's that path Evan mentioned. Want to check in there? We're still missing a lot of pieces."

Monroe's sweaty hair stuck to his temples and the nape of his neck, the matted locks giving him a grumpy appearance. He'd scratched his knuckles climbing around a tractor. "After the last path we followed? Where we found an armed giant? Count me out. And you're not going alone, either."

Guess I earned that. "Fine. We'll head back. Being outside wasn't all *that* bad, was it?" I asked as we walked back to the car.

He flexed his fingers, exercising the joints. "My pay grade is above doing this. Evan should've inspected this stuff."

"Wayne asked us to do it, so we did. We want the least number of people involved as possible."

Monroe glanced over, a tired scowl on his face. "Someone sure is perky after an afternoon of humidity, dirt, and grease."

"This *someone* enjoys being outside," I said. Wayne would be here in two hours, and my energy came from anticipation, not fresh air. My fingers itched to call his number and check his status, but Monroe seated two feet away made me think twice. Now I pitied him abandoned in the motel later. "You want to eat dinner with Wayne and me? Doesn't have to be seafood."

He kept his glare on the road ahead. "Got nothing else to do."

The heat didn't agree with him, or at least that's what I told myself.

Around four thirty, we scooted back to the motel to take showers, knowing rush hour would bottleneck traffic on and off the islands.

As warm water beat on the back of my neck, I watched swirls of suds go down the drain. If Monroe didn't get over this new pouty behavior, he'd complicate our working relationship. That's what I'd always loved about him, the simplicity of friendship where we could banter and not worry about innuendo.

Dried off and hair fluffed, I donned my tightest jeans and a forest-green plunging T-shirt, my best color. I knocked on Monroe's door. "I'm headed to the lobby to wait for Wayne. You ready, or you want me to go without you?"

"Give me a second. Getting my shoes on," he said, retreating back into the room. "Slade? When can we find some time to talk?"

I glanced into his room. "We talk all the time, Monroe."

"Slade?" said a voice from another direction.

Backing out of the doorway into the hall, I turned.

Wayne swaggered up from the direction of the lobby. I jogged to him, throwing myself around his neck. He planted a hard sweet kiss on my passion peach-painted lips as he squeezed me. His palm ran over my hair, until it rested in the middle of my back as he glanced over my head. "Hey, Monroe. You coming with us?"

Monroe appeared. "A man's got to eat," he said, pulling his door closed.

"YOU ALL RIGHT?" Wayne asked me, his mouth full of fried flounder. The two of us sat on one side of the booth, Monroe on the other. "You're not eating much."

I drank my water and took my time with a diminutive shrimp cocktail set on a plain white plate. "Just not that hungry. Got a lot on my mind." The choice of tight jeans reined in my caloric intake, plus I anticipated an après-dinner activity without a dinner-paunch belly. We were away from my children, together on a case again, with opportunity to enjoy each other's company. Like the affair we'd once been accused of. I'd built up my expectations all day.

"So what have you two found?" Wayne asked. "Who gives you the most concern?"

When Monroe didn't speak, I raised my eyebrows. I wanted Monroe to shine, since he'd uncovered the problem. He finally took the hint and filled Wayne in while I nibbled on a cracker. A few minutes later as I played details through my head, I caught Monroe's words.

"A complete waste of time." He tossed his crumpled napkin on the table.

"What was a waste of time?" I asked.

"The trip to that obscure dock, the marina, talking to Evan, to Savvy . . . even you coming down here."

What the hell was this? "You found a legitimate problem, Monroe. We haven't solved the case, but we've ruled out things. We accounted for part of the security. We know that they're sensitive about something out there. If nothing else, we learned that we needed the IG."

"We agree on that. I'm not interested in more gun surprises."

Wayne shook his head. "Damn, Slade."

I shook my head in response. "No. It wasn't as bad as he said. Finish telling him everything, Monroe. This time forgo the drama. We did a lot."

After another ten minutes of Monroe's explanation and me paying enough attention to fill in the gaps, I suggested we leave. It was only seven thirty, Monroe wasn't on his best behavior, and I wanted personal time with Wayne. He'd been doubly pleasant tonight, downright respectful of Monroe's and my investigative efforts. For some reason that made me horny.

Wayne grabbed the ticket. "Y'all keep this case to yourselves for now, okay? I'll decide who does what, who knows what."

I agreed.

Monroe finished his coffee. "Sure."

At the motel, Monroe promptly excused himself. I touched Wayne's sleeve and started down the hall toward my room. "Let me check in," he said, drawing away. He stopped at the counter and gave the clerk his credit card.

Stunned at his need for a room, I walked toward the dining area where the free breakfast imbibers gathered each morning for instant grits, cereal, and hard, dry pastries. The empty tables and chairs gave off a ghost town appearance this time of night with blank counters and cold, empty coffee dispensers. A basket held three apples and an orange. I grabbed an apple with fleeting fancy to throw it at the back of Wayne's head. Another room? What was wrong with mine?

"Ready." He shoved his credit card in the back of his badge. "I'm in room one twenty-four. Where are you?"

"I'll show you where I am." Slinging my purse over my shoulder, I marched down the hall to room 130. I slipped the keycard through too fast, giving me a red blinking light. I repeated the motion. The lock clicked. Wayne followed me inside.

"What's wrong with you?" He secured the lock.

"Geez, Wayne. We barely see each other as it is. Here we are in a motel, away from kids, and you get your own room?" Our one chance for downtime, and he wasn't all over me.

"You're crankier than Monroe. What's going on?"

"I don't know what's going on. I don't know whether to trust Savvy. I loathe Teddy."

He wrapped an arm behind my head and the other around my back, snapping me toward him in one quick motion. Breath whooshed out of my lungs before I could inhale. He kissed with a hungry heat that threw my heart into double-time thumping way down in my ears. I reared back for air, and he leaned over, retrieving my mouth with his. The clash of emotion dampened my eyes as I discarded anger for passion.

He stopped, stepped back, and exhaled. "Not here. Not now," he said. "Not yet."

"What?" I replied, completely off guard.

Oh my God, déjà vu the beach last year. He'd kissed me during a stressful day when I'd escaped to my sand and surf to collect myself. Fighting our attraction for each other, we agreed that an affair during a bribery and, ultimately, a murder investigation wasn't wise. We couldn't afford the scandal and jeopardize our work. A week later, he returned to Atlanta, and I focused on children who'd just lost a father.

He'd said almost these exact words back then.

"Not at the beach and not here," I repeated. Animated, I glanced around the room, then reached out to either side of me, arms stretched wide in frustrated confusion. "If not here, then where?" Then I paused. "Is there something you're trying to tell me?"

My arms fell to my sides. Were we banned from having anything to do with each other whenever there was a case? How the heck was that going to work if we ever expected a relationship? We were investigators, for God's sake.

Another thought caused me to ease back half a step. Oh no. I remembered the tactical words of Agent Beck, the man who'd interrogated me for hours last year, pushing me to the point I trusted nobody, even Wayne for a while. Beck had suggested . . . please don't let there be another woman. I'd feel like such an idiot not seeing this coming for the second time in my life.

To think just days before, I'd worried about whether I could afford a serious relationship with another man. Now that I felt on the brink of something catastrophic, I couldn't imagine not having him in my life.

I plopped on the edge of the bed, deflated, almost afraid to get mad for fear of screwing something up.

Wayne smiled softly, almost empathetic. He reached out. "Come on, Slade. We need to talk. Here's just not appropriate."

"Guess not," I grumbled. Anger, disappointment, and a dash of pain threw up my defensive wall. I stood and picked up my purse. "So where are we going to have . . . this conversation?"

"Trust me," he said, and we exited the room.

"Guess we don't want to invite Monroe?"

Wayne snorted once. "No, we don't."

He motioned for me to lead the way, still the gentleman. "Care if I drive your car?" he asked. "I have a government car, and you know the rules. Work only."

I threw him my keys. "Why do we have to go anywhere?"

"You really want to do this here?" he asked, serious.

"I don't know what we're doing," I said, and got in the car.

We drove through Beaufort and across the bridge to Lady's Island. I'd quit counting the times I covered this ground already with Monroe. Then we traveled farther, for fifteen miles, all the way past Coffins Point, Wayne talking about one crime or another, then reliving the backstory of Zack's broken arm and Daddy's attempts to move furniture too heavy for him. Chatty as a magpie. Almost as if he felt compelled to fill in the void, maybe to avoid a weightier subject.

We crossed Harbor Island, and soon pulled up to Hunting Island State Park. Wayne paid the entrance fee, the uniformed attendant winking at the badge. People did that a lot.

Families ran helter-skelter, children in bathing suits, parents in beach clothes, carrying back everything they thought the kids had needed, but didn't. Wayne meandered my car around campers and campsites to the main parking lot. We got out, and he came around the car to collect me.

Now I was scared. He was about to dump some crap surprise on my head and wanted a neutral setting to control my response. Unless . . . surely he wasn't about to propose?

God wouldn't play that trick on me, even if I didn't attend church. I liked the guy—really liked the guy. But tie the knot this soon? Of course I'd turn him down, but what would that do to our feelings for each other?

My eyelids scrunched together. Shit, shit, shit.

Wayne led us toward the ocean. He knew I adored the coast, having grown up playing on almost every beach between Myrtle and Hilton Head. I'd visited Hunting Island, but never stayed overnight, only enjoying it long enough to experience the lighthouse, climbing to the top to see the semi-tropical coastline much as it was experienced a hundred years ago.

Churning saltwater summoned me. I'd cleansed my cluttered head many a time mesmerized by whitecaps and curling waves . . . usually alone, sometimes with the kids, always when my thoughts needed some sort of release.

Wayne started to wrap himself around me, and I shrugged out from under it. "What are we doing here, Wayne?"

He sucked in a lungful of salt air. "Remember when we went to the beach before?"

"Yeah," I said. "I'd busted my toes on a desk and soaked them in cold saltwater while you told me you'd watched the whole event on hidden cameras in my office."

He grinned. "Besides that."

I turned into the wind, giving the noise of the sea my attention, and started walking. Wayne followed.

Despite the summer heat, the breeze cooled the shore to tolerable as the sun lowered. We must have walked over a mile, past most of the tourists, when Wayne scurried around me and stopped. He laid his forearms on my shoulders. "I have some news."

"Oh Jesus," I said, back muscles tensing.

"What?" he asked, a playful smirk on his face.

"You're building up to something I don't think I'm going to like," I said. "I hate surprises."

He laughed. "I can see that. You've been in knots for the last half hour. Enjoy the setting."

"Not until you spill the news," I said. "I'm not budging until you do."

He strolled those cowboy boots of his through the sand about twenty yards ahead, while I stood fast. Then he veered right, to the edge of palmetto trees and some scraggly junipers until I couldn't see him.

I waited, craving to tap my foot, a difficult attempt in sand.

A squawk sounded in thick vegetation to my right. I jerked around in time to see an egret lift off, angry at visitors. Crickets and other wildlife began to sing as dusk settled. The ocean took on a grayer hue. All tourists were gone.

"Wayne?" I followed his tracks, so unmistakable even in the dimming light. What the hell was he doing? God, I hated surprises.

Chapter 13

ROLLERS SLID IN slow and easy, black in the evening with their phosphorescent crests. "Wayne?" I called again, almost reaching the tree line, now fifty feet from the water with the low tide. Then my hand rose to cover my mouth, agape at the scene.

Wayne took my hand to aid me in the quickening dark. I tried to withdraw, but he held fast. His warm, dry hand held assurance, however, something I needed for this moment, so I clung to it.

A pale-blue blanket, thermos, and two white ceramic cups with faded motel logos lay on the sand, abutting a five-foot-tall dune guarded by palmettos and brush.

My eyes teared as the wind smacked my face.

Lids closed, I inhaled down to my navel and held it. Then I let it go. This moment was perfect. Regardless of where it went from here, this man prepared the proper setting to elate me, let me down, or deliver whatever news he held. I was grounded.

"Would you hold me a minute?" I asked, lids still shut. "Nothing else. Just hold me. Before you say a thing."

His embrace crawled around my shoulders from behind. Sea breezes whistled as we interfered with their race down the coastline. "You have me, you know," he said in my hair.

I crossed my arms to rest my hands on his.

We separated after a few moments. Judging the tide's progress from the hardness of the beach, we owned a dry place out of sight from all but the most curious tourist. Nothing in sight but a horizon.

I straightened the blanket corners and settled in. Wayne dropped beside me. Twisting my bottom, I hollowed out a spot in the sand.

The surf murmured. Wind dropped to a wisp, and the ocean sparkled like a zillion tiny stars danced across the top. The humidity wrapped me in a soft summer hug.

"Thirsty?" Wayne asked. "I brought the perfect quencher."

Opening the thermos, he poured iced coffee and handed me a cup. My hands wrapped around the ceramic as the tension eased. Finally, a private moment. I gave my other senses full rein. I raised the cup to my lips.

"This is great! What is it?" I drank a second, long swallow, the burn wonderful. The combination of coffee and alcohol tingled me down to my painted toenails. "It isn't your Wild Turkey, I know that," I said, recalling the man's favorite, knowing he always kept a bottle in his motel room.

He laughed. "This is a concoction I learned from a manager with Agriculture in Tennessee. He owned a great place on the lake, and this drink was his wife's specialty for wrapping up the week. We normally drank it hot, in the fall, but with it being summer, I gave it a twist."

"I need this recipe."

The second cup warmed my insides. I nestled into the blanket. Wayne's reach moved behind me, then around.

"You working on a buzz?" he whispered, breaking the hush.

"Aren't you?"

"Takes more than six ounces of spiked coffee to take me down." He set his drink aside. I finished my last sip, and he placed my empty mug beside his.

His finger traced my jaw line, then leveraged my mouth to his. I reached around his neck this time. He laid me down with gentleness as intoxicating as the coffee. He unbuttoned my shirt and wrapped his arms under it, around me, radiating heat.

Doubt nudged at me, not knowing the news he harbored, but the setting, the spiked coffee, and the hunger to be with him consumed me. I needed this so badly I ached.

"I've wanted you since day one," he said, kissing my neck. "Even with your goddamn husband in the house." I lay my head back. He buried his face in my collar, squeezing me tighter.

When he let loose, my hands brushed over his shirt then down his abdomen, and he released a barely audible moan. I opened his shirt one button at a time and ran my fingers back up along his bare chest. He raised my hand to his face and kissed the palm.

Now I understood. *Not here, not now* became right here, right now.

My fingers raked through his dark hair. Step by step we entered each other's fantasy. Hands reached and stroked, delved and explored places we'd craved, each knowing the other had imagined this moment many times before.

His hand traveled to my waist, and then below. I came easily in anxious shivers with his first touch.

He withdrew his touch, and I calmed and leaned into him. We rolled over, and he lay on his back as we kissed with impatience and tongues that couldn't taste each other deep enough. I drew him tighter, reaching down to awaken him, my own yearning coming back for seconds.

He hesitated. "Are you all right with this?" he whispered.

I paused to study his eyes, and then touched his cheek. "Are you kidding, cowboy?"

My instincts rang true. Wayne had protected me from the start, never wavering. Even now he patiently searched for acceptance in my eyes, giving me time to choose. I smiled from the heart and gave him no reason to doubt. He quickly rolled and poised over me.

"You sure?"

I nodded and drew him down for a kiss . . . and then more.

Darkness cupped us in its hand as we lay wrapped in the blanket. Waves rolled in, stole grains of sand, and retreated into the night. Constellations crossed half the sky before the tide returned. Midnight arrived, and we rose to head back, hating to break the spell.

BACK AT THE motel, at almost one in the morning, the only sound for ten minutes came from panting, an occasional moan, and one brief pop as I underestimated the number of buttons on his shirt. One date on the beach didn't come close to satisfying our ten months of long-distance patience.

The spread slithered down toward the foot of the bed as we moved one way, then another, until it gave up and slumped to the floor. When the blanket became too heated beneath us, Wayne yanked me up with one hand, my legs around his waist. He stripped the vellux cover out of our way and laid me back gently on a cool sheet. A shiver crossed my back and ran down inside me. Muscles in his shoulders tensed, supporting his weight over me. My hands reached and clasped behind his neck, then crept into his hair.

"You make me nuts, you know that?" he grunted. "Why the hell did we wait so long?"

"Back at you, lawman."

Damn right. We closed the distance between us. The sheets lost their chill.

The evening surpassed my many nights of imagining this moment.

Later, I rolled over and closed my eyes, spent and deliciously fatigued. The air conditioner whirred, and the wall reverberated from a slamming door on our side of the hall. I read the red digits of the clock bolted to the nightstand. "Oh my gosh, it's two a.m." I missed calling the kids. Not that they'd notice my absence these days.

Wayne sat up and patted me on my bare belly.

"I missed you," he said, getting up and heading to the bathroom.

"You wanted sex."

"Like you didn't."

He returned wearing gym shorts, a glass of water in hand. I drew a pillow to my torso and hugged it. "Still don't understand why we have two rooms."

He stood at the foot of the bed. "How would I explain that I came down here and bunked with you while working for your agency?" He chuckled. "Anyway, we need uninterrupted sleep at some point."

I rested my head on another pillow, enjoying the view and the simple talk. I never wanted to go to sleep. "You never told me your all-so-important news." For some reason it didn't seem so urgent or disturbing, and I no longer feared the thought of a surprise.

"Oh," he said, busting into a laugh. "I forgot."

"So?"

A grin cut across his face. A big one. "I've moved to Columbia."

I half rose, scrunching the blanket in my hand, surprisingly nervous. "What?"

He leaned forward, a knee on the bed. "I've been reassigned, Butterbean. They decided to open a resident office in Columbia. You're seeing the guy who'll run all the Department of Agriculture's cases from there." He cocked his head, happy with himself. "I just signed the lease to an apartment in the complex you just left."

"Seriously?" I hesitated, thought about getting up to hug him, then withdrew the idea. Not while I was naked. I needed to pay attention to this.

"They mentioned adding resident agent offices outside of headquarters to put us closer to the action, save travel, distribute our image better in the field. Three two-man offices in the Southeast. When I saw Columbia as a possible consideration, I volunteered. Don't have a partner yet, but all in due time." He glanced sideways at me. "I sense reservation."

"No, no, not at all," I said. "Zack will be ecstatic."

"What about you?"

I reached out, and he entered my hug. Of course I was glad. I kissed, then rubbed the side of his face like I would Zack. "I'm happy for you. And we'll so enjoy having you around. A month between dates is rough, but just understand . . . I mean, it was hard dealing with life after Alan's death, plus the kids have gone through some adjustments . . ."

He tapped me on the forehead, which was turning into a habit I wasn't sure I liked. "I'm not asking you to marry me, Slade. Just be glad I'm no longer two hundred miles away."

"Then I'm tickled pink," I said as I unraveled myself from the bed and moved toward the bathroom.

Wayne raised his voice as I pushed the door semi-shut. "Your dad was pleased when I told him. Zack was a hoot, saying something about telling the kids at school."

"Yeah, I can see that," I said. Geez, this was the first step toward us trying to be a couple. Admittedly, I'd imagined us as a serious arrangement someday, but the shock of the here-and-now left me somewhat stunned. Another major change. Good, but still, an adjustment.

"It's been ridiculous moving me here and maintaining my workload, though," he said. "I've been butting heads with bureaucrats while loading and unloading furniture. I've got some government hacks that need to be in jail more than their crooked clients. This one guy thinks . . . you listening?"

"I'm listening," I said from the bathroom, staring into the mirror while juggling mental images of Wayne with me, the kids, Christmases with my folks.

I came back in the room and curled up. Wayne sat on the bed again, against the curve between my thighs and stomach. Some neurological energy coursed through me as our skin touched. I rubbed up and down his spine. For the moment, this was good enough. The future was something to think about tomorrow.

He turned to face me, moving from my reach. "Now talk to me about this Heyward business. Monroe's head was someplace else, so let me hear it from you." He stood and reached for a T-shirt. "What was his problem anyway?"

I sighed and scooted to the edge of the bed. "Let me get my notes. Don't worry about Monroe. He just spent a long day in the hot sun."

My thoughts returning to the case, I felt a tad wicked I'd enjoyed my night while trouble hounded Savvy, but this night had been a long time coming. Heck, she'd probably tell me it was about time.

I threw on a nightshirt then spotted the clock. "Crap, it's three." My seven o'clock wake-up call wasn't that far away.

"Want me to go so you can get some sleep?" he asked.

I shook my head. "No. I'll go through Heyward one more time for you." I owed it to Savvy.

THE NEXT morning, Savvy's attention moved from her keyboard toward me as I walked in a few minutes late, bouncing on the balls of my feet.

"Where's Wayne?" she asked. "I can look at you and tell he's in town."

I slung my purse strap on the back of a chair. "He said he needed to check out some leads before he came by. Said the coroner contacted him about the bodies."

"Concerns?" she asked.

"Yeah," I said. "Don't spread that around, though. But they might have a murder on their hands." I leaned forward and whispered, "Might overshadow the application irregularities, huh?"

Her long, tanned neck lengthened, and she froze, like a heron at water's edge. "Wayne say that?"

"No. Just my spin on it. And maybe I shouldn't have spoken about it."

The slow slump of her shoulders told me she'd dared wish I was right. I wanted to kick myself for raising her hopes, but mine rode a high wave, and I'd wanted her to enjoy some of the same. She didn't seem to have much fire in her.

With Wayne on the ground, and my day contingent on his findings, I left Savvy and rolled a chair up to Monroe's desk. "Let me help you finish this audit. What can I do?"

Showered, rested, and easier to get along with than he'd been the night before, he dumped a stack of files on me. Not to be bested, I dug in to demonstrate I still possessed a keen grasp of figures. Paper shuffling, pen scribbling, and the infrequent slap of a file atop another served as the only disturbance for two hours. I barely heard the first rap.

"Takes a mutated DNA gene to make someone enjoy what you guys do."

I smiled before raising my head.

"Savvy in?" Wayne asked. He wore his business expression, with his favorite boots and a lightweight windbreaker even though it was July, a guise for the weapon on his hip. Unlike the FBI guys, who often flaunted suits, IG agents dressed for the setting, and with Agriculture, that meant casual enough for mud.

Savvy appeared from her office, pen behind her ear and sultry humor on her lips. "Come on in, big boy." She gave him a hug that tested my reserve, but she loved like she lived . . . with an extra squeeze. "Just wish you were here to check out more than my farm files."

"Hey," I said in mock concern.

Wayne rewarded us with half a smile, then quickly dismissed it. "Need to talk. Slade'll come in for part of it, then I think I'll let her get back to Columbia. I'm sure the state director has a punch-list for her to do."

My stomach clenched. We didn't agree on my returning home, but now wasn't the time to debate the issue. "Sorry, Monroe. Gotta go." I slid unfinished files toward my loan partner, then stepped across the threshold in front of Wayne. He closed the door behind me, and we took seats in front of Savvy's desk.

He covered the basics, speaking to her as if she didn't understand investigations, informing her he was there to check for inconsistencies and identify any criminal activity. I remained silent, like a personal assistant ready to follow instructions.

"First, do you have any questions?" he asked.

"No," Savvy said. "I trust you to do your thing. All you can blame me for is working too fast and getting scammed by some dead farmer." She held it together. I slipped her a wink.

"I'll be scouting around, interviewing people here and out in the field," he said in a fatherly tone. "I won't tell much about what I find, Savannah. That's for me to report to my headquarters and your state office to use. I'm just a tool uncovering the facts."

She nodded before he finished speaking. "That's fine. Slade told me you might check out a murder, and that the coroner had questions. I'm not the least bit nervous you'll find me involved in any of that."

Wayne's head pivoted toward me, and I bit my lip. I kept my mouth shut, something I should've done earlier.

Still eying me, he spoke to Savvy. "I want to ask you a few questions. First, though, let me walk Slade outside to her car, and I'll be right back."

I grabbed my purse and started to hug Savvy, then thought it best I just leave. "See ya, Savvy. Behave while I'm gone. Call me when the doctor tells you something."

She read me. "Will do. Drive careful."

I thanked Monroe for his assistance and warily walked outside. As Wayne and I reached the parking lot, I turned and leaned on the hood of the car to receive my reprimand, but the summer heat jolted me upright away from metal that would scald a tree.

"It's hot out here," Wayne said. "Go ahead, get in, and crank up the air. I've got a minute."

Relieved he didn't sound too mad, I did as he suggested.

He clicked the fan down to medium to be heard. "I'm disappointed in you."

I scratched behind an ear, tucking my hair in the process. "Yeah, I gathered that. I didn't say anything damaging. Guess I just wanted her to feel better."

"By the way, none of that information you told Savannah was true."

I snapped around in his direction. "What?"

His face was as stoic as I'd ever seen it. My heart fell into my gut.

"I haven't talked to the coroner," he said. "I have no clue what they've found."

"So why'd you tell me that last night?"

"I wanted to put that leak out to see where it went."

Damn. *Double damn!*

"I would have told her that tale about the coroner if you hadn't, to see where she took it. Unfortunately, you did it for me, in record time I might add."

I fought to withhold the brewing rage over him playing me, and playing me well.

He took a deep breath. "Damn it, Slade. I needed to know how you'd handle yourself. You broke a confidence. What if that information was crucial?" His hard glare pierced confidence I fought to hang onto.

Jaw clenched, I faced the front window and watched a customer collect her toddler before entering the building. My nails dug into the steering wheel. I'd been used. At least concerning Savvy. Presumably nowhere else.

"Go home, Slade. Don't poke your nose in this case again. In the future, think twice about taking on an investigation where you're too close. It compromises your credibility." He reached for the handle. "I'll see you this weekend."

"How dare you."

He sat back. "Truthfully? I almost told you how I planned to approach Savvy last night. Then again this morning. But after listening to you talk about Savvy, and seeing how torn you were about this case and how intent you seemed on finding her innocent, I planted the coroner's story with you, to see if you'd run with it."

I glowered at him. Truthfully, he said. What the hell did that mean? Truthfully, Slade, you're a pain in the ass and you need to go home. Truthfully, Slade, you don't know what you're doing.

"Go back to Columbia," he said, and paused. "I'm sorry."

"I'm supposed to assist. Dubose told me . . ."

"Told you what?"

I could say she told me to watch him, but I didn't really want to let him know that now. "She told me to help Monroe and watch Savvy."

"Not wise. I'll call you with updates. You can brief Dubose. That ought to pacify her." He opened his door and turned around, as if wondering how we should part. "Be safe," he said, then exited and returned to the building.

He never glanced back.

I waited for logic to kick in and justify my actions. Did I march back into the office and dress down Wayne, then explain to Savvy? I'd do more damage trying to undo what I'd done. My fists pounded the steering wheel half a dozen times before the pain registered. "Who gives you the right to tell me to go home?" I screamed and hit the wheel again.

Gripping the handle, I thrust my door open and hit the car beside me. "Goddamn it," I growled, and then slammed it back shut. Not knowing what to do made me even madder.

"Screw you, Wayne," I yelled again and yanked the transmission into reverse. Then I jerked it back into drive and scratched gravel as I left the parking lot.

I may have screwed up, but why had he set me up to do so?

After deliberating options for five miles, I called the state office and placed myself on leave for the rest of the week. To hell with it all. I'd neglected my half-moved-in house long enough. Since Wayne had dismissed me from Beaufort, I'd unpack crates and hang pictures for a few days. Settle down and rehash what had just happened. Good thing we'd tumbled in bed last night, because it'd be a cold day in August before we did it again.

Chapter 14

TEN P.M. FOUND me alone in bed, a Sue Grafton alphabet mystery open on my stomach. The memory of Wayne leaping off the sofa last weekend, startled at the Amicks' sudden visit, induced another bout of sadness. I closed the book. His mumbled embarrassment at meeting them was a harsh contrast to his stern demeanor today in my car. To top it all, Ivy seemed disappointed at my earlier-than-expected arrival. She ran back over to Dolly's for blueberries and stayed the night, uttering something about clues.

Unaccustomed to letting someone down, shame gnawed at me. My bitterness, however, grew from the belief that Wayne shouldn't have tested me. Sure, I'd failed, but how dare he play games with me? I sighed. But I had proved him right.

This job was anything but straightforward. Lesson learned, but I was still pissed.

The book went back on my nightstand. I dragged a limp Madge the cat next to me, then tossed for hours before falling into a fitful sleep.

The next morning, suffering a headache and bags under my eyes, I unpacked boxes, breaking them down and storing belongings in closets and cabinets.

Lunch came and went unnoticed.

Alone, I did my best to enjoy the new surroundings by walking barefoot on unrutted carpet, almost worshiping the virgin bathrooms with no mildew in the grout. Part of me wished Wayne would call. Other parts breathed a sigh of relief at the distance . . . the silence. I didn't want us to regret words, not now. But that tinge of disappointment in him still subtly rubbed me raw.

The front door sensor dinged. Wayne had all but forced me to install a menagerie of security paraphernalia on the house. Ivy strolled in without so much as a hello and headed toward her room.

"Can I go shopping this weekend?" she hollered halfway down the hall, her words echoing, reminding me to finish hanging the curtains.

"For what?" I shouted back.

"A different bathing suit. Mine's a one-piece. Star has a bikini."

"Good for Star," I mumbled. *Star*. The pretty name fit the tall, dark-haired, blossoming fourteen-year-old child of my next-door neighbor.

"I'll think about that." Let me adjust to the idea was more like it.

The Branton boys lived across the water. A herd of five, always barefoot, shirtless, and tanned with sun-streaked hair, and my daughter intended to parade herself like some catwalk model in a bikini. How much flaunt would take place when I went back to Beaufort? *If* I went back.

Zack would like the boys, however. My phone call to him went well. He and Daddy were heading to Lake Moultrie to fish for crappie. Gobs of enthusiasm and no sass, he sounded leaps and bounds better. An ache formed in my chest. I missed his dusty footprints across my hardwood floors. Heck, I almost missed the attitude.

Twisting around to put away my turkey platter, I knocked my head on a cabinet. "Damn it!"

"I heard that," Ivy said, her flip-flops smacking the floor toward me. "All I said was 'hell' and got totally busted when Grandpa was here." She leaned on the counter. "Who gets to bust you?"

Wayne. He'd busted me good. I slammed the cabinet door.

She twisted a shock of her hair. "Maybe it's Beau the ghost, Momma."

"Boo Beau." I shook a dishtowel left then right in a semi-ritual. "I hereby banish you."

She laughed. I laughed.

"Mrs. Amick used to like Beau," she said. "I mean, when he was alive. She talks to me about him when Mr. Amick isn't around."

I scowled. "Don't meddle. You're a guest over there."

"Oh, I'm not." She hopped her butt on the counter. "But I'm learning lots of stuff. We do have a ghost. I mean, seriously."

I set up canisters and poured flour into the largest. "How do we get rid of him? Not sure I like having a stranger in the house, unless he's willing to pay rent or wash the dishes." I stopped. "What if he sees me naked?"

"That might scare him away."

I wadded up paper batting from a box and threw it toward her, where it softly bounced off her belly.

An hour later we walked our sandwiches, chips, and iced tea to a table on the gazebo at the water's edge. I started the ceiling fan to blow away mosquitoes. Before we finished half a sandwich, a boy yelled Ivy's name. Star stood on the Branton's dock and motioned.

Ivy's cheeks blushed pink, and she cut a glance at me, as if waiting for me to ruin an opportunity.

I waved toward the floating dock. "Go on."

Ivy scurried off after a double take at me, like I'd morphed into a creature she'd never seen before. Alone with my pimento cheese, I watched a pair of mallards tip bottom up and grab dinner off the lake mud. A wasp lit on my bench, searching. Finding nothing, he buzzed off.

"Yoo-hoo!" Dolly waved from her dock. "How's the move coming?" We lived forty yards apart across the water, but voices carried like stereo speakers in the cove.

"Pretty good. You want to come over and have a sandwich? My company deserted me."

Ten minutes later she drove her golf cart down my drive. She walked onto my gazebo in coral knee pants, a floral tee, and gold sandals, toenails painted peach to match. She offered me the tallest glass of bourbon and Coke I'd ever seen. My iced tea glasses weren't half that big. "I try not to let the sun set without one of these," she said, her long drawl laced with matronly charm. "Where's your guy?"

I took a huge swig at the mention of Wayne. The burn seemed appropriate for the topic. "Beaufort. Working."

"He's quite the fine young man." Her penciled brows rose as she wiped condensation off her glass, avoiding direct eye contact. "Where'd you meet him?"

Half a glass later, I'd unloaded my history, all but the present issue. The light ringing in my ears warned I'd reached my buzz level. I started to set the drink down, then didn't. What good was a home if I couldn't drink without reservation? I was off tomorrow anyway. "You mix a damn fine drink, Dolly."

"Thank you, sugar. We so enjoy your daughter. She's an angel. You have any weekend plans? I'm open to babysit."

"Afraid not." I raised the glass to my lips.

She clucked her tongue. "I thought so. What'd y'all fight about?"

I still couldn't decide who shouldered more fault, Wayne or me. Who should apologize first? "It's a long story," I said, as another option abruptly crossed my mind. Maybe we weren't the match we claimed to be.

Her feet propped on a bench. "I've got no place to go." She sighed in satisfaction after a sip. "I'm a good listener."

Evening began to fall and crickets chirped. An early tree frog croaked an enormous *baroke*. We'd been talking for almost three hours.

I blinked, then refocused. "Let me run something by you."

"Do tell, honey. Do tell."

Amidst assorted rants and raves, and her *oohs* and *aahs*, I shared my concerns.

She eyed me sideways. "If I was your age, I'd be going after that hot piece of backside."

"Hmmm."

"At least show him up. Moping around here doesn't seem productive."

A plan swam around in my drink. "How about tomorrow?"

She swung her short legs back and forth over the edge of the bench, like a girl one-quarter her age. "I'd be plum delighted to watch Ivy for you, if that's what you mean."

I was plum delighted as well, only not sure why. What would I do back in Beaufort? I slouched on the bench, relaxed as hell. One thought at a time, and at the moment my whiskey stood at the front of the line. "Your turn. Talk to me about Beau."

Dolly flashed a devilish grin. "Beau Wessinger went to high school with me. Of course Buddy swept me off my feet, but Beau remained ever true. Nothing ominous, though. Buddy tolerated him because he was such a pitiful soul living alone over here." She lifted her glass toward my house. "He loved to drink, that's for sure. Only he favored wine."

The sad sparkle in Dolly's eye told me Beau had stolen a piece of her heart before he'd left this world. She gazed out at my yard. "He'd have liked this place you built."

"When did he die?"

"Twenty-five . . . no . . . twenty-six years ago." Her giggle rebounded and chased away the melancholy. "Bet he's powerful thirsty by now."

"Dolly?" We jumped as Mr. Amick rambled down the walk. "You aren't supposed to carry the tumblers out like this, especially driving the golf cart. You'll make people think you're a drunk. Hope she hasn't talked your ears off, Slade."

I stood and prayed he'd missed our conversation, shifting my sweaty glass to my left hand, wiping my palm on my clothes in order to shake his hand, moving slow in the process of too many steps. He smiled at my dilemma. "Sit down before you fall and bust something, gal. Dolly, you've done liquored up our new neighbor."

Mrs. Amick rose to leave in perfect balance, her glass three-quarters full. "You don't drink much, do you, hon?"

She'd sipped for effect, like any good Southern lady. I'd guzzled like a lush.

Driven up the hill to the house in the golf cart, I thanked them both and agreed to deliver Ivy in the morning. Dolly scrunched her nose and grinned as she left, making me snicker. I wondered how many secrets lay buried with Beau.

Several hours later, Ivy strolled in with pink, sun-kissed shoulders. Lost in her enchanted afternoon, playing teenager, she showered off the lake water and prepared for bed. I rocked on the back porch, clearing my head and rethinking my plan, the ringing in my ears reduced to a distant drone. Maybe it wasn't Wayne I needed to go after when I got back to Beaufort. Maybe it was Purdue.

The state director had told me to watch her back, yet I'd let Wayne shoo me away. God, he'd made me appear a limp noodle coward. A fire rekindled in me again. A fire to prove I could do my job as well as be a loyal friend to Savvy.

I'd tell Ms. Dubose I came home feeling poorly, bounced back, and returned. Assuming I told her anything at all.

THE NEXT morning, halfway to Beaufort, I placed a call.

"What happened?" Monroe said. "You just disappeared."

"Hush. Anybody there?"

He lowered his voice. "Savvy's in her office. Wayne's in the field. Haven't seen him much since you left."

"I'm on my way back. You want to meet me at the motel?" I asked.

"The motel?"

Fried crickets. That didn't come out right. "Meet me at the motel and let's take one car back out to the farm. It's Friday. Bet Purdue is at the house sorting wages for his pickers." I wondered what Monroe picked up on in my absence. "Wayne talked to you since I left?"

"Just asked me where the farm was. I drew him a better map than that thing in the file."

Exit 53 flew by me. "I'm outside Walterboro. Meet me in an hour. I'm in my personal car, so we'll take yours."

"Why aren't you in the government wagon?"

"None available." Truth was I didn't want to set foot in the Federal Building for fear of being asked to report on my progress, or lack thereof. "You meeting me or not?"

"If I let you go out there alone, Wayne would pound me into the ground."

Wayne would pound him more for letting me go, but I thanked Monroe and hung up.

I reached the motel and circled the parking lot for Wayne's Impala. Thank God he wasn't there, because Monroe had parked in the middle of the lot and stood by the car, as obvious as the Dixie battle flag in a New Jersey bar.

I rolled down my window. "All you need is a bull's-eye taped to your shirt."

He shrugged. "What am I hiding from?"

"I'll park my car at the Dairy Queen, back near the dumpster, next to the bushes. Come get me."

Once in his car, I buckled up and told him to head to the farm.

"You had to hide your car?" he asked.

"You know why."

"I'm not going to like this, am I?" he said, barely doing the speed limit. When he slowed behind an elderly couple poking along in a black five-series Beemer, rather than passing, he just followed. "What exactly am I aiding and abetting?"

I ignored his question. "If we find Purdue, we can ask where the tomatoes went. Why were there two shrimp boats instead of one, and what happened to this year's profits? We have the right to foreclose. Purdue might want to avoid the hassle and pay us off, or at least assume the loan." I sank back in the seat to enjoy the marsh scenery as my plan began to come together; although at Monroe's pace, we wouldn't get there in our lifetimes. The slow speed, however, gave me time to formulate what I'd ask Purdue. The loan issues were in my jurisdiction. Wayne could do his thing, and I could do mine.

Monroe threw me a skeptical glance. "Savvy's not totally exempt here."

"Yeah," I shrugged, "but I've been in her shoes."

"And the state director's going to knock you out of yours if she finds out what you're doing." He made the first turn on the island.

I studied a thumbnail. "She told me to watch her back. No rules broken. I'm sticking to the loan stuff."

Monroe shook his head.

We reached the outskirts of the Heyward property. He parked near the entrance, on the sandy edge of the road.

"Go on in," I said with a wave. "If Purdue doesn't cooperate, we'll threaten foreclosure. Wayne can deal with him then."

Monroe craned his neck and searched the field. "Aren't any pickers around."

"Maybe they're getting paid near the house."

We approached the Tidewater home. The place appeared deserted. Marie didn't even answer the bell. "Maybe they don't get paid here," Monroe said, as if cheering me up.

"Let's drive to the other tracts where we found the equipment."

We did. Not a soul there, either. I slapped my lap. This was ridiculous. I refused to return home empty-handed. "Let's rattle doors at the house again." As we drove up to the homestead, I snapped my fingers. "Whoa, what about Podville? I remember a store back there. Maybe someone meets payroll in that shed with the sign nailed to it."

Monroe turned the car around. "I hate that place, Slade."

I gripped the steering wheel, and he stopped. "It's not my favorite place, either," I said, "but our options are running out. We made a wasted trip if we don't check."

The tires bumped over the dirt road once again, past where the pickers had observed us a few days before, past the house where we'd practiced our Spanish. Like before, the underbrush and overgrowth raked our car as we followed the meager path.

Monroe stopped where it widened at the thicket's edge. "Now what?" he said under his breath. "What if we're caught?"

"Why are you whispering?"

He rolled his head to one side in disgust. "You're the one who hid her car, remember? It's what you do when you're sneaking around somewhere you're not supposed to."

Having him as a partner was like dragging along my mother. I left the car, walked to the first shed on the left, opened it, and peered in. Thin, stained mattresses piled in a corner, the kind of mattresses seen in movie jails, striped and about three inches thick. I imagined water bugs, the big ones, waiting for a meal in the wadded batting.

"No one's home," I said, glad Monroe had finally gotten out of the car and was checking out the adjacent shed. "Let's check out the store."

"Disgusting," he said. "How do people live like this?" He shoved the door closed with his shoe.

"I imagine they take what they can get," I said.

The store building rested on a layer of concrete block twenty yards across the community courtyard, if one could call it that, with scorched places that marked the remains of cooking fires. The shed stood on a one block riser, with white walls, a fiberglass top and a sign screwed into the metal. I tested the padlock. It held fast, so I knocked. Nothing.

A thump from the shed to our left snared my attention.

I eased toward the structure, wiping the first trickle of sweat off my temple.

Monroe moaned, "Unh-uh. Don't go over there, Slade."

I tried the lock to no avail, but I heard muffled voices inside. When I stood back, I heard them better as their words floated up. Had to be a roof vent.

"Now what?" I asked. "There are people in there. Maybe we ought to call the cops."

Monroe dialed his cell. "No service. Let's go. We can call the authorities on the way. I don't like standing around here waiting to collect shotgun pellets."

"Don't be a wuss," I said. "Wait here and keep your eyes peeled."

I worked my way around the tiny windowless building. Of course, Monroe followed me.

The source of air appeared to be small slits between the metal and the fiberglass. Surely they needed more breathing access than that. A sour odor wafted from the structure.

"Boost me up," I said low.

"Are you insane? No," he replied. "Let's go. I'm melting out here."

"What if those poor people need our help? Could you sleep sound walking away from that?"

He glanced left and right, then over his shoulder. "Just for a second. Then we leave here and call the authorities."

He laced his fingers and stooped. As I held onto his shoulder, noting signs of muscle, Monroe cupped his hands under my foot. He wasn't a huge guy, but he made no sound as he lifted me high enough to scramble on top of the shed roof.

"Sorry, dude," I said as my other foot left a dirt swipe on his khaki pants. He gave my butt a final shove. I shimmied toward the center of the shed's cover, closer to a vent.

"Make it fast, then let's go," he said in a harsh whisper.

Just as I thought, a crude hole appeared rudely cut in the fiberglass top, a piece of plywood to the side, probably used when it rained. I grabbed the edge of the hole, hoisting myself further. The smell of urine, sweat, and God-knows-what-else hung heavy, rancid and acidic. Sweet Jesus.

Though the hole measured only six inches across, I could make the shapes of at least eight people seated on two stacks of mattresses. A wet corner held a pile of something I didn't want to guess.

A young man rose and stood beneath the hole, staring up, his face stiff with anger. "*Kaka!*"

Didn't know the lingo, but I recognized cursing when I heard it. The accent was directed at me in thick Caribbean. This guy wasn't one of the standard workers, not with such an arrogance. Chances were he'd angered the bosses one too many times for them to confine him like this. Five black-skinned women in their twenties and thirties stood and leaned against one wall. Two men, maybe five years older than the speaker, sat against another, their knees pressed to their chests, threadbare clothing fastened with a couple of buttons. All rose to peer up at me through the small opening.

"Who are you?" I asked.

"*M rele Rene.*" If the conditions hadn't been so repugnant, I'd have taken a moment to enjoy the way melodic words as they rolled off his tongue. A dialect that belonged on a beach where warm breezes blew about linen shirts and gauze skirts in bright colors.

"I'm from the government," I said, which sparked rapid exchanges amongst them. "No, no, I'm not immigration. I came to find the boss . . . Purdue Heyward."

"Slade!" Monroe said with urgency.

"*Gen you moun la,*" said the guy calling himself Rene. "*Pinda!* Be careful," he added in English.

"He said someone's coming," said Monroe. "It's Creole French." So his high school French lessons had come in handy after all.

Raising my head carefully, I caught sight of the black hulk as he stopped to inspect our car. "Crap. Monroe. Hide, then when you can, run for the car. Right now just hide."

The goon whipped out a switchblade and punctured our tire. Air hissed, then faded. My partner flattened against the side of the building. "Dang it," he whispered.

The knife stuck tire number two with more of a pop, then again, the hiss. The Hulk stiffened and scanned our direction. My heart pounded, hurting my chest. Before the huge man took two steps, I softly muttered to Monroe, "Run. Please. Get somebody."

"Oh God, Slade."

"Go!" I whispered.

Monroe broke from his flattened stance, the structure between him and the Hulk. Then with more stealth than I expected of him, he slipped into the woods ten feet away. I was alone, eyes tearing, quaking as I lay on a stupid roof on a stupid hut.

"I know you're out here," the big man boomed. "Might as well come out now 'cause you ain't going nowhere in that car."

My limbs drew up close to my body, praying the people in the pod beneath me knew to stay quiet. I covered my mouth. I couldn't stop breathing heavy.

Chapter 15

ABOUT EIGHT FEET off the ground, the corrugated, fiberglass roof sat on a slight angle atop the Heyward shed, just enough to handle runoff and hide me from the overseer. Two hundred and fifty pounds of mahogany muscle stomped toward me as I hid and wished for my phone on the dash of Monroe's car. And the gun in my glove box back at the Dairy Queen.

A broiling summer sun beat down on my bare arms, but the pine trees shaded my legs. My presence bothered several eight-legged critters, but thank heavens, nothing slithered.

The beast of a man inspected all four sides of my hiding place. I squeezed my eyes shut, ceased breathing, and imagined his thick biceps reaching up and snatching me off the roof. I'd barf from fear before I hit the dirt. My heart caught in my throat when I spotted Monroe hiding behind an old oak instead of beating it toward civilization like I'd told him.

What the heck was he doing?

Waving once, then twice at him to go, I almost lost my grip. All he did was scowl harder.

"Where you at, bitch?" The overseer's deep resonant voice summoned images of cracked femurs and busted teeth.

He tromped from one shed to another, rattling locks, banging doors, and cursing. There were twelve, if I recalled right. What was he going to do when he couldn't find me? I sucked air in a slow rhythm to stop my body from shaking apart.

His footsteps returned. He kicked the side of my shed. The thin metal vibrated under me. Despite the ninety-degree late afternoon heat, goose pimples crawled down my legs.

Keys jangled, the lock clanked, and hinges creaked. He ordered the occupants into the sunlight. "Y'all hear a woman out heah?"

Some mumbled *no*. I prayed the rest spoke no English.

"Hurry to the shit house," he yelled. "Get a drink outta the hose. Then get yo' asses back heah." I peeked. They scurried to the four-by-four unpainted outhouse.

One woman dared peer over her shoulder barely covered with a ragged blouse; a man jerked her forward. My pulse leaped at the possible realization that they protected me. I shot a glance toward the woods, but couldn't see Monroe.

In a five-second plan, I envisioned running the path to the house, then cutting along the tomato fields to the highway. Woods weren't an option. No telling how many bogs lay out there, with squiggling, reptilian inhabitants. What if Monroe met up with a water moccasin or a copperhead . . . an alligator? Help might not find him fast enough.

Liquid splattered in the outhouse hole, then water sloshed, slapping the ground, smacking puddles and mud. Someone slurped. If I could only get to the path that led to the Tidewater house.

"Time's up. Get back over heah," the Hulk shouted. "Bring that hose with ya."

The group filed into the shed. I ducked as the thug turned. My suspicions were right. This was a prison of sorts, and the Three Musketeers I'd seen a few days ago were sentinels of human property.

The deep voice hollered, "Pick up the mattresses."

I jerked in surprise as water thundered against metal walls. Hulk ordered one poor soul to sweep out the water. I froze, praying the person didn't peer up at my shadow through the opaque roofing.

The sound of water gave me an urge to pee and increased my thirst. I couldn't think of one without aggravating the other.

The door slammed. A lock clunked shut. "Hey, Wink!"

Footsteps approached.

"What's with the car, man?" Wink said.

The Hispanic accent told me Wink might be one of the Musketeers who'd chased us away a few days ago. The one who raised his gun and aimed at our Taurus.

"Think it's that damn agriculture woman who poked around here earlier. Ain't found her yet."

My stomach knotted on the word *yet*. The roof released a small pop under my weight. I stiffened. The men's laughter about something the slave tenants did hid the noise.

"Man," said Wink, turning serious. "You better talk to the boss about this. I'll be back in an hour. The crew oughta be done pickin' at the Whitehorse place."

"She ain't goin' far on foot from way out here."

"Probably in the woods," Wink offered.

"You stay put, Spic. Clean out those other sheds while you waiting. I'm gonna keep an eye on the road and watch for the boss," Hulk said, his voice carrying toward the trees. "You might as well come on out, bitch. You're fucked!"

The threat sent shards of shivers through my ribs.

He walked far enough away I could see his back. He strutted past

Monroe's car like he carried music in his head, hitting the tire with the butt of his shotgun as he disappeared down the small, rutted road.

Wink stood a foot shorter than his six-foot-plus partner and sixty or seventy pounds lighter. A Glock resting crooked in his belt confirmed I wasn't going anywhere.

Night was a couple hours away. I'd make my move then.

Wink took a man from my shed and forced him to wash out the other buildings.

A whisper rose through the hole in the roof. "Madam."

I eased toward the opening and peered down at the young woman from the outhouse.

"*Ou pale kreyol?*" She hiked her ripped blouse up over her bare shoulder again.

I whispered. "No comprendo."

She shook her head, working her fingers as if the effort helped reword her sentence. "Let us out."

Letting them out was desirable, but I wasn't James Bond. I laid my cheek on the rippled roof. "I'll get away when it's dark and bring help." We needed to remain quiet.

But she kept speaking. "We come to pick, make money for passage. But we put in here. Rene. My brother. *Move moun* beat him." She struggled to correct herself. "Bad person."

I read about smuggling Mexicans but not Caribbeans.

"We from Haiti. Our boat break near Abaco. Refugee camp there, but everyone poor, and the Bahamas no like us. No give us work. A man promise work here."

Of course he did. They'd been scammed. And she needed to quit talking so much, or we'd be heard.

My knowledge about the Caribbean islands wasn't all that great. My high school senior class went to Nassau, but who remembered geography amid free-flowing booze and hormone-engorged teenagers? A few years back, journalists covered stories of Cubans washing up on Florida beaches, claiming safe haven. Thanks to a law passed in the '90s, if they could plant their feet on American soil, they could stay. Those people risked their personal safety and left family to start a better life with opportunity.

Family.

Ivy was probably helping the Amicks with dinner about now. My mother most likely cuddled Zack at her stove, too, teaching him how to cook something simple like grilled cheese.

Wayne didn't even know I was here. Our fight seemed so frivolous now. Just like I'd done in Charleston, I took him for granted when he was my best ally.

Damn, I felt stupid.

Shade covered me now, and the temperature cooled from broil to low bake. My sweaty shirt stuck to me like skin.

Stiff from lying still, I moved and peered in the vent. "Who brought you here?"

"*Yon moun fou*—a crazy person," said the woman. "The one with flamin' hair."

Well, that was clear enough. A Heyward. I rolled over a little to get the kinks out of my hip. Taking careful, abbreviated moves, I moved my weight just millimeters, from one position to another, feeling the roof give. I had no clue how much weight this structure could hold. The flimsy material probably did little more than keep out the weather and wasn't constructed to support a 130-pound woman. Okay, maybe 135.

"Out!" Wink yelled.

I started and slid a couple of inches. Gripping the edge of the roof, I envisioned steel claws extending from my fingers, like that X-Men character Zack loved. Heck, in that case I'd jump down, goring, slicing, and disemboweling these captors. I closed my eyes, gritting my teeth. God, I had to pee.

Wink ordered the women to exit and fix something to eat. He allowed them a small fire, which explained the assorted scorched areas dotting the courtyard. They started a pot cooking faster than I could've lit the match. Something tomatoey filled my nostrils. That figured. These were the Bubba Gumps of the tomato business. I imagined them eating tomato this and tomato that three meals a day.

I twisted to risk a new view of the situation below. As Wink picked his nose, the Haitian refugees hunkered on their haunches and ate out of metal tins with dirty hands. From the indignation in his eyes, I identified the beaten brother. He turned toward my car. A herd of like-colored workers filtered in. They shuffled around the Taurus, staring like it was an alien spaceship.

Wink kicked dirt toward the eating Haitians. "Time's up. Back in the shed." He rested a palm on his weapon. They gulped down the remnants of their meal, all except Rene, who threw his plate to the ground.

"Rene not go," he said, spit on his lips.

Wink shoved him toward the others. "Get your ass in there, or I'll put another hole in it."

They hustled forward, glancing over their shoulders at the incoming workers. Some of the field hands glowered disdainfully at the refugees. I presumed they weren't fond of the malcontents who made their lives harder. I spread myself flatter against the roof. The chances of my discovery just rose twentyfold with so many more eyes in the compound. The sound of sirens would be welcome about now.

My cheek pressed deeper into pine straw as I tried to ball up and disappear. A nest of granddaddy-long-legs with its hundred babies peered back at me, two feet away. The thought of all those feet on me, climbing in my clothes, guts squishing on me as I fought to hit them off, creeped me out. I shuddered, then stopped when the mama spider moved.

The dense woods held the campfire smoke hostage. The fire reflected off surrounding sheds, flickering shadows contrasting as dusk fell and workers fixed supper. My stomach grumbled. Lightning bugs glimmered against the backdrop of trees, another next to my shed, then one beside my head.

Sweat soaked my underarms. The muggy evening blanketed me as ninety percent humidity stuck my hair to my forehead and my underwear to my butt. My watch said Monroe had disappeared two long hours ago.

Where the hell was he?

My left ankle itched. I used the other to rub it, maybe chase away a critter. Pain bit me. The sting crescendoed to a burn, then a yellow jacket flew away. Damn it. That meant there was a nest nearby. My deodorant and hair spray would draw them like a magnet.

A different voice rose above the others, and I froze. "Make 'em eat fast. We gotta get these damn people into hiding." The speaker sounded Caucasian.

The Hulk spoke up. "It'll take that nosy bitch a while to walk through the bog to the road, then a long ways to the highway."

"Cops won't do nothing," the Caucasian said. "It's picking season. Damn islands are covered with migrants. So she makes it to the road and hitches a ride. We'll move 'em to another place as a precaution. These idiots won't talk. Not and risk getting deported."

The people under me mumbled at the mention of *deported.*

"Start loading them up in the trucks," said the boss. "Each of you take a different barn."

"Shit, man," Wink said. "I've spent all damn day in this sun."

"Tough."

A Zippo-type lighter clicked with a flame. The poignant scent of a thin, fruity cigar reached my nose. The Zippo snapped closed.

"You guys are pulling night duty," said the man. "Any of 'em give you trouble, chain 'em to a tree and burn them. Can't afford to lose one tonight. Got to finish the Whitehorse picking tomorrow, then the Perry place the day after. We're behind."

Pale gray smoke rose six feet in front of my shed. "Make these obstinate ones pick tomorrow, too," he said, banging the shed under me. "They don't cut it, we'll deal with 'em at the end of the day."

A truck arrived and brakes squealed to a stop. Diesel fumes mingled with outhouse scents. "Where you want me to take the first load?" shouted a white guy. The white Musketeer, the redneck from that same trio of hired hands. Dang if this place wasn't diversified to the hilt.

"Go over there and tell Hank what we're doing," the boss told the black man.

I recalled the conversation from the marina where the wrinkled seaman Quincy told us Hank was the guy who'd pulled farmer Heyward's body parts out of the ocean.

Cigar smoke drifted away from me. I could just make out dark red wavy hair. He opened the store and inspected whatever stock it held, then stepped back out. "Got that truck loaded yet?"

"Yes, sir, Mr. Purdue."

"Take Louis with you. He can keep an eye on that batch. Then get back here."

So Purdue *had* arrived.

The truck roared to life and drove up the single-lane path. The straw boss hung on the back. He reached in across the tailgate and slapped a worker as the vehicle disappeared through the trees. Guess Mr. Straw Boss was Louis. Never would've matched him to that name.

"*M pa konprann.*" A woman's whisper rose through my peephole.

I ran the words through my head, but couldn't understand. "Shhh," I told her.

A fist or foot hit the side of the shed. "Shut up in there." Wink still stood guard.

I shrank down.

The truck returned faster than expected. They weren't traveling more than a few miles. The second load of bodies boarded and disappeared with Hank. That left the people in my shed. Purdue managed no more than twenty or so migrants. With so many sheds, he'd obviously harbored more at some other time . . . unless he was building up his, um, herd?

Hulk spoke up. "What about the store, Mr. Purdue?"

Keys jingled then stopped as someone caught the toss. "Go get my car."

As the big guy strutted to the house, Purdue lit another cigar. Dusk made the flame's glow reflect off the white of the shed beside me. The metal lighter clicked shut, and I pictured him doing so with a whip of his wrist. "Miss Whoever-You-Are, if you're still out there, I need you to hear me."

Ice water surged through my arteries.

"Ah, here it is. Ms. Carolina Slade, Special Projects Representative with the United States Department of Agriculture. You pass these business cards around like candy, don't you? Third one I've seen this week."

My limbs stiffened, willed to freeze as if they would make me invisible.

"Sure appreciate you letting me know who's fucking up my operation," said Heyward as smoke curled up and rode away with the humid breeze. "I'll be in touch. I can promise you that."

I'd met one murderer in my life, and a familiar alarm ran through me. I could smell my own fear. Come on, Monroe.

Chapter 16

THE MIGRANTS locked in the shed beneath me began a hum that grew into words I didn't understand. Here in the dark, with a thousand mosquitoes sucking my blood, cramped after hours on a roof, an eeriness crept into my marrow. The Haitians sang as if to beckon spirits or strength from a higher power.

And I still had to pee.

Purdue's guffaw scared the singers quiet. He sang back at them in an out-of-tune, bastardized version. "Oh yeah, so hard. We should've stayed home. Shit happens and life sucks sooooo bad." His laughing slowed to chuckles and he sniffled. "Shit, I'm funny."

Headlights hit the trees. The Suburban from Perry's Landing cruised into the open area and stopped by the store pod. Purdue unloaded six gym bags out of the store, slinging them to Hulk, who loaded the backseat.

"Let's get this stuff back to the boat. Wink, stay here and see if there's any chance that nosy bitch is still hiding somewhere. We know she didn't make it to the road." He nodded toward my shed, and I ducked, grateful for the night. "We'll send the truck back for you and the last load of pickers when we finish. Then you can take your turn at watch."

Hulk wedged himself in the driver's seat. Purdue opened the passenger side and stood on the running board, facing the woods. "Hope to see you real soon, Ms. Slade."

I wanted to yell, "What makes you think I'm still here, you idiot," but I was here. Who was the idiot?

The green Suburban bounced as it left, red taillights reflecting off the tight thicket of greenery. Wink hunkered down and searched along the edge of the woods, scouting for what I presumed to be proof of where I went, was, or had been. He extracted a small flashlight from his camo pants and darted into the brush, leaving only the sound of crickets rubbing their legs together in chorus.

I leaned over the hole. In the dark, I couldn't see anymore. "I'll try to help if I can get away."

"Rene fights too much," said one man.

Another man whispered harshly at the first. "Hush yo' mouth, I say. If we stand our ground, we get free. We are more."

"Fool," said a younger man. "We be killed."

"Or burned," said a woman from the corner.

"We be killed for sure if dat woman is found on our roof and we didn't say."

Silence fell like a rock.

I still couldn't wrap my head around the fact Monroe and I stumbled onto human slavery. The Immokalee slave ordeal in Florida was common knowledge in the migrant agricultural community, and human *coyotes* hauled Mexicans to Arizona and California, but I never imagined such activity in my state.

"Do they mistreat women?" I asked. I never met a woman who sold her body for money, much less personal safety, but with slavery came other sins. Like the homeless in the parking garage at home, I never took notice of poverty for fear of germinating a tinge of guilt.

The girl who spoke the most replied. "We go to big *kayla,* the house, and lay in soft bed for one hour. Helps pay debt."

That concept hung a moment before it registered. Oh my gosh. She probably got charged for room and board while she lay on his comforter, too, with her legs spread.

Rene whispered up to me. "Woman, if you are good person, you free us."

Damn. I didn't know how to get myself out, much less them. "If I get out of here, I'll bring back the authorities to set you loose."

"No police!" he hissed.

My body quivered in fear at the man's subtle threat to violate my covert position. My heart banged like a band through my chest, and into my ears.

A female told Rene to hush. Thank God for one ally.

"She's here," Rene shouted, no longer holding back.

I jerked, and slightly wet my pants.

The structure vibrated as someone shoved someone once, then again.

"Don't," I whispered. "Please be quiet."

It had been three hours since Monroe left. I'd hate him if I wasn't afraid he'd been caught, or injured, maybe lying on the side of the road. And where was Wayne? This was Heyward Farm, for Christ's sake. The reason he was even in Beaufort. I wasn't home, wasn't in a motel. When the hell would he get wise enough to come out here?

"What's the problem?" Wink was back.

All the occupants below me spoke at once, shouting, arguing.

Visions of Ivy and Zack shot through my conscience. This wasn't the time, but I missed them. Missed the routine of being a family, telling them not to do stupid things like I'd done.

Every muscle tightened. I wanted to shut my eyes, but I also wanted to see if this guy ever wised up enough to look up.

Shouting continued below me. Someone fell into the wall.

Wink hit the shed. "Like a goddamn pack of dogs," he grumbled. "Shut up before I burn you."

Everyone shushed.

Oh my God. They protected me, overriding Rene.

Wink appeared twice more, skulking, checking inside the open pods with a flashlight. "Come on out, lady. You can trust me," he said. He stood still for a moment, then returned to the woods. When the truck rambled up, he jogged out of the trees like a rabbit hound leaving the trail upon hearing his master return.

Wink and Hank shuffled my pod-mates onto the truck bed, the young woman peering back in my direction. The two-ton truck cranked and left, Wink sitting on the tailgate, one leg hanging down. Taillights backlighting him, he placed a finger against a nostril and snorted the contents onto the dirt.

I was alone. I wanted to scream and cut loose the tension, but instead I slapped the life out of the mosquitoes sucking pints of my blood.

The crickets quieted. I tried to shift, and the noise of my movement amplified four times over in the dark. I chewed on whether or not to slide down and run or wait for help. The moon hung like a fingernail sliver, the clouds moving in and out covering what little light it gave. I didn't know if I could find the road in this pitch. If I did, who would give me a ride? When visions of killer types inflated my imagination, the safety of my roof made more sense.

Besides, if I got down, I'd never be able to climb back up. Where was Monroe, damn it? I curled up tighter, embarrassed, scared, and debated if I wanted Wayne in my rescue party.

A few long moments later, I prayed for him to arrive.

I lost track of time. I almost jumped down again, but Monroe would hunt for me here. That's when I saw the headlights—three sets of them reflecting on the brush, and then on my shed.

Wayne jumped out of his Impala. "Slade!"

I eased up, my joints stiff. "Wayne!" Mother Granddaddy Longleg and her brood shoved away, I kicked pine needles off the fiberglass ridges. "I'm over here."

Hands wrapped around my calves. I went over the edge as someone caught my waist and hoisted me down. "Are you all right?" Wayne asked.

Gravity took over. Wayne tried to hold onto me, but I shoved him off balance into the metal side of the pod with a reverberating echo. I staggered as blood returned to my legs, then I struck out in a run to the outhouse.

"What's wrong?" he shouted to my back.

"I've got to go," I screamed, urine streaming down my legs. The outhouse door slammed shut behind me. I squatted, hovering above the hole, holding the door shut, wondering what lived below my backside. I finished my business and zipped up. Now what did I do? An audience awaited me and my wet britches.

With no danger, no physical demands, and the protection of God-knows-how-many cops, the weight of the night crashed down on me. Tears pricked my eyes, and I stifled a sob. I stood stiff in the middle of the facility, afraid to touch the walls. Finally my breaths returned deep and steady, the hitches gone.

I tripped over the threshold coming out, to the amusement of informed deputies. Wayne waited, the only one without a smirk. He was mad. I almost preferred the humor and humiliation.

"Is Monroe okay?" I asked.

Wayne pointed toward his G-car. "He's in the backseat with a bag of ice. He wrenched his knee pretty bad but insisted on directing us here to see that you were safe."

"Thank God he's okay. I worried a snake bit him, or worse."

Wayne pushed a bottle of water at me, nudging it into my stomach.

"What's your problem?" I asked low, trying not to draw more attention.

"You sure you're okay?"

I studied a smoldering campfire. "Yes, other than my pants, and a gazillion mosquito bites. I've got a lot to tell you." I tipped my head toward the uniforms inspecting the sheds. "Should I file a report with them?" I scratched my ankle.

A fortyish deputy walked up to me. "Ma'am? Where is everyone? We heard there were others out here holding you hostage."

"There were. I was," I said. "You missed them by half an hour."

"Guess they didn't tell you where they went?"

"Listen," I said, angry at their lack of concern. "Heyward Farms has slaves. Did you know that? Some are forced to service the owner."

The deputy repeatedly pushed his palm down, a sign to chill while his colleague held a flashlight beam on me. "Hold on. Migrants aren't slaves, ma'am. Around here, we get Guatemalans, Costa Ricans, Mexicans, you name it. Every picking season. When they're done, they move on to other states, other farms."

I shook my head. "No. They're locked in these sheds. The women are taken to the house for sex."

Another deputy came up. "Nobody here." He shined a light in my face then lowered it when I squinted. He then bounced the beam off several of the sheds. "I don't see any locks. Did the girls say they were raped, ma'am?"

"They struggled with English, so not exactly," I said, exasperated. "Take a whiff. Smell that? Who lives like this?" I eyed Wayne for support amongst these strangers.

The second deputy started to roll his eyes and caught himself. He rejoined the other two standing near their squad cars.

"Ms. Slade, we'll let your special agent friend here explain the circumstances to you," said the fortyish guy. "Where are the immigrants?"

"Heyward moved them, thinking I would escape and bring trouble. They didn't know about Monroe." I twisted the bottle cap and chugged several deep gulps before coming up for air. I wiped my mouth on my sleeve. "He mentioned barns. They also plan to pick two other farms; one called Whitehorse, I believe. You checked the house?"

"Nobody there but a Mexican woman."

"They couldn't have moved the Haitians far," I said. "They didn't take much time between loads, and they only used one truck." I gave directions to the other land tracts and described the truck. No one took notes.

"We'll have a chat with the caretakers and the workers, but frankly, unless the migrants want to complain, or unless we see them chained, caged, or abused, don't know what we can do." He shrugged. "It's just that time of year."

How would he like to be tied up? How would he enjoy sleeping in a shed full of crap and pee with nothing but straw for a pillow? I drained the bottle and tossed it in a metal barrel next to the store shed. "So it's my word against theirs?"

"Pretty much. We don't deal with illegals unless they break the law. Of course, you're trespassing on Heyward's place, so don't know what he'll say about that."

"Wait a second. You mean . . ."

"We'll be in touch. You heading back with Agent Largo?"

Wayne spoke to Monroe through the back window of the Impala.

"Guess I am," I said. "You can reach me through him." I was tired of passing out my card. "What about our car?"

"Tow truck's on the way. I'll leave the other unit and a deputy with you until it arrives. Have a good night, ma'am." The deputy walked away and patted the second uniform on the back. They gave the courtesy brotherhood nod to Wayne. After speaking into a radio, they turned their car around and left. I doubted they'd speak to anyone before dawn, or noon, maybe even their next shift tomorrow evening. If ever.

The waiting deputy leaned back in his seat, hand dangling out his window.

Wayne opened the Impala's passenger door. I shook my head, wanting to stand for a while to gather my thoughts, collect my composure . . . and cool my temper. "Why didn't you speak up?"

"I believe you, but you *are* trespassing."

"So we do nothing." I turned to Monroe, my back to Wayne. Monroe and I acknowledged each other's safety with a quick few words.

When I spun around, Wayne faced the car, leaning on the hood, head down. "I don't have to say how—"

"No, you don't," I said. "Not a word."

A whippoorwill broke the mood with his three-note call. A second later its mate answered.

Wayne sighed and turned, this time leaning his butt against the vehicle, crossing one boot over the other. "So what *were* you doing out here?"

"Hunting for Purdue."

"On top of a shed?"

I faced him, fists on hips. "Aw, bite me. I couldn't talk to the people in the shed without climbing on top or yelling my fool head off. Purdue's man caught us by surprise. But none of that's the point."

He stared. "Well, enlighten me."

"The point is the hired help stay armed, and they order the field hands about as if they're chattel. You should've seen them cower, Wayne. It's disgusting. Those poor people said they came here to make a living, but were forced to remain with Purdue until they earned their passage. I think they've been tortured with fire." I sighed heavier, reenergized by a need to stop the abuse.

"But you saw Purdue?"

At least he had one ear open.

"Yes, and he threatened me. After he moved his stock out of that shed," I said, pointing to the store. "He used the shrimp boat to bring in these people." I gestured toward the deputy on his radio. "I know they won't do anything, but what can you do?"

"Not a lot," he said. "I can call immigration and tell them what you think you saw."

I rubbed my bug-bitten, flustered face. "What I think I saw?"

"Don't get me started. Not here." He glanced at the patrol car and lowered his voice. "That ridiculous logic of yours could've gotten you killed tonight."

Anger rushed in, and I didn't care how loud I got. "Ridiculous?"

"You got it."

"So you agree there's something bad enough going on to worry about?"

"No, I agree you walked into a potentially dangerous incident without your head on straight. You investigate with a plan, Slade. You don't just wander around unawares as chaos breaks loose in your path."

I inhaled, ready to assault him with more of my *logic*.

"I'll call ICE for you," he said before I could speak. "But it's not our case to solve. I work for Agriculture. So do you. You let people best qualified for the job *do* the job."

"Don't forget the part about the gym bags . . . at the boat and here. Could be drugs," I said.

"Or could be shrimp, tools, or somebody's clothes."

The tow truck pulled up before I could tell Wayne to soak his head in the outhouse. I pushed off the car, more than ready to go. "At least let me get my purse and cell phone out of the car."

Wayne drove like a robot back to the motel, sharing no conversation. We retrieved my car from the Dairy Queen. Thank God he didn't question why it was there. My temper held my exhaustion at bay. I sat on a notepad to keep my wet pants from staining his seat.

Once Monroe was settled in his room, motel ice bucket next to his bed with a plastic bag, towels, and two bottled waters, I hugged him, thanked him again, and left.

Wayne stood in the hall, arms folded.

I dropped my bag on the floor and mirrored him, leaning on the opposite wall. "You better?" I asked.

"Do I have to list all the scenarios that could've played out tonight?" His jaw muscles worked hard under the skin.

"I just wanted to talk to Purdue to see if he'd be willing pay the loans." I fought not to shift my weight, to stand as rigid as him. My thoughts weren't lining up right. Standing in a carpeted, wallpapered, centrally cooled motel removed all sense of urgency from my mission, the night's memory tinged with visions of a whimsical fiasco. I switched arms, crossing them differently, fighting to stay mad with him, ignoring the fact my pants stank.

"Don't do *anything* else on *this* investigation," he said pumping his pointed finger toward the floor. "I mean it. I'll go to your boss. I can't afford your screw-ups."

I eased off the wall, leaning toward him with my index finger planted in his chest. "And I'd tell her you blocked me from working on her behalf. I don't work for the IG."

My conscience told me to shut up, but my pride kept stepping in. To a degree Wayne was right. "I know it got stupid, but I wasn't doing anything wrong!"

"I can't function with you operating behind my back, Slade."

"But it's not about you."

"Yes, it is. And it's about you, Monroe, Savvy, and anyone else involved. Go to bed. I'm not in the mood for this conversation. We'll both regret it." He turned and strode three rooms down to his. Before he stepped in, he glanced back at me, almost said something, then shut the door. I heard the clasp and the deadbolt locks clunk into place.

Wonderful. Two o'clock in the friggin' morning, and I didn't have a room. I could get one, but no telling what the desk clerk would think about my aroma, and I didn't want to find out. No way I'd knock on Wayne's door. I was too tired to deal with him again. I turned around and tapped the door behind me, waiting patiently for Monroe to hobble over.

"Who is it?"

"It's me, Monroe."

He slowly opened up and hopped backwards a step, braced on the wall for balance.

I offered a sheepish grin. "Did I wake you?"

He eyed the empty space behind me. "Are you kidding? With all that noise? I'm surprised no one told you two to get a room." He paused. "Wanna talk about it?"

"Wanna go to bed."

Monroe studied me. His locked expression made me hesitate. For a long moment, we stood on either side of the threshold, wondering what the other was thinking. All I wanted was to clean up and sleep. The later it got, the grumpier I became. "I'm tired, you have two double beds. Wayne hasn't offered his place, and I'll be damned if I'm begging him."

"And you need to talk." He backed away with two more hops. "Come on in."

After he flopped on his bed, I shut the bathroom door and turned on the shower.

My night wear consisted of a soft pink gown with a plunging lace bodice, completely inappropriate, packed in the off chance Wayne apologized. So I'd taken up Monroe on his offer of boxers and an extra-large T-shirt. I washed my clothes in the sink and hung them on the shower curtain rod.

The water ran hotter than I liked, but I left it that way, sterilizing the day's stench off me. The shed, outhouse, mud . . . each thought a layer of crud I scrubbed away. I let the steam cook me, down my back, through my hair, and along my legs.

A half hour later, I stepped out onto the cheap thin rug, my pink flesh radiating heat.

I opened the door, letting the steam out. Monroe eased down and drew up the quilt to his chin. His leg poised on a pillow under the covers. "You sleepy?" I asked and pulled down the sateen quilt on the other bed.

He gave me that smile usually saved for five o'clock when I vented at the end of a work day. "I'm awake. Spill."

I propped up on pillows, slumber-party style, one held in front of me like a stuffed animal. Words poured out of me. Soon I paced the floor, melodrama in my waves and steps. We talked about the women who exchanged sex for an hour just to enjoy a mattress and clean sheets, the men who couldn't speak up about their living conditions. Those subjects frothed me into a new frenzy. Then before I broke down in sloppy tears, we changed subjects.

Monroe indulged my conscience, then patiently listened to my concerns about Wayne. A half hour into my lawman tirade, he interrupted me. "You're unbuttoned."

I'd returned to the bed some time ago and crossed my legs Indian-style. A gap grinned in the boxer shorts. I grabbed the pillow again. Buttons? Wayne wore briefs.

Monroe stood and retrieved a pair of drawstring sweat pants from his closet. "Don't make me limp over there. Come here."

Following instructions, I walked to him. He held the pants up in front of me. "There," he said. "Put these on so you won't distract me."

I stepped into the pants, my face flushed.

He eased back on the bed. "So, what were you saying about Wayne being a pond scum-sucking bonehead?"

I fussed anew, asking for feedback, seeking support and absolution.

"Wayne had no right to lead me on, Monroe. No right at all. Especially after we . . . after I let him . . . I mean . . ."

Monroe held up a hand. "I get it. No point painting a picture."

"Sorry." I'd once again treated him like a best friend, forgetting he was a guy. "So, what do you think?"

"I doubt I'd have used you like litmus paper and told you a lie to take back to Savvy, but you sure proved his point, Slade. And you know how I feel about you snooping on Heyward Farm."

I caught myself whining and recognized it was time for bed. Monroe's eyelids had drooped twice already.

"Go to sleep," I said, getting up. "Need another ice pack?" His knee stretched big as a grapefruit. A doc probably should take a peek at it on Monday. I took the trash can liner, filled it with more ice, and wrapped it in a fresh towel. After placing the fresh ice pack on Monroe's leg, I gingerly straightened the quilt and covered his swollen knee. He lay still, gazing at me as I smoothed out the wrinkles.

Then Monroe grabbed my wrist. "You scared me to death tonight. I ran like a frantic fool, wrenching my knee on some swamp hole like a moron. I never should have left you there."

"You're my buddy, Monroe. I was scared, too. But it's over. You did good!"

He rubbed my forearm and my insides panicked, nerves pinging. "If I were Wayne," he said, "you wouldn't have to ask about staying with me. I'd—"

My other hand covered his mouth. "Don't."

He kissed my palm then removed it from his face. "He rode in like the white knight, with me crippled up on his backseat." He swallowed hard. "I shouldn't have left you, Slade."

With both my wrists held, he drew me down. His lips tenderly covered mine.

Before I realized it, I closed my eyes and kissed back. So familiar, so comfortable. Then softly resisting, I pulled out of his grip. I shook my head, unable to find the right words. He smiled.

I retreated to the bathroom, shut the door, and sat on the closed lid of the toilet, my head resting on my arm. I caught a glimpse of myself in the mirror, reached up and shut off the light.

Chapter 17

SINGING IN THE bathroom stirred me awake. Trying to clear my sleep-deprived head, I squinted at morning light seeping in along the edges of the thick, rubber-backed drapes. My eyes flashed open—then I covered them with my hands. Chicken spit! Wayne didn't sing. My chest stirred at the memory of a kiss.

A knock sounded. "Monroe, it's Wayne. You there?"

Damn! I leaped off the bed, glanced in the mirror, and combed fingers through Medusa hair. Monroe had the hair blower going on those thick white locks, and mine resembled wadded crepe paper.

I ran to the corner of the room, like that would help, then back toward the door, stepping from one foot to the other, turning one way, then another. Where could I hide? Crap, that was stupid. Should I answer? What would I say if I did? My fists wadded up in my shirt. Damn, Monroe's shirt! Oh God. My overnight bag was in the bathroom, with my clothes.

The hair dryer continued, Monroe ignorant to the imminent catastrophe.

Wayne knocked again. "Monroe? Call me on the cell if you can't get out of bed."

Crap. Nowhere to go.

Taking a second to breathe, I marched forward, released the deadbolt, counted to three, and turned the knob.

Wayne started talking the minute the lock clicked. "You know where Slade is? I called the front desk, and they said she never checked in."

"You found me."

Puzzlement filled his eyes, and I cringed as if caught in the act. He studied my attire, then scanned behind me, squinting. Collecting evidence.

He strode into the room, tension in his wake. I shut the door, watching him take in the setting. "Don't overreact, Wayne."

Monroe stood in the bath's entryway, his weight on one leg. He wore the gym shorts he'd slept in and a fresh T-shirt. Blood left his face as he saw Wayne standing between our two beds. "Oh, God."

"Quit, Monroe," I said. "Mr. Investigator left me in the hall with wet, pee-soaked pants and no room. What did he expect?"

Wayne turned away from me and rubbed the back of his neck.

"Definitely not this," he said.

"Wayne." Monroe limped around the end of his bed toward the lawman. His foot caught in the spread puddled on the floor, and he fell forward. Sprawled across the cheap carpet, he yelled, "Oh geez," sucking air through clenched teeth, holding the injured knee.

Wayne spun but did not reach for Monroe. Instead, he hovered over my writhing partner. "Here, let me really help you."

"Wayne!" I reached for Monroe. "I'm so sorry. Can you get up?"

"Nothing happened, man." Monroe moaned again, inhaled, then released it in a huge exhale. He closed his eyes, rocking on the floor. "Geez!"

"Help him up, Wayne," I said. When he didn't react, I yelled, "Help him up!"

The two of us aided Monroe into his bed, and I grabbed the ice bucket, sloshing melted ice water down the front of my T-shirt. "Be back in a minute with more ice." I headed to the hall, flapping my wet shirt away from bra-less breasts.

"Not looking like that." Wayne snatched the bucket from me and stomped out.

I dropped onto the bed next to Monroe. "I'm so sorry."

His face was no longer contorted, but the pain showed clearly in his frown. "Don't let stupidity break you guys up, you hear?"

I reached to stroke his face and caught myself. "Not your problem to worry about. He acted like an ass. You didn't do anything wrong."

Wayne walked into the room and hesitated before bringing me the bucket.

Monroe took the ice pack from me and held it on his leg. "Listen, Wayne. Slade didn't have pajamas to wear."

"Quit, Monroe," I said, uncomfortable between the two men. "Like he said, Wayne, nothing happened. Don't even try to make something of this after leaving me alone last night."

Wayne sat quiet on my bed, a clash of feelings evident on his face. I almost hugged him, to remove the conflicting emotions bouncing around his brain. So we fought at times. We clashed at stressful moments. Still, we had so much going for us.

But Monroe was my best friend next to Savvy. Slipping into a kiss wasn't the end of the world. And he'd injured himself fighting to get help for me. Who wouldn't want to kiss him after that, and then clean up the damage later?

None of us spoke for a long moment. Ice washed around in the plastic bag on Monroe's knee. I grabbed a couple of cubes and rubbed them on the mosquito bites dotting my legs, holding one cube longer on the yellow jacket sting. Both men watched, and I wanted to tell them to quit studying my anatomy.

"Well, enough of this ridiculous scene," I said, standing. "Sitting here all wet in Monroe's clothes doesn't help the mood. I'm going to change."

"Take my key," Wayne said. "Go to my room and use my bathroom."

He held out his key card. The moment was more important than Monroe understood. Wayne and I clearly recognized the crossroad of the offer, and I hesitated.

Then I took the key. Monroe's room wasn't the place to make a long-lasting decision.

"I'll see if the motel has aspirin," Wayne said, his voice husky, the Alpha male. "I think breakfast is still being served in the lobby." I left them coordinating Monroe's morning.

When I came out of Wayne's bathroom a half hour later, he rose from the unmade bed. "Let's go eat. And talk."

"You asking or telling?"

"Didn't think I needed to work that hard to get along with you," he said. "Guess I'll call it asking."

I wasn't a natural follower. Daddy reared me to lead or get out of the way. Wayne continued to shove me out of the way, metaphorically speaking. It was time for a come-to-Jesus meeting with the lawman.

At Blackstone's Café, we dined at the same table Savvy and I had shared a few days earlier. Waitresses darted past with their balancing acts of dishes, while silverware clinks echoed from the kitchen. Diners ate and eyed their watches. Someone broke a glass behind the counter.

Only two sips into my coffee, Wayne started in on me. And here I thought that talking meant *us*—him and me.

"This isn't about you this time, Slade. This is about Savannah and the agency. You can't run renegade with a crime that may end up in federal court. You don't have the authority, and you've been trained enough to know this is my jurisdiction."

"You're right. It isn't about me. It isn't even about Savvy. It's now also about twenty other people living in squalor on Heyward Farm. Plus I was only asking about him paying the loan. Geez."

He sighed. "You can't go carrying every torch you find. You don't know how the law works. Chances are you'll damage more than you'll help."

"Damage your situation, or ours?"

He set his cup down and leaned back, his steely gray eyes fixed on me. "You will get hurt."

I ignored the comment. "I'm not trying to pee in your sandbox, Wayne," I said. "I have an interest in what Heyward's up to, and since all this can incriminate my best friend, my heart's in it as well."

"Is it still in us?"

"Listen," I said, to slow myself down as well as him. My next words nudged a tear, but I blinked it back. "It hurt so damn bad that you baited me with the information I gave to Savvy, you know?"

His lips flat lined, as if he were choosing his response carefully, too. "Well, it bothered me that you didn't respect me well enough to keep a confidence."

I crossed my legs, touching his. "But it was a lie," fell from my lips.

"But you didn't know that," he said, his jaw taut. He sighed. "I'm sorry. Maybe I stepped a little out of line." He reeled back on the *sorry*. Hesitating a bit on the *maybe*.

In all my years with my husband, I never heard him say sorry. But I bit back telling Wayne everything was rosy. I needed more, an assurance we wouldn't travel this road again. "Promise me," I said.

"Promise what?"

"Promise me you'll respect me, my job, my logic." I tapped the table with my spoon. "That you'll never use me again."

He scowled, like I'd fed him an unripe persimmon. "What do you think I am? I apologized."

I clenched my teeth. "Just promise, Wayne. It's so friggin' simple."

His eyes tried to read how deeply he waded by repeating the phrase. "I promise."

That's all I needed to hear. "I'm sorry, too. And I vow to think before I do something stupid like hiding on a shed . . . or betraying a confidence."

This patched up, jerry-rigged, make-up moment couldn't undo all we'd done and said, but it was a start. Time to tread slowly and patiently watch for confirmation that he meant his promise . . . and would keep it. He'd be watching me, too.

"No more secrets, okay?" I said.

He returned my smile. "Agreed."

The young, spectacled waitress pushed her glasses up on her nose and warmed my coffee almost without missing a step to the next table. I poured another pack of sweetener, stirring it for something to do. We let our compromise settle around us for half a cup's worth.

"Are we going to discuss Monroe?" I asked.

"Do we need to?" Wayne replied.

"It was as I said, a room shared by two people, not a bed."

He winked. "Then we're good."

Thank God. No way would I mention Monroe's kiss.

I'd just broken our promise. I sipped the last of my coffee. "It just amazes me that the feds will go after Savvy for a forged signature, but they won't deal with slavery."

Wayne pressed his lips to a fine line. "See? Do you see why you excuse yourself from an investigation when you're close to the parties involved? You do her an injustice just being around."

"You didn't excuse yourself from my bribery mess last year."

He shook his head. "Totally different, and you know it. We were fighting idiots." He evaluated me a second. "What happens if she's indictable?"

"Good gracious," I said, falling back in my chair. "You're not listening."

He set down his cup. "Some of her mud might stick to you. You could get accused of trying to aid and abet."

What was wrong with trying to show she'd been hoodwinked? An investigation would unearth the facts anyway. What difference did it make about my attitude and beliefs if the end result was the same?

"I get what you're saying," I said. "Not that I agree."

The corner of his mouth slid up, and his gaze softened. His arm came off the chair and both elbows laid on the table in acknowledgment of my attempt to compromise. "Listen . . ."

I shook my head and waved. "That's fine. I get it. There's a halfway decent brain up here," I said tapping my forehead.

"Halfway," he said, grinning.

"Signatures on loan papers are falsified. Savvy doesn't know why. Evan doesn't know why." I took a fast breath before he could interrupt. "The farmer's dead, but owes us money. The crop is gone, and we don't know if we'll get paid. The only shrimp boat blew up, yet there's another shrimp boat in use for some reason, which almost doesn't matter since Savvy didn't perfect the lien on it. That second boat shipped something to the farm. Purdue was worried enough to move it back to the boat once I'd interfered with their plans. My guess is drugs."

"Wouldn't shock me," Wayne said.

He cooperated, so I kept rolling, touching upon the other subject. "But the migrant workers . . . totally unexpected." To Wayne's credit, I caught a hint of rankle in his facial lines. I fell in love with the man partly because of that strong sense of right and wrong.

"Slaves, Wayne. In the twenty-first century. In the United States, for God's sake."

"I said I'd talk to ICE. We, you and I, don't have the power to get involved. Let's be sensible enough to pass it to someone who does."

This was Saturday. Monday seemed ages away when each second was brutal enough on those people. With a hardy exhale, I shifted topics. "Teddy. You never met him, but he's the biggest piece of filth walking on two legs, and he's back with Savvy."

"Not *my* concern."

I sat back disappointed. "That's a bit cold." I almost completed the thought with *she's a friend*, but caught myself.

"You know what I mean," he said. "It's not a professional concern. I like Savannah, but I'm not about to get involved with who she sees. Especially now."

Shifting forward, I pointed my spoon at him. "Ah, but I think Teddy *is* a professional concern. He insured the boat that blew up. He inspected the crop for Savvy. He gave her a Mercedes. He's too connected to ignore." My palm flattened on the table. "And that's my *professional* opinion."

"I could give a probable reason for all three of those."

"Yeah, but you should investigate them first. I'm shoving you clues. You can pursue them or I can." He'd have to check out the son-of-a-bitch now. I pinched off a piece of toast crust and ate it, like a period on my sentence.

He straightened. "Don't give me ultimatums, Slade."

He knew how to push my buttons, but I also knew how to push his. My daring side both intrigued and upset him, as his did me. "Ditto, lawman. Respect, remember?" I took another bite and brushed off crumbs from my lap. Still glancing down, I asked, "So, what have you found out while I've been gone? I've certainly spilled my guts to you."

I glanced up, taking in his eyes, regretting last night's missed opportunity to be alone with him, remorse rising a teeny bit about Monroe.

"All I've done is confirm what you've told me. I did talk to the coroner, and he's doing a DNA test to be sure it's Dan. All he's got is pieces of somebody."

"You found Purdue?"

"No, but I will—when I'm not chasing you."

I snickered.

He brushed my hand with his fingers. "I couldn't get along with Pam because of her daredevil antics. Please tell me I don't have to worry about you, too."

Pam? "You're comparing me to your ex-wife?"

"At least she was trained in self-defense. You strut into the middle of a crisis without thinking. One day you won't strut out."

This father-figure behavior pissed off his ex, stifled her, drove her to socialize with peers who loved to walk into gunfights so she could stretch her own muscle. I better understood that now, from her perspective.

"I'm not Pam," I said slowly.

"No, you're not. I don't want you to be. But I want you safe."

His duties could scare me to insanity, yet I understood and accepted the nature of his work. I wouldn't want him to shy away from his responsibilities. I was proud of him. So why couldn't he be the same for me? I wasn't trying to get in trouble.

"I said I'd dodge the stunts, remember?" I might not be trained in hand-to-hand, but I wielded an analytical intelligence and common sense that carved my way to the present just fine. I ached at this clash of wills; or maybe it was wits. I laid my napkin beside my plate. "Just let me work this case, too, okay?"

"As long as you don't interfere."

He left money on the table and reached to slide my chair out. I stood on my own and walked to the exit, saddened at how much we still weren't quite communicating. In the car, he kept glancing at me. I faced straight ahead, not sure how I felt.

Wayne received a brief call then hung up.

"Monroe's G-car will be ready on Monday. I'll get Savvy or Evan to help me get it if Monroe still can't walk," Wayne said. He headed back to the motel. "Drive careful on your way home. I'll keep you updated." He nodded once. "I promise."

Home? That made three times. Three goddamn times he'd shooed me away like a freshman on prom night. He parked next to my car, turned off the ignition, and smiled, like we remained all hunky dory.

I tried one more time. "The state director said I should stick around."

"The state director would have a fit if she thought you complicated matters. I'll wrap this up quickly, then hurry on back. Let's go to Hennessey's when I get home. You like *fancy* every once in a while." He leaned over to kiss me, like what he'd said provided the perfect icing on the cake.

"Don't let me hold you up then." I got out and threw my bag into my car. "I'll sit home and iron my favorite Sunday dress. Maybe I'll even get my nails done." I slammed the door and started the engine. When he walked around the car to address my response, I hit the lock.

A text came through on my phone. My daughter was still snooping about Mrs. Amick's old boyfriend.

Can U stay in luv with a memory? Mrs. A can't stop talking re: Beau. Luv U. Ivy.

Sure you could, I thought. Sometimes I wondered if that's what I loved—the memory of a knight in shining armor, with cowboy boots.

I drove off, teeth grinding. Wayne leaned on his car, his belt badge glinting in the sun.

Chapter 18

I TORE OUT of the motel parking lot, headed in the opposite direction from home, ignoring the temptation to check again for Wayne in my rearview mirror. Rushing through downtown, I debated returning to St. Helena. I didn't have a mission. I snorted at my use of Wayne's words discounting my presence on the case. Still, that rushing, too proactive rationality had already thrown me in enough of a quagmire to make me think twice about striking out alone. I may be hardheaded, but I learned from my mistakes.

A breeze whipped in from the nearby Beaufort River, rattling the fronds of stocky palmettos. Gulls floated aloft in suspended animation until they broke ranks and dove for herring. The thick, humid air carried the briny marsh odor that was Beaufort, and even the air conditioning couldn't sanitize the smell.

My six-month stint in the early years of my career had taken place right here, under Savvy's oversight. Her deadbeat brother had hit on me, and she'd given him a tongue-lashing for flirting with her employee. Years later, Deadbeat Jeremy had become a successful real estate broker in Atlanta. My loss.

Saturday traffic ran sluggish. With streets barely wide enough for two cars, downtown was clogged with tourists, local shoppers, and nautical enthusiasts headed for the marina.

The weekend drew tourists to Fripp, Harbor, and Hunting Islands. Yankees comprised half of them. Not that their money didn't spend well down here, but we tended to move slower on the highway than they did and didn't believe in nudging a horn except to wave hello.

I couldn't catch a break with the lights, so I called Ivy. I'd never answered her text, the one that mentioned her amateur sleuthing efforts on Mrs. Amick's old beau. My daughter answered, breathless.

"Miss me?" I asked.

"Sure, Momma." A squeal echoed in the background. "Just a minute," she said. The phone plunked down. "Okay, I'm back. When you coming home?"

"Not sure. What you up to?"

"Swimming, cooking, feeding Mr. Amick's chickens. Just stuff."

"I called to check on you," I said.

"No you didn't. You're feeling Momma-guilt. I'm fine." Music blared in the background. "Miss Dolly is teaching Star and me the jitterbug. Can I go now?"

"But you texted me," I said.

She lowered her voice. "That was so yesterday, Momma. Now I'm collecting clues."

"Well, excuse me. Guess I'll let you go."

Ivy hung up. She was happy, which meant I should be too. I wasn't.

Drumming fingers on the wheel at the sixth red light, I glimpsed Kamba, the Gullah priest, as dignified as a person could be atop his plastic crate.

I lifted one of the conjure bags from my purse. After a circle around the block to park, I walked to the corner, stood, and listened politely.

Sweat streamed down the preacher's face and neck. Periodically, he wiped his forehead with a handkerchief and deftly returned it to his hip pocket without a pause in his message. He threw me a few sideways glances. A family of tourists took his picture before walking on.

I was about to interrupt him when he stepped down, picked up his crate and dropped his pamphlets into it. As I wondered how to open a conversation, he approached me.

"What can I do for you?" he asked in a melted chocolate voice.

"I'd love to buy you a cold drink, unless you need to be someplace." I held out the conjure bag. "And I'd appreciate it if you could tell me the meaning of this unexpected . . . gift."

His white teeth shone beneath tired, yellowed eyes. "Ah. Now how'd a nice lady like you go and get hexed?"

He escorted me to a sandwich shop tucked beside an art gallery flaunting local scenes of boats, egrets, and girls in billowing dresses on the beach. He chose a wrought-iron table away from the sun-drenched front window, and we sat against a whitewashed wall adorned with iron sconces brimming with ivy.

"Care for something?" I asked.

"A Coke, please."

I ordered his drink and mine, a sweet tea. His sandaled foot slid his box under the table. Long, thin fingers reached for the glass, holding a straw to his mouth. He sipped long, and then dabbed his forehead with a napkin from the dispenser. "Thank you."

"I imagine it gets rather warm out there," I said.

"Yes'm. It gets hot at times." He grinned, his dark face a stark contrast to the walls. "Now, what you done to earn a conjure bag?"

His words rang of formal education, but some parts of his speech indicated otherwise. I pictured him preaching to the congregation in a country church, the members captivated. Hand fans fluttering in the thick summer air, grasped by women in pastel dresses and floral hats, keeping fat flies off their toddlers asleep in the pews.

I laid the bag on the table. He picked it up, undid the hemp string, and sniffed the contents before dumping them out on a napkin.

As he studied the blend of pennies, poppy seed, and goodness-knows-what-else, I scratched mosquito bites and took small sips of tea, savoring each one as it soothed my throat. A damp night atop the shed, coupled with the campfire smoke, did little for a summer malady trying to take root and grow.

His forehead creased. "You fighting a cold, young lady?"

I let loose the straw. "Nothing bad, but yes. How'd you know?"

"The way you swallow. You need some *life everlasting*."

I doubted a quick shot of religion could cure my cold. "And where would I get this *life everlasting*?"

"Used to be in drugstores long ago, but doctors outlawed it. Didn't like the competition from hoodoo grannies. Got some at the house, though. You comin' by here on Monday? I could bring ya' some."

Not directly a drug offer, but no telling what the heck was in his homemade concoction. I hesitated and decided not to bite.

He chuckled. "Don't act so scared, miss. You know plants?"

"I have an agriculture degree."

"You know cudweed?"

The light came on in my befuddled brain. "Rabbit tobacco?"

"Ah, you *do* know. Boil it with some whiskey and lemon and you'll feel better."

This time I laughed. "You worried me there, Kamba, is it?"

"Yes'm. And your name would be?"

"Slade." I held out my hand. He shook it with a smooth grace, the back of his velvety from age. "Not sure I'll be here Monday, but thanks for the offer," I said.

He winked *you're welcome*. "So how'd you come by this bag?"

"Someone left it on my car. My friend and I have cars that look alike, so we don't know who it targeted."

"Two pennies. It's for both of you."

"Is the hex real?"

"The intent is real. Someone is fightin' you in your quest, and that's what's important." He bowed ever so slightly and drank again.

I didn't believe in hocus-pocus, but curiosity tugged at me. "Where would someone get this stuff?"

"A root doctor's medicine cabinet or a corner Piggly Wiggly. Just takes a little knowledge. The power is in the motive."

"Well, they wasted their time and energy." So much for leads, but with half a drink left and no clues to investigate, I could kill time. "So tell me, what's *your* mission, Kamba?"

He lifted his head, back straight, as if about to preach. "My people. Most importantly, the youth led astray by drugs brought into our community." He paused with a twinkle in his eye. "Not cudweed."

I couldn't help smiling.

"Buckra needs to know," he said. "I want the youth to know. The Gullah people can't afford to allow drugs to poison the few of us left on the island."

"Buckra?" I asked.

He smiled this time. "White folk."

I acknowledged him. "What about the police?"

"They arrest a son here, a daughter there, but nobody reaches the dealer. My sons try to help."

Ah, maybe connections I could use. "Are your sons police officers?"

"No. I saved two boys from drugs a few years ago." He closed his eyes for a couple of seconds. "A grassroots energy, we call it, to turn youngsters around while searching for the person who sold them drugs. But the flow keeps coming."

A grassroots group might know scuttlebutt on a neighbor. "Are you familiar with the Heyward farm?"

His forehead creased. "Slave owners."

"Yes," I exclaimed. The clerk's head behind the sandwich counter snapped up, and I began again, more discreetly. "Nobody believes me. I was out there yesterday. Purdue Heyward was a nasty man."

"He burns his people."

Before Rene made her shut up, the young Haitian girl had mentioned burning. "He brands them?"

"No, he holds their arms in fire to make them behave. That's why, even in this heat, they all wear long sleeves."

I set down my glass. "Good God." The other day Monroe noted the wide-brimmed hats, long pants, and long sleeves in the tomato field. I assumed the clothing guarded them against the sun or brush. I figured everyone burned if left in the sun from dawn to dusk, day after day.

The subject matter seemed inappropriate for such a public setting, but the old man piqued my interest. My sixth sense didn't pick up any vibes of deceit in him. Instead, he seemed all-knowing. "You have a ride back to St. Helena?" I asked.

"Yes, I have my truck. Why?"

"I could come out and sample your *life everlasting*. If someone's coming after me, I'd just as soon be ten-eight. We can chat some more."

"Ten-eight?"

Geez, Wayne's cop language now infiltrated mine. "It means the ability to work full speed."

"Be happy to have you." He stood then bent over for his box. "The okra's coming in, and my wife should have stew ready when we arrive."

"Don't want to interfere with your supper," I said. Then remembering my manners, I asked, "Do you want to call ahead and tell her company's coming?"

"One more does not matter," he said. "We feed whoever sits at the table."

I dumped the conjure bag and its contents in the trash with our cups. "By the way, you know about haints?"

I ALMOST LOST Kamba in the line of cars leaving Beaufort proper. Once in the country, however, he led me down side roads, and a sandy track ended at a small brick-boxed home under two old oaks so massive they dwarfed the residence.

"Anyika, we have a guest," he said, as he held the screen door open for me. A tomato aroma greeted me in the drive, and now I smelled cornbread. The overhead fan whirred with a slight hum, and three young men relaxed in the small, pine-paneled den.

A short, plump, dark woman fussed in the tiny kitchen. Her hair hid in a white kerchief, and tight curls of black and gray peeked out from the edges. Sweat beaded on her forehead, glistening across corpulent cheeks as she put the final touches to dinner. The only air conditioning came from a window unit in the room where the boys waited. A portable fan in the kitchen created circulation, a good move since pots on all burners raised the room's temperature to a level almost matching outside.

She wiped her face with the back of her apron, and then motioned for me to come in. "Sit, sit. Always room for another."

Kamba directed the largest, muscular boy to move to the vinyl sofa beside the other guys so I could have the upholstered chair. Two in their twenties and one a teen, the young men laughed and jeered each other, joking about sports, music, and girls. The youngest turned out to be a grandson, Jamie. Kamba introduced the two big guys as the protégés mentioned back in town.

Not long after, the matriarch called us to eat. We dined around an old oval maple table with its leaf intact, large enough to accommodate eight with a tight squeeze, tighter with the shoulders of these boys. Quilted floral placemats, faded from frequent washings, adorned each setting.

Kamba stirred okra gumbo in a big soup pot, and then ladled it into bowls. The cornbread went around on a green floral plate, mismatched from the yellow trimmed ones on the table. Chairs creaked as the guys rocked in laughter or passed a plate. Someone's chair owned an unlevel leg and it occasionally thumped on the vinyl floor.

Kamba filled his bowl last, and then accepted the pepper shaker from a boy. "Slade works for the Department of Agriculture. I ran into her downtown."

Anyika's smile accented wide white teeth. "Always glad to have a guest fo' dinner. Yo' work in Beaufort?"

"No, ma'am," I said, biting into my cornbread. "I'm on an investigation. I thought Kamba might help me. So far he has." I stirred the okra around, but it still threatened to burn my mouth.

"She asked about the Heywards," Kamba said, eyes on his meal.

Spoons dropped.

I wiped my mouth with a folded paper towel serving as my napkin. "I went over there to inspect the crop and discovered a bunch of Haitians. A few talked to me, but the owner of the farm wasn't too happy I'd come to visit. Neither were his overseers."

"Umm, umm. You best watch yo'self, baby," said Anyika. "People disappear over there." The boys agreed and mumbled to each other. I halfway expected an *Amen*.

"Nana, can I tell her about that girl?" the teenage boy asked.

Anyika waved permission.

The teen leaped in his seat at the chance to talk. "A group of us was playing ball at my friend's house when this girl came exploding out of the woods. Her arms was all scratched up from the bushes and stuff, and she also had burns on her. Like she'd fallen in a fire and used them to stop her fall, you know?" He pointed to different areas on his forearms. "She had 'em like here and here. Then this big brother tore out right behind her." The more the boy talked, the more animated he became. "Dude caught up to her right at the driveway where we'd been shooting hoops. We were all nice size guys," he said reaching out, "but this monster was crazy huge!"

I suspected the boy was right. Hulk could shade a small herd of cattle. "So what happened?"

"We tried to, you know, show him our stuff and keep her away from him, but he snatched her away saying she was his wife." He shrugged. "Like, what could we do?"

Kamba spoke up. "I talked to the police, but they did nothing."

The boy turned to his meal. "That girl ain't been seen since. Probably got really burned up when they got her back. They don't let nobody loose back there. They come out feet first or not at all."

I lowered my spoon and gawked. "They kill people, too?"

"Jamie, dat's 'nuff," said Anyika. "Shut mout'." I honored her wish as well and held my questions. Besides, the stew was eatable now and proved quite good.

After dinner, I ran water into the sink. My cell phone rang from my pocket.

"You take care a yo' bizness," Anyika said, rolling her ample hips forward to take my place. "I take care of deez dishes."

I grabbed the cell on the fourth ring and headed outside. The humidity smothered me when I stepped through, even in the shade of the porch. "Hello?"

"Where are you?" Wayne asked. "Thought you'd be getting home about now and wanted to make sure you made it." Like he'd forgotten the manner in which we'd parted ways at the motel.

"I'm still in Beaufort."

He sighed. "Where?"

"Visiting friends. I ran into someone. He invited me to dinner with his family."

"Okay, but exactly where?"

I had one daddy already, thank you. I was a grown woman who didn't have to answer to anyone anymore, but out of respect and something I couldn't name, I answered him. "St. Helena."

Kamba walked out and glanced at me. The two young men who'd kept silent through supper sat on the porch in formed rubber chairs. Over the top of Wayne's fussing, I said, "Listen. I'm fine. It's just dinner with friends. Talk with you later." I closed the phone. On second thought, I shut it off.

One man started to get up, and I waved him to keep his seat. Instead, I rested my behind on the porch railing. "Thank you for dinner. The food and company were excellent." They smiled, like they already knew.

The tallest and darkest gentleman, Martin, seemed the most introspective. "What exactly you investigating at the Heyward place?" he asked, a dialect almost nonexistent.

I couldn't say, per the rules of investigation, so I asked a question in return. "Do they deal drugs?"

"Yes'm. Purdue Heyward's known for that. Dan Heyward, too."

"So what's with the slaves?" I asked.

He shook his head. "Cheap labor. Our concern is the stuff. We're close to being sure they make the exchange out at sea, but we've never seen local distribution. But someone is supplying these islands. Might not even be him."

The stouter man puffed up at the comments. "Drugs is drugs, Martin. He might not be supplying our people, but he's delivering to somebody's people. And I'm sick of them locking up workers."

Martin sighed as if retreading old ground. "I'm not risking what happened to Kamba again—him or nobody else. We have a focus."

Kamba watched Leghorns scratch bare ground under one of the oaks, the birds clucking contentment.

I studied Kamba's illegible face. "What happened to you?"

He raised his sleeve. A puffy, multi-shaded brown scar appeared from under his shirtsleeve. Even healed, the distorted, raised skin appeared painful. "I approached the Heyward place last year to protest the way they treat people, especially after that girl tried to escape. A guard up and burned me with hot wood from a campfire, like I was one of theirs."

I tried to hide my surprise. What if they'd caught me on the shed roof? First Rene and his crowd, and now Kamba. God knows what happened to the girl Jamie mentioned at supper. "Please tell me the cops did something."

"A deputy spoke to them. They said I was trespassing, possibly stealing from their store, stirring up trouble with the workers. They said when I would not leave, they threatened to chase me off the place, and I tripped and fell into the fire."

"Oh, good grief," I said, recalling the deputy who accused me of trespassing.

Kamba went back to watching the chickens. "You be careful, Miss Slade. You don't know what you're dealing with. Whatever you are chasing is not worth getting hurt over."

The heavier young man stood, tipped his chair back, and marched into the house, slamming the screen door behind him.

"Don't mind Jumper. He gets fired up at times." Kamba glanced at the sun beginning to dip behind the woods. "If you're headed back to Columbia, you best be getting on the road soon. Let me fetch you that cold remedy first." He stepped inside, leaving me alone with Martin.

"Didn't mean to aggravate your friend," I said.

Martin dispelled my apology with a head movement. "Don't worry about him. He lets emotion override his sense at times. When you've been there, you get the itch to stop as many sisters and brothers as you can. We'd like to think Heyward supplies this island so we knew who to target, but after two years, we've never seen the first clue."

I frowned. "Two years?"

"Yeah, since Purdue joined up with Mr. Dan."

My gut turned, with nothing to do with okra and cornbread. The timeline added up. Savvy's loan to Heyward had most likely funded drugs.

Chickens peered up as Kamba came back out and rejoined me on the cozy front porch. He gave me a cheesecloth bag full of broken, dried leaves. "Boil it and add lemon and whiskey. Fix you up."

Any drink with lemon and whiskey would work for me, but the cudweed couldn't hurt. I said my thanks and goodbyes and strolled with the older man toward my car. Shadows brought dusk skulking in.

"We never finished our talk about your haint," he said. "He good or bad?"

I laughed. "Beau seems innocent enough. He's my neighbor's ex-boyfriend who liked his wine. He used to live on Lake Murray, on the same place where I built my new house."

"Ah." His head dipped. "He had no family?"

"Don't think so." I popped a mosquito on my shirt and flicked it to the dirt, and the sight of him started my zillion bites to itching. "Lived his life near his childhood sweetheart, my neighbor Dolly, who married someone else." Maybe Kamba grew a secret for mosquito bites, too. I felt like a pincushion after last night.

"Gunpowder and salt sprinkled in the house might keep him at bay." An arthritic hand ran across his chin. "Find where he's buried, break something he liked on the grave, and leave it there, like a bottle of his favorite wine. Helps keep a tempestuous soul at rest."

He accepted my shake, the grip dry, even in the humidity. "Thanks so much. You've been a generous host."

His head bowed. "You just be careful."

Seeing my cards in the car ashtray, I passed one to Kamba. "Oh, here's my number if you think of information I might need."

He saluted me with the card and patted the roof of my car as I eased out of his yard.

I headed home, still not happy I followed Wayne's orders. If he was the only reason I'd headed north, I'd turn around, rent a motel room, and get in his face. But I owed Ivy momma-time, I missed Zack, and this was a weekend. I punched in my parents' phone number.

"Your father's taken him in the backyard," Mom said. "They're having a long talk, baby. Want me to interrupt?"

I could tell from the age-old tone I'd grown up with that she preferred I didn't. "No, don't bother," I said. "Just tell him I called. How long you think he'll be with y'all?"

"Carolina." The warning tone rang clear. "It's been less than a week. There's noticeable progress taking place between the boy and your father, but he's your son. You decide."

Torn up about not being the solution to whatever ate at Zack, I chewed the inside of my cheek. I felt impotent about him, and having another adult tending to him ate at my gullet. Yet here I was up to my neck with Savvy's melee, unable to give my son my full attention. "Let him stay another week," I said. "I'm on a nutty case anyway."

"I think that's wise, sweetheart. Sometimes it's harder to back away than to take charge."

"Yeah, well, thanks, Mom." Though I sure as hell couldn't recall a time she backed away from me.

Halfway to Gardens Corner, I stopped at a Jiffy Mart and picked up an ice-cold Coke for my throat. When I got home, I'd fix the tea. The whiskey part sounded real good.

Chapter 19

I ARRIVED AT the Amicks' home around ten. Ivy chattered with energy to spare, but I could've slept standing. I wanted to drag my worn out body to bed. Dolly, Buddy, and Ivy studied a Scrabble board as though it held the answers to world peace.

"So how's it going?" I asked. No tiles left in the box. Good. The game was in the home stretch.

"Shhh, Momma," my daughter scolded. "I'm concentrating." Dolly Amick cut a glance at me and smiled. Ivy laid down five tiles and hit a triple word score. "Pow! Y'all beat that. P-R-A-N-K."

"I'll be danged." Buddy's fingers drummed on the table. "I can't beat that."

"She's sharp," I said. "Did y'all have a good time?"

I spoke to Ivy, but Dolly answered. "Oh, baby, we've shared the grandest time. Let's see . . . we picked blueberries and made pancakes with them. We gathered eggs."

Ivy jumped up. "They've got baby chickens, Momma. Teeny ones," she said squealing as she cupped her hands. "And I can put a chicken to sleep."

Better time than I had.

"I think I learned something about Beau," I said.

Ivy shook her head and threw me a wary look. Dolly's face brightened, then she caught herself. "How's that?"

I relayed the story about the Gullah man, the spirit world, medicinal plants, and hexes, holding back the discussion with Kamba about Beau after seeing Ivy's reaction.

"Can he put jinxes on people you don't like?" Ivy leaned her elbows on the kitchen table, her foot swinging. She'd perked up at my story, as if seeing me in a cooler light.

"You ready to come home, Ivy?"

"Aww, Momma," she whined as only a preteen girl could. "My bed here has huge fluffy quilts to sink into. It's like being a princess. Can I stay, please? We planned on going to Sunday School in the morning if you didn't get back in time."

Buddy walked over to me. "It's no trouble, Slade. It's a Presbyterian church in Chapin. We thought she'd meet some kids her age."

Watch what you wish for. I'd asked for a local babysitter and found the perfect one in the Amicks. Problem was, and I'd be selfish to consider it a problem, the Amicks appealed to her more than I did. "Of course I approve." A pang shot through my heart.

Buddy studied me. "We're just being neighborly, sugar. You're welcome to come."

I smiled. "Spent a fitful night in a bad motel after a long hard day at work. I'll take a rain check."

"You sure?" he asked.

I waved aside his concern. "Positive. I'm lucky to have you two around."

After ordering my daughter to behave, out of pure habit, since she appeared to be a perfect angel, I drove around the corner to home. With tea water on the stove, I ran to the bedroom to slip into gym shorts and a tie-dyed T-shirt. The water was boiling by the time I returned to the kitchen. I steeped the *life everlasting* weed into a tan tea, strained the liquid into a mug, and added a tablespoon of lemon and a healthy jolt of sour mash. On the porch in the dark, ceiling fans blowing away insects, I listened to tree frogs and the occasional plop of a bass leaping out of the lake.

I picked up the phone and dialed Wayne's cell. The call went straight to voice mail. "Hey, it's me. I'm home." My voice seized at what to say next. I love you? I miss you? I'm what to you? The voice mail timed out and I closed my cell.

I went back to the kitchen, grabbed some paper towels and hot spicy potato chips, then returned to the porch. Madge the cat climbed in my lap. With a whiskey toddy on the stool beside me, and red, cayenne pepper-spiced fingers digging into the potato chip bag, I returned to thoughts of Beaufort.

Purdue had arrived too conveniently in town when Savvy closed the Heyward Farm loan.

A yawn escaped. For now I hoped Kamba's *life everlasting* gave me sleep everlasting, without dreams.

An hour later, I dozed, still in the rocker. An owl awoke me at two a.m. I dragged myself inside, fell into bed, and slept the sleep of the dead. Not a single solitary dream.

CLOSING THE door of the state director's huge office behind me felt like entering a bullet-proof limo: luxurious and buffered from the real world.

Today Ms. Dubose wore charcoal-hued slacks and jacket with a red, silk blouse and rich, pointy black heels. Sharp as shit.

She stood at her window. Nine times out of ten, that's where I'd find her, peering across the Columbia landscape from her tenth-floor perch. Whether a conscious tactic or not, it worked on me, as though she contemplated what I'd say before I even entered the room.

I briefed her on my meager findings once she returned to her desk. I caved and told her about Wayne's attitude, minus the spat. Better to make the preemptive strike in case Wayne called her to rein me in, in which case I'd be royally pissed.

"So, Mr. Largo doesn't like you down there?" she asked.

"No, ma'am, he doesn't. Thinks I'm too close to Savannah Conroy."

"I don't get it," she said, tapping the same gold pen as always—a Montblanc. "Why should he care?"

I grasped for an answer. "Maybe I distract him?"

She breezed past my comment. "I received a memo about Monroe. He reported quite the eventful weekend. Twisted his knee on Friday?"

"I saw him that evening," I said, not exactly coming clean. "He walked through some woods. Someone slashed the tires on his car."

She pursed her lips. "Monroe led me to believe it was more than that. What's going on down there?"

God, I hoped she didn't know about the shed ordeal. "The dead farmer has a partner about as honest as a politician." I caught the reference and almost blushed. "No offense."

Luckily that garnered a laugh. "None taken."

"Savvy has medical issues. Her head isn't quite on straight, either."

"And you fell out with your boyfriend."

Was that a hint of humor? "Excuse me?"

"Harden told me."

I analyzed the last few days in speed mode. Who fed information to Harden? Savvy? Couldn't see that. Even if I disappeared, Wayne remained, and I served her needs better than he did. Evan? Didn't have a clue about him on a personal level, but he'd tried to help me, and I detected not one shred of inappropriate behavior from him. He supported Savvy. Unless she and Evan operated together?

Surely not Monroe?

"Who's reporting on me, Ma'am?"

"Have no idea."

"Why not? How am I to do my job with someone gossiping behind my back?" My blood pressure rose a bit. "Unless you don't trust me and have someone watching."

That could be it. I'd seen it before—experienced it. Tables turning on the person turning over the rocks for clues.

"Ms. Slade." She sat, leaning closer, waiting for me to reply.

"Yes, ma'am."

"It's no secret you're down there, and by now, enough people know why. Focus. You think I don't have constant eyes on me, whether I want them or not?" She pointed her pen in my direction. "Your concerns are this investigation, my reputation, and your job. Deal with them."

I chewed the inside of my cheek. "So what would you have me do?"

"Go back to Beaufort and watch Largo. Keep me apprised so I'm not surprised by any damaging discoveries. And since I'm wary enough to realize you'll struggle with that assignment, I'm putting Monroe in charge. You can go there under the guise of helping him with that audit. He said he'd love to have you back."

My stomach dropped. "You've already discussed this with Monroe?"

"Don't get sidetracked, Slade. You're my real eyes and ears."

Who else had heard that *real eyes and ears* speech? "I appreciate the trust," I said, the sarcasm costumed.

She rolled the soft leather chair back. "You'll earn it, I'm sure."

She dismissed me with *have a good trip.* I wasn't feeling quite as gold-plated as before.

I walked past my office, stopping long enough to let Whitney know where I'd be. My cell phone rang on the way to the parking garage.

"Hey, girlfriend." Savvy sounded tired but closer to her old self. "Heard you came and went and missed me this weekend."

"Hey, yourself. Yeah. Had to help Wayne do something. How you holding up?"

She cleared her throat. "Can you come to the doctor with me tomorrow? They'll have test results."

What about Teddy rested on the tip of my tongue. *Have you ratted me out to the state director* almost fell out as well, but I repressed the urges and said, "What time?"

I ARRIVED AT Savvy's office at ten thirty. Ivy was tickled over staying with the Amicks again. At this rate, they could claim her on their tax return.

Savvy's appointment was at eleven thirty and only five miles away. Raye smiled at me this time when I entered, and I showed myself past the counter into the main office. Monroe leaned back in a clerical chair, knee propped on a straight-back from the lobby, files to his left and right.

I opted to go neutral, uncertain what played out behind my back.

"How's the knee?"

"Doc says I sprained it. Nothing torn." He placed an open file on the stack beside him. I studied his mannerism, his voice, his eye movement for hints.

"You talk to Largo since you left here Saturday?" he asked.

"No, I haven't," I said, my words clipped.

He continued reading his files. "I haven't seen or heard much from him, either. Got my car fixed, though."

"Wonderful."

His eyes filled with concern after hearing my sarcasm. "Doesn't matter who's in charge of this two-person operation, Slade. It was Dubose's idea, not mine."

"Whatever." He could've called, given me a heads-up. One kiss and I felt like I'd argued with a boyfriend.

Only Monroe wasn't pumped up with ego. He'd never betrayed me.

"Savannah in?" I asked.

"Yeah, she's been on the phone. You just missed Evan. Surprised you didn't see him outside." His crow's feet seemed more noticeable.

"You need something? Lunch on my way back? I'm headed out with Savvy."

"You haven't been too reliable with food delivery."

"Take it or leave it. What do you feel like?" My defensive posture was slipping. Monroe had always been a compatriot. Dubose most likely backed him in a corner on this *in charge* thing.

He smiled at my concession. "Surprise me. Any food is welcome."

I walked the few feet down the hall to Savvy's office and poked my head in. "Hey, you ready? I'm in a G-car, so we have to take yours to the doctor."

My girlfriend focused hard as she jotted notes. "Just a sec. Trying to get this stuff down while it's fresh in my head." I stood against the wall and read her diploma and a few awards I already knew by heart. "There," she said. "That'll hold me until I can get back and fill in the gaps."

"Well, come on. You don't want to be late."

She shut down her computer.

"What are you working on so hard?" I asked.

The Windows operating system jingled its shutdown tune. She cradled her mouse. "At dinner last night, Wayne said I needed to record my thoughts about Heyward. About everything that happened, going way back to two years ago."

Dinner? "Are you also writing about Teddy inspecting the crops?"

"Sure. We talked long and hard about all that, losing track of time until they raised the lights and mopped the floors. But I promised to be honest about it and document everything I could remember." She reached in her file drawer for her purse.

"You tell him about your health?"

"Since he asked me to be open, I felt that meant the illness, too."

I nodded. "Open is good." Too bad few people were these days.

She winked at me as she rose. "You're lucky."

Huh? "How so?"

She gave me a wolf whistle. "That's one cool man you've got there."

"Yeah, well, we gotta go."

Savvy and I reached the parking lot and turned toward her Mercedes. My fingers slipped on the handle. I wiped my palm on my shirt and eased the handle sensibly, to cool any residual frustration.

Maybe dinner was simply dinner. Not everyone harbored ulterior motives. I felt no deeply rooted reason to be angry, yet here I was rankled at the world. A blinding flash of the obvious split through me. This was how Zack felt. Nothing was normal. His familiar environment gone. He'd lost his father and moved from a home he'd known since birth. Today all my friends shifted, too, eroding trust I'd considered unconditional. Or was it me unwilling to trust? Suddenly I wasn't too proud of my attitude of late.

Movement caught my eye in the far corner of the parking lot. Savvy saw me and followed my attention. Evan pointed to the office. Teddy laughed, a file in his hand. Evan slapped Teddy's chest and reached for the file. Savvy's ex knocked the effort away, a glower on his face. He gave Evan nasty gestures as a heated conversation ensued. Tight faces and clenched fists appeared on both. I couldn't make out the words between the men, but their body language clearly indicated a hostile, male face-off.

My logic went into frenzy mode with ideas why Teddy and Evan debated with such animation in broad daylight. I turned to watch Savvy's take on the confrontation, but only caught the top of her head dip as she got in the front seat. I dropped into the car and fastened my seatbelt. "Do they always fuss like that?"

"On occasion." Savvy backed up the car then shifted into drive. "They're talking Braves baseball, for all I know."

I played innocent. "Wow, they fight like that over baseball?"

"Figure of speech, Slade."

"They working together?"

"We share a lot of clients."

While their spat wasn't my business, my radar stayed overactive these days. Both men hovered along the edges of this investigation. Instinctively, I sided with Evan, because experience taught me Teddy couldn't pass for honest if his life depended on it.

I twisted in my seat, almost expecting punches, but Evan was stomping back toward the building. Teddy still stood, eyeing Evan, red-faced.

"What do they normally argue about?" I asked, turning back around to face Savvy.

"Let it go, Slade. Just let it go."

Chapter 20

SHAG MUSIC played on Savvy's radio. Traffic moved easy as Savvy drove through the streets to her doctor's appointment, giving me a little time to sort my thoughts, my behavior.

Wayne and I had originally met on a bribery case and soon became an item in spite of our collective common sense saying otherwise. In an effort to sabotage me, one of Wayne's adversaries lied that my lawman tended to fraternize with the victims. Now my hot-to-trot buddy, the current victim, had met him after hours. Not that either one would tackle the other, but the mental image of two of the sexiest people in my life doing dinner irritated me for a reason I could not pinpoint.

Wayne preached professionalism, but his taking Savvy to a restaurant felt too close for my comfort. Somebody could see them together and misunderstand. People wouldn't misunderstand seeing Savvy and me. We were friends, and both women.

I bit my lip, as realization caught me by surprise. Socializing with Savvy probably made her misinterpret my purpose in Beaufort. That's okay, I argued. Right now on the way to the doctor's office, she needed me to be her friend, regardless of how close anybody thought we were to her case.

Savvy was living and breathing Teddy anyway, so Wayne shouldn't be an issue, not that Teddy was anywhere near as good a substitute. Guess I simply didn't like Wayne going out to eat without me. Yet I'd dined with Monroe many times ... and kissed the man. A walloping load of guilt smacked me. Wayne would be crushed.

Savvy raised her voice, "Slade!"

"What?" I said, returning to the present. "Just thinking."

"No joke. What about?"

"What did Teddy think about your dinner with Wayne?"

She flashed a split second of hesitation I recognized only because I understood her so well. "I didn't tell him. Wayne told me not to—at least until the case is over. Does our dinner upset you?"

"I'm struggling with it," I said, watching out the window as we rolled past the Civil War-era homes.

"Oh, come off it, Slade. I oughta whip you. He's damn fine, but he's yours. He's an agent. I figured his clandestine activities were appropriate."

She nudged my leg, playful. "If I wanted a piece of him, I wouldn't tell you we went out, now would I?"

I flinched at her mentioning a *piece*. "I know it's his job, Savvy." I crossed my arms. Aware I'd challenged her with my face-off mannerism, I unfolded them. "Forget it. This is about you and your doctor's appointment."

"Damn right," she said. "My blood pressure's already on the rise. I might have an aneurysm and drop dead on the spot."

"Geez, Savvy, shut up. You make me feel like I've cussed in front of my mother."

"Good, you ought to." She turned into a strip mall of medical offices.

We came in sight of the place. A lump formed in my throat as this illness got real. If the doctor delivered bad news, I'd be there for her.

When we entered the doctor's reception area, a mom and two grade-schoolers sat on one side and a couple in their seventies on the other. All of them glanced up at us as if they knew our reason for being there. The nurse finally called for Savvy. I held onto last year's *People Magazine* and remained in the chair, uninvited.

Savvy walked two steps and turned. "Come on, Slade. I didn't bring you here to sit in the waiting room."

I trotted to stand with her.

The nurse smiled and asked Savvy, "Is this your sister?"

"As far as I'm concerned, yes."

The plastic smile stuck firm to the nurse's pudgy face as she turned on rubber soles. Like an airline stewardess who told you it'd be fine after the plane dropped an engine. "Follow me," she said.

Savvy gripped my hand, and I squeezed back.

The doctor wore a smart blue tie beneath his white coat. The expensive tie-up shoes probably came from a highbrow downtown Savannah boutique, maybe Hilton Head. Everything about him suggested a creased and neatly placed appearance, as if he ironed his underwear and socks and flossed three times a day. I resisted exhaling into my cupped fingers for bad breath.

He gestured toward a matching pair of cherry-finished chairs with raised embroidered, filigreed upholstery. "Sit, ladies." He opened the file, straightened his glasses perpendicular to his patrician nose, and tilted his head to see through the upper part of the bifocals. We poised rigid. He said "*hmm*" and silently read the top page.

His stare switched from the paper to Savvy. "We have good results. It isn't a tumor." He smiled.

Neither of us smiled back. Savvy lost her pent-up tension for a second, then gripped the chair and leaned forward. "So, what is it?"

He returned to the paper. "Your symptoms are most likely caused by stress, possibly coupled with your choice of birth control. Appears you are premenopausal, which exacerbates the stress and sleeplessness."

Savvy cut loose a squeal I'd never heard.

I scrunched her fingers. "What can she do about her headaches?"

"Simple lifestyle changes and hormone replacement therapy. Eat a good diet. Get lots of calcium."

Savvy released a huge sigh underscored with a moan. If the situation hadn't felt so dire, I'd have laughed out loud at her theatrics. "So that's it?" I asked.

The doctor grinned. "That's it."

My girlfriend's words sprayed across the good doctor's desk. "I'm not old enough for . . . for menopause."

"Savvy," I said, rubbing her back. "It's not a tumor."

She yanked me from my chair and wrapped me in an anaconda grip.

"Hey," I said, stroking her hair. "It's okay." I'd never seen her this undone, at least not since she divorced Teddy. Over good news, no less. No telling how much she'd bottled up her fear of this diagnosis.

The doctor cleared his throat, and Savvy released me. "Doc," she said. "I'd like to say it's been a pleasure, but I'd be lying my ass off. You have a good day. I'm out of here."

She turned to leave, and I grabbed her wrist and held her there long enough to retrieve her marching orders and prescription, me writing the information, knowing she wasn't hearing any of it. Then we walked out and busted into the summer heat.

In the car, I relaxed, relieved at the verdict.

Savvy refreshed her makeup and primped her hair, as if defying the diagnosis. "I'm too friggin' young for this crap."

"Actually, you're not," I said. "It happens to women younger than you." We fell back into our old familiar banter. "Bugs me he couldn't make that diagnosis sooner. He obviously put you through hell because I've never, *ever* seen you act like that."

"Yeah, well, it's not his fault that tests take so long."

I flicked her. "When this Heyward stuff is over, why don't you get a second opinion? Maybe go to someone across the river in Savannah, or Charleston. We can do an overnighter."

She started the engine. "My head sure hurts for it being just the *M* word."

"It's the *PM* word, remember? Premenopause. Take the meds and see what happens." With tensions easing, the other reason I was in Beaufort rushed back. An idea formed. "How about we not tell Teddy about the results, at least not yet."

"Fine by me," she said. "He'll think I'm ancient."

I laughed. She was eight years older than me, mid-forties, far from ancient. But her diagnosis made me measure my own years. Sex appeal, however, wasn't why I wanted her to keep the doctor's disclosure close.

She squinted. "You don't think he'll be happy about this, do you? You don't trust him."

"I don't know, Savvy. I want to keep as many factors the same as we can. He's having spats with Evan, maybe regarding the Heyward ordeal. Who knows what else is going on?"

She avoided eye contact.

"Savvy, don't get mad at me again."

"I'm not. It's just . . ."

I tugged her earring. "During a moment of weakness, you fell back into what was once comfortable. Am I right?"

She scrunched her nose, frowned. "Don't know that I'd call it a moment of weakness. He'd had a bad day. I'd ended a long week. We ran into each other in the parking lot after everyone else went home on a Friday. He flirted like the old days, and, well . . ."

I snickered. "You flirted back. You can't help it. It's in your DNA."

Her laughter sounded nice. "We started remembering fun times and carried it to Dockside. Once they closed, we took it back to my place. It was like our history started all over from the beginning." She exhaled. "He's tried hard, Slade. There's no doubt he missed me."

No doubt, but Teddy always turned selfish sooner or later. Savvy was having selective memory. My girlfriend possessed all the confidence in the world, except when it came to this imbecile.

"I'm not as convinced as you are that he's changed his stripes," I said. "But before you bite off my head, just know that my concern is for you, not against you." The next words rolled around in my head a second longer before I let them loose. "I believe right now I'm remembering the past a little clearer than you, and I don't trust the man."

And just when I expected sarcasm, she hugged me to her chest. "You are so good to me," she said.

The shock raised a laugh. "You, too." I snickered again. "That medical stuff screwed with your head, didn't it?"

She rolled her eyes. "You have no idea."

Yes, I did. Teddy had wormed his way back in by capitalizing on Savvy's anxiety. He knew her inside and out from ten years of marriage, and the moment she got scared, he'd honed in on the scent. Drugs, cheating, and vanishing money had exploded their relationship before. I predicted it was just a matter of time before it happened again.

"Well, I'm here for you," I said. "I mean it. Call me next time."

Her smirk came back. "Instead of running to Teddy?"

"Did I say that?"

She laid both hands on her chest. "Honey, please. Your face is like a marquee in the mall, you can't miss the message."

"So we agree not to tell Teddy for now? About your health or whatever else," I said.

"I guess I can do that," she replied.

Relief swam through my body. "Listen, if you don't trust my suggestion, run it by Wayne. Only don't tell him I'm down here. Let me handle that."

The creases around her eyes deepened. "He told you to back off, huh?"

I severed eye contact, studying a late-model Chevy pickup as it drove in and parked two slots down. "Yes."

"And you're not going to, are you?"

I turned toward her. "I want to see your name cleared."

"Damn, honey." She grabbed me again, the console jutting into my ribs. "I'm sorry."

"Me, too." Tears welled. So great to have her hugs back.

"That was pitiful," she said, pushing back and wiping her eyes dry with her sleeve. "Dang it, got mascara on my blouse." She glanced at me with feigned innocence. "Think it's hormones?"

She put the car in drive and moved on. "Want to update me on what you know?" she asked. "Say it slow. Since I'm getting old, I might forget."

She zipped through traffic. Her mood danced for a change.

"Savvy, I don't have a thread of evidence on this Heyward deal. I feel like I've completely wasted my time down here."

"Aw, hon." She eased the car into a driveway and shifted it into park. "Your turn to talk to me."

My heart pumped harder at the chance I would say too much. But she'd asked me to accompany her to the doctor. Didn't that prove our friendship ran deeper than our conflict? She wanted me near, even if it meant listening to me bitch about Teddy.

I started. Then I stopped, weighing what to say.

"Slade," she said. "Don't tell me stuff that'll get you in trouble."

Our gazes met. She waited, patient. I replayed fifteen years of unwavering friendship. A car drove past and honked, and she didn't budge. "I'm fine either way, honey," she said.

I told her almost everything, trying to decipher what Wayne would interpret as too much information. I briefed her about Heyward's farm, the slaves, the hint of drugs with no evidence, the missing crops, and getting stuck on the shed. However, not Monroe's kiss. I couldn't handle that psychological can of worms on top of everything else.

I shrugged. "So there. What do you think?"

"Did you go to Sweetgrass Shed?"

"No, but I'm sure Monroe called them in his checking around."

She picked up the cell phone and told Raye she'd be out of the office for the afternoon. She hung up. "We're going out on the island. I went to high school with Mel Cribb. He holds an annual fundraiser dance at the shed on the concrete loading dock. I help with the plans. He'll talk to me." She rubbed her forehead.

"Headache?"

"Yeah. Getting old's a bitch."

I slapped her leg. "You just need caffeine, stupid."

We grabbed coffees at a drive-through and headed to the island. When we drove into the gated facility, the upkeep stood in stark contrast to Triple R. Sweetgrass flaunted pride of ownership. While many sheds were caked in dirt and grease, here unused crates were stacked neatly, tools were in place, the grass mowed around the building.

Savvy waltzed in like she owned the place, flashing a bright spirit. The sorters and packers were easily recognized by their uniforms—meaning any material that stayed buttoned or zipped—dirt often holding the threads together. Savvy found some barrel-chested honcho in a polo shirt, obviously management, and asked for the boss. He pointed toward the back of the facility.

A tall, fiftyish guy strolled out as we approached. "Savannah, darling, come on over here and give me a hug."

She did. Thick tanned biceps in rolled-up shirtsleeves surrounded her. His khakis lay flat, encircling a middle used to the gym. She patted his arm and drew back, but not before planting a kiss smack on the mouth. "Got a minute?"

"Sure, sugar, come on in."

She gestured toward me. "Mel, this is Slade, a very good friend as well as a business associate. We need to talk shop with you about some tomatoes."

His office was styled around cheap paneling and office warehouse furniture. The pine desk held neat stacks of papers and chintz curtains hung on the window. An inexpensive oval rug lay at the foot of a small, plaid sofa. We took our seats.

We gave him just enough details to let him know we were tracing a missing crop, not an uncommon topic for a packer accustomed to lenders, bankers, and the feds hunting hidden money. But when we mentioned the name Heyward, he shook his head and cranked back in his chair like the conversation was over.

"I don't do the Heywards," he said. "Dan and I fell out way back, when he wanted me to write the checks out to any name other than his." He winked at Savvy. "He got emergency loans from you guys, didn't he?"

Savvy nodded in a flirty way.

He brushed fingers through wavy, auburn curls woven with gray. "I know I'm talking out of school here, and I got nothing to validate the feeling, but chances are Dan lied about his losses so he could get hard cash at that low interest rate you guys offer. He lost money like everyone else out here—that year was seriously hot and dry—but he always seemed the type who thought he could stay a step ahead of you. He's just too smart for himself."

Savvy leaned over and teased a lock from behind his ear. "Now, off the record, what do you know about that place, Mel?"

"Don't know nothing as fact," he said, sitting still, enjoying her touch.

Savvy dropped her voice an octave, and this time she brushed his knee. "I'm not asking for fact, just what you hear."

His tongue licked his lower lip. "You're something, you know that?"

She smiled crooked, wide, with one dimple.

"Word has it they're no account," he said. "I'd bet two week's net they deal drugs out there. And I don't know what the hell's going on with the labor. He farms them out to other places. Migrants usually coordinate through their own foreman, but that place practically owns theirs." He lowered his voice. "He won't hire a white face. Wait. I take that back. He won't hire a local, white or black. Everyone's dark in his fields, but I'm not talking Lowcountry dark. Like imported dark. Real odd arrangement."

I took everything in, amazed that the community ignored whatever the Heywards did. "Triple R says they don't have but a few acres' worth of sales," I said. "Any other shed would require a haul, and gas ain't cheap."

He turned to me. "Maybe you ought to take another gander at Triple R."

"Why?" I asked.

He shook his head, no longer humorous, nor intrigued with our mission. "Sorry. Last thing I need is locals thinking I snitch on their business. It'd be like rerouting tomato trucks directly to Rabon's place."

"Rabon?"

"Triple R," Savvy said. "Used to be three brothers ran the place. One died in a car accident, another sold out and left the state in a huff. The baby brother owns it now, and he's semi-retired—only shows up to meet payroll on Fridays."

"That his kid that Monroe and I talked to? Might be all of twenty-one?"

Mel snorted. "That would be Doug. He plays at running things. He doesn't have sense enough to know one grade tomato from another. Daddy might check in on him on his way to or from the marina or the golf course."

Savvy stood. "Thanks for the info, Mel."

"Don't be a stranger, sugar. My divorce is about final, you know."

"Told you no in high school. Why ruin a good friendship trying to make it something it isn't?" She patted him on the cheek. "But I still love you, bud."

Wow. Sounded like Monroe and me.

We picked our way through the conveyor lines, tables, and wooden boxes. I felt his eyes on us, or rather Savvy, all the way to the parking lot. I touched her shoulder at the car. "Sssss. Still hot as ever, I see."

"Humph." She swung her butt around the car's bumper. "Mel loves everyone. Ask me one day why he's divorced. It's a long tale with a longer list." She beeped open the Mercedes. "Want to ride over to Triple R?"

"I'm glad you feel better."

"Me, too," she said. "Bet you ten bucks we solve this idiot investigation. Whatcha say?"

I shifted my shoulders, and dipped my chin best I could sitting in a car. "Sucker bet, hon. Sucker bet. I know we're gonna crack this thing open. Just don't speak a word to Wayne until we've done the deed, okay? I want him to owe me."

But at the same time I wondered if I didn't have a dose of whatever it was Savvy had that made her weak-kneed around a particular man, too often letting personal feelings cloud my common sense.

Chapter 21

THE DRIVE between Sweetgrass Shed and Triple R took five minutes.

As Savvy and I walked into the complex, the acidic odor of green tomatoes hit us, mingled with the scent of motor oil and mechanization. Conveyor belts carried cooled and washed crops in an assembly line fashion past sorters who graded the number ones, number twos, and culls. Once semi-dry, the boxed vegetables went into refrigerated trucks parked against the concrete pad, for wholesale delivery up the eastern seaboard. Five-foot diameter fans cooled workers and vegetables alike in the raging heat of a Southern afternoon, spinning so fast they emitted a roar too loud to think, much less talk over.

We found Doug Rabon in the air-conditioned office same as before.

This time I took the lead when he opened the door and flashed my administrative badge. "Carolina Slade, Mr. Rabon. We spoke a week ago?"

His youthful blue eyes shone fresh and bright, complementing his freckled red nose and sun-baked complexion. "I already told you all I know. I'm needed on the packing floor, or my workers will cull everything or nothing."

"Fine." I angled to the left to see over his shoulder. "We can wait in your office. Take your time. We're government employees. We've got hours."

His eyes darted from Savvy to me then past us, as if backup hid around the corner. "Can't let you wander around here. Company policy. OSHA, too. You'll have to wait in the parking lot, or your car."

I straightened the boy's collar, which fell from my grasp as he drew back. "Doug. The heat is ungodly out there. What would your momma say about you making two ladies wait in such stifling conditions?"

His eyes narrowed. "Okay. Only a few minutes." He retreated back into the much cooler office. We followed, Savvy's wink giving me a virtual high five.

"Thank you," I said, as he motioned to the chairs. Young men raised even halfway proper in the South caved to older women. "I told Ms. Conroy you were so helpful before, we'd definitely learn more the second time. You have met Ms. Conroy, right?"

"No . . . maybe . . . I think . . . um," he stuttered.

Savvy reached out and pumped his hand enough times to make him uneasy, unsure when to let loose. "Charmed to meet you, Doug." Upon release, Doug slid his chair back a few inches.

Savvy sat and played the next move. "You might remember my assistant, Evan Canady. He does most of the field work for our agency."

Four straight-backed chairs lined the long wall of the twelve-by-fifteen room. Posters from old Water Festivals stuck on the cheap paneled wall. A farm supply calendar hung next to an ancient framed print of a shrimp boat. Doug's chair groaned as he shifted and bumped it against a pressboard desk probably thrown together with an Allen wrench and Chinese instructions. He probably wished he'd sat behind it by now.

"Doug," I continued, overdoing his first name to keep him docile. "We've run ourselves ragged tracing the Heyward tomato crop."

"I can call you Doug, too, right?" Savvy scooted closer before he could answer. The boy blushed and nodded. Savvy's voice flowed sweet and thick as she lightly touched her shirt at the neck and slid her fingers down the lapel to the top button. She paused for the boy's response.

He recrossed his legs. "Yes, ma'am. I mean, Doug's fine, ma'am."

Savvy smiled softly and dropped her hand. "Okay, Doug. Focus. You can do that for me, right?"

"I'll try, ma'am."

"Good," Savvy said. "I made a loan to Mr. Dan Heyward. Well, not exactly me, you understand, but the Department of Agriculture. Now the money's floating loose, the crop's gone, even Mr. Heyward's gone, poor soul. Guess you heard he died on his boat. Anyway, when we tried to find the tomatoes—"

"Everybody told us, 'Talk to Doug,'" I said, completing her sentence.

The boy's jaw dropped and his eyes widened. "Me?"

Savvy shrugged, exuding innocence in her effort. "I mean everybody, Doug. From other farmers to workers to town people. So I figured you knew these parts. You know, gifted with the ways of the island."

His gaze followed her movements. "I don't know about the Heywards, not since Mr. Dan died."

"Thank God it's cool in here." Savvy lifted her shirt away from moist skin and fluffed it twice. "Think you can tell me something about those tomatoes so I can quit traipsing around in this heat?"

I rested elbows on the arms of my chair. "I figure you were in such a rush the other day you may have skimmed your records too fast. My unannounced visit wasn't quite fair to you."

He swiveled to his desk and opened a notebook. "Um, maybe I can find a few more sales." He flipped back and forth through the pages and settled on one. "Oh yeah, here's four loads in Purdue's name dated three weeks ago. Think those came from Mr. Dan's fields?"

"I think so," I said, knowing he knew they did. "How much?"

Like extracting teeth, we coaxed about half the crop out of the boy, with an admission to one check issued in Purdue's name, one in Dan's, and the rest in an entity called Runabout Incorporated. We could now order an audit. Doug's father would wish he hadn't dumped his duties on his baby boy.

"Aw, Doug," I said. "We have a lien on that crop. We send you a list of mortgaged crop each season, trying to help you keep up. Must be rough managing a packing shed on your own."

He froze in a daze, like a kid caught skipping school. "We get busy 'round here," he said.

He knew better. He knew we knew it, too. A tomato shed disposing of mortgaged crop could be held liable for the dollar value. No different from a person buying a car with a debt still owed to the bank. The difference with the feds was whether the U.S. Attorney felt it worthwhile to pursue legal action. Unless the crop disposal approached six figures, they usually didn't bother. Irked me to a fare-thee-well. Farmers and purchasers of their commodities weren't stupid. Skimming could happen, and nobody would do a thing about it. People like Savvy, Evan, and me spouted federal violations usually with no one backing us up. I hoped Doug was naïve enough to remain ignorant of that reality, and frightened enough to cooperate.

As if I had all the authority in the world, I slapped hands on my thighs, flaunting a grimace for Savvy's sake. "I know where this is going, don't you, Ms. Conroy?"

Savvy nodded.

I faced Doug and hammered him with innuendo. "Purdue's going to say Runabout wasn't his company. Maybe you took that money for yourself. Maybe your daddy has a game going here with false names and companies. Heck, I could probably find Runabout, or whatever other company name you claim in there, stamped on the side of a sailboat or a set of golf clubs." I stood. "We're wasting our time here, Ms. Conroy. We need to speak to Big Daddy. Funny how nobody fingered the father, just little boy Doug."

He blinked with a forced pretense of composure. He blanched, however, and sank front teeth into his bottom lip. "Don't talk to Daddy. He doesn't know anything."

"About what?" I asked, restraining any excitement at a break. "We already know you cut several checks in illegal names. It all falls on your head. And Doug, prison ain't no kindergarten for babies like you."

"Mr. Purdue said I had to do as I was told. He knew I'd skimmed money off crop sales for Mr. Dan, and he'd turn me in if I didn't follow his orders. Told me I had to be busy when his people come in with tomatoes."

"Busy?" I asked.

"Yeah. Not walk the floor. Stay up here until he stacked his crop in the trucks."

A knock thumped at the door, and he hit his leg on the desk as he stumbled by me to answer it. A Mexican worker wearing disheveled clothes older than Doug grumbled about a jammed conveyor.

"Be there in a minute," our young man said in a deeper voice before turning back.

In that moment, the boy's leap to overseer snapped him out of the young man we'd controlled. His face regained color. "That's about all I intend to say to you ladies. Now if you don't mind, I've got work to do." He waved us toward the door, insuring we walked ahead of him so he could lock up. "Bring the law with you next time, along with a subpoena or search warrant. You're done here."

Savvy threw him one last sultry glance.

He smirked as if to say she could quit wasting her time.

Back outside, we climbed into the Mercedes. Without a word between us, Savvy reversed, turned, and drove toward the road. From my vantage gazing into the side mirror, Doug stood on the dock and watched as if insuring we left the premises. A husky dark man sidled up to him. I recognized Jumper, one of Kamba's boys.

Savvy affectionately punched me. "We missed our calling, sugar."

"That was amazing." I took a deep breath. "Almost addictive. No wonder cops can be so arrogant."

"You're telling me. Just wish he'd kept talking." She paused then exclaimed, "Oh my gosh."

"What?"

"I'm going through menopause and just flirted with a boy young enough to be my son."

Days of frustration burst from me in teary-eyed laughs until I was spent and breathless, my ribs sore. "Face it, girl, you've still got what it takes."

Savvy started laughing again, this time uncontrollably, and had to stop in a church parking lot. She reached into the glove box and found tissues. "Dang, that was fun."

"Doug, the flirting, or the laughing?"

"All of it. Especially the flirting. Do you think he got wood?" she asked, her sniffle twisting her grin.

"Control yourself." Then I busted a gut laughing again.

"What do you think he was about to tell us?" she asked. "What the hell does one do with tomatoes other than sort and ship them?"

Her cell phone rang. She studied the caller ID and quickly eyed me. "Hello, Wayne."

I adjusted the visor mirror to straighten my makeup, doing my damnedest not to show interest.

"Oh, the doctor's visit went fantastic. Nothing serious." She gushed genuine delight. She had a right to. "All I need to do is take little pills, eat right, and I'm hunky dory. Dinner?" She eyed me again. "Um, okay. Same place tonight at six thirty. Fine. See you then." She hung up.

Dabbing at my mascara, I asked, "Dinner again?"

"Seems that way. Don't get pissy. I promise to be good."

My phone rang. "Hello?"

"How's my girl doing?" Wayne asked.

My thoughts train wrecked.

"Slade?"

How'd he know where I was? Wait, maybe he didn't. "I'm here."

Savvy faced away.

"We need to clear the air, CI."

"Hey, Wayne, I'm good. I get it. You don't want me around you during a case."

He cleared his throat. "Why don't I take a break and come back home tomorrow? We can go out and eat barbecue. I don't like this hanging over our heads."

"Can't," I said, almost feeling guilty. "I'm scheduled to be in the field until late, and you should finish the case. Savannah's not just anybody, you know." This would bite me later, but I didn't relish the thought of a lecture. Not now that we were making headway.

Savvy pivoted toward me at the mention of her name.

"I'll see you whenever you wind things up in Beaufort." I closed the phone and looked up to see tender emotion in Savvy's eyes. "What?" I asked, already telling myself I hadn't actually lied. Theoretically I *was* in the field.

"Honey, you're gooder than grits."

Savvy needed not just Wayne but all the assistance she could get to unravel this quandary. I needed to be here. "Just try not to pant over Wayne tonight," I said.

She wrapped an arm around me. "Sweetie, I'm after twenty-year-olds these days. You know I'll behave with an old dude like Wayne."

"Yes, I do," I said, drawing back. "Your problems are deeper than any of my insecurities anyway."

After a pat on my back, Savvy readjusted herself in the seat. "Let's find you a place to stay. I can land you a bed and breakfast that beats the pants off that fleabag motel and keep you away from Wayne and Monroe at the same time. You need an evening to yourself."

"It's not a fleabag. It was a decent place. No water bugs."

She sped up to merge with the traffic. "By the time I finish talking to these friends of mine, you'll kick back in a four-poster antique bed with a mint on your pillow for the government per diem rate."

"I can handle that."

We drove a few miles, me asking about her parents and her idolizing my kids, enjoying our rekindled friendship. The scenery ranged from whitewashed juke-joints to trendy native gift shops, several I recognized from my past dealings in the area. Newer modern places stuck out like a six-foot pigweed stalk in a field of soybeans. Guess folks banked on the hope that the long stretch between Fripp Island resort and Beaufort would eventually build up to a higher standard. A lot of history and agriculture would disappear if it did.

We crossed a creek and passed a dive I'd seen many times and never felt the inclination to visit: Sand Briar Bait and Tackle Tavern. The weather aged it more than time, but regardless, the general appearance fell on a sliding scale between seedy and dilapidated.

"Over there," I pointed.

Savvy snared a glance as we breezed by. "That's Teddy's car," she said. "What's he doing at that shack?"

"Don't stop to find out. Our day's been too good for me to get into a hassle with him now."

She drove on, my guess being she didn't care to deal with Teddy and me together on the same piece of ground. She'd question him later, and I'd ask her what he said. Hopefully now she'd be more inclined to tell me.

But Teddy wasn't alone. And with Savvy driving, she probably didn't see the other guy. I'd seen Kamba's son Jamie peering in the car window, talking to Teddy, who sat behind the wheel.

"Did I tell you I spent last Saturday at Kamba's house?" I asked to distract.

"The Gullah guy? Seriously?"

"Yeah. Nicest man. He gave me a dried plant that kicked the heck out of my sore throat."

"Do tell."

For twenty minutes, we drove, an ease to our conversation we hadn't enjoyed in forever, but between sentences I fretted over what we'd seen. The closer we drove to Beaufort, the more worry wormed its way back into my head.

Savvy drove into the River Inn gravel lot. Good to her word, she landed me a room at the government rate. From the taste of the period furniture, lush drapes, and Victorian rugs, I'd nabbed a deal. Then we shot back to her office to retrieve my car, anxious Wayne may have dropped in and noted my vehicle.

"Aw, crap," I exclaimed as we arrived.

"What?" Savvy's eyes darted, seeking the problem.

"Monroe. I promised him lunch and it's . . ." I peeked at my watch. "It's after four. Wonder if he ate?"

"Let me drop you off at your car. I'll tell him the doctor's office was backed up."

"Thanks," I said, ready to jump out and bail.

"Yeah, I owe you, hon." She rolled her window down as I walked around the car. "Hey, don't worry over me with Wayne, now. We're all business."

I leaned on the door to say adieu. "We're good. Especially if you can feed Monroe."

"Slade?" She slid my name out slowly. "You think Monroe's, um, fond of you?"

"Why, what's he said?"

"He asked me about how you and Wayne met. Wondered if you had this thing for cops." Her gaze dared me not to lie. "What's going on?"

Uneasy about the question, I rubbed my neck and followed my hand as I wiped sweat on my slacks. "We've been friends for ten years. Sure he's fond of me. I'm fond of him, too."

"Not what I meant, and you know it."

I paused, like she'd accused me of being vegan knowing how much a twelve-ounce sirloin sent me to heaven. "Oh shoot, no. I'd have seen it. Call me, okay? I need to figure out what we're doing tomorrow, and I don't need to run into Wayne. Figure out what he's up to, if you can, so our paths don't cross."

The split second pause said she'd park the conversation about Monroe for another time. "Bingo. Have a good night overlooking the river. Wait."

"What?"

"Don't I need to tell Wayne about Doug and the missing tomatoes? It's my ass on the line here. Give me a chance to redeem myself."

She was right. This was getting complicated.

Now was my chance for redemption, too, and I'd gone and misled Wayne into thinking I wasn't even here. Why the hell did I even do that? Heyward was still a conundrum, a much bigger mystery than a few stolen tomatoes, but I wanted to use Savvy to uncover some of it. Wayne might not approve, but girlfriend and I had always been a formidable team.

"If you have to, go ahead and say what you uncovered," I said. "My fear is that it'll appear like you went out there to cover up."

She scowled. "But you were there."

I didn't need or want to run into Wayne, but Savvy's reputation carried more weight. "Play it by ear, Savvy. Don't volunteer. Just answer his questions. If it comes up, fine. If it doesn't, we'll have bought time to gather more information and beg for forgiveness later."

Savvy shrugged. "You're the investigator."

She was probably the only person who thought so.

After she parked, and as I watched her backside strut into the office, I second-guessed my judgment. There was no right or wrong answer here, and whatever she said could backfire.

The inn's owners had my room waiting when I arrived. The white-painted, eight-foot door opened into a scent of gardenia, my favorite floral aroma. The cream-colored ruffled valances, floral wallpaper borders, and satin, crimson-striped bed coverlet proved everything an enchanting B&B should be—minus the right man.

Stripped down to a T-shirt, underwear, and socks, I sank into the quilt, thinking of Ivy at the Amick's place. I rested the television remote and my dinner on a lap desk to avoid staining the history for someone else. My fingertips floated over the satiny spread. A pitiful waste of a romantic getaway. Switching channels for sitcoms, all I could find in the early evening were twenty-year-old reruns. I slid off the high bed, heavy hearted.

I had uncovered a teeny crack in this case. I could think about that.

Leaning against the window sill, twirling lace in my hand, I watched birds and water, making myself relax, forcing long deep inhales. Ten breaths did nothing, so I tried twenty. By fifty, time felt slower, my nerves consoled, my head clearer. I let the curtains fall back into place. Walking over to rummage through the room's bookcase, I found *Prince of Tides*. Of course they'd have Pat Conroy's books since this was his neck of the woods. Of course I'd read them all. I threw *Tides* on the bed and climbed up on the coverlet, muted the television, and skimmed to the good chapters.

But I couldn't read. I got up for a glass of water, then reached for a notepad in my purse. I wrote a name at the top of several pages, to include all the players in the Heyward case. Dan, Purdue, Doug Rabon . . .

I relocated to the divan. An hour later I wrote standing, leaning over the tall bed, papers spread out, as if a new position aided discovery. A while later, my back tired from bending over, I sat at the cherry desk. Finally I returned to the divan, dashing down ideas about motives and who to play against whom.

About three in the morning, my eyes straining, I set down the pen. But my head still whirred with dilemmas on who to see, how to find them, and what to say when I did.

Prince of Tides lay on the end table. I picked it up in hopes the familiar story would shift my gears. The descriptions captured me. Enveloped in the lyrical phrases, I slowed down and digested the story, the visuals so distinctively lucid from my current travels around the region. I dozed off about the time I reached the part about the caged tiger in the backyard, and thought how stimulating to be so close to something beautiful yet so dangerous. In my dream, Monroe warned me to be careful, to quit standing so close to the bars.

Chapter 22

FOR THE LAST twenty minutes, I'd enjoyed the chance to primp and feign affluence in an old-fashioned B&B, the sun filtering through embroidered, filet crochet curtains. Enthusiastic from yesterday's success and buzzed from all my ruminations last night, I air-kissed my reflection in the bathroom mirror, smiled at the silliness, and returned attention to my lashes.

Savvy had most likely orchestrated the dinner with Wayne last night to her advantage. I was sure of it once I awoke, the sunrise having burned off my nighttime fretting like the dawn fog. I anticipated a hard day of chasing people and connecting the dots with her today. Proactivity was empowering.

The mascara wand stabbed the corner of my eye as a heavy rap caught me off guard. With my hair embroiled in a battle on my head, I hastily fastened two blouse buttons to avoid sharing views of my white, lacy bra to some innocent kid delivering morning pastries.

My breath caught as I opened the door. "What're you doing here?"

"You going to invite me in or stand there flashing your underwear?" Wayne asked, flicking a finger at the missed button on my top. "By the way, here are your crumpets or scones or whatever they call these flaky excuses for breakfast."

Savvy would not have revealed my location, so he'd routed me out on his own. He needed to finish our conversation and understand why I was in town, and he was striving to be cordial. I rather liked that. Frankly, I could use this opportunity to reveal my prowess at getting the info out of Doug Rabon yesterday. The setting couldn't be more perfect to work some things out between us.

"May I come in?" he asked.

"Sure." I stepped aside.

He entered, nudged crystal knick-knacks aside on the cherry desk and set down the tray. Pinching off the corner of a croissant, he popped it into his mouth. "Still warm."

"Nice place, huh?" I pinched a bite from the other end of the croissant, then strolled back to the bathroom. "Don't eat more than half. I like that stuff, and nobody ever bakes for me." I licked my finger, tested the curling iron, which sizzled appropriately, and looped a thick lock of brunette hair around it while my heart break-danced. As I waited for him to talk first.

He scouted the room, taking in my notes on the table beside the divan, on the divan, and across the bed. The unslept-in bed. Decked out in my underwear, I'd spent the night on the little sofa, my ingenious ideas scattered around me, *Prince of Tides* on the floor where it fell off my belly.

He reached over and picked up one note, read it, then studied another. He turned around and leaned in the opening of the bathroom. He crossed one boot over the other, tucking hands in his pants pockets. "Pretty obvious what you're up to, Slade."

"Maybe not." He did know, but heck, I possessed official orders from the state director.

"I came back to take Savvy to the doctor," I said, twisting awkwardly, reaching over my head with the curler. With my hair in place for a second, I glanced over at him. "Great news for Savvy. I'm so relieved."

He nodded once. "Yeah, she told me the details at dinner."

Obviously, he waited for me to ask questions. I wasn't about to. Watching my reflection, I managed the control on my face and remained benign. A hiss escaped from my curling iron as I wrapped another tress.

He let me finish that shock of hair then grabbed the appliance and set it on the counter. "She didn't tell me you were here."

"She wouldn't," I said, leaning my butt on the bathroom counter.

"We just talked about the case."

"As you should." My nerve stood rock solid. I picked up the iron again.

"And you should've come to my motel room instead of Monroe's. That was just wrong the other night. If you'd knocked—"

"If you'd asked before you dead-bolted your door."

We stared into each other's eyes, dares hanging in the air between us.

"Why didn't you admit you were in town when I called?" he asked.

I waved the iron at him like a giant finger. "You probably already knew I was here. You probably called to see what I'd say." As I slammed the iron down on the granite sink, the tip broke off and slid across the counter. "I'm not one of your targets. I am *not* to be played."

"Trust is important, Slade," he said, his jaw squared.

"Exactly what I said at breakfast the other morning. How does it feel, lawman? How exactly does it feel not to be trusted?"

He blew out long and hard. His lack of words pleased me.

"You want me to keep quiet, say so," I said. "You want me to tell the truth, be honest with me." Wayne backed up to my step forward. "Planting that lie in my head so I'd tell Savvy was horrible. Then calling me to see if I would admit my presence in Beaufort . . . explain how that's trust, Wayne?"

"How is misleading me trust, Slade? I don't know whether you're coming or going. Or who's chasing you at the same time."

I saw his point. Just wish he kind of saw mine. Hands up in a truce, I replied, "Okay. Henceforth there will be no more deceit, no more jumping on sheds, no guys with guns. Just let me work the case. Dubose just reemphasized she wants me down here. Don't blow me off." I blew out a breath. "I overstepped lines. I know that."

Staunch resolution held us both at bay, five feet apart, his control versus my stubbornness. Intent on being the bigger person, I edged back to the sink. The mirror showed fat waves of hair standing all over my head. I picked up the brush and raked my scalp as I transferred annoyance.

He stepped back into view of the mirror. I tilted my head down, brushing the back. His grip around my wrist halted the strokes. "I can't do this anymore, Slade. I love you too much to see you get hurt, or see you screw up your career."

At his touch, heat ran through me. I suppressed an instinct to jump him and cry uncle. The setting lit me afire with all the period lace and cherry wood straight out of a Harlequin romance. Please, Wayne, say something right. Just agree to trust me. That's all I asked. I'd promised to stay out of trouble, and actually had since I did.

For a second, his gaze softened. *Come on, Wayne.*

He walked back to the bed and lifted one of my notes. "I can't keep worrying about you," he said. "This is Pam all over again." Before I thought of a quip to the mention of his ex-wife, he opened the door into the hallway.

"Why do you keep picking at me?" I asked, with an urgent desire to run after him.

"Please, stay out of the way," he asked, resolute yet with a plea entwined in the obstinacy. "I can't juggle you and all the players in this case at the same time."

Where will I go? What will I do? echoed in my thoughts—Rhett Butler leaving Scarlett in their entryway, donning his dapper hat only to disappear into the fog. "You'd dump me because I'm too much to worry about?"

"I don't know what I'm doing around you, Slade. This isn't the game you think it is."

Bitter, hot exasperation rushed into my cheeks. "A game? Murder and fraud involving my best friend, and you think I'm playing games? After all these months you don't know me, do you? I'm just the little lady with the toy badge pretending to be important."

He hesitated in silence, so detached it scared me. He didn't even tell me to keep my voice down so others wouldn't hear.

"Don't worry about me," I said. "I can take care of myself. Been there, done that. Next time, talk to the state director if you want to investigate. I'll stick to catching employees milking sick leave for ballgames and ditching the office for the mall. By all means, don't let me stand in the way of your *professional* law enforcement."

"You done?" he asked.

"According to you I was done three days ago."

We faced off, him outside and me in, knowing our next moves were big ones. He stared, and I fought not to be the first to turn away.

"If you interfere anymore, I'll have no choice but to talk to your boss," he warned.

"Go right ahead."

He took a half step away, halted, then continued down the hall.

I slammed the door. No way the owners would give me a government discount at this place again.

I finished buttoning my shirt with weak fingers. Fingers that then balled into fists, nails into my palms. Back in the bathroom, I shut off the iron and brushed my hair, not caring how it parted, then threw the brush into my bag. The zipper snagged on my best pair of panties. When I jerked it back, a snag ripped a quarter-size hole.

Pastries meant to be savored were wolfed down and chased with cool coffee. The not-yet-cooled curling iron went on top of my bag between the handles. I snatched my purse and left the inn, grateful for automatic checkout.

THIRTY MINUTES later I still sat in my car in the River Inn's gravel lot, facing the Beaufort River as stupid gulls squawked in the sunshine, coasting on a sweltering breeze. My .38 hid in the glove box, and I pushed aside temptation to take shots at the dipping, diving aerial targets.

With Alan, life had been simpler. Nasty days filled with arguments, but simpler. Nobody won a fight. Nobody made up. Nothing was really at stake because we'd both accepted the marriage was a sham. The union eventually dissolved thanks to his drug addiction, his cheating, and my inability to deal with it all. Real relationships were supposed to be give and take. I didn't know how to do that anymore.

I tensed, shoulders hunched reliving ancient history. Maybe I needed to be more accepting, more understanding of people's mistakes, more compromising. But damn it, I'd vowed never to be taken for granted again . . . or used. Maybe I shouldn't have told Savvy details about Wayne's fictitious story about the coroner, but still.

Thanks to all my brainstorming last night, more ideas swirled around on how to solve Savvy's problem than how to act with Wayne. Whatever happened next might even be the deciding factor in the future of our relationship . . . unless I . . .

The phone rang.

"Hey," Savvy said. "Enjoy the room?"

"Nice place, but wasted on me."

"Why?"

"You want to come go to St. Helena? I could drive."

"Sure. Probably need to update you about dinner, too." She paused. "We're going to talk about Wayne, aren't we?"

"Yes, we are," I said. "When I calm down. I'll be there in a few."

I started the car and headed her direction. Changing scenery, and the crazy events of the past few days, stirred me to ponder my actions.

Slaves, drugs, and floating dead bodies. Blown up boats. Fraud. None of this was a game. But I'd exasperated Wayne with my zealous methods. Okay, overzealous. Monroe and Wayne both had tried to temper my cavalier investigative style. Savvy, as loyal and loving as she was, had said let the IG do what they had to do.

I drove through Beaufort, pondering my next steps, and if they would be conceived as smart or too Slade-ish.

Finding Kamba's street corner vacant, I checked off that task and made his home the first call for the day. I wanted to see if Savvy's inherent knowledge of the area, partnered with his, could develop a coherent theory about the Heywards and their set up. And Kamba was safe.

Savvy waved me to the curb and got in. "I didn't tell him where you were."

"I know. He wouldn't push you about me. Plus you wouldn't let the badge sway you."

She playfully pinched me. "Honey, please. I know what's under that badge. He can't play that . . ." She froze. "Of course, you know I mean the thoughts behind the badge, not what's under—"

"I know what you meant." I turned onto Carteret Street. "Doesn't matter anyway. He's all yours if you want him."

Her giggle escalated into a belly laugh. She toned it down when I didn't join in. "So what did he do to set you off, Miss Priss?"

"He hinted I was up to something, and all but said I ought to quit playing at investigations and let a real lawman do the job."

She wiped her eyes. "Did he say all that . . . really?"

"He compared me to . . . his ex-wife." Saying it hurt more than hearing his words this morning.

Her eyes widened. "He didn't."

I gripped the steering wheel tighter. "Um, yes. He did."

"Boy's missing brain cells, honey. That's just not bright." She shook her head. "Thought agents could read thoughts or something. You know, interpret people."

"So they'd like you to believe," I said.

"He's right, though," she said with a curled lip. "You *are* up to something."

All those brilliant plans scribbled during my high last night seemed no more than chicken scratch in the light of day. I turned onto the bridge.

Still, those ideas had no choice but to work.

KAMBA'S OLD truck was in the hardscrabble drive.

Anyika swept the dirt yard with a worn, woven straw broom, her long ecru housedress swaying with her movements. Clucking chickens scattered out of her way with every other swing. When we drove in and parked, her broad, white-toothed grin coordinated with her skirt as well as any strand of pearls. "Come, come." She leaned the broom on the oak and fast-waddled toward the porch. "Kamba?" she yelled. "You decent? We gots company."

When we stepped inside, her husband appeared from a back room, lean fingers adjusting his tunic. "Hello, Slade. Nice to see you again so soon."

"Kamba." I smiled at our sleepy host. Deep summer heat enticed naps under a fan, a Southern habit dating way back and about forgotten with central air. "This is a co-worker and close friend of mine," I said.

Savvy held out her hand. "Savannah Conroy."

Kamba took it and covered it with his other. "Nice to meet you."

"A pleasure," she said. "I've seen you in town. Been meaning to stop."

He laughed. "My ramblings aren't meant to beckon a greeting, just deliver a message."

I gestured to the porch. "Can we sit and talk?"

"Yes, yes," he said. "Anyika, can you bring—"

"Already ahead of ya', ol' man," his wife shouted from the kitchen. Ice clinked, and I heard a refrigerator shut.

Our hostess brought out heavy, clear glasses, already slick with moisture. We thanked her and she disappeared into the house. The hard plastic chairs scrubbed the wood planks as we settled. Hot air swung gray Spanish moss dripping from the massive trees in the front yard.

"I take it your cold is better?" Kamba asked.

"Much. *Life everlasting* works well."

"Yes'm. It does its job." He set his drink on the railing. "What brought you out here, Slade? It's not like I'm on anyone's beaten path."

My fingernails clicked against each other as I commenced with Plan A.

"I have some questions about something I saw yesterday."

Savvy eyeballed me over her glass. She was ready to ad-lib or chime in as needed.

"We saw one of your boys when we visited the packing sheds," I said. "I can't remember his name."

"My grandson, Jamie?"

I shook my head. "No. One of the boys who works for your mission. Not Martin. The stouter one . . . the one who fussed the other day."

"Jumper?"

I mulled that one around a second. "Jumper? As in the rabbit?"

"That's Thumper, Slade," Savvy said.

"Oops, that's right. Is that his real name?" I asked, fearful I'd call him by the bunny title next time we met.

Kamba's smile was the epitome of a sage teaching the novice. "That's his community name. The Sea Islands often give their children names that represent the ways of the child. Lester can't sit still, and when he did drugs, he was even worse. Doubt too many people remember his birth name anymore."

"Anyway," I said, "Jumper was at Triple R talking to Doug Rabon yesterday afternoon. We left just as he appeared. Don't believe he even saw us pull away."

Kamba remained silent.

"Just found it odd he'd be friendly with young Rabon," I added.

"And why would that be odd?" Kamba asked, his drink now resting on his knee.

"Doug all but admitted shady activities at that packing shed. I could understand Jumper chatting amongst the packers and drivers, trying to learn if activities affect y'all's drug fighting work. I'd infiltrate places like that, too. But why the boss?"

"You asking because Doug's white?"

My mouth opened, then shut, unsure how to respond.

"Mr. Kamba," Savvy interjected. "Slade isn't that way. I've lived in Beaufort and worked on these islands since I could swim and paddle a boat. I shrimped and sunbathed in these inlets. Went to school here, and now I help people build houses and fund their farms and businesses." She paused, letting her words sink in. "Speaking as a native, it seems unusual someone working for the righteous would fraternize with a party we suspect is up to his neck in inappropriate activity. I don't like drugs on these islands any more than you do. Illegal is illegal, regardless what color you are."

"Plain-spoken woman," he said.

"Best kind," she answered.

He gave us a laugh from deep within his soul. Anyika peered out.

"My plain-spoken woman," he pointed, and laughed again.

"Standin' ri' heah," his wife sassed through the screen. She snapped back with a short sentence I didn't understand, and left.

Savvy chuckled.

I glanced at Savvy, unable to interpret what the older woman said.

"She says he chatters like a crow," Savvy whispered.

"Oh." I replayed the words I'd heard, trying to catch on. The accents from my Charleston days didn't match the thicker, concentrated dialect here.

"I'll speak with Jumper, but I trust him," Kamba said. "That all you came for?"

No it wasn't, and I braced myself for the next message. "A few miles down the road, we saw Jamie. He met a white man in the Sand Briar parking lot."

Kamba's forehead furrowed at the mention of flesh and blood. "At the Sand Briar? The bar?"

Savvy's gaze snapped toward me.

"Yes, sir. He met with Teddy, um, Theodore Dawson. How do those two know each other?"

Savvy's posture stiffened. "Where you going with this, Slade?"

My lips pressed together briefly before I plowed on. "I don't know. Just wondered how Kamba's son knows your ex-husband. Who better to ask than the guy himself?"

"Then ask the real man himself," said a voice from inside the house.

We jerked around. Jamie stood behind the screen.

Chapter 23

KAMBA'S GRANDSON, Jamie, leaned in the entryway, a sneer on his face. He opened the screen door, walked out, and let it slam. His hip propped on Kamba's porch railing as he scanned me in a half-squint, his chin raised in challenge. "You gotta problem with me talking to a white man, lady?"

Kamba stood. "Jamie!"

"What's the big deal about meeting a buckra, Granddad? This lady is making something out of nothin'."

"My problem is with your manners, and you being at a bar," Kamba said. "What's this about?"

"Specifically, what is your business with Teddy Dawson, Jamie?" I asked.

He shrugged.

"If you won't answer the lady, you answer me," Kamba demanded.

Jamie's braced stance was one I recognized in my daughter. It spoke of teenage spite and headstrong willfulness. "Teddy meets with Jumper sometimes," he said, glaring at his granddaddy. "You're so high on those two who aren't even your kin. I'm just a pile of meat and bones that eats from your table."

Holy cow, I thought as the conversation pivoted. I'd stomped a fire ant hill, and now all I could do was stand aside and stay clear of the stings.

"I love you, boy." Kamba spoke like he'd talked about this before. "I don't want you involved in this dirty business." He cupped his hands, as if they held the dirt.

"But Martin and Jumper work alongside you."

"That's different," Kamba said. "You're my grandson."

"You don't know what it's like having kids rag me at school about my granddad standing on a street corner ranting like some crazy fool." Jamie took a quick, furious gulp of breath. "If I was part of the mission, that'd be one thing, but I'm not."

I sat transfixed, studying the turmoil I'd stirred. Savvy's eyes glowered indignantly.

Jamie grasped the railing and studied the dirt yard. "I decided to probe around on my own. Jumper talked to Mr. Dawson before, so I got the man's number from the insurance magnet on our refrigerator. Told him I was interested in whatever he was dealing."

Kamba's horror was obvious. "You what?"

Savvy fidgeted beside me in her seat.

The conversation continued to sour. "So what happened with Dawson?" I asked, selfishly wanting answers.

He smiled smugly, as if he ran a step ahead. "Actually, this is the *second* time we met. The first time, he just wanted to listen, find out who I was. I told him I was a kid in school and needed money for college. Didn't figure he'd cooperate if he knew I was connected to Granddad. He said he'd think about it. We met again yesterday." He beamed. "He believed me. He thinks I'm willing to deal."

"Deal what?" Savvy asked quietly.

"Crack," he said, his chin raised in pride. "The real stuff."

"Oh no," I whispered, more for Savvy's sake than any surprise on my part.

A hot breeze drifted across the porch, doing nothing to dissipate the tension.

"He said I could make good money selling at the high school, 'specially at my basketball practices." Jamie straightened, proud. "We can set him up. Bust his ass!" The boy swung a fist through the air, light on his feet.

The rest of us sat like wet sacks of feed. The child didn't grasp the severity of his words.

"Where's your proof?" Savvy replied, then faced me. "We don't know this kid. He could be lying to get back at his family."

"I'm not lying," Jamie said, stepping toward her. "And you're right. You don't know me."

Kamba rose from his chair. "The boy is not a liar." He eyed Savvy then faced his grandson. "This stops now! This isn't a competition with Martin and Jumper. This poison eats people's lives. I won't have you touched by it." He rounded toward Savvy and me. "And I won't tolerate you two making empty accusations, baiting my boy."

Anyika watched from inside, wringing a dish towel.

Jamie spit over the railing. "I'm eighteen, Granddad."

"And I'm your guardian 'cause my son hooked your mother on this stuff and killed 'em both." His voice echoed across the porch, scattering chickens.

Jamie had forty pounds on the man, but the boy still flinched.

Kamba's exclamation hung heavy in the air, silencing everyone. Embarrassed that my selfish need to pry led to a family storm, I picked up keys and gestured to Savvy. I stooped to set my glass on the floor next to my chair and stood. "We should leave. I'm so sorry to have . . . we'll see you some other time."

The old man's sigh made his shoulders appear weighted. "You're always welcome. Sorry I lost my temper."

I smiled uncomfortably. "Don't worry about it, Kamba."

Savvy and I got in my car, backed into the dirt yard, turned around, and drove toward the highway. I kept telling myself I'd done the right thing.

Savvy said nothing. A thick shroud of disillusionment hung over her. None of the dozen useless phrases running through my head fit the moment.

Teddy represented a serious lack of judgment on her part. If she let her common sense slip gears for Teddy, what else fell by the wayside? Worse, if drugs drove Teddy's behavior, what drove hers? She'd abetted a crook—two of them, Teddy and Heyward, but not intentionally. I recognized that. The way events deteriorated, however, would anyone else believe her innocence? I stood in Wayne's shoes now, in his perspective.

I wanted to hug and throttle Savvy at the same time; instead, we watched in silence as the saltwater countryside passed by. Savvy's Beaufort home put magical spells on people, taking them into a tropical Garden of Eden. In the waters along Seaside Road, it wasn't unusual to catch the flip of a dolphin's tail as it chased herring for dinner. The dirt roads led to eight-hundred-thousand-dollar homes and two-bit shanties, their entrances off the highway identically marked.

"Money's killing this area," Savvy said, subdued. "Yankees buying up land, prices going through the roof. I can hardly afford my own property taxes. And with all this comes shit like cocaine."

"I'm sorry."

She covered her mouth. "You tried to tell me." She pointed toward the side of the road. "Pull over."

I stopped at the nearest drive. She leaned out and threw up, waving me back when I tried to hold her.

I leaned toward her anyway, aching for her loss. Gently, I touched her shoulder and dared to rub it lightly. My poor friend. Once again, she saw Teddy for what he'd always been. Seeing her puking her guts and heart out, I would have gladly chosen to silently hate the bastard's guts if he made her happy.

Teddy was a goddamn jerk.

After a long drive in silence, with me hiding any feelings, I dropped Savvy at home.

"Call me," I said as she shut the door.

Her nod was almost imperceptible as she turned and entered the house.

With a fury, I started punching Wayne's number on my cell, as much to vent as to update him. The phone rang from another number before I could finish.

"Slade," Monroe said in a huff. "Where are you?"

"Hello to you, too. I've been dealing with a few calamities, but now I'm on my way back from Savvy's house. Why?"

"Everything came undone over here."

My nerves tingled as I pictured Heyward doing something crazy, or one of his flunkies threatening a crippled Monroe. "What? Inside the office?"

"No, the parking lot," he replied. "Evan and Teddy just beat the life out of each other. Someone called the authorities, and two cops hauled them in."

Nope, I didn't misread the tension between those two yesterday. "Who won?"

He paused. "I can't believe you asked that."

"If you knew what I knew, you'd understand." Traffic backed up, like everything else in my world these days. "Is Wayne around?" This wasn't going to be easy, but our personal differences needed to take a backseat.

"Yeah. Hold on."

My stomach clinched at the cool sound of Wayne's voice. "Slade?"

I closed my eyes, almost smelling the man. "What happened?"

"Your guy Evan about beat the crap out of Teddy."

"Good for Evan," I said. "Was he hurt?"

"He's bloodied, but nothing bad. The rest depends on whether Teddy presses charges. Nobody saw who started it."

I didn't know Evan well enough to make that call, not that it mattered, but Teddy wouldn't start a ruckus. Too much jelly in the spine. "Don't think Evan has family to call, not that he'd want them to know he lost his cool."

"If you want, we can go to the station," Wayne said. "Savvy with you? It'd be nice to have Evan's boss come in and . . . well, maybe that's not a good idea."

"Doesn't matter," I said. "She's at home taking time off. I can represent the employer."

"She okay? She's not sick, is she?"

"I'll tell you when I see you. I'm five minutes away. Meet me outside."

As I drove up to the office, Wayne stood at the curb. My gaze took him in like a deep drink of water after a midday run.

He climbed into the car. We left the office, heading toward the station, and Wayne listened to my revelation about Teddy's entrepreneurial venture on the islands.

"I'll inform the sheriff's office when we get done here," he said.

"That's county jurisdiction."

"So what do we do about him?"

"Nothing." He rested his arm over the back of my seat.

I hesitated at the one-word response. "Please don't give me attitude about going out there," I said, slowing for the car in front of me.

"I'm not." He tickled my earlobe.

"Ooo-kay."

Then he patted my neck. "Seriously, Teddy has nothing to do with Heyward and Savvy."

"Oh yes, he does. He dated someone who's being scrutinized for falsifying a loan file, maybe disposing of illegal loan funds. Since when do money and drugs not mix?"

He pointed to the government complex on our left. "Turn here and park in front of the building."

I turned off the motor and reached for my purse.

"Not so fast," he said. "You just pitched an argument against Savannah. You've been butting heads with me saying just the opposite from day one. What gives?"

I relished possessing the upper hand. "Once upon a time, someone taught me to follow the money. Savvy's not guilty of anything except being taken advantage of by a farmer and a boyfriend. Teddy got too cozy too fast. He may seem to have nothing to do with all this, but I'd bet on my grandmother's life that he does." I halted for effect. "If we remove him from Savvy's equation, we make this whole affair cleaner and easier to solve."

"Uh huh." He peered back at me like he always did when attempting to get in my head. Only this time I'd laid it all out for him. "You're pretty sure she's clean," he said.

"I'd bet my firstborn on it, lawman."

"I don't need your whole family moving in with me."

The humor was nice.

He grinned. "One day I'll learn to give you more credit."

I almost tripped getting out of the car.

We entered the police station, walking past the secretarial sentinel who'd stonewalled me a week ago. The police didn't have Evan or Teddy behind bars. We found them seated in a waiting area over to the side of an open lobby. The testosterone in the place could choke a bull. Unisex uniforms strutted around as if they owned the power to flip a switch and upend anyone's existence. The vests, guns, leather, patches, and badges caused visitors to give them extra berth.

Wayne went down a hall with a portly, middle-aged officer and left me supporting the opposite wall from Evan, Teddy, and a few others. A seat would make me feel like one of the guys in line, so I stood. Evan waited three chairs away from Teddy. The two men shot venomous side glances at each other over the backs of the guys seated between them.

After ten minutes of watching them laser each other, I strode over beside Evan and thumped his shoulder. "Quit acting like a child. What's wrong with you?"

He caught my eye then snatched his attention back to Teddy. "That guy crawls under my skin. I can't lay eyes on him without wanting to beat the snot out of him."

"So quit staring at him," I said.

Teddy leaned forward, gazing across the laps of two other troublemakers. "Keep your nose out of my business, kid. I warned you."

Evan bent at the waist to meet Teddy's glare. The men in between leaned back. "Bring it, old man."

"Shut up, Evan," I said, to interrupt a potential second round of fists. "Sit back and be quiet. Pay attention to where you are. Teddy has an excuse. The powder's probably fried his brain to a crisp."

Teddy gave me a caustic stare. "Go to hell, Slade."

The oldest detainee between them stood and moved against the opposite wall, out of the line of fire.

"What is with you two?" I asked. "You got a beef about a parking space, a wager, a woman . . . what is it?"

Evan shut his mouth and snorted hard through his nose.

Teddy stood and stepped to within two feet of me. "Nobody made you God. Mind your own goddamn business for a change."

I ground my teeth.

Wayne came out of an office and waved at us. "Hey, Evan. You too, Slade."

I led Evan away and gladly left Teddy standing in the middle of the floor.

Wayne spoke low. "Dawson isn't pressing charges. Give them a few minutes to finish your paperwork, and you're free to go."

Evan fidgeted, shifting his weight. "Somebody ought to do something about that son-of-a-bitch. He—"

"Can the lip, son." Wayne gripped the younger man's shoulder. "This happened on the job, Evan. Your boss has the right to discipline you, regardless of who's right."

"Savannah wouldn't," Evan said.

"He's not talking about Savannah," I said. "He's talking about the state director, and I'm her representative. Chill."

He held up his hands in surrender. "Fine."

Half an hour later, we passed Teddy still in his chair.

"You all right, Teddy?" I asked, as we walked by.

"Fuck off."

Wayne tugged at me. "Come on, Slade."

"Just trying to be civil," I said over my shoulder. We stepped outside onto the concrete landing. Evan gave me a discreet high five.

I touched a bruise on his cheek. "You don't look so bad. Your knuckles sore?"

He flexed fingers, studying the red marks and swollen knuckle. "I laid him out good. So worth it."

At the car, Evan slid in the backseat behind me.

Wayne climbed in front and turned around. "Now what was that all about?"

"I've had a bellyful of that bastard screwing with my boss," Evan said, his tongue running over a swollen lip. "He's in and out constantly. Only when you guys aren't there, of course."

"Of course," I said.

"He reeks of alcohol all the time," Evan said. "Savannah's stressed out, but he continues to smother her."

"Amen to that," I said.

Wayne sighed. "Slade."

"He's a crack addict, for God's sake." I'd repressed my opinion of Teddy until I was about to bust. "He's still using, isn't he?"

"Bet my paycheck on it," Evan said.

"Well," Wayne said, "beating the hell out of him won't change matters. Except maybe make things worse for Savvy." Wayne let that sink into Evan's head a moment. "What else you know about Teddy and Savannah?"

Evan leaned back. "Not sure I want to talk until I speak to Savvy."

"Evan," I said. "We're already keeping your minor-league boxing match secret from headquarters. No point in letting the state director know and have her go ballistic. Right, Wayne?"

"Probably right."

Good. An amen from the lawman. "So help us out, Evan."

He grimaced. "Alright. Savvy is a straight arrow. Teddy, however, is as crooked as a dog's hind leg."

"Involved in what?" Wayne asked.

"As in his company insures anything and everything," Evan replied.

"We know that," I said with a scoff.

Evan gave a dimpled smile. "Yeah, but I was the one who talked to his agency about the shrimp boat. I read that interim loss report in the file. Seeing his name on it, I started taking notice. He's the agent on hundreds of housing policies and a good many of the farming operations. He insures the Triple R shed."

I frowned. "What does that have to do with our business?"

Evan undid his seatbelt, leaned forward, and draped over the back of the front seat. "Triple R is the only shed doing business with Heyward, right?"

"Yeah, but that's too thin. Doesn't mean squat." I was about to get frustrated with his amateurish sleuthing. Guess that's how Wayne felt about me.

"Well, what would you think if Purdue Heyward took out partnership insurance with Dan Heyward . . ." he said, "and Teddy Dawson was the agent?"

"Meaning?" I asked.

"Meaning Purdue gets paid if Dan dies."

Chapter 24

WAYNE AND I left Evan at the office around two p.m. with a stern reminder to steer clear of Teddy. Evan agreed, but only after we assigned him the farm files, to determine which ones involved Teddy's insurance company.

Outside the agriculture office, I stated the obvious. "The Heyward file says nothing about partnership insurance. No one knew Purdue was involved with Dan's farming until recently—at least no one outside Triple R, Kamba, and probably the neighbors." I caught a whiff of Wayne's skepticism. "Guess that means everyone but us, huh?"

He leaned against the car and flashed a crooked grin. "Appears that way. If Savvy had inspected that farm once or twice in the past year, instead of relying on Teddy, Purdue's involvement might have come to light."

"Yeah," I conceded and sneaked a peek at my phone to see if she'd called. I wanted to head back to her house and check on her emotional state.

"It's appearing she may have been used," he said, "but the agency could still hold her accountable."

I gave an appreciative smile, enjoying that we operated on the same wavelength for a change.

He pushed off my car and strolled toward his Impala. "It's too humid to stand around out here, and I've got work to do. Catch you later."

I fought whether to go to Savvy's, out to the island, or inside for more god-awful paperwork. Then I marched toward Wayne's car. "Mind if I ride <u>shotgun</u>?"

Wayne paused but kept walking across the lot, a hint of confrontation in his boot heels as they crunched across gravel.

I jogged to catch up, reached the door, and gripped the handle. "Come on, it's friggin' hot out here."

He studied me, then did as I asked. Once inside, he turned on the engine. "So, are we heading out to St. Helena by any chance?"

"Seems like the thing to do."

He sucked the inside of his cheek, a habit I'd come to recognize as one of indecision, or an effort to carefully choose his point. "There's a reason I don't want you snooping around on your own," he began. "Remember the last time you did that?" He held a finger up, then drew it back as in afterthought, probably realizing how demeaning it seemed. "I don't even want you accounting for the rest of the equipment. I wouldn't send another *agent* to that farm now with what we know."

For the first time he didn't give me a direct order. Amen! He was making an effort. I could, too.

"Thanks for seeing me as an asset." I left off the part *instead of a liability*.

His gaze drilled into mine, past all the work details. "I still see someone I care deeply about putting herself in harm's way."

It was nice having him not drop ultimatums. "I know our agency. I know farming. I know lending. I know how to put pieces together."

He held up his hands in surrender. "Yeah, I realize all that."

"And yet you can't see past me being your girlfriend."

"I didn't say you're not good at your job."

I raised my arms in the air and sang to the heavens. "Hallelujah, it's about time."

A smirk spread across his face. "Guess I might as well keep you in my sights."

The state director would be proud. "Where we going first?"

"To Triple R. You can fill me in on the way. And tell me a little more about this voodoo guy."

I rambled on about the packing shed and had started in about Kamba before it hit me. Wayne wasn't babysitting me, was he?

"Slade? You stopped in mid-sentence. Where'd you go?"

Where was I going? I hadn't decided what I'd do this afternoon, he had. However, I now could keep my eye on him. Who'd been the wiser?

"You were telling me about Kamba? Earth to Slade," he said, tapping me on the head.

"Don't," I said, brushing him away. "I have a headache."

"You've been chomping at the bit to get involved. Talk to me."

A livid debate played in my thoughts. My dark side screamed I'd been had, discreetly conned into being watched, deterred from sleuthing on my own. The other told me to grow up; the guy had made a noble gesture.

"What have I done now?" he asked.

"Nothing," I said. "I'm just woolgathering." Heck, no wonder I confused the man. I wasn't so confident about my decisions myself these days. I made myself tired.

WAYNE HELD his credentials out for Doug Rabon. "I'm Senior Special Agent Wayne Largo with the US Department of Agriculture's Inspector General's Office. Might I have a word with you?"

Closer to my height, Doug peered around Wayne's shoulders at me with a what-the-hell-is-this expression, his raised blonde eyebrows barely discernible against his tan. Oil stained his khaki shorts. He'd obviously done more than supervise today.

"Hey, Doug." I reached out for a shake. "Carolina Slade, remember me?"

He heaved a dramatic sigh. "I see you brought clout with you."

I ignored his refusal of my hand and fought to hide smugness. His last words were something like "bring back some legal authority next time." The boy let us in.

He lowered himself into his creaky wooden chair. Wayne and I sat in the same two chairs Savvy and I used the day before. I felt taller next to a six-foot badge.

Wayne withdrew a notepad from his shirt pocket. "Doug, tell me exactly what you told Ms. Slade when she came to see you."

Doug crossed a leg and played with the laces on his Docksiders. "Like I told the ladies, the Heywards sold very few tomatoes here. If they're up to something, I know nothing about it."

Wayne took notes. I took mental notes on how to get someone's attention for a better interview. From what I saw of Wayne's technique, I dragged more out of the kid using Savvy's feminine wiles.

"I see." Wayne reached over and slipped a pen from Doug's fidgeting grip and laid it on the desk. He then returned to his notes and scribbled something on a page. "Now, tell me everything you *didn't* tell Ms. Slade."

The kid watched the pen but left it alone. Then as if in defiance, he acted as he did with Savvy and me, at ease in repeating his *I know nothing* line. Behaving as if he held control and nobody could prove otherwise. Silly child.

"Aw, Doug," Wayne said, shaking his head. "I came here all polite and respectful, willing to sit down in your office and chat. You can be my friend, or not. Your choice."

The boy's body turned rigid, hands on his thighs.

Wayne rested a boot atop the opposite knee. "What about the Heyward farm? The tomato shipping."

"What about it?" Doug said, staring down at the orphaned pen.

"Aren't you upset your business partners are jerking you around? Taking advantage of you?" I asked.

Doug frowned at me, as if I single-handedly threw him in this mess. "They aren't jerking me around. They're only farmers."

"Dan asked you to make out those tomato checks in another name so he wouldn't have to pay the government," I said. "He's dead now. And here's Purdue still trying to use you. Doesn't seem fair, does it?"

Wayne shot a wary glance at me before he scratched through something on his pad and rewrote it. I hushed. I'd had my shot at the kid. Guess this moment belonged to Wayne.

Lawman faced Doug. "Now you have a chance to make things right, son."

"I have nothing to say." The words came out softer than I'm sure the boy intended, because he cleared his throat after he spoke. A contemptuous grin split his smooth, twenty-one-year-old face. "You don't have anything on me. You're fishing."

"It's obvious you don't want to be my friend, son." Wayne stood and produced his cuffs.

My eyes grew as wide as Doug's. The boy jumped up and stepped back, hiding his arms behind him.

Wayne scanned the body language. "You see, Doug, the cost of not being my friend translates into years of your life. Each check you wrote with a wrong name on it earns you five years of prison time."

Doug's gaze flitted desperately between Wayne and me. "I'll be getting Social Security by then."

"You're better with numbers than I gave you credit for," Wayne said. "There's no parole in the federal system. You get fifty years, you serve fifty years, unless you get seventy or eighty . . . but you get the point."

Dang, I wished I could do that . . . scare people with snappy lines about jail time.

Doug waved, twitching. "I'm only given instructions," he blurted. The backs of his legs bumped his chair, rolling it two feet away. "They don't let me know anything. I simply ship the tomatoes. I'm not sure what's happening on the other end. That's the truth," he said. "I'm not allowed to step outside of this office when a Heyward load comes in, or one they picked for someone else."

"Wait a minute," I said. "What do you mean someone else?" Memories of that evening on the shed roof came back. Wink mentioned something about the Haitians picking a crop at another farm. "How often does that happen, a farmer bringing in another's harvest?"

"I don't ask questions," Doug said, gripping the arms as he fell into the chair. "When're you gonna get that through your heads? They call and say they're coming. I tell the floor workers and stay here in the office." His voice cracked, as if the stress had thrown him back into puberty.

Whatever Purdue did in the packing shed involved a cut of crops from other farms around the island, probably in exchange for providing labor for picking. But what was so secretive about packing those tomatoes?

"Doug," Wayne said, as if helping his son learn how to throw the perfect spiral. "You're doing good."

We needed tangibles, though. "Do you have cancelled checks for everything you paid either of the Heywards?" I asked.

"Not the checks, but I got copies of the fronts like they send in our bank statements."

"How about getting those for me?" Wayne asked. "I'll sit right here and catch up on my notes while you do that."

"I'm not sure I . . ."

"Call the dad," I said. "He's the real owner."

"I got the damn statements here," Doug said. "Daddy doesn't—" The fight in him withered with the realization his father could be dragged in. He stood and walked to a closet housing two rows of filing cabinets, and he rifled through papers.

"What now?" I whispered to Wayne.

He threw an arm over the back of his chair. "I have to sit here until he produces everything."

If I remained here twiddling my thumbs, I'd go nuts. With Doug broken, the game lost its glamour. "Mind if I walk outside?"

"Stay close."

Some of my summer jobs as a kid involved packing sheds. I wanted to wander around and imagine what the heck Purdue could be doing. I eased out, quietly closing the door behind me to avoid traumatizing Doug any further.

Only one semi-trailer stood cooled and ready at the dock. It contained a couple dozen boxes of washed, sorted tomatoes. The truck wouldn't fill to the top, as the loaders had to leave room between rows of boxes for air circulation to avoid rot. The water used to rinse produce on the line multiplied the humidity under the shed, with moisture at the level of a hard rainfall.

Laborers sorted at their leisure without the frenzy that came with a peak delivery. One by one they eyed the stranger on their turf. Most faces were darker than mine, both Hispanic and native island, with enough white faces amidst the crew to seem out of place. I walked around the outside of the activity and recognized Jumper off to my left. He saw me, grinned nervously, and then disappeared to the far side of the shed, but not before pointing at a sign.

No visitors on packing floor.

Kamba's words of trust for the young man echoed again. I wondered if he was a nexus of some kind, a plant in the shed to monitor activity. The big question was whether he was on the good or bad side of the equation. And why hadn't Kamba told us Jumper worked here?

Nothing appeared out of the ordinary. To avoid contaminating or violating anything, I returned to the office.

Wayne stood next to Doug at the desk when I walked in. "I was about to come hunting you," he said. "Junior here turned real cooperative." He patted Doug on the back. "Here's my card. Call me the next time Purdue phones about a shipment."

"How much will it help me if I do?" the boy asked.

"You've done fine so far. Don't screw it up. I think you understand."

He lowered his gaze. "Yes, sir."

"Nice meeting you, Doug." Wayne held out his hand. The young man shook it like they'd concluded a business meeting, but his face remained sheet-white.

Wayne pocketed his pen and put Doug's papers in his notepad. "Keep this between us, like I said. Prompt Purdue, or anyone else in his corner, and you can start counting those years, plus some."

"Or wind up at the bottom of the sea," I said.

"Ms. Slade's right." Wayne patted the boy's back again. "Thanks."

We exited down the stairs to Wayne's G-car. "I've never watched a pleasant interrogation before," I said. "Different."

Wayne wasn't the type to puff up and brag, but I caught a whiff of pride. "Common sense. Make someone like you, or at least treat them fair, and you get a lot more out of them." He reached in his glove box. "See this?" He held up a leather wallet, stamped with a design and the initials WL. "A guy I put away made that for me while he was in prison. Said he owed me for respecting him." He slipped it back in the compartment.

"Remember Jumper?" I asked.

"Yeah. One of Kamba's boys—the one you saw here the other day."

I nodded toward the shed floor area, resisting the urge to point. "He's in there working."

"Maybe he has a job."

I scanned the floor. "You know how you said sometimes you've got to go with your gut?"

"Yeah."

"My gut ain't feeling so good about him," I said. "I think he dodged me in there."

He started the engine. "Then let's go do something about that. Where's Kamba's place?"

"Take a left," I said. "Go about five miles. I'll show you." I turned on the radio and started to hum. All this action left me jazzed. Whatever the reason Wayne had invited me along, I was pumped.

THE SUN BAKED the landscape even this late in the evening. When we arrived at Kamba's, the place lay as still as a cemetery. Even the chickens had found shade. We parked under the large oak.

By the time we reached the front porch, Anyika appeared behind the screen. "You gettin' be reglar 'round 'ere."

"Yes ma'am. Still working hard. Is your husband home? Please tell me he's not standing on a box preaching in this heat."

"He be nappin," she said. "But it time he rose up." Before I could say don't wake him, she hollered. "Kamba? Roust yo'sef up. Company's here."

"Come in, come in." Anyika beckoned us in. She cranked up the window air conditioner a notch. A minute later, Kamba appeared buttoning a white, short-sleeved dress shirt, his eyes puffy.

Anyika hustled up glasses of soft drinks. Wayne sat on a lap blanket that lay across the vinyl sofa. I eased next to him. The roaring window AC unit forced us to raise our voices.

"A federal agent?" Kamba said from his recliner. "This about drugs, slaves, or tomatoes based on what I've heard so far from Ms. Slade?"

"Slade tells me you have knowledge about the drug activity out here. She explained how you're fighting the influx of drugs on St. Helena. That's mighty commendable."

Kamba eased a bit, but he was a far cry from laid back.

"I'd like to pick your brain on what else you might know," Wayne said. "I've got lots of pieces to a puzzle, with no idea how to connect them."

I took a long swallow of my Sprite. "Saw Jumper at the shed again today."

"Miss Slade, I told you 'bout those boy's backgrounds—how far they've come—the good they're trying to do."

I didn't feel the same warmth from Kamba as I had before, a feeling I attributed to my exposing Jamie and practically calling the boy a liar. "It's just we're learning more and more about that packing shed," I said, wanting to make amends. "What happened with Jamie? I feel bad about causing problems."

The man smiled at the mention of his grandson. "Think we remedied that situation," he said. "Glad you brought it to my attention, or the boy might of stepped in over his head."

I sighed with relief. "So did he cancel the meeting with Teddy Dawson?"

"No. Knew better than to ask for total abstinence. Got to thinking maybe the boy was partial right. Maybe I should let him work for the cause."

My gut turned. I looked at Wayne, wondering if he felt an ominous dread, too. Kamba wiped the side of the glass on his pants when the moisture dripped on his wife's braided rug. He ran a slippered foot over the water spots.

"So what did you do?" I asked.

"I told Martin to go with him and keep the meeting. Figured the two of them might be able to get more information from Mr. Dawson."

Wayne's eyes narrowed at Kamba's disclosure.

I fell back against the sofa. "Oh my gosh."

Chapter 25

WAYNE HELD HIS composure better than I did at the news Kamba had sent his teenaged grandson into an undercover drug deal. "The time to go to the police was before this meeting. You need to call your boys and cancel such foolishness," Wayne said. "Teddy Dawson could sink them up to their ears out of pure spite." He glanced at me. "And Dawson *will* go down."

I should have been pleased Wayne stood on my side now about Teddy, but my concern was for Jamie. How could Kamba do such a thing?

Wayne perched on the edge of his seat. "Sir, it'll be hard convincing the police that the deal was a ruse."

Kamba scowled anew and turned his head, glancing sidelong at the lawman. "The police know us and what we stand for."

Wayne touched his forehead a moment before speaking. "What do you actually know about the drug culture around here? Go to the police first. Don't let your grandson and . . . who?" He turned to me for help.

"Martin," I said, hoping Wayne would instill fear in Kamba about this crazy plan.

Wayne nodded and turned back to Kamba. "Just stop this."

The older gentleman appeared unfazed. "According to the kids on the island, some buckra supplies the drugs."

Wayne squinted.

"A buckra's a white man," I said.

Kamba wriggled. "He slips in and around here like a snake. We never see him, only the drugs and their damage."

Wayne retrieved his notepad. "What do you have Jumper and Martin doing?"

Kamba hesitated. "Jumper works at the tomato shed. Martin does too, at times. He's more in the school and community groups. We planned to present our drug findings at the sheriff's office and show them what is happening in their own backyard."

Wayne laid the notepad in his lap. "That's awful risky, Sir."

Kamba's back went rigid. "They know me."

"Do your boys have a past?" Wayne asked.

A pain crossed the old man's eyes. "Yes, and it's a past long gone. Martin and Jumper did drugs with my son. When he died, they approached

194

me at his funeral and asked what they could do to find the evil that took him. I refused them at the time. When my daughter-in-law died a month later from the same poison, they offered their services again, and entrusted themselves to me one evening in the praise house." A sigh escaped as if the memory aged him more. "That was five years ago."

And here I thought he'd just started their just-say-no club. "These guys have worked for you for five years?"

Anyika appeared from the kitchen. "No. They just start dis mess two year ago. Dem babies too young." She turned back toward the kitchen with a swish of her hips. "They too young for all dis."

A cabinet slammed. We rested in silence a moment, respecting her frustration. Again, something that started two years ago. When Purdue came to town.

"Like she said, they are indeed young," Kamba said. "But they are wise about the street . . . too wise for their years. But we wanted to go to the police with facts, not just whine and fuss. These boys know what they are doing."

Wayne made a note. "Does Jamie do drugs?"

"No, suh," hollered Anyika.

Like Anyika, I assumed Jamie was clean. Wayne's question made me realize my too-quick assumption and forced me to consider what else I took for granted. I pondered how Kamba had dealt with his son and daughter-in-law's failures to lead clean lives. God, was Jamie born addicted?

I rubbed my forehead. What questions did Kamba and Anyika ask themselves each night?

Wayne flipped a page, the pen dwarfed in his large fingers. How did he remain calm, focused, choosing the right questions, not reacting to the answers?

"Slade said you don't think Heyward's involved with Teddy or anything going down with your boys. How do you know?" Wayne asked.

Kamba leaned an elbow on his chair. "In the two years since Purdue Heyward arrived, we've never known him to deal local. I'm sure there are enough fools in this county who could claim that territory."

"Is it that bad, Kamba?" I asked. The saltwater inlets, the white sand parks, the heavy-laden mossy oaks seemed too beautiful for such systemic evil.

"Any drugs is bad, Ms. Slade. But Beaufort is the most beautiful county in this state." The ugliness of the past conversation melted away as I recalled Savvy's almost exact description. "There is not a place I would rather live and die. I wake up smelling pluff mud and blessing God for planting my feet in it. Don't mind me. Sometimes the fight overwhelms all else." He patted my knee. "It's gonna be all right. Life is still sweet on these islands."

"So Heyward only does *slaves* locally." My sarcasm spilled over. This area had worked hard to grow past the slave days and civil rights upheaval. Now it embraced the Gullah culture. Heyward was a throwback of the worst kind.

"Authorities need a complaint and hard proof about that business," Kamba said. "Otherwise they won't listen."

"What about the Three Musketeers?"

Both men gave clueless stares.

"The big black guy, Wink the Hispanic dude, and Hank. They deal drugs?"

Kamba tipped his head, recognizing the descriptions. "Wouldn't surprise me." He sipped the bottom out of his drink and set it on a Disneyworld coaster on the pressboard end table. "That white boy is trouble."

"That would be Hank," I said. "He enjoyed knocking the tomato pickers about in the back of the truck the night they relocated the slaves away from Podville." I leaned toward Wayne. "Hank was the one who brought Dan Heyward's body back with pieces of the boat."

"And you believe that?" Kamba asked. "He retrieved a body," he said. "But who knows how that body died out there on deep water?"

A shiver raced across my shoulders. Who were these people? Hunting deer or slaughtering hogs was one thing, but capturing humans and doing God-knows-what with them was a depth of dark character I didn't want to examine.

Wayne stood and handed one of his cards to Kamba. "I'd appreciate it if you'd call me when you find out the boys are all right. Please don't let them do this."

Kamba slid the card in his shirt pocket, unread. "Thank you kindly."

I wandered into the kitchen and hugged Anyika, apologizing if we upset her. Her ample dimpled cheeks rose in acceptance. She yanked me to her chest. My mother was thin and lithe, all light hugs and quick kisses. Anyika's warm, plump embrace surrounded me with a homespun, quilt-smothering peace. As I pulled back, she patted my cheeks. "I likes you, girl. Take care a yo'sef."

"You, too, Anyika. Jamie will be okay. I just know it."

Wayne and I said our goodbyes.

The day's pace and all its baggage weighed on me like a wet, wool blanket. Wayne backed the car out of the silt drive.

A last minute thought struck me. "Wait. Head back the other way down the highway. I want to show you where Monroe and I saw Heyward's boat parked last week."

"In the water, by any chance?" he asked.

"One would think so," I sassed back.

We cruised down the asphalt while I studied the many pieces to this jumbled madness. All we were supposed to do from the outset was identify false signatures, determine if clients spent loan money appropriately, and insure employees weren't involved. Hopefully, we'd clear Savvy's reputation. But we couldn't tell where the case started and stopped. "You realize how many of our business cards are scattered around?" I said. "We'll be better known than the governor if we keep this up."

"We're better known than we need to be, thanks to a certain lady I know." He cast me a droll look. "If the bad guys weren't alerted before, they damn sure are now."

I held up a defensive palm. "Enough lectures. I'm beginning to forgive you."

"Forgive me?"

"Turn left here." We coasted to the place Monroe and I had sped away from before. Naked, without a boat, not even a bucket resting on the pier. "Guess they're out."

"Or they've found another dock," Wayne said. "You kind of stirred things up, Butterbean."

"Drop the vegetable names."

"What about fruit?" He laughed as he backed us out and headed toward town.

On Highway 21, we faced the sun again and lowered our visors.

Wayne thumped the folder beside him. "These receipts from Triple R give us handwriting samples for both Purdue and Dan. We have Savvy and Evan's signatures. We'll probably learn who number three is on your loan papers if we ever pick up Purdue and get him to talk."

"He committed fraud, isn't that easy enough to prove?"

"Yeah, but for the U.S. Attorney to prosecute, we have to prove Purdue committed the offense, that it was a material offense, and that the government was harmed."

Again, the intense red-tape and gotta-win mentality of the U.S. Attorney. "He falsified a signature, operated alongside Dan on the farm, which we can confirm with the partnership insurance and packing shed records, and the loan is delinquent. There. I just made your argument."

"What if he pays current, or better yet, pays your agency off? If he's into drugs, he might have the means."

Mighty good point, but I wasn't having it. Right was right, and wrong was worth pursuing. "He still falsified paper. We need to take his butt to court."

This seesaw reaction always flared when Wayne played devil's advocate.

"If the government gets paid in full, why bother with the expense?" Wayne asked.

"You saying he could pay us off and skate charges?" I asked.

"It's possible."

"What about the partnership insurance?"

He smirked. "What's that got to do with anything?"

"What if Purdue took out the insurance then killed Dan? What if Dan was the good guy, and Purdue moved in and took over, snuffing his partner?"

His laugh threw his head against the headrest. "Snuffing?"

"Wouldn't you get credit if you caught him *and* landed a murderer as well?"

Still grinning, he nodded once. "Sure I would, but we don't have a murder. And we don't want to hunt for a murderer. The locals deal with Dan's death, which is unofficially accidental. We reported the Haitians. I'll speak with someone in Columbia about that. But now we deal with signatures and money. Keep it simple, Slade. Don't stray."

"I know."

"You keep telling me you understand, but I'm not sure you do," he said, turning into the Beaufort Memorial Hospital parking lot.

"Where are we going?" I grasped the armrest at the crisp, unexpected detour.

"Patience." He weaved around to the back of the complex and parked under a light.

I caught the strap of my purse, threw it over my shoulder. "You know somebody in here?" I got out, rummaged to find my lipstick and run a brush through my hair.

"They won't care about your hair. Come on."

We walked under orange sodium fluorescents through the automatic glass doors. They slid shut, sealing us in the hospital's vacuum. The sun had set an hour ago, taking with it a lot of my stamina. If I stood still for ten seconds, I'd fall asleep after my almost-all-nighter at the B&B.

Wayne escorted me down one hall, then another until we reached the elevator. He hit a button.

"Where are we going?" I asked again.

"You'll see."

My experience with hospitals involved someone either being born or having a bone set. I wondered if we should've brought flowers or at least a card. And who would Wayne know in Beaufort? My sixth sense rose to level red.

After an endless walk, we reached a plain sign indicating the morgue.

So much for the lipstick and hair. Wayne hit the buzzer and flashed his badge in the window. A green-garbed man let us in.

A dry chill greeted me internally and externally to the point where I didn't know which was climate controlled and which apprehension. "What are we doing here, Wayne?"

"*We* are learning what kind of a guy Purdue Heyward is."

I froze in place. "I don't want to see Dan's body parts. Let's go. I haven't eaten since breakfast, and I'm tired."

Wayne ignored me and proceeded through another set of doors. I decided being with him beat standing alone. I stepped through. Big mistake.

Wayne stood next to a shrouded corpse atop a stainless steel table. He lifted the sheet slightly to reveal an arm. Per the television shows I'd seen, its pasty shade of gray indicated someone dead for a day or two, the skin bloated. I didn't care to see more, but my feet weren't receiving the message to leave.

"Come on, take one look, and I'll get you out of here."

I clutched my purse to my body like it held me steady. "This is mean, Wayne. Why would I want to see anyone in here?"

"You don't, but this is a Haitian immigrant. Illegal. No family. You heard the talk about Heyward, you've seen Kamba's scar, yet you still think this is a straightforward problem needing your personal, often unaided, attention. This body was burned, then dumped in a marsh for the alligators. A fisherman found it."

I'd never seen a body before—at least not cold like this. My ex-husband died by shotgun, blood everywhere. I constantly shoved the memory back into my subconscious.

This was so different, though. This person, fifteen hundred miles from home, would probably lay unclaimed without a relative to pray over him as he was buried. Would he even be buried? I might be the last person to care, before they did whatever they did to nameless, homeless dead people. Pity dragged me closer, but not close enough to touch. Wayne stepped forward and held my arm at the elbow.

"Don't yank on me," I said, pulling away, unable to take my stare off the sheeted mound.

His voice turned gentle. "Just see if this is anyone you saw at the farm the other day." He eased me around for a better view.

I covered my mouth. The bloated face of the young girl who'd spoken to me through the shed roof lay as if sleeping. I tried to explain to Wayne. "She was . . ."

His grip on me tightened, but I felt lighter than a breeze as my face turned cold and someone turned out the lights.

Mrs. Amick's Beau hovered in the alcoves of my dream setting, wherever the hell that was. I shooed him with a dish towel, as I did in the kitchen with Ivy. He vanished, but I sensed him behind me, no matter how many directions I moved.

As my senses crept back to the present, air whooshed from overhead vents. They sounded sealed, contained with no depth, like traveling on a plane. Amazing how I couldn't detect odor. My eyes stayed closed. I didn't care to see the body again.

This girl had spoken to me about escaping Haiti. She'd equated sex with an hour in a clean, soft bed. I hadn't done enough to save her. Tears welled behind my closed lids.

"Slade. I know you can hear me. Your eyes are moving. Open up, or I break out the smelling salts."

As I opened my eyes, tears spilled down my temples. "That wasn't right, Wayne." I tried to hold back a sob, but couldn't. "She's dead because I didn't act fast enough. Y'all wouldn't listen to me."

Wayne took both my hands and lifted me from the floor. He swaddled me as I collected myself, buried in his shirt. When he was sure I could hold my own, he took my bag from the attendant and escorted me out, my arm firmly held through the crook of his.

"She isn't your fault, honey," he said softly. "If you let criminals make you second guess yourself, you'll go crazy." He quick squeezed me when we reached the parking lot. "You feel like eating?" he asked, setting my purse in my lap as I sat in the car. "Scratch that. I'm getting you something anyway." He shut the door and walked to the driver's side.

Such a short life for that poor girl. No telling what she'd sacrificed to reach here. I brushed more tears away. Why did I feel like a failure? This had nothing to do with me, other than to remind me of what happened when people looked the other way.

Empty of cars, the dark streets gave the town a quainter appearance than it held by day. I envied Savvy's roots. Hometown flavor embedded this place in every avenue, business, and front porch with wrought-iron signs, quaint knick-knack shops, and azalea-filled yards. And that dead girl didn't get a chance to see what that was like.

Wayne's cell phone chirped, startling me from a depression spiral. I readjusted in the seat and deep-breathed myself to a calmer place.

Wayne listened intently, glanced over at me, then stiffened.

"What?" I asked, fearing for Ivy or Zack.

"Slow down, Kamba," Wayne said, his business voice firm. "At this point, tell the police everything, absolutely everything. It's terribly important right now for them to know all the facts so they can do their job."

As he drove through Beaufort, Wayne gave orders. "Tell the police the boys met with Teddy Dawson at the Sand Briar. Explain your plan, and show them my card." He listened, squinting. "You can handle it, Kamba, but I'm here if you need me." He hung up.

I was afraid to ask. "What's wrong?"

"Jamie and Martin didn't come home after the meeting with Teddy."

Chapter 26

GRIPPING THE dashboard, I twisted to scan behind us, as if I'd see all the way to St. Helena. "Turn around, Wayne. We've got to go back."

"No," he said, too calm for my surging panic. "The local authorities don't want us meddling."

A missing child conjured horrific nightmares from my past. To lose a grandchild entrusted to you by a dead son was just as bad, or worse. "But Anyika needs somebody with her."

Wayne's gaze softened. "You need to eat. Rest. Sorry, Slade. You know why we can't be there. And I shouldn't have to remind you why from your own experience."

He pulled up at a burger drive-through.

The memory of a deranged farmer stealing Ivy and Zack last year flashed vivid at Wayne's reminder. A farmer had hid them for three days as I drove myself mad waiting, searching, listening to everyone tell me all would be fine. I craved to soothe Anyika and Kamba, but I also recalled a house full of people driving me insane. I'd wanted to focus on finding my children, not be consoled by people standing around doing nothing.

Wayne paid for our food and left. Three or four minutes later, he eased the car around the motel to a space just outside his room. He always preferred the first floor, so he could watch his car. He turned off the engine. "You appear about as exhausted as I feel. Kamba will call us when he can."

"Aren't you worried?" I asked, wound tight at the sudden feeling of uselessness.

"Sure I am. But we can't rush in and hope to put the pieces in order. Sometimes they have to fall into place on their own. Tonight we let someone else sort things out." He tipped my chin toward him. "We can't carry everybody's torch. I've told you that."

"I could vouch for Jamie."

Wayne's breath brushed my face, rousingly close any other time. "The word of a woman rescued from the top of a shed after she trespassed makes for a superb character witness."

I sighed and recognized my need to be proactive, a personal desire that didn't necessarily serve Kamba's purpose. "Then I just want food and sleep. And please don't make me get another room."

He studied me, then traced the curve of my jaw, and then my chin. "I won't."

With the AC off, humidity had built up within the car. He gave me a peck of a kiss then picked up the bag of fast food. "Let's go inside and eat."

The image of bloated flesh filled my head. "Don't think I can stomach that right now."

He reached in the bag. "Sip your Coke. Maybe that'll help."

I took a drink. The windshield shattered. Glass pelted my face. My back hit the seat, a seatbelt rammed into my spine. Wayne wrapped around me like a shield. My nose wedged against Wayne's neck. I couldn't get air as two hundred pounds pressed me into the upholstery. Then just as abruptly, the chaos ended, and routine night noises resumed.

Wayne rose to peer out the front and side windows. Random bits of glass fell. "You okay?" he whispered.

My wits awoke and scanned my body, nerve endings unable to locate any pain. I wasn't even afraid. "I think so. What happened?"

"Stay down." He slipped his Glock from its holster and eased from the car. He gently closed the door behind him, and tiny pieces of glass dropped, tinkling each other.

After minutes of agonizing wait, I itched to move. Opening the glove box, I reached for my .38, then sighed with disappointment as I realized this was Wayne's G-car.

Five minutes later, maybe less, blue lights reflected on the windshield, growing stronger with each flash. I lifted up to see a police cruiser slowing, with headlights directed straight at me. Two uniforms exited the vehicle and ran toward my car, with Wayne hurrying over to meet them, mustard and ketchup smearing his shirt where he'd mashed the burgers between us.

"You okay, ma'am?" asked a bald cop about my age.

I shut the glove box. "Haven't found any blood."

The cop helped me exit the car, but I stopped at the edge of the seat. I was afraid to stand.

He touched a bullet hole in the upholstery. It couldn't have missed me by more than inches. "Somebody was sure watching over you tonight." Reaching for the soft drink, leaning into Wayne, whatever, the small move had removed me from the line of fire.

I swallowed hard and held onto the car door. My legs seemed like jelly.

Wayne reported details to a second uniform about ten feet away. "Caught the glint of a muzzle flash from the end of the parking," he said, pointing east. "Saw a late-model, dark Pontiac race out of the parking lot. Didn't catch the plate."

After his rundown to the cops, Wayne returned to my side of the vehicle. As I moved toward him, at his coaxing, glass pieces the size of ice cream salt poked my midsection.

Time caught up as I rose. My muscles randomly twitched from adrenaline, and I didn't want to stand still. The patrol car lights made me squint. "Turn your head that way again," Wayne said, pointing toward the LEDs.

"I don't want to. The lights give me a headache."

"Close your eyes, then."

I did as told.

"You need to sit down."

An officer walked over. "Need an ambulance for the lady, sir?"

"Might not be a bad idea," Wayne answered, serious tension in his words.

My eyes flew open. "I'm fine. Don't embarrass me, Wayne." I related with Savvy in the office, fighting with paramedics.

He pressed his handkerchief to the side of my neck and then drew back a two-inch wide, dark stripe of blood on the cloth. His lips moved, but I heard nothing but a high-pitched whine as I went down.

Someone tugged at me as I searched through my kitchen cupboard. I tried to turn my head, but he held me tight, winding my strands around his hand. I fought to get away. Beau needed to find someone else to haunt. I tried to swat him, but my effort passed through nothing but air. Then he grabbed me.

"Slade. Look at me." I felt Wayne's hand grip mine, and came to the realization my head lay in his lap. "Don't move until a medic checks you out."

"Am I shot?" War movies always showed the guys stunned a few seconds before Technicolor anguish contorted their faces. I touched my ear, my jaw—nothing. When I eased my fingers down to my neck, however, the sting announced a problem.

He jerked my hand away from the wound. "Leave it alone." Wrinkles deepened around his mouth.

I tightened at his sour expression, wondering what he saw that I didn't.

Another face appeared above me, the street lamp backlighting him, for a second hiding his identity. "Slade?"

"Monroe?" I was so glad to see him. Wayne acted too serious. Maybe Monroe would talk to me. "Does it seem bad? I don't want to go to the hospital." The only one in Beaufort held a Haitian girl in the morgue.

The halogen lights gave Monroe a tanned appearance in contrast to his hair. He sneaked a glance at Wayne who moved his head in a don't-say-anything fashion.

"Stay there. Don't move," Monroe said. "I think I saw the car, or at least one that hauled butt out of the parking lot past my motel window after the shot."

I frowned at him. "You shouldn't leave your curtains open at night."

"Shut up, Slade," they said in unison.

AFTER WE SPENT three hours in the emergency room, Savvy arrived to cart Wayne and me to the motel. She tried a couple of jokes, but her attempts at humor fell limp. I could hardly think through all the exhaustion and pain meds. Wayne went to retrieve my overnight bag from the car as Savvy walked me to his bed. Monroe hobbled over from his room across the hall.

"You look like shit," Savvy said. She moved onto the bed against me, as if to guard me from anyone else.

My stitches pinched. The bullet had parted skin along the right side of my neck just below my jaw and nicked my ear. A huge white bandage adorned the side of my head. Pieces of my hair caught in the adhesive.

Monroe sat on the other side and touched my other arm. "Slade."

"I didn't die, Monroe." I scrunched back against the headboard, out from under everyone's claustrophobic touch. "It's just a few stitches. He barely cut meat." A headache that once jackhammered behind my retinas began to fade as the pills took effect. But even through my fuzziness, I caught Savvy analyzing Monroe.

Lousy time for her curiosity to pique about Monroe's attentions toward me.

"How you holding up about Teddy?" I asked to divert her attention. "I'm sorry I just dropped you off like that after you found out about his extracurricular activities."

"He ain't changed." She arched her back and stared at the ceiling. "I was so goddamn stupid."

I wasn't sure I could add anything to that statement. "Exes are like that."

Her faux chuckle couldn't mask the disappointment. "I was so insane to drag you into this."

"I came because of a farm file. It wasn't your call."

Monroe moved to the foot of the bed and stretched out his swollen knee. "What the heck happened? Thought I was supposed to be in charge."

"You said in the office that no one was in charge."

Wayne entered with my bag. He set it on the dresser and excused himself to the bathroom.

"Guess I need to go," Savvy said. I moved to walk her out, and she pressed her hand against my leg. "The old lady can still find the door. Don't get up."

I smiled. She'd turn menopause into a string of jokes for weeks to come.

"Wayne? You decent yet?" I called.

Water ran, but I heard him blow his nose. He came out and stood there smiling too hard. "What do you need, CI?"

"Can you walk Savvy to her car? I don't like her going out alone."

He waved her over. "Glad to." He took her arm in that chivalrous manner I loved. "I'll be right back." Pointing to me, he told Monroe, "Keep an eye on her, okay?"

My partner nodded, oddly quiet. As soon as Wayne left, Monroe limped to where Savvy had sat. He stroked the side of my face. I didn't have the strength to stop him.

Every molecule in me lay prostrate and spent, but my heart beat a hint faster at his touch. Monroe seemed to know it, too. He bent over and gave me a gentle kiss. He drew back, his smile as troubled as his eyes.

I gave him that one, in the name of friendship. But then he kissed me again with serious passion, his lips tasting mine like it was the last chance he'd get. Scared to withdraw and stretch the bandage, I resisted him with a slow shove to the chest. "Get a grip, Monroe. You're in Wayne's room, for God's sake."

He seemed to not hear me, showing no reaction, so I made the point clear. "I'm seeing Wayne."

"Yeah, well, you scared me. Again."

"You have a weird way of dealing with fear." Humor seemed the best way to cope. I moved to a different position, in spite of the stitches, to remove temptation.

He lifted hair away from my face with a finger. "Relax. I'll just sit here until your boyfriend gets back." His fingers continued to stroke my hair, so sweet and tender. The room turned silent as remnants of my energy drained into the mattress. I closed my eyes. My body melted, eyelids unable to open. "We need . . . to . . . talk . . ."

Next thing I knew, Wayne was easing my shoes and jeans off. "Get under the covers, CI."

I heard him double-check the locks and click off the lights. The mattress gave on his side, and he slid over, spooning against me.

"You need some *life everlasting*," I slurred. Then I faded out again, and he placed a loose protective arm around me and kissed my hair.

THE NEXT morning, Wayne closed a gap in the curtains, in spite of an exquisite sunny day. "If you didn't need rest, I'd pack your ass back to Columbia."

I moved to the chair. "I'm not going home and baiting someone to follow me to my house and family."

"That's a stretch."

"Farmers have shown up at my house before."

Wayne stood in the middle of the motel room as I stiffly slid on socks, attempting not to wrinkle the bandage on my neck. A spasm raced across my back as I pictured my carotid bleeding out in the parking lot. Providence had again smiled on me.

"Listen to me," he said.

I sat up. "I'm listening."

"Lock the doors." His finger pointed to the floor, rising and falling with each word. "Stay . . . in . . . this . . . room."

"I know."

He set fists on his hips. "I hate it when you say that."

"What else do you expect me to say?"

"Your 'I know' doesn't mean 'I know' like it's supposed to. It means you won't necessarily do what you're supposed to do."

"How about 'I know and I promise to stay in this room until you come back?'"

"Better. Someone might be hunting you out there, and I don't want to take a chance. Be back in a minute. Told the babysitter I'd be right over." He left.

Babysitter? Did he expect me to sit in this room all day with a damn stranger he paid by the hour?

A rap sounded. The bearded lawman stood on the other side of the peephole. I allowed him access into the "safe room." Someone stood behind him.

"Monroe's in charge," Wayne said. His words sounded like mine before leaving the kids on a Friday night.

Last night's romantic moment called up my defenses. Couldn't Wayne tell Monroe was acting odd? I moved back toward the bed. How were we going to handle this? "Can you go get us biscuits or something? I haven't eaten since a bag of glucose in the hospital. You squished my burger."

Wayne placed the Do-Not-Disturb sign on the handle. "No maid service today, either. Just deal with the unmade bed. If no one gets shot or kidnapped by dusk, I'll take you guys out for dinner and drinks. Send out for lunch and be careful before you open the door."

I reached up and hugged him, keeping my eyes locked on Monroe as I did. Surely this moment left no doubt in his mind. "I'm serious. I'll be right here," I said low into the hollow of Wayne's neck. "You be careful. What're you going out to do today?"

He held me out from him and checked my bandage. "Talk to Purdue Heyward and check on Kamba. Then I'm going by the sheriff's department.

It's time to close this thing." He gave me a second hug. "God, you scared me, Slade." He touched his forehead to mine.

"Me, too," I whispered back. "Oh, and Savvy's coming over, too." No way I'd hide in this motel room all day with just Monroe. Too damn weird.

Wayne tapped my nose and left. I called Savvy. Monroe remained in the easy chair.

"So," I said, spreading out the wrinkled sheets, tossing the coverlet over pillows. I crawled back on the bed. "Are we going to talk about it or pretend it didn't happen?"

"Pretend it didn't happen." He turned the chair around and propped his leg on the bed. It wasn't as swollen as before, his limp less noticeable.

Not the answer I'd expected, nor one I'd accept. "How am I supposed to act around you now?"

"How do you want to act? Seems to me that all this is up to you. Either you like Wayne or you don't. If you want to see me, you will. In the meantime, we work together. I can deal." He showed no hesitation, no hint of self-doubt. Just a tiny working in his jaw. "I made my feelings known. End of story."

My attraction to Wayne remained undeniably strong, reinforced by this new trauma, just like when we met. We shared an intense history, which had forged a fire between us. His gentle strength captured my breath when he walked into a room. He loved deep, willing to protect what was his. After an ex-husband who thought my biggest assets were spaghetti sauce and bathing the kids, Wayne represented the crown jewel of partners.

Monroe, however, respected me. We clicked as a team at the office. He was who I ran to when work backed up, or the state director doubted my abilities. When my ex-husband was alive, he never suspected how much of my lateness resulted from evening chatter with Monroe. His personality fit easily into my life. I never thought of him as more than a cohort, though. Maybe a male version of Savvy. That is, until he'd kissed me. Then suddenly he'd appeared with a potential I'd never seen before.

"Hey," he said, breaking the silence. "I'll be here either way."

Why did that scare me?

I hadn't fought the advance. Monroe was safe and comfortable, that's all. Subconsciously, maybe I wanted to test Wayne, make him jealous. I grabbed the remote and scanned television channels, ignoring the nerves in my stomach.

"Nothing's changed," he said as he studied me. "Quit worrying."

I muted the sound and dropped the remote. "Don't embarrass yourself with a statement like that. You know better."

He leaned forward, elbows on his thighs, his gaze unfaltering. "I'm not embarrassed in the least, Slade. But it's obviously embarrassing you. Maybe you need to rethink your relationship with Wayne. He's a good guy, and all that, but he smothers you."

"Sometimes, but we click more than we clash."

A corner of his mouth lifted in a confident grin. "You and I . . . feed each other."

A cold ache crept through me. Damn him. I gripped the remote again, wishing I could mute him, change his channel. I cut eye contact and watched the silent television. "I liked your first answer, Monroe."

"What's that?"

"Let's pretend it didn't happen."

Chapter 27

HOW WOULD I explain to Wayne that Monroe now lurked, primed to swoop me off my feet? Or should I even let him know? I hadn't dated in eons, so what were the rules these days? Were there any? Yeah, the kiss was pleasant. Who hasn't wondered what it would be like to kiss someone off-limits? I recalled an English professor whose hair swept his collar. I used to come to class early just to watch . . . wait a minute.

"Monroe."

He lowered his newspaper. "What?"

"Why'd you kiss me last night?"

He grinned like he did across the table at Columbia staff meetings. "Because I always wanted to."

Time to define his limits—mine as well. "What if you were presented with the chance to crawl in bed with me, right this minute." I flipped an edge of the spread aside. "Would you do it?"

Shock swept across his face.

I giggled, my smile so wide it hurt. "You don't want me. You want the excitement, the daring gesture of sneaking in while Wayne's back is turned." I scoffed. "You just want to know what it's like to smoke that joint you never tried."

Expression sober, he folded the paper and slid it across the table. "You're not marijuana, Slade. Not some kick of the moment. I'm real flesh and blood. When will you see that?"

The hurt on his face stabbed me as I regretted my humor. "Monroe, come on. You've known me for a dozen years. We're buddies."

As he bit his lower lip, his stare moved from my face to the wall behind me. Sympathy swelled in my throat. Silence filled the room. Muted newscasters reported the weather on television, their waving animations exaggerated. Someone got out of a car outside and a maid's vacuum started up down the hall. I sensed the crescendo of important words about to be laid at my feet.

I wished I hadn't laughed.

"Monroe?" I said softly.

He wouldn't look at me.

"Talk," I said. "You can kiss me twice but don't have the guts to discuss it?"

His glare took me aback. "I don't know how to approach you."

I held up my hand in a wait-a-minute move. "And you're confusing the heck out of me. Wayne and I are *not* a casual couple. I haven't hidden that fact." I paused. "What's with you? Why now?"

He cleared his throat. "Maybe because you were married before? You meet Wayne, and you dump Alan, with no downtime in between. I was taught not to pursue a married woman. Wayne apparently had no qualms about doing that."

"Whoa, no fair." I crossed my legs, fists resting on my thighs. "That's out of line. I left Alan for reasons solely related to him. Wayne picked up the pieces. We have a genuine attraction." I huffed a sigh. "That was a year ago anyway."

Monroe moved to the edge of the bed, and I inched back.

"We've always had an attraction for each other," he said.

"Yes, friendship and respect. Don't let bullets and cops turn that into something amorous. Been there. Danger's an aphrodisiac. The real deal is when life slows down and the spark still lights."

He touched my knee. "Maybe I needed the fear of losing you to recognize how I feel. Near-death experiences have a way of opening eyes. Mine are officially open."

A key clicked the lock. We turned.

"Don't do this," I said. "Don't screw up our friendship."

"Just saying I'll always be here."

"Why couldn't you just be gay?" I whispered back.

Savvy entered with Wayne behind her.

Flustered, I felt guilty by association and couldn't decide where to settle my gaze, on Monroe or those entering the room.

Savvy squinted, like she read our thoughts.

The room suddenly seemed thick with unsaid words.

"Well, the glass guy just left," Wayne said. "They replaced that windshield . . ."

Monroe walked out without speaking.

Savvy knew better than to ask questions, but Wayne didn't. "Where's he going?"

In precious truth-or-consequences seconds, I weighed how to answer such an elementary question. I could say Monroe forgot something, wanted coffee from the lobby, or needed his cell phone. I could feign ignorance and say I didn't know.

Savvy recognized Monroe's sulk. An uh-oh expression rolled across Savvy's face as she gave me her back and eased around Wayne toward the hall. Knowing her, she'd wait just outside, the door not completely closed in order to catch every word.

Wayne blinked hard. "So where's she going?"

I waved flippantly and rose off the bed. "Everyone's on edge; wearing feelings on their sleeves. Two days ago you were even ready to dump me, remember?"

"No, I wasn't."

"Wayne," I said, softly. "How do you think I feel about you going back to the island alone? I think they're giving us a moment before you leave. Last night was a bit traumatic, don't you think?"

"An understatement, but yes."

I moved to Wayne. With pressure on his shoulder, I lowered him to sit on the bed. My body maneuvered between his legs, as I held his head against my belly just under my breasts. His embrace encircled me. I stroked his beard, his neck, behind his ear.

"Well," I said. "I only have a scratch and six stitches."

"Less than an inch from bleeding out. And by a bullet," he said.

My fingers wound in his hair and gently eased his head back, face up. I lowered my lips to his, sucking his top lip lightly twice to tease. I exerted pressure, then harder to drive my point home, my tongue tasting his.

He pulled me down to the bed slowly with careful strength, rolled me to my back and cradled the side of my face in his hand. After nuzzling the unscathed side of my neck, his mouth covered mine, hungry, anxious, driven to prove I was his. He ran his lips below my chin, down to the valley between my neck and chest.

"I'm still here, lawman," I promised as I fought not to give in. "I'll prove it to you later. Now, let Savvy back in before her ear suctions to the door."

Wayne smiled, left the bed with a bounce and let her in. My girlfriend strolled across the carpet, feigning ignorance.

"What about Monroe?" I asked.

Wayne straightened his shirt. "What about him?"

I shook my head. No point drawing attention to what we'd just diverted attention from. "Guess he'll come back when he's done with whatever he had to do," I said.

Only a couple minutes later, Monroe strolled back in, with only a hint of a falter. Savvy and he sat in chairs near the window. I posed on the corner of the bed, tense. Wayne stood guard near my side.

"So we're here today, and you're going where?" I asked Wayne, patting his leg. Monroe noticed.

"Purdue, Kamba, and the sheriff's office," he said. "I'll try hard to wrap everything up this evening."

Monroe seemed mildly deflated, in a half-hidden way. Someone trained to read people would have no problem understanding that language, but the lawman seemed oblivious. Good. I'd try to keep it that way. With Wayne in the field, I would mend feelings with Monroe, or kick his ass to the moon and back. Savvy would provide comic relief. What else did we have to do for a day? We sure didn't need more controversy.

"I'll walk you out," I told Wayne.

He cut his eyes toward the other two. "Y'all behave," he instructed, stroking my back.

"Like we don't always," Savvy said.

"Right," he answered dryly.

In the hall, I stopped him. "I don't like you going to see Purdue alone," I said. "He's not stable. Go by the sheriff's office first. Take a deputy."

He studied me. "This is my job. I know what I'm doing."

I snorted. "I normally tell you that. We've switched roles."

That raised a grin out of him. "Well, you don't have to worry about me."

"Why not? Do you worry about me? Do I worry about Ivy and Zack?" Emergency room sounds still vivid in my head, I'd delegated last night's close call to the furthest recesses of my brain, not wanting the seriousness of the threat to eat at my resolve. Or remind me what could happen to Wayne. "Purdue is a bad guy. Teddy's a bad guy," I said. "Will you at least check in a couple of times?"

He tapped me on the head. "Yes, I will. You take it easy while I'm gone." He kissed me lightly and headed down the hall toward the motel lobby, turning to grin once as he exited the building.

Once I returned to the room, Savvy fastened the lock, and then pushed me toward my bed. "Get off your feet." She returned to her chair, pulled out the cards and poker chips, and tossed a chip at Monroe. "Now, who wants to play?"

The remaining audit files sat on the dresser. They never moved.

She dealt playing cards and threw in an ante, but after several hands, I lost interest. I called the state director's secretary to provide an update. She slapped me on hold, then put me directly through to Margaret Dubose. My finger sliced across my throat at Savvy.

"How's the situation progressing, Ms. Slade?" asked the boss.

"Someone shot at me last night, ma'am. Bullet just grazed me, though." I enjoyed saying the cliché movie line and waited for the gasp.

"Good Heavens," she exclaimed. "Do you have anyone with you? I could send someone to pick you up." She paused. "Good Lord."

Ah, the advantage of an injury in the line of duty. "The police want me to stick around. So guess I'm on sick leave or workman's comp, not sure which."

"How are you feeling? You sound rather collected."

"You should've seen me last night," I said. The pretense of jocularity lifted Monroe's crankiness off me. "I'm sore, but okay. I'll stay here in Beaufort, if that's all right. Monroe's here, and Wayne is available." Savvy's presence probably wouldn't sit well with Dubose, so I held that one back.

"Of course it's all right," she said.

"May I ask if Harden is still reporting behind my back? I'm concerned how he's gathering his information."

"Don't worry about him. Just take care of yourself. When you see Mr. Largo, tell him I need an update. Need to hear from Mr. Prevatte, too."

"Yes, ma'am." I flipped the phone closed with a sigh of relief. My misfortune had diverted her from asking questions she would now direct to Wayne. But I yearned to know the identity of Harden's informant. I ran down the list of ten or so people in Savvy's building, which included a fair share of good old boys.

"Everything okay?" Savvy asked, shuffling the cards.

"Yeah. Harden's undermining me, but that's not unusual." I pointed my cell at Monroe. "She wants to talk to you sometime today."

Monroe stood. "Anybody want a Coke?"

"Um, sure," I said. Savvy nodded.

He pulled out his cell phone. "I'll be back in a minute." He left the room, his footsteps disappearing down the hall, soon muted by the carpet.

I dashed aside the brief thought that Monroe was calling Harden. No. Monroe wouldn't do that. Damn. A kiss could so twist up one's head.

I so wished I was back in the field.

Chapter 28

THE MOTEL ROOM door had barely clicked shut behind Monroe before I opened up to Savvy. "Monroe kissed me once last week, and again last night. What should I do?"

She sifted her cards, a smirk just below the surface. "He's got the hots for you, girlfriend." She tapped the deck on the table. "What now?"

"Now is definitely not the time for this conversation," I said, changing my mind to go into the details. "I'm here to help save your career, remember?" I ran a finger over the bandage on my neck, a subtle reminder of the seriousness of things.

"Again, you forget who you're talking to, hon. I see what's going on."

"And you forgot what a scumbag Teddy was, yet you won't spill on him."

She sneered. "Nothing to spill, and what does Teddy have to do with Monroe? I was just making light conversation."

I scratched around the bandage, pretending it irritated me. I shouldn't have snapped at her, but we weren't exactly here for a slumber party. "Teddy doesn't have Heyward's loan file by any chance, does he?"

"You lost it?"

"No, someone stole it."

She organized the cards in a neat stack, sighed, and set them down. Then she came to the bed and sat. "Stop. Calm down. You've endured too much crap to let a flirt upset you. Someone shot at you. Your nerves are frayed. If you want me to kick Monroe's fanny for taking advantage, I'll be happy to, but it's no big deal. Don't worry about it right now."

I rubbed my nose, embarrassed.

She chuckled. "Trauma makes people react in all sorts of ways. You of all people ought to know that." She held out a tissue from the desk. "Monroe's a decent guy. He'll understand. And he'll still hang around as your buddy."

Monroe entered and stopped. "What's wrong?"

"Déjà vu about last night," Savvy said as she accepted a Coke can from him. "She's fine."

He moved toward me, but Savvy stepped between us. "Here, let me open that drink for you, fella." She punctuated her attention to the chair with a head dip. "You best prop up that knee."

Damn, I could almost date *her*.

Monroe kicked back, put the knee up, and Savvy returned to her chair.

"Who'd you call?" I asked as Monroe shifted around.

"Work," he replied.

To strike him off my list of suspects, which he wasn't really, but still, somebody had leaked info to Harden Harris in the past, so . . . "Who at work?" I asked.

Savvy peeked over invisible bifocals.

Monroe threw me a dose of disgust. "You take this in-charge stuff seriously, don't you?"

"No, I just—"

"You told me to call Dubose, so I called Dubose. Satisfied?"

I scrunched down further on the bed and crossed my arms. Then I unwrapped them, leaned over, and grabbed my cell phone. I'd worried about Kamba off and on all morning, so I decided to call and ignore Monroe's temperament.

Centering myself, I steeled myself as the call rang. When Kamba picked up, I caught Anyika's wails in the background. I swallowed anxious concern as I identified myself.

"Jamie's still missing," Kamba said abruptly, without any social introduction.

Geez. I so wanted to be there, but then again, I didn't. Again, the memories. Letting Jamie meet Teddy turned into the trouble I'd expected. "I'm so sorry," I said. "I'd come over there right now, but there was an incident last night."

"Are *you* hurt?" Kamba asked. Before I could reply, the phone clanked.

A different voice came on the line. "Hello?"

"Who is this?" I asked.

"Jumper."

My body tightened. I pictured him standing on the Triple R tomato platform next to Doug Rabon, my trust in him shaken.

"Kamba's a bit tore up about Jamie right now, Ms. Slade. He can't talk no more."

"I truly understand." Voices exchanged in the background.

"I take it you didn't hear the news?" he said.

"No . . . I've been . . . um, no. What?"

His voice cracked. "They found Martin's body."

My pulse kicked, throbbing beats into my ears.

"Someone shot him last night at the Sand Briar, where Martin went with Jamie to meet Dawson," he said.

I stared wide-eyed at Savvy, ice water surging through my veins. "Oh my, God." She and Monroe stared, worry etched in their faces. "What about Jamie?"

"Still ain't found him."

Jamie gone, Martin dead. "Anyone seen Teddy?" I asked Jumper.

"No one's seen that son-of-a-bitch, but they're hunting him," he replied. "They found crack in Martin's fist, probably planted by the sorry piece of—"

"Jumper. I . . . I gotta go." I disconnected and contemplated the numbers on the device as if reading messages, not wanting to meet Savvy's stare.

"What is it?" she asked.

Hesitating, I peered up.

She recoiled a bit. "Don't mess with me, Slade."

"You remember us mentioning Martin?"

"Yes, Kamba's guy, adopted son or something," she said, as if waiting for me to lower the boom.

"He's dead."

She rebounded backward. "Oh my gosh. Teddy?"

"Nobody knows about him." I figured no need to add more. She'd fill in the blanks.

She then cursed a blue streak. "Last night was the first night he hasn't called in weeks," she said. Red blotches showed on her neck. "I was primed to chew his butt off after Jamie told me Teddy was still dealing. Now he's up to his ass in trouble." She jerked her head at me. "And I know he's involved with Martin somehow, so no tiptoeing around me."

"Well," I said. "Maybe it's good he didn't call. He might have pulled you into all this."

Tears slipped out as she voiced regret ever knowing the bum. I suspected, however, she still feared for his life despite his sorry, poisonous habits. She'd want to catch him and tear him a new one herself.

I rubbed her back until she reduced her rant to heavy, chafed breaths. As shock eased out of her system, it stockpiled in mine. If Teddy had shot me, as indicated by the blue Pontiac Wayne had seen, he could have killed Martin too. I didn't dare speculate about Jamie.

Savvy picked up the cards and smacked them on the table for solitaire, each card taking a beating for some past sin of Teddy's.

"You going to call him?" I asked.

"No."

She'd handle this. I'd seen her weather more. Teddy was a personality easy to forget, in my opinion, and she'd soon learn to move on without him, again. Right now, she probably needed time to let the big picture settle in before she dealt with the details.

A couple hours later, sitcom-, shopping-channel-, and card-game weary, I worried why Wayne hadn't touched base. Interviews occurred at their own speed. I understood that. If I called, I could interrupt some fact-finding, deep discussion with Purdue. So I called Daddy. I'd delayed too long checking on Zack and getting an update.

"What's wrong?" Daddy asked when I said it was me.

"Don't get upset and don't call Mom to the phone."

"Ivy all right?"

"Yes, sir, but I might be in Beaufort a few more days."

He paused. "Savannah okay?"

"She's fine."

He sighed. "So what the hell's wrong?"

"I got shot."

Once I talked him down off his lecture, which included the question "where was your gun?" I explained my seclusion in the motel for the day, behind double locks, with my .38 in the nightstand. Mom overheard a piece of our chat, took the phone, and asked what was going on. I excused myself, blaming another phone call.

I wished there *was* another call. Hopefully, Wayne had found Purdue. If the stars aligned right, we'd have answers, maybe even payment, before he finished with the red-headed bastard, and we could go home and leave this muddled madness behind.

I called the Amicks, needing to hear my baby's voice. Ivy rattled on like the teen she almost was. Her report about the kids on the cove, chickens, and stories of Beau linked everything together in one breath. When she asked about me, I didn't have the heart to tell her anything other than that I was fine. I loved hearing her alive and excited, describing the eggs she collected, the hydrangea she cut for a vase on the dinner table, the quilt she curled up in under a ceiling fan on the porch. She became the bright moment to my stressful day. I smiled and envisioned the wrinkling of her freckled nose as she replayed her adventures.

She hung up. And dark concern for Wayne replaced Ivy's sweet conversation in my mind.

"Call him," Monroe said, flipping a magazine. "I'm not a complete idiot. You're worried."

Our gazes met. My old buddy read my thoughts.

I dialed Wayne. The perfunctory recording said he couldn't accept a call.

"Try again," Savvy said. "He might have bad reception. You got something for my headache?"

"Taking your prescription?" I tossed her my bottle of aspirin, and then tried the call again. Same thing—zilch.

I dialed the number of the deputy who'd given me his card last night, then the sheriff's office, and finally Raye.

Nobody knew Wayne's whereabouts.

I made another call. The sheriff's office confirmed the murder, but not Wayne's locale.

Martin's death led to uglier thoughts. A migrant, Dan Heyward, and Kamba's protégé, all dead within two weeks—deaths that touched me and people I cared about. If Wayne hadn't reacted so swiftly last night, a bullet would have made me the fourth.

Savvy grabbed her purse off the floor and slung it over her shoulder. "Get your pocketbook, Slade."

"Why?" I wasn't liking this.

"We're going nowhere," Monroe said with a deep voice that made me jump. He jabbed his finger into the soft bed beside him. "We need to stay put."

Savvy slapped his foot. "Sitting around here sucks. We're going out."

"Wayne ordered us not to leave," he said. "He won't like it."

"He's right, Savvy. Wayne expects us to stay here, and I promised we wouldn't leave the room." And I'd promised him I'd use more common sense.

"I'm going to the Sand Briar Bar with you or without you," Savvy said. "Teddy's a worthless SOB, but he wouldn't kill anybody."

I envisioned Wayne's facial muscles hard, his neck tensed, pissed at all of us, but especially me. But I couldn't let Savvy go by herself. And I sure as hell couldn't stop her. "Wait a sec," I said. I called Wayne again. Voice mail. Then I put on my shoes.

"Then we try to find Wayne, too," I said. "All we're doing here is wallowing in what-ifs and whys." I turned to Monroe. "You coming or not?"

"I'm not sitting around here for Wayne to find alone," he said.

He walked to the door and held it. "What if he shoots at us?"

"Who?" Savvy asked. "Wayne or Purdue?"

"Or Teddy," I added.

"Does it matter who?" Monroe asked.

"I'll let you hold my gun if that makes you feel better," I joked, going back to retrieve my .38 and slip it into my purse.

He blew out a laugh as I eased past him, then he hobbled into the hall.

We headed toward the island in Savvy's Mercedes, with Monroe and his bad knee stuffed in the backseat. Martin's death altered everything. I shoved away the reasonable argument that told me another murder underlined the need for me to stay locked in the motel room. It'd be different if Wayne was around to emphasize it, but he was absent, the tiebreaker that convinced me to hit the field with Savvy and watch her back . . . keep her from making stupid decisions. Like leaving the motel really ranked up there as intelligent.

Twenty minutes later, we parked in a deserted lot down from the bar. Crime scene tape and a sheriff's vehicle blocked most of the bar's parking.

"Slouch, act redneck, or something," I said low as we exited the vehicle. The concrete block dive sported wrought-iron bars and a loud array of neon beer signs in the windows. The deputies gave us a once-over as we approached.

"Place still open?" I asked loud, summoning my worst hayseed drawl. "Nothing happened inside, did it?"

"It's open," one deputy said. "Just don't cross the crime scene tape out here."

I feigned appall, touching where my poor little old heart would be under my shirt. "Honey, I ain't worried what's out here; the beer's inside."

We opened the screen door, stepped in, and let our eyes adjust to the dark. We were the only customers. The bartender weighed us from a vinyl-covered chrome stool at the bar. Guess his regulars didn't care to breach the cop brigade parked outside, which told me I probably didn't fool anyone with my playacting.

Two pool tables stood to the side, the felt worn to the slate in spots. Four varnish-glazed pine tables showed legs filthy from dirty mop water. The matching pine bar had belly-worn wood around its edges. A coolness rose from the dank concrete floor, blotched from slopped beer. A soap opera played on a small flat-screen in the corner. We were girl scouts in a strip joint.

"What you need?" the bartender said, stepping off his stool and sliding behind the bar.

"Information," I said from our stance in the middle of the floor.

He growled in what sounded like a laugh. "You ain't cops, you ain't drunks, and I ain't no information hotline," he said. "You drinking or not?"

"Gimme a beer." I took a stool, wondering what alcohol would do with the pain meds I'd taken an hour ago. "Draft. You got a happy hour?"

He ignored my question, which I took as a no.

Savvy slapped her purse on the bar. "I could sure use one of those."

"Diet Coke," said Monroe.

The barkeep nodded. He set the three drinks on the bar and charged us fifteen bucks.

I chugged half of mine in one long draw, then reached in my purse. The bartender's eyes flashed wide at my badge, the low-light accenting the gold and inhibiting the administrative wording, as I'd hoped. "What can you tell us about what happened out there?" I gestured toward the crime scene.

He rested elbows on the bar. "Guy got shot in the parking lot. Don't know him. Don't know who killed him. Any more brilliant questions?"

"My husband was supposed to meet a guy out there last night," Savvy piped up. "I need to know if he was here and if he's okay."

A hint of surprise skimmed the bartender's face, then disappeared.

"His name is Teddy Dawson," she said.

The man's eye twitched at Teddy's name.

"Do you know him?" I touched my bandage. "He shot me last night."

Savvy held it together, acting redneck and saucy, letting me accuse her ex of attempted murder.

"How——?" The barkeep caught himself. "The dead dude came in with a kid. He asked for Dawson, but that's all I know. I ain't seen Dawson, and I didn't see what happened outside. Once I heard a couple of pops, I knew better than to care." He sneered a lopsided smile. "I didn't give him a chance to cap my ass."

Our host wiped the counter and moved back to his stool. Chin on his palm, he returned to the soap.

We wandered outside. Squinting in the sun, we shaded our eyes, craning to see the blood on rock and shells behind the crime tape, as if we could analyze it better than the forensics already performed.

"I don't think Teddy did this," Savvy said, her gaze affixed on the huge brown stain. "The bartender's guessing."

"Heck, he said he didn't go outside, so what does he know? Call Teddy," I said. "You've got him on speed dial, for goodness sake. Ask."

She drew out her cell, opened, then shut it. "Not here," she said.

The deputies watched us leave the lot, then went back to their gossip. Inside the Mercedes, Savvy cranked up the air conditioning.

"Where would Teddy go?" Monroe asked. "Surely he didn't return home, and I hope he isn't hiding out at your place."

Savvy flipped open the phone. "He might not be *hiding* anywhere." Hitting speed dial, she buzzed her ex.

"Hey," she said. "Where are you?"

Monroe and I raised wide eyes at the fact Teddy had answered.

"What do you mean you can't say?" Savvy's scowl hardened even more. "Just tell me if you had anything to do with this murder at the Sand Briar. I know you met with two guys there last night." She listened. "And the drugs?" she asked. "You're dealing again, aren't you?"

I'd labeled Savvy a potential adversary in this venture, but she pulled off the call with Teddy like a damn trooper.

"Don't call me anymore, Teddy," Savvy said after a lengthy dissertation from the other end. She dropped the phone in a cup holder beside her.

"Don't call?" I repeated.

"The idiot peeled off one lie after another," she said, spitting the words. "He said he wasn't at the Sand Briar. He wouldn't tell me where he was, nor when we could meet. Said he'd call me, not to call him." She snapped her head back against the headrest. "Shithead." She cut a glare at me. "But that doesn't mean he's a murderer."

Understanding only she could bash the man, I reached to fasten my seatbelt, but Savvy opened her door and marched back to the bar. Monroe and I scrambled out. She yanked open the screen, stretching the rusted, coil hinge to its max.

"Teddy claims he was here last night," she said like she was about to call a rustler into the street for a showdown.

The bartender reached under the bar.

"Who did he meet?" she demanded.

I gripped her arm in warning.

"Two black guys came in asking for him," he said. "Later he came in and asked about a kid." He rested a shotgun on the counter. "You ain't cops. Now get out of my place."

Monroe and I led Savvy back to the car, expecting an emotional episode from her about all of Teddy's flaws. Instead, she started the engine. "Let's go." Gravel crunched as she exited the lot and hit asphalt, heading away from town.

"Where we going?" I clenched the door handle in case she swerved. "I gather you're mad."

She choked the steering wheel, lips tight. "Haigh Creek. My jerk ex has a fishing spot there, where he hides when he doesn't want to deal with shit."

Stunned, I pondered the goal at the end of this knee-jerk movement. My hand brushed my neck and fingered a loose end of medical tape. I wasn't sure I was ready to meet the guy who may have tried to shoot my head off.

"So what is this Haigh Creek?" Monroe asked as Savvy drove ten miles over the speed limit. She barely slowed to hang a left on Dr. Martin Luther King, Jr. Road.

"A small river," she said.

"Not a creek, huh?"

Savvy passed a pickup loaded with crab traps. "It's where the idiot disappears to drink, snort, or screw someone he doesn't want me to know about."

Okay, so she wasn't naïve about Teddy. That just made her moronic to have rekindled their relationship, but that was over, thankfully. Especially considering the demonic temper she flared at us now. And the string of expletives with it.

My cell rang. Ivy.

"What's wrong?" I said breathlessly into the phone. We'd spoken only a couple hours ago.

Savvy veered a sharp right on Lands End Road. My purse toppled to the floor.

"Anything wrong?" I said again. "Speak up, Baby. It's crazy where I am."

"Mrs. Amick says she misses Beau. Is she allowed to miss a boyfriend when she's married?" Ivy asked.

"Ivy, leave the poor woman alone," I scolded. The speedometer read fifteen miles over the limit. "Slow down," I hissed to Savvy.

"I'm investigating like you, Momma," Ivy continued. "This is a cool mystery. I'm learning all sorts of goodies about the Amicks."

I exhaled, adrenaline rising at Savvy's driving and my daughter's inquisition with a sitter I sorely needed to keep. "You're being nosy. She's allowed to miss him. Even if he's an old boyfriend," I said in Savvy's direction.

Savvy cut her eyes sideways at me. Then she slowed behind a rusty sedan in no hurry, skirted our car to the left, and weighed a chance to pass.

"Ivy, I need to go. Back off Mrs. Amick, okay?"

"I'm subtle," she said.

Who knew my daughter understood the word? "I mean it."

"Chill, Momma. Talk later." She hung up before I could squeeze in an "I love you."

Savvy passed the car, and I pretended to need my purse to avoid the other driver's scrutiny.

Sunlight flickered through gaps in the oaks like a disco ball. I lowered the visor. A small bag of white material fell into my lap.

"What's that?" Savvy asked.

I picked it up and held it so Monroe could see. "I'd say cocaine, but it could be coffee sweetener for all I know."

"That son-of-a-stinkin'-goddamn-bastard!" Savvy pummeled the steering wheel. The car jerked right, front wheel dropping off the pavement. She grasped the wheel again and straightened the tires. My heart pounded a Mexican hat dance.

Savvy didn't know Teddy had put the dope there. Teddy would most likely deny it. I rolled down the window and tossed it. The bag disappeared into a creek we passed over. One good tide and a foot of pluff mud would bury the stuff.

Savvy turned down one dirt road, then another, before traveling toward the creek. She slammed brakes, her whirlwind chase ending in silence and billowing dust. Tide was in. Teddy's car sat parked at the edge of the water, the driver's side wide open.

Chapter 29

SAVVY PARKED next to Teddy's car on the edge of Haigh Creek, staring statuesque out the windshield. She then released a huge sigh, followed by a mild tremor, and got out. Monroe followed and leaned against the car, and I went after Savvy. I prayed Teddy wasn't lying dead beneath the dashboard. Drunk or high, however, would suit me best—a big fat bow on his romantic demise with Savvy. Anything but a cold body.

No one lay in the front or backseat. Dark red splatters dotted the vinyl inside the driver's door. A small red trail drooled over the seat's edge onto the floor, then the running board. Blood that might belong to Martin, Teddy, Jamie, or anyone else.

I flinched with a shiver.

Monroe caught up, and we left Savvy stewing in her juices, furious and fretful, cursing to herself as if speaking directly to Teddy. We moved away from the found car, snapping pictures of the area with our phones like we were professionals. I hated putting blood pictures on my phone beside cutesy, hip-cocked poses of Ivy and Zack flexing nonexistent biceps.

"Don't remember this work in my job description," Monroe mumbled, clicking his phone.

We noted multiple sets of footprints plus the tracks of another vehicle. Grass and sandy gravel kept us from telling who walked where and did what.

"Can you tell how many people this is?" I asked.

"I'm used to tracking my game in the mountains, Slade, not in the grass. Takes a special kind of skill to track quarry in vegetation," he replied.

I halted. "Say what?"

He blew out in exasperation. "No, Slade, I don't have a clue how many people were here. I don't even know what I'm taking pictures of."

That's when it hit me. We bumbled like clods, stomping around a crime scene when bad guys might not be all that far away.

I dialed Wayne again, praying he'd pick up, but the call rolled to voice mail. In the presence of blood and an abandoned car, my fear for him escalated.

Antsy to leave, I walked over to Savvy and draped an arm around her. "Teddy's not here, hon. Just think about that." I didn't speak my complete concern, the part screaming murderers could be scoping us out from behind the brush.

Monroe limped over. "Should we call the sheriff?"

"And get stuck out here?" I said, imagining eyes on us. "What time is it?"

Savvy turned her wrist up. "Five thirty."

Only two to three hours of daylight left. "Let's go," I said.

"Call the dang sheriff, Slade," Monroe demanded. "We shouldn't leave the scene of a crime."

"I think it's perfectly fine to leave a scene where there's recently spilled blood," I said. "We can call from down the road."

"You're scared," Monroe said. "We can lock ourselves in the car if it makes you feel better, but the authorities won't be too thrilled we noted everything, left tracks, and took off."

"Fine." I said, climbing in the car. "Call the friggin' sheriff."

Savvy got behind the wheel, and once Monroe placed his call, he slid into the backseat.

For twenty long minutes, our windows down halfway for ventilation, noises in the bushes kept me on edge as I tried not to worry about Wayne. How the heck had Monroe's signature discovery escalated into murder? But what creeped me out more was what we had yet to uncover. I so wanted all of this to move into somebody else's lap. Trouble was, Savvy stood in the midst of the crap, which was a game changer. I had vowed to remain in this for the duration.

Two patrol cars pulled up. We stood as four deputies strode over. "Mr. Prevatte?" asked one uniform.

"Yes," Monroe said, rebalancing with a hobble outside.

"You can sit back down," the young guy said. "And who are you ladies?"

We exited the car. He wrote as we made introductions, grinning slightly in recognition of Savannah. She could identify everybody in this damn county, except maybe those doing the killing, and I worried I was wrong on that count.

It took less time than I thought it would to tell them what we knew. We came, we saw, we walked on some of the evidence, then we called. But Savvy knowing Teddy intimately caused them to ask her a few more questions as Monroe and I waited in the car, me reading headlines on the phone between texting and calling Wayne.

"Finally," Savvy said, returning to us.

I got out and walked to the lead deputy, who'd asked most of the questions while the others scanned the area, took pictures, and made notes. "You got a minute?" I asked, then before he could respond, I added,

"There's another person in our party, Special Agent Wayne Largo. Have you heard from him? Seen him? We expected a response hours ago, once he completed an interview. It's not like the man to remain out of touch." I rambled for several minutes, striving to build the intensity I needed to make this officer feel as worried as I was.

"Ma'am," he said once I took a breath. "I hear you, honest I do. But it hasn't been ten hours, and you say he had to run Heyward down and then convince him to give an interview. What if Agent Largo missed Heyward? Or it took him four hours to find him? They might still be interviewing. He could have his phone on vibrate, or off even, so they wouldn't be interrupted."

"No," I said. "You don't know this man. He would not turn off his phone, and he would return my calls. See this?" I pointed to my neck. "Someone shot me last night. If someone tried to shoot your . . ." I searched for a wedding ring, ". . . wife, and she was home in bed, wouldn't you take her call?" His stoic patience drove my nails into my palms.

"Calm down, ma'am. He's probably fine."

My voice deepened. "*Probably* doesn't cut it with me."

"Settle down, ma'am."

Savvy's hand slid around me. The other deputies regarded us now.

"He's a federal agent," I said. "He's not some drunken spouse who hasn't come home. He's alone and out of reach—for too long, so don't discount his absence as routine." I exhaled with a force to accent my point.

"She's right," Savvy said.

He turned toward her, the calmer voice. "I can put out a BOLO. Give me his car description. But listen," and he turned back to me, "if he's having cell problems, don't you think he'd be trying to contact the motel? Or have someone else get word to you there? Go back. If you don't hear from him by midnight, call us."

"Midnight!" I exclaimed.

"Come on, Slade." Savvy led me back to her car. "I can't deal with you and Teddy in my head at once."

That statement set me back to right. I'd think more clearly if I composed myself anyway. We loaded into her Mercedes.

"Back to the motel?" she asked, starting the engine.

"Stop by Heyward Farms," Monroe said. "It's not far out of the way. See if Wayne's car is there."

At that moment, I could've curled up against Monroe's shoulder, so damn grateful he understood.

Minutes later, we drove up the dirt road toward the Tidewater house. No cars. Not even Purdue's Suburban. I made Savvy ease back to the pods. We slunk around without exiting the car and were about to turn to leave.

"Stop," I said. I left the car, and they followed. We made the rounds to each pod, my nerves on edge, waiting for a booming voice to catch me. I avoided the shed where I'd been glued to the roof for hours. Monroe caught me glancing, his own neurosis probably awakened at the memories of that night as well.

As Savvy checked the outhouse, Monroe brushed my elbow, his face coming within inches of mine. "Leaving you was not the thing to do, and I'll never forgive myself for it."

I eased loose. "You did exactly what needed to be done, Monroe."

"But—"

"There is no 'but.' If you'd stayed, you might've gotten caught. I might've been found. It all worked out. Damn, you were the only casualty," I whispered. "Stop it. Wayne spoke highly of what you did."

Savvy jogged back. "Nothing here."

"Then let's go," I said, fast-walking to the car and getting in. "He's got to be back at the motel."

Once Monroe fell into the back, we left. Driving faster than comfortable on a dirt and gravel road, Savvy reached the pavement, and we turned toward town. I cursed silently for the next thirty-five minutes to the motel, aching to see Wayne's Impala parked safely in the lot, his temper red hot because we left against his orders.

His car wasn't there.

Back in Wayne's motel room, I opened the file and found Purdue's phone number, then Dan's for good measure. No answer at either one.

"We wait," Monroe said, before I could speak.

"You can, but I won't," I said. "You can't walk a hundred yards, so stay here in case he calls. We're going back out."

Savvy tossed her purse on the bed near Monroe, where he'd already propped his knee up. "No, it's dark, and we can't see squat. Better we wait."

An October night ripped into my head. Rain had made roads slick. Daddy rode with me, Wayne following in his government car. Daddy had scolded me to end the search, saying I couldn't find my missing children in the dark. I should go home and wait. That pain tore my guts out, and I'd collapsed in a field, wet and muddy, shattering my flashlight on a fence post at the despair of leaving my children lost. I'd fallen unconscious with exhaustion into a warm, soft, dry bed back at home. The kids had spent that night locked in an old house, cold, with only each other for warmth.

Keys at the ready, I prepared to leave. "I'm going out. It's almost ten. I'm not spending two hours watching television."

A quick knock sounded, and I jumped.

"Someone answer the door," Wayne hollered.

The lock guard jolted me as it caught. Slamming the door shut, I fumbled with the chain and freed it.

Wayne grunted as he endured a rib-bruising hug, before I reared back and fussed. "Where the crap have you been?"

Down the hall, a woman and her two kids paused at the elevator. I dragged Wayne into the room. He sank to the edge of the bed and started pulling off his boots. Dried mud tracked across the carpet.

I plucked a piece of brush from his hair. "What happened?"

"Car mired up after a three-hour discussion with Purdue, once I found him. I swear he stayed one step ahead of me. Tried rocking the car out of the muck, and the damn cell phone rang. I dropped the thing in the mud. Walked two miles to find a place to call a tow truck."

"What about Purdue?" I asked.

Wayne finished suctioning off the other boot and turned toward Monroe. "Any problems today?"

"I asked about Purdue!"

Monroe picked up on Wayne's insinuation before I did that we were discussing the case too openly. "No problems."

"Good. Y'all care if I shower before dinner?" He glanced at Savvy, the sting of hate and concern about Teddy still evident in her demeanor. "What's wrong?"

"Not many restaurants will be open by the time you shower," Savvy snapped, stuffing her feet in her shoes. "Maybe some all-night breakfast place."

Monroe reached for Savvy's hand. "Clean up, man. We'll wait for you and Slade in my room."

Wayne peeled off his wet socks smacking with mud the consistency of chocolate pudding and the odor of a paper mill. "Works for me."

After the two left for Monroe's room, Wayne faced me. "Again, you're forgetting Savvy's still under investigation. Don't ask me about Purdue in front of her."

I winced, dropped my head back and sighed. "Sorry. I keep thinking we're all in this together. It's been a hell of a day."

Wayne walked into the bathroom. "In a motel room?"

"People are dying, Wayne. Martin's dead." I flopped in the chair Savvy vacated near the narrow wall air conditioner under the window. "Guess the sheriff didn't tell you."

He peered out, shirtless, awe on his face. "What?"

"Finish and get out here, so I can explain without yelling."

"No," he said, coming out and sitting across from me on the bed. "Tell me now. What happened?"

"Jamie's still missing. Martin's dead. I think Teddy did it, but that's just my gut talking."

He gaped at me.

"They found dope on Martin's body. Someone shot him in the bar parking lot where Jamie intended to meet Teddy."

Wayne grimaced. "That explains Savannah's mood. How's she taking it?"

"She's beyond furious, and scared, too. But there's more." I stopped talking to let that settle.

He leaned elbows on his knees. "What part of this am I not going to like?"

"All of it."

I told him about the trip to the bar, Savvy's chat with Teddy, then the bag of dope above the car's visor.

He straightened at the mention of drugs. "What did you do with it?"

"Tossed it out the window into a creek. Don't remember which one," I added.

"You disposed of evidence."

"It was Teddy's, so it doesn't matter. We have bigger issues," I said, holding back sarcasm. "Can't believe I'm the one telling you that."

He frowned. "What else happened?"

"We found Teddy's car on a creek, abandoned, blood all over the inside."

His eyes closed, as if he counted to ten, then they opened. "*You* found it?"

"Yes, me . . . and Monroe and Savvy. We notified the cops. We tried calling you, but . . . never mind." I got up and moved to collect his dirty boots and avoid that glare. "So what exactly did Purdue say?"

He rubbed his eyes, despair in his shoulders. "Jesus, Slade. You were supposed to be in bed."

I set down the boots, walked over, pulled his hands away from his face and put them around my waist. "Quit worrying, cowboy. Now, answer my question. What about Purdue?"

He sighed and let loose of me. "He claims he doesn't know anything. He says he didn't know about the mortgage on the crop." Wayne rose and tossed the boots in the bathroom. "Of course, he knows nothing about drugs, but he heard that Kamba rants about *somebody* dealing on the island. He'll be glad to assume the mortgage to keep the farm. Anything to please us, he said. Says he's an honest, law-abiding citizen."

"Yeah, right." However, we did need Purdue's signatures on paperwork before he developed selective memory loss. Making him obligated for Dan Heyward's debt could save Savvy's hide. I worried how much criminal activity we would have to overlook to protect the government's financial interest.

Wayne seemed to follow my thoughts. "Let's assume Purdue takes over the mortgage and pays the account current," he said. "What do you think Dubose will do about Savvy?"

"As little as possible," I said. "I still think Teddy dealt drugs under Purdue's wing and Martin died saving Jamie."

Wayne stood. "We don't have a smidgen of proof to back up those assumptions. Who knows who killed Martin. And so far Purdue's guilty of nothing except selling tomatoes that weren't his. We can make that claim easy enough, but if the agency wants him to assume Dan's debt, it may have to mitigate any charges. Otherwise, you've no choice but to foreclose."

I stretched my neck. "Yeah, then we lose our shirt."

"Come over here," he said, studying my bandage. "Your bouncing around has your neck bleeding." He disappeared into the bathroom and returned with a fresh bandage. "I looked around best I could, trying to find your slaves and get an idea on the residual crop. I found nothing but a bog that tried to eat me and my car." He rubbed the new tape flat then crunched up the wrapping and old bandage in his fist.

I waved toward the bathroom. "Go take a fast shower. Monroe and Savvy are sour enough, without having to wait so late to eat."

Steam soon drifted into the bedroom. Not five minutes later he appeared in stonewashed jeans and eased on a soft yellow polo shirt. Fully dressed, he donned the badge and weapon on his belt and pulled me up from the chair. As we turned to leave, he stopped mid-stride. "Let me call the sheriff and see what's happened in the last hour or so." He paused again, smoothing the adhesive around my wound.

"Thanks," I said, sitting back in the chair.

He stood there.

"What?" I asked.

He crossed his arms. "I need to get something off my chest first."

I leaned back and waited for it.

His lecture started about me not following through on my promise.

"We don't need to get into a tit-for-tat about who's honest and who's not," I said, in an attempt to diffuse him.

"Don't even try to argue with me," he said. "What if whoever caused that bloodletting at the creek had still been there when you arrived? What about your neck? The doctor said be still for several days. Do you know how close that bullet came? I swear, next time I'm cuffing you."

I apologized. "But Savvy insisted on leaving alone when she heard about Teddy. We couldn't let that happen." Not waiting for his response, I passed him the motel phone. "Call the sheriff. Let them know they no longer have a need for that BOLO . . . on you. I was worried stupid."

He shook his head in disbelief and dialed.

Wayne's safety lecture gave me the urge to check on my children again. I speed-dialed the Amicks, one eye catching a glimpse in the mirror of my pout that so resembled my daughter's.

Dolly said she and Ivy had spent the evening studying old photo albums. "The baby drifted off on the floor right here at my feet," she said. "Mr. Amick's relaxing in his chair next to us, and everything's real quiet around here," she said softly. "Well, at least peaceful," she chortled as I heard the snores. Sounded like a Hallmark movie.

I reached Zack for the first time since he'd left my watch to stay with my parents. "Momma, guess what?" he exclaimed. "I caught a striped bass! He wasn't twenty-one inches, so I threw him back 'cause that's the law. Guess he wasn't grown up, needed to make more babies, whatever. Dang, I wish I'd brought a camera. Grandpa's phone doesn't take pictures, can you believe that?" A loud yawn interrupted his storytelling. Poor baby. I had called late.

"Go to bed, sweetie," I said. "You're tired. I'm so glad you're having a great time. Love you."

As I heard the click on his end, regret pierced my heart. I missed my kids, and I wanted them to miss me.

I had stifled the temptation to brag to Zack about my cheating death last night. The comfort of hearing his jubilation over a fish overshadowed my need for praise. Neither child needed to revisit old fears from their kidnapped days I reminded myself, gripping the phone, wishing I lounged on my sofa with Ivy experimenting with my hair and Zack running over us with Matchbox cars.

Then I realized Wayne had hung up. "Slade."

"Sorry. What did they say?"

"No one has found Jamie or Teddy. Tomorrow they'll organize search parties and canvass the county, particularly St. Helena. Anyone willing to search should report by eight. I think I might go."

We collected Savvy and Monroe, who were quiet and obviously uncertain about what had gone down in Wayne's room, and left to find something to eat. At the late hour, Waffle House won by default. Our bones weary, we fed our souls on comfort food of bacon, eggs, and waffles.

I ran my bacon through puddled syrup in my plate. If Purdue paid up Dan's account, we could close a major chapter. If I hung around another day or two, I might be able to meet with Purdue and clean up the loan, removing a lot of heat from Savvy.

In the meantime, I couldn't toss the vision of a teenage kid; a young man hiding in the bushes, scared for his life.

Wayne waved with a piece of bacon. "Want to come with me to search for Jamie tomorrow? I don't know the area like you guys do."

Savvy's brooding expression eased at the thought. "Yeah, I think I do."

Wayne intended to use the search as an excuse to pick the brains of whoever he could at the sheriff's office. Before we left Waffle House, we all decided to comb the island for Jamie, regardless of what anyone at headquarters thought. For the moment, a missing young man took precedence over Savvy's future. She was living and safe, her career a concern for later—a small worry considering that Jamie was possibly dead.

Chapter 30

AROUND TEN after eight the next morning Wayne and I arrived in the Impala, Monroe following in his government Taurus in case the sheriff needed more cars for the search. We met Savvy at the station. Bodies and faces of all shapes and colors hustled in the main entrance of the red brick building, as if there was a sale on Get-Out-of-Jail-Free cards.

The united effort to hunt for a native boy did my soul good. By the time we arrived, I'd missed seeing Kamba and Anyika. Earlier, they'd brought pictures of Jamie and begged those assembled to find their grandson, then returned home to wait. My gut twisted at their heart-wrenching vigil.

Walking into the building, Monroe held the door open for an older woman before stepping into the lobby. He turned to Savvy. "Just thought of something. Would Evan want to help search, too?"

"I don't know," she said. "Not sure what he's got going at the office."

A coordinating deputy overheard the conversation. "He got a boat?"

"Evan? Sure," she said.

"We could use him, then." The man walked toward a group of other deputies who packed a forty-by-fifty lobby. Teams came together, identified on a dry-erase board.

Savvy searched in her purse. "Aw, damn. I left my cell on the kitchen counter. I ought to at least ask Evan if he wants to help." I threw her my phone. She still wasn't thinking clearly. A half hour later, as we stood around watching too many people try to organize, Evan arrived. Savvy briefed him, including the part about Teddy. "Jamie might have been snatched in the middle of a drug deal," she added. Coffee finished brewing in the forty-cup urn on a foldout table, and she left to pour a cup.

"Teddy's messed up in this?" Evan whispered to me.

"Maybe. Found drugs on Martin, blood in Teddy's car."

"Good riddance to Savvy's moron," he said, his eyes rolling. "And the drugs were a big surprise."

"*Shhh,*" I said as Savvy returned, a glazed Krispy Kreme in her fingers. "Where's mine?"

"With all these cops in here, I feared they'd tackle me if I picked up more than one."

"Raye sure acted strange this morning," Evan said.

"Do I need to go to the office?" Savvy asked.

He shook his head. "No, she's fine. When I came in first thing, she was crying. I offered to call her husband. She said it was something personal, cut off the faucet, and straightened up."

Savvy sighed. "God, I hope she's not pregnant. Last thing I need is to have to hunt for another clerk."

A salt-and-pepper-haired man in uniform cleared his throat. In ten minutes we owned our marching orders. Evan and Monroe left to man Evan's boat, since Monroe's knee made walking difficult. Deputies paired up and left the room. As the din evaporated, I poured two cups of coffee to take with us. Right before I turned around, a unique voice in the mix sent a chill through me.

"Sheriff Goff, I'm here to offer five of my hired help in the search. Tell me what we can do."

I cut my eyes right and caught sight of red hair. With my back to the man, I made my way to Savvy, since she was closer than Wayne. I thrust the cup at her. "Here. Don't be obvious."

"But I already have coffee."

I shifted my eyes toward the guy. "*Shhh.* Don't you know him?"

She sipped from her cup and studied the room, making a point not to linger on any one person. "The guy who just came in? No."

Wayne strode over. "You ought to move on out." He rubbed my back. "You feeling okay to do this?"

"That's Purdue Heyward over there," I said to him.

From his deepening crow's feet, Wayne affirmed the identity. Savvy's face blanched.

Her expression told me she'd probably witnessed the real Dan Heyward sign the loan, diminishing the likelihood she had anything to do with fraudulent signatures. I knew Heyward by voice only, and he knew me via my overzealous distribution of business cards. I wanted to keep it that way. Wayne, however, worked through the crowd toward Sheriff Goff. Unfortunately, so did the farmer.

Wayne tapped the sheriff's shoulder as I caught up. "Goff, may we have a word with you?"

"Sure," he said, but as any gent taught by any decent Southern mama would do, the sheriff first introduced us to the other man walking up. "Y'all met Purdue Heyward?"

I almost groaned aloud.

"We've met," Wayne said.

The farmer's red hair curled around the edges of a baseball cap with the emblem of a pesticide company. Poison. How appropriate. He smiled at

Wayne and held out his hand. Wayne passed on the shake and dipped his chin. I glanced away, as if someone in the throng caught my attention.

Wayne stared hard at Goff. "Can we talk privately?"

He nodded. "Come into my office."

"Might I borrow a cup of your coffee?" Purdue asked with a cavalier smirk.

"Help yourself, Heyward. Right over there," Goff said before he led us down one of the halls.

Wayne shut the door to the big room adorned with wooden, brass, and gold accolades on the wall. Lots of gratuitous slaps and shakes in photo moments and plaques dating back twenty years praised the man for his crime-fighting exploits.

Wayne moved to the center of the room. "Sheriff, you know I'm checking into Heyward's business activities concerning serious irregularities. Jamie's disappearance most likely connects with the drugs making their way around St. Helena, Heyward's home turf."

Goff slumped into his chair and toyed with the silver pen on his desk. "And you know as well as I do that without proof I can't do a blessed thing. Don't read me wrong. I ain't for or against the man, but—"

"Excuse me," I said, "but this is the man who threatened to *come after me.*" I leaned on the massive polished walnut desk, and Goff seemed to muse over my hands crossing some invisible boundary, daring to touch his esteemed property. "He's got honest-to-God slaves on his farm." The Haitian girl's dead, blotchy face came back all too clear. "I talked to one of them, and now she's in the morgue. She warned me that Purdue tortures them and kills the ones who open their mouths."

The barrel-chested sheriff moved his mouth around like he tasted my words, sorting them to spit back at me. "Miz Slade," he said, emphasizing my name like a teacher about to critique my tardiness. "I've got a missing boy. If the devil offered to help find him, I'd take him up on it. Heyward knows a lot of people, as well as the terrain."

"Probably all the cons and misfits, too," I said.

"Look," Wayne said. "Our department wants to cooperate with yours, but . . ."

Footsteps walked up and down the hall, as if telling us to hurry back to where real business took place. Goff's thumbs tucked inside his belt. "I appreciate your help, but I also appreciate Heyward's. Let's try to keep our concentration on finding that boy." He turned to Wayne. "Agent, that kid is still a person of interest in that bar murder. I'm not gonna have any trouble out of y'all, am I?"

"Absolutely not," Wayne said.

"What do you mean person of interest?" I asked.

Leather and springs groaned as Goff rose and released his chair from the burden. "Let's get to it. We can sort Heyward later." He left the office, expecting us to follow.

I stopped Wayne in the hall. "Jamie wouldn't kill Martin. That's ludicrous."

Wayne started back toward the lobby. "We've lost enough time, Slade. Let's find Jamie."

As we entered the lobby, Purdue fingered an unlit cigar as the sheriff reached out to shake hands. "Be glad to accept your help, sir." They shook like business partners. I wondered.

Purdue's threat resonated too clearly from my night on the shed roof. I wanted a piece of the scum, but as the deputies explained, the sheriff could just as easily lock me up for trespassing.

As we tried to walk past, urgent in our effort to leave, the farmer gave me the iciest stare I'd ever seen over a smile. "Excuse me, Sheriff, but I didn't get the lady's name."

Wayne stopped, which meant I stopped. Unfortunately, all three men turned toward me, including Wayne, damn him.

The sheriff touched my shoulder. I steeled myself not to shirk his touch. "This is Ms. Carolina Slade. You met before?"

Purdue's expression was saccharin-coated. "There is something familiar about her." He held out his hand. "A pleasure to know you, Ms. Slade. Have we met?"

I resettled my purse on my shoulder, a stranglehold on the straps. "No."

"Nice to make your acquaintance then." He dipped at the waist ever so slightly and touched his ball cap.

I spun and stomped away. Stepping over to Savvy, I pinched her shirtsleeve and tugged her to go outside. "Get me out of here." A deputy followed and chatted alongside Wayne as we exited.

"What a load of chicken crap," I said, blowing hot air through puffed cheeks. "The crook helping the cops."

At Savvy's car, a young deputy introduced himself. "Deputy Drew Harley," he said. "They assigned me to your group. Your car or mine?"

"What?" fell out of my mouth and "huh?" dropped from Savvy's.

"A law enforcement official's assigned to almost every search party," Wayne said, walking up. He gestured toward a patrol car and turned to Deputy Harley. "Think you can manage them in your vehicle?"

He laughed. "I'll try. Y'all ready, ladies?"

"You're a lawman," I said to Wayne, recognizing his posturing to supply us with a bodyguard. "Why can't you go with us?" Then checking out the squad car, added, "And who gets to be the person in the backseat?

Behind the cage?"

"Don't argue, please. You've already cheated a bullet once. Accept the protection." Wayne opened the back door for me. "Y'all stay together. I'd prefer you not get out and walk around."

My gaze twisted left to the handle-less confinement, and in front to the cage, the Plexiglas over the back of the front seat. No leg room. "Is this how you intend to control me?"

"Never crossed my mind." He leaned over and kissed me. "I know you think you're fine, but I still don't take anything for granted. You've got your phone. I've got Monroe's. Call if you see anything."

He peered in the front seat. "Savannah, make her behave."

She winked. "Sure thing, lawman."

"I'm not believing this," I grumbled.

Wayne closed me in. "Since Heyward's decided to get involved, thought I'd pair up with one of Heyward's boys, just to see if they're up to anything." He strode a couple steps away. "Y'all be careful."

As we drove off, I nervously watched Wayne greet someone who resembled Louis, the Straw Boss, but I could've been mistaken.

All search teams were instructed to reconvene at the sheriff's station no later than five p.m. My watch read nine a.m. Our assignment included a stretch on Seaside Road. Savvy, Officer Drew, and I intended to drive every road and path we could, and walk the ones we couldn't. It's not that I didn't care what Wayne said about staying in the car, but a boy's life was at stake.

Zoning didn't exist in this area. Unless one lived in Beaufort, on Fripp Island, or around the many parks and reserves, a person bought a piece of this semi-wet dirt and built, hoping someone of similar financial means bought the neighboring land.

Longtime residents and heirs burrowed in, protecting what was theirs, knowing the two- and three-story dream homes constructed next to them raised property taxes. The older owners went to bed at night praying they could pay the tax collector another year. This saltwater haven was too beautiful for anyone to let go. It pitted the haves and have-littles against each other. In our search for Jamie, we needed to knock on both kinds of residences.

At the first stop, Drew and Savvy stepped out, ready to make inquiries.

"Hey," I yelled from the locked cage. "I can't get out."

Drew jogged back, smirking. Savvy threw her head back in a laugh.

"Not funny," I said as Drew released me. "Don't you even think about keeping me in there; I don't care what Agent Largo said to you."

Smile still on his face, he escorted me to the first house. "I won't tell if you don't."

Six houses, then twelve, then twenty. We hopped over chains blocking paths, stopping just short of disappearing in waist-high weeds. We stood on several docks, studied thickets of reeds, under piers, and among waterlogged tree roots. Drew pretended not to notice the .38 hidden in my pocket, in case of snakes.

On the south side of the road, paths dead-ended at the water with marsh seeping in and out of vegetation. We sullied up the Crown Vic's floor pretty bad.

Drew approached homes alone, Savvy and I in tandem. The recent number of bodies made me pause before meeting each stranger, and I didn't like the feeling. Maybe Wayne had planted that fear. Regardless, I hated it. I'd inspected many a property, called on many a property owner in my last job as a loan manager, and this should be no different. I started flashing the badge and speaking bolder, saying we were investigators with the sheriff's office searching for a missing teenage boy. While it made people listen, no one offered information.

Around two p.m., Savvy and I stood on a dock that reached over the water then branched left and right like a large *T*. I popped a pain pill and chased it with bottled water.

"You all right?" she asked.

"A pinch here or there, and a headache," I said. But this wasn't about me, and I wanted nobody taking me back prematurely. "So, weird-looking dock we have here."

"Chandler Nugent owns this half of it," Savvy said.

"The billionaire?" I said. "Can't he afford the whole dock?"

"Estate thing. The previous owner's kids sold the acreage and one sold his end of the dock. Chandler bought it."

I glanced sideways at her. "Chandler, huh?"

"Oh yeah," she said, brushing some kind of weed seed off her pants. "We've met. Dated the guy who helps manage the place for him in the winter."

"Aren't you special?" Here I stood on a billionaire's dock, facing a billionaire's island with concrete block houses to my left and a dilapidated brick ranch to my right, both abandoned. "Think we should check those houses?"

We peered in windows, calling Jamie's name. A quiver scurried down my back at the memory of hunting my children through run-down shacks like this. This one, however, was beyond redemption, and we didn't dare risk entering for fear of roof trusses caving in on our skulls. We climbed through a locked fence and followed the shell and gravel path back to the Crown Vic. Drew leaned on the car hood, after having checked a small brick house across the road.

"I just don't see how we're going to find him," I said. "If you snatched someone, would you dump the body somewhere easy to see?"

"I'd dump him in the marsh, or better yet, out at sea," Savvy said, climbing in the vehicle.

"Like the Haitian girl? Like Dan Heyward?" I replied.

"You never know what people'll do," Drew said, folding into the driver's seat after banging his sandy boots against the threshold.

Savvy stared in her rearview mirror and winked at me. "What do you think about that murder at the Sand Briar, Drew?" she asked.

He adjusted yet again to a comfortable position and started the engine. "I expect a drug deal gone bad."

"Who do you figure did it?"

"When it comes to drugs, no telling," he said.

She twisted sweaty curls. "You heard Theodore Dawson's name mentioned?"

"It's been tossed around."

"So has Jamie's," I said and watched a mockingbird strut on a pine bough to my right. "What she's asking, Drew, is who do they think killed Martin?"

"Too soon to tell," he said. "Let's cover the next road, okay, ladies?"

Savvy pouted and put a final twist to her hair.

Drew pulled onto another side road and stopped. "Want to drive it or walk it?" We already dripped from the humidity and heat. My back seat jail ran several degrees hotter than the front.

"Leave the AC running," I said and punched a number on the cell. "I want to check in with the sheriff's office."

"No, let me," Drew said, reaching for the radio. "Search team eleven needs an update. We've covered our area."

"Hon, we've got a mess." The woman sounded collected yet busy, like I imagined police station people would. "Someone'll be right with you. Anyone not searching ran over to the packing shed. They've got a hellacious disaster over there."

"Triple R or Sweetgrass?" I hollered for her to hear, but Drew had to repeat it. Either choice meant bad news. One was an ally, the other full of evidence.

"The Rabon place," she answered. "Place burned clean to the ground this afternoon. Young Doug's in rough shape."

I trembled briefly from the combination of chilled air, moist skin, and the news. Our case grew more ominous and invasive with everything we touched.

"No one has found the boy," she said. "Finish your assigned area and report back so we can mark the region complete. Dispatch out."

As badly as I wanted to find the kid, our search efforts held slim to no chance for success at this point, in this area anyway. Guess we were done.

"I'm calling Wayne," I said. A recorded message indicated no service. "Crap, forgot his phone got blitzed in the mud last night. He's got Monroe's." I called the other number. No pick up.

I made Drew call the station back. The same tired woman answered. "Have the other teams checked in?" he asked. "We're interested in the Wayne Largo party. We're unable to raise them."

"Just one moment."

We sat still, waiting to hear.

The woman came back on. "Largo's party last checked in at three."

Drew nodded. "What did they say?"

"They hadn't found anything. But it's about time everyone came in. Only three out of ten parties haven't—yours, Mr. Largo's, and two deputies caught up in an emergency."

Drew hung up. We drove back. It was a little after four. I was probably too edgy about Wayne not calling in, especially after yesterday's scare, but cell reception proved iffy in spots and it hadn't been that long since he'd reported. Twenty or so cars filled the parking lot when we arrived back at the sheriff's office.

My phone rang. "Slade," I answered and smiled as a deputy nearby said "Go Tigers" upon hearing the ringtone.

"You aren't gonna believe what we saw," Monroe said.

"Seen or hear from Wayne?" I asked impatiently.

"Listen, Slade," Monroe continued. "We think we saw the shrimp boat."

"The one we saw the other day?"

"Yeah. Nowhere near where it was before. We found a different spot."

Evan spoke loudly in the background. "They're up in Story Creek near the old Pritchard place," he said. "Nobody on it, but we didn't want to risk being seen. We drove close enough to see a Georgia registration."

"You hear that?" Monroe asked.

"Yeah. You really think it's the same boat?" I asked.

Evan took the phone and put me on speaker. "Hey, it's me. And yeah, I think it's the one I appraised for the loan."

"Wait a minute," I said. "How do you know that from two years ago?"

"Because I know boats. Because every shrimp boat is custom-made. I recall the shape of that cabin and the bow. Profiles are distinctive—the way they ride in the water, the height of the outrigger. The name might say *Magic Moment,* but that's the same boat we listed as *Magnolia Lady.* I took a picture for the file. Didn't you see it?"

Evan didn't know the file had been stolen.

"There's no picture in the file," I lied.

"I might have an extra in my desk," he said, not questioning the missing picture. "I save copies."

"No need if you can point it out for us," I said. "Hold on a minute." I turned to Savvy. "Can you register a boat in two states?"

"And insure it, and use it for collateral?" Savvy added. "The simple answer is no."

I raised a finger. "Purdue drives a Suburban with a Georgia tag. What else do we know about Georgia while we're brainstorming here?"

"It's the Peachtree State," said Monroe.

Savvy rolled her eyes and shook her head. "Raye's from Georgia," she then said.

We waited for the connection.

"She wasn't even here when we made the damn loan, Savvy. Scratch that," said Evan.

"Scratch anymore brainstorming," I said. "Someone's going to hurt themselves."

Savvy spoke up. "Speaking of Raye, did you check in with her?"

"No, you're the boss," Evan replied

"I didn't have my cell phone."

"You could've used Slade's."

"Forget it," I said. "Let's go see that boat. Can you get us there by land?"

Everyone went silent. Exasperated, I said, "I'm not letting today set on a clue like that. As long as Wayne is still out with Purdue's gang, hunting for Jamie, we can check out the boat without Heyward catching on, hopefully. You coming or staying?"

Savvy slung her bag over her shoulder. "You know I'm coming, hon."

Evan said, "Got nothing better to do."

"My knee kind of throbs," Monroe said.

"Oh, geez."

"What a wuss."

"Whatever."

"Fine. I'll come," he agreed.

"Meet us at Jake's Landing," Evan said. "Savvy knows it. We're almost there now."

We hung up, climbed into Savvy's Benz, and struck out. I wasn't sure what we hoped to accomplish. However, if it was the same boat, Heywood had two lies to account for: why disguise the boat to begin with, and how did cousin Dan actually die? I'd let Wayne and his kind take the reins once we nailed this boat as the *Magnolia Lady*, alive and well and not in pieces at the bottom of the Atlantic Ocean.

Chapter 31

MONROE AND EVAN were leaning on Evan's boat trailer when we arrived.

Savvy scanned the interior of her vehicle. "My car's rather obvious, don't you think?" she asked, as the men approached. "Can we unhitch your SUV and use it? It's a bit more nondescript."

In five minutes, the trailer was parked to the side of the landing's lot, and the four of us piled into Evan's Jeep. Evan described where they'd seen the boat, Savvy nodding with each reference point.

"Anybody on the boat?" I asked.

"No," both men said.

"Okay, listen," I said, a finger tapping on my chin. "This is what we're gonna do. Purdue and his hands are still out with Wayne. Before we go see the boat, let's do one more thing. That isolated tract of land where they keep equipment is only three miles down this way." I pointed as if we'd turn left from the parking lot. "Purdue pretty much hates Monroe and me, and probably Savvy by now. Evan, you're guilty by association. Since there're four of us, and with the farmer preoccupied, we can determine how much equipment is out there and be done with the place, while we have good daylight."

Wayne would be proud of my safe logic, plus I didn't want to have to come back to this farm ever again. "Sound good?"

Everyone agreed. Accounting for equipment and livestock was mundane, easy work, and four people would knock it out in no time.

The sun shone immensely bright, and I'd forgotten my sunglasses. Soon Evan jostled us over bumps and holes to park us in the shade outside the small enclosed shed attached to a twenty-by-forty open pole barn where Monroe and I had walked before.

"There are some new pieces out here," Monroe said, opening his door.

Evan retrieved a notepad from his glove box and gave us each a sheet of paper.

"You take that side," I said to Savvy, nodding toward the west. "Monroe the back, Evan east, and I'll take the stuff in front of the barn."

We climbed over harrows, tractors, wagons, and spreaders for twenty minutes, eager to gain closure on this part of our job, with this particular farmer.

"Evan," I said as he went down on one knee to study a plow. "How come you don't know Purdue and those lunatics that work for him? You knew how to get out here, so why didn't you know they had that huge dude with a shotgun and his nutty friend Hank?"

Savvy walked up. "I'm done. And I want the answer to that question, too, mister."

Evan slapped a gnat off his neck. "We've got a hundred farmers on our books. Even Savvy doesn't know them all."

Savvy twisted her mouth in thought. "I know ninety percent of them. But you're my eyes and ears in the field, Evan."

He rose, looking serious and folded his paper, tucking it in his shirt pocket. "In good faith I took an application from someone who I thought was Dan Heyward. Never saw him or his cousin after that. I knew where the crops were from county agriculture files and where the equipment was from when I first valued all of it for the loan." He stared at me. "Am I a suspect now?"

Frankly, I didn't see him as culpable for anything, but neither was Savvy. Evan had originated the loan, which could easily mean he helped orchestrate the whole affair and had been handsomely paid. He could've been duped. Someone had assisted the Heywards. Evan's head was on the block as much as Savvy's. I'd tell Wayne when I caught up to him. Hell, he probably already knew.

"I hear you, Evan," I said. "Just get this equipment categorized and let's get out of here. We need to go check out that shrimp boat."

Evan walked to the Jeep, where Monroe already stood, making notes on his list. Savvy nonchalantly moved next to me, pretending to read her paper. "Need I worry about Evan?"

"Not sure," I replied. "He can't recall what Dan Heyward looks like, but knows the farm? Then he remembered that shrimp boat like he'd appraised it yesterday."

She glanced at his back. "Yeah."

"How well do you know Raye? And Melanie, for that matter, since she was the one who closed the loan."

Savvy looked surprised, if not a tad hurt. "You saying I can't run my office?"

I grasped her arm and walked her away to a quieter spot. "I've had staff backstab me before. It's easy to miss when they don't want you to know . . . and you think they're on your side. You're the one most in the dark on this farmer, hon. Think about it."

Monroe rubbed his forehead with the back of his hand. "Slade, it's hot and I'm tired of this idiotic case."

Evan folded his pad. "You and me both. I imagine they'll be foreclosing all this stuff soon."

"We're done here," I said. It was too hot and sticky for a mutiny. Savvy and I walked to the Jeep. I peered across at Evan. "Purdue said he'll take over Dan's obligations. Better study this place thoroughly, because you'll be inspecting it on a regular basis from now on."

He threw an insincere grin at me. "At least Teddy won't be around."

Savvy's expression tightened to anger. "What the friggin' hell does that mean?"

Evan went to get in the vehicle. "I just don't like the lying bastard."

"No, you hold on. All Teddy did was report back to me if the tomato crop did well." She jerked her hand back and forth as if showing how they were on opposite ends of a spectrum. "Heyward . . . Teddy. Teddy has nothing to do with Heyward."

So why did I think he did?

A man's scream erupted from the woods.

Birds flushed into the air. All four of us froze like a clipped movie film.

Fear crawled up my spine, and Monroe's shock-filled eyes met mine, his mouth agape.

The scream erupted again. A nerve grinding sound of someone in extreme agony.

Evan darted for the tree line.

I jumped into the driver's seat and shouted, "Get in."

The terrible sound came again, a death-filled screech.

"Get in the damn car!" I yelled, fighting the vision of a Haitian being tortured. I threw Monroe my phone. "Call 9-1-1."

Monroe jumped into the passenger side, Savvy in back. I fumbled with the key, then cranked up the motor and floored the gas, pointing the car at the origin of the macabre noise. Evan ran like a damn deer and was almost at the woods. We mashed Johnson grass out of the way, grasshoppers flying, not thinking of what the hell we'd accomplish upon reaching the desperate soul.

Monroe pointed. "There he goes."

I drove white-knuckled as the wheels bounced along the rutted track shaking us all to hell. Evan reached a dense stand of wax myrtles having the advantage of a beeline versus our curved road. Shrubs and limbs suddenly split apart as a truck exploded from the woods. Evan dove behind a tree, and the vehicle missed him by inches.

Migrant men packed the old Ford pickup from bumper to bumper inside, on the running board, seated in the open windows and spilling out of the bed. Their whoops filled the air as they pumped fists and beat the truck's metal with sticks.

Rene drove and hollered out the window with the loudest of them.
Our Jeep blocked the one-lane path.

They sped up.

Metal tore against metal as the Ford raked the side of our Jeep. I veered off the path plunging through grown-over tomato rows, bouncing, hitting the roof as we came off our seats. My ribs struck the steering wheel, knocking wind out of me just as my head hit the rim of the driver's window.

About the time I thought I could regain purchase on the old path, a sickening bang resounded from the undercarriage. The floor vibrated, and an explosive *pow* filled the air as we jolted to an abrupt halt, throwing me to the floor, my knee resting on the brake and my back bent against the seat.

As I clamored back onto the seat, I twisted to locate the truck. It veered right, onto the two-lane, and flew toward the end of the island, probably to rendezvous on a stolen boat since there was no other way to escape.

Seeing Monroe, a gash on his head, blood everywhere on his shirt, sobered me. I turned the engine over again until it coughed to life and shoved my foot down. The dangling mirror bounced like a marionette, held only by a wire. Whatever struck the bottom of the Jeep had turned the gentle purr of the engine into an intermittent chugging noise, but I still had acceleration. Twenty feet later, however, the vehicle died, listing awkwardly to the left.

Evan had vanished. Monroe moaned and kept his eyes shut, as if holding a migraine at bay. I glanced at Savvy, crawling up off the floor of the backseat. "You okay?"

"I'm good," she said, huffing as she breathed hard. "We should've put on our seatbelts."

Monroe's face initially looked a mess. I slid over and pulled his hand away from the one-inch gash. It didn't appear deep, but the whack had disoriented him. He reached up, trying to clear blood from his eye.

I flipped open the glove compartment, fished out a first aid kit we were required to keep in any of our cars used in the field, and pressed a dressing into Monroe's hand. Savvy leaned over, helping.

"Just sit there, then," I said, hunting for the phone that seemed to have vanished in the mayhem.

I rolled down the windows. A motley assortment of bugs flitted in. Then a waft of something acrid caught my nose. A column of gray cloud spiraled from inside the tree line.

Evan yelled from somewhere in the brush. "Slade! Monroe! Help me!"

My blood turned cold. "Evan?" Then realizing the distance, I hollered, "Evan?"

"Oh, God, please help!" he cried again, gasps breaking up his words.

In a split second, I chose to leave the other two in the car. And I ran. Hard. At the woods' edge, I held out my arm for support against a gum tree, doing my damnedest to listen between panting breaths. The smell had become a stench, and it was powerful.

"Evan?" I called, hearing labored breathing and grunts.

"Over here!" he cried.

I crashed through the brambles, and dead wood cracked beneath my feet. Coughing, eyes watering, I scurried to a clearing where a bonfire licked and crackled, smoke now swirling around me. The odor flipped my stomach, crawling into my sinuses, my chest.

Evan struggled madly to kick logs off the fire. The two of us kicked dirt into the flames. I fell to my knees, scooping and tossing handfuls of dead leaves and soil. Savvy appeared and joined in, her face sheet-white.

In the meantime, a man burned.

No more screaming.

No movement at all.

Just a deep, putrid mix of a sulfurous, burnt, steaky smell we could taste.

Sweat pouring down our faces and backs, we scraped up and flung soil. When our hands wouldn't work, we kicked again as we frantically, randomly moved the dirt in any way possible. Evan found a branch and knocked burning logs away. It was like spitting in the ocean, expecting the tide to rise.

Eventually we dampened the fire and dropped to the ground, drenched with sweat. Savvy stared into the woods, tears coursing down her red cheeks. Evan, his filthy hands gripping his knees, sunk forward, his head bowed from exhaustion.

I stared at the smoldering body.

A ten-foot creosote pole rose from a shallow, ash-covered pit. This wasn't the first fire burned here. How many poor souls had met the same horrendous fate?

The body of the man, skin crusted black, slumped about four-foot high amidst smoking limbs and ashes, his hair burnt away. The arms stretched taut behind, bare of any shirt, charred, eaten by fire. Random pieces of cloth melted into muscle, shreds of some material held on due to a leather belt. Loafers still on his feet. Even tethered to the pole, the body curled in an effort to reach a fetal tuck, frozen in place, now crusty and black. None of Purdue's men wore Docksiders.

"Call 9-1-1," I shouted, falling to the ground spent, soaked through to my underwear. "Call 9-1-1," I said again, leaning my forehead on the dirt.

"Already have, Slade," Monroe said as he knelt beside me and placed a gentle hand on my shoulder. At his touch, I bent over and sobbed muffled cries into the dust. Savvy slid beside us, soot covered and out of breath.

"Did you see him?" Evan cried, pacing, pointing deeper into the pines. His steps hesitated as he thought about running toward whatever he imagined. "I saw somebody. He could have started this fire."

Choked from smoke, tears, and dirt, I lifted my head. What the fuck was wrong with him? "Evan, the people who did this ran us over. I recognized the driver. I saw his sister in the morgue yesterday." My words came out raspy from the smoke. "They got even," I said more for myself, no louder than a mumble.

Then I stiffened at the new image before me. Evan lifted a still-smoldering log with bare hands, as if some specter might rise up and challenge him. His eyes stretched wild with fear. "Did you see him, Slade? He might come back."

In a quick rundown of all the players, I deduced he might mean Hank. Hank tended the migrants. Hank wasn't at the sheriff's office. Hank seemed the most squirrely of the lot. Glancing back at the smoking pillar, I'd bet my job that the burned body was Teddy's.

Identifying the smoldering carnage, hair lifted on the nape of my neck. My gaze darted from tree to tree, like Evan's. "Oh, Jesus," I whispered, infected with Evan's paranoia, half-expecting Hank to run out. Maybe even the Hulk with his almighty shotgun.

Monroe rose, standing between Evan and me. Savvy seemed unusually quiet.

"Get down," I hissed, tugging Monroe's pant leg. "Don't stir him up."

"Put down the log," Monroe said calmly.

Evan stepped forward. "I'm not the bad guy. I tried to save Teddy," he shrieked.

When Savvy didn't freak at the mention of his name, I knew she knew.

"We understand," Monroe said. "Hand me the log or drop it. Just get a grip on yourself, man."

"Would Hank be out here, Evan?" I asked.

He gripped that log like it was his last link to this world, in spite of burning pain I could only imagine.

"Hank's got nothing against you, Evan," I said.

Evan's stare bored into me. "Hank's bad news. Real bad."

"I get that," I said.

He spun around and grabbed his hair. "Goddamn, what the hell happened here? I didn't know they killed people."

"Monroe," I said slowly. "Give me the phone."

Evan lurched at Monroe, lifting the log. "Don't!"

What exactly did Heyward have on Evan? I rose to my knees. "Evan, sit down. Tell us what happened."

He wiped furiously at the sweat and tears running down his face, leaving smears of ash and blood on his cheeks and neck. "Teddy did this." He shook his fist at Savvy. She retreated, complexion paling.

"The bastard held those papers over me," he said. "I seriously thought Purdue was Dan when I first took that loan. What was I supposed to do with Teddy threatening to say I set up the deal?" Evan grumbled. "Then he made me send him insurance business, telling people they had to use him."

The idiot had kept quiet, willing to let Savvy go down for this mess.

Savvy clenched her hands together in front of her, against her chest. "Evan, why didn't you come to me? I could've handled Teddy."

He snickered with a half-grin. "Seriously? The way he manipulated you?"

Bingo at that, I thought. Teddy blackmailed Evan and distracted Savvy. All that was left was Raye. As timid as she was, Heyward surely held her under his thumb, too. This whole damn office was infested with the Heyward virus.

An ember popped. Evan spun to face it.

Monroe reached down to help me up. Evan, seeing the movement from the corner of his eye, swung in a roundhouse move, laying the wood across Monroe's upper back, clipping the back of his head en route. My partner dropped, taking me down with him. Savvy scurried backwards on her butt several feet until halted by a tree.

Monroe lay face down in the dirt. I rolled him over and brushed the debris off his cheeks. My fingers worked deftly yet frantically through his hair to the back of his head. No cuts. No blood. Good. But a scary knot already rose behind his right ear. I glanced up, fighting to hide the uncontrollable shivers of alarm in my shoulders as our plight took shape. I'd only been skeptical of Evan before. Here on my knees, I feared him.

Evan watched, the log acting as a fulcrum as he rocked side to side. "Why did he move like that? I didn't mean to hit him."

"You son-of-a-bitch," I said, with a slight catch in my voice.

Evan's eyes darted between me and the barbecued body. Teddy's demise had shoved him over the edge. Good and bad bled together now, and Evan lashed out at anything.

"Evan," I said, fighting for peace in my tone, to keep him from being so skittish. We ought to be hearing sirens any moment. "You recognized that the *Magnolia Lady* was the original boat when you found it with Monroe. That's when you started putting pieces together, wasn't it? You're the bigger detective on this case."

"Like I said, boats are customized." The log lowered lazily as he spoke, then he brought it back up, as if waking up from a nod in Algebra class.

"There was no picture in the file, so we had to rely on you. Good job."

His brow raised as he turned toward me, appeared genuinely surprised. "You found the file? Where did Teddy put it? The bastard wouldn't tell me."

I recalled the argument again between the two men in the parking lot, Teddy holding papers over Evan's head.

As I looked down to study Monroe's face for signs of consciousness, he moaned and opened his eyes. Thank Heaven. He groaned again. I brushed a couple ants off his cheek. "Lay still."

Clipped whoops of a police siren sounded from the road. I heard automobiles reach the barn, one navigating toward us.

I turned to study Evan's reaction, expecting him to explode yet again. Instead he spoke on his phone. The log rested atop the fire. "Yes, we've had a bad situation on a distant tract of the Heyward farm . . . oh, wait, the police have already arrived."

Deputy Drew broke through the trees and six other uniforms followed, poised on holstered weapons. One deputy halted and ran back, hollering, "Bring me a fire extinguisher and make it quick!"

Drew helped Monroe stand. "What in heaven happened out here?"

"Goddamn," exclaimed a middle-aged black deputy. "What the hell is that?" He walked in hesitant steps to examine the cadaver closer.

I stood on the other side of Monroe, my arm looped through his in case he wobbled.

Evan reached over to shake a deputy's hand, and the deputy obliged, pissing me off.

"We were just checking equipment, and we must've interrupted something. Damn Haitians tried to run us down. Then we found Teddy on fire and busted our asses trying to . . . put him out." Tears formed in his eyes and ran down his dirty face. "I overreacted when Monroe made a sudden move . . ." He choked up and patted Monroe's back. "Sorry, man."

Monroe stared at him from behind a flat-lined mouth.

Evan had cleanly transformed from aggressor to victim.

Drew turned to Savvy and me. "Are you ladies all right?"

I wiped a sweaty trail of grunge off my face, my insides somersaulting at the deception playing out. "Just marvelous. Monroe really needs a doctor, so we need to go."

Another deputy with more brass on his chest walked up. "An ambulance is on its way. They'll take this gentleman back to town, along with that one," he said nodding toward Evan. Savvy's assistant held his hands in front of him now, open for all to see his wounds, everyone assuming him the martyr from trying to put out a fire bare-handed.

Monroe caught my gaze and held it. Our shared, near-catastrophe put us on the same wavelength, even if he knew nothing of investigations.

Bottom line: we couldn't pin anything on Evan. Our word against his.

I glanced at the cooked Teddy Dawson. I had no more tears for the guy.

After some questions, Drew led Savvy and me away from deputies who were analyzing and studying the crime scene, the senior of them on a radio.

"Over here!" shouted one. We stopped in our tracks.

Three uniforms ran to where he stood in the far part of the clearing, behind myrtles and pines, vines snaking around them all. "Got us another body! This one's not burned. Anybody know him?"

People moved to the woods' edge, Savvy's hand clutching my wrist and cutting off circulation. I had one arm wrapped around her shoulder, fingers twisted in her shirt sleeve. Drew rested a hand on each of our shoulders as we took slow steps in that direction.

"It's Hank!" Evan yelled.

I blew out a hard breath. We'd take his word on the identification. The migrants had given back as good as they'd gotten from that particular Musketeer, and I didn't care to see their handiwork.

We turned around just as a deputy walked up . . . with Jamie.

"Found him tied in the shed over there," the badge said, nodding toward the barn. "Perfectly fine. Just scared and hungry."

"I ain't scared," the boy said.

Elated at something good resulting from the day's disasters, I broke away and hugged Jamie as if he were my own. "Oh my God, I'm so happy to see you healthy," I said, emotions building up in me again. "I bet you have a story to tell."

"Yes, *ma'am*," he exclaimed. "Did you catch Teddy Dawson?"

"No problem, Jamie," I said. "That business is taken care of."

"I saw their boat, Ms. Slade. They almost shipped me out to sea!"

"What kind of boat?" I asked.

"Shrimp boat," he said. "Teddy hid me on it. Some Mexican man about shot us for trespassing, and we hauled ass to get away. Teddy said he'd show 'em, so he locked me up here, on Heyward's farm."

Sharing the blame for the kidnapping, I guessed, but all of this still didn't make sense. This boy shouldn't be alive. "Why didn't Teddy ki—, um, hurt you?"

Jamie lowered his head, and when he peered back up, his eyes misted. "I never should've agreed to meet with Teddy Dawson. It was all a mistake. Martin got mad. Teddy got madder. Martin threw a punch then pulled out a knife. Teddy accidentally killed him. Martin woulda killed him otherwise. Teddy must've apologized to me a hundred times."

Not the best testament for Teddy Dawson but one that proved what I said before. Too much jelly in the spine. This time I was glad the man was too much of a coward to kill a teenage boy.

Placing myself in front of a tearful Savvy, I held both her forearms. "Did you hear that? Teddy might've screwed up, but he couldn't murder a kid. Just like you said."

Forget the fact he did kill Martin and I suspected he shot at me, but with Teddy dead in such an atrocious manner, saying the words to her seemed malicious.

Savvy didn't cry, didn't turn red-faced, and didn't throw me over the hood of the nearest car. Instead, she just said, "I know what Teddy was, Slade. And I'll deal with it." And with that, she walked to where Drew stood beside his patrol car.

Before I left, I drew the boy by the arm, closer. "Was Evan involved, Jamie?"

"Evan who, Ms. Slade?"

Chapter 32

ONCE AGAIN I sat in the caged backseat of Drew's police cruiser, the deputy giving particular attention to Savvy, who seemed unusually quiet.

"They'll want you ladies to give statements at the main office," he said.

Savvy just stared out the window.

"Mind if we get our car first?" I asked. "We left it at Jake's Landing. I imagine someone will have to help Evan retrieve his boat there, too. But we'll meet you back at the SO. Nothing we'd like better than to help you put pieces together against Purdue Heyward."

He glanced at me via his rearview mirror. "Not sure Heyward gets drawn into this, Ms. Slade. Just because a murder took place on his property doesn't make him guilty of anything."

Falling back in the seat, I studied the ceiling and sighed. What did it take to connect the dots for these law enforcement types? Didn't anybody follow their Spidey-senses anymore? Had gut-instinct gone the way of Dragnet reruns? The car slowed. "There it is, over there," I said, hitting my hand on the cage as I tried to point to Savvy's Mercedes.

"Sweet ride," he said, pulling up next to it.

"Come on, Savvy, I'm driving," I said. "Let me out of prison and give me your keys."

"Don't be long," Drew said, releasing me from my containment. "We'll be waiting for you."

It wasn't dusk yet, but light was fading. Lights came on around the outside of Jake's store. "Savvy and I need a Coke and a minute to allow our stomachs to settle down. Then we'll see you at the station."

As the patrol car reached the road and turned right toward town, I turned to Savvy. "You need a soft drink? If so, get it, because we need to run."

She gave a deep, weighted sigh. "Thought we had time. You just said—"

"We need to find that shrimp boat."

FIFTEEN MINUTES later, I shut off our headlights and cruised in the dusk. I parked a half mile past the gravel path to the tucked away dock that supposedly moored the *Magnolia Lady*, and pulled the snub-nosed .38 out of my purse to slide it into my pocket.

Savvy and I exited the car, half hidden in draping vines and undergrowth that infringed into the skinny two-lane road. We kept to the edge of the asphalt for a half mile. I prayed we wouldn't see someone and have to dive into thorns and heaven knows what. It was that time of day when the sun hadn't set and the night hadn't yet absorbed the colors, when the scenery carried reddish hues, and sights and sounds weren't always what they seemed. We stayed silent for fear someone in a shanty or behind a thicket would hear. The stand of trees and brush blocked the waning sun.

No-see-ums found us without any trouble—the tiniest of tiny gnats that swarm on human flesh in airborne clusters. We swatted at them, knowing it did no good, rubbing our noses, digging in our ears. One of the few flaws of Lowcountry living was insects. You didn't get rid of them; you learned to live with them. Or you moved.

We edged off the gravel to moist ground to muffle the sound of our shoes, Savvy in the lead. Green briar dug into my jeans and flesh. Once I ran into Savvy when she halted, stepping on her heel.

"Do you realize we don't have a phone?" she whispered.

Crap. Monroe had mine, and Savvy'd left hers at home. "Well, it's too late to worry about that now."

Like Keystone Kops, we trekked around pines, oaks, and bald cypress, tripping on myrtle and wild olive, hoping to avoid snakes and fire ant mounds. We prayed we'd hear a gator before it heard us. Finally we arrived at the edge of the vegetation, facing the saltwater river.

The boat was docked exactly where Evan and Monroe said they'd seen it earlier, but now people moved around on it, dammit. There was no mistaking the shape of the Hulk.

My eyes adjusted to the encroaching darkness. We huddled behind an ancient oak and scanned the makeshift parking area of weeds and rock. Fifty feet away sat two cars side by side, one a Suburban that could only belong to Purdue. Even in the dim light I made out the red hair.

By now Wayne was probably pacing at the sheriff's office, cursing me for all he was worth, pestering the stew out of Monroe on my cell phone.

Savvy and I focused on the boat.

The muggy air formed droplets under my clothes, tickling as they ran between my breasts. A gnat found its way under my shirt, and with tense muscles, I fought the desire to fish it out.

Under the dim orange glow of a lone lamp on a pole, the Hulk loaded gym bags similar to those I'd seen them move before. He spoke to some guy in the hold, but I couldn't make out the words. Purdue motioned for the huge man to come help another flunky still working with something in

Purdue's car. The Hulk marched off the dock onto the gravel. Out of the back of the Suburban, the dark beast lifted a blanket-wrapped bundle, waving Purdue's partner aside.

Purdue lit a cigar and in the flash of light I recognized Wink. I wondered if they missed Hank yet.

My blood froze in spite of the heat.

Savvy touched my leg. "Oh my God, they're carrying a body."

I narrowed my eyes as I prayed this person wasn't another Haitian. We saw the men escape. Could this be one of the women? Straining hard to see through the dark, I angled to see the face, skin color. All I could see were feet.

And then I recognized those cowboy boots.

"Who is it?" Savannah whispered.

I knelt beside her, moisture from the damp forest floor wetting the knees of my pants. I squinted through the falling darkness. "Oh my God, it's Wayne," I said, a catch in my throat.

She gripped around my waist.

My thoughts raced. He wasn't dead. I'd know. Or rather, I hoped I'd know.

"Holy shit, hon," she said. "What do we do?"

Savvy's concern was spot on. "I don't know," I said under my breath, my chest constricted, eyes glued to those boots. Wayne didn't get blindsided. That concept wouldn't register in my head. He was always the guy who won. My thought processes hit a brick wall as nothing made sense during a time I knew seconds were of the essence.

Savvy tugged on me. "Slade, what now? We don't have a phone!" Her whining, foreign behavior suddenly grated on me like a slow, rusty hinge. "What do we—"

"Stop it. Let me think." I covered my ears with fisted hands.

She let go of me. "We can't go after those guys. Not the two of us. Let's go get help," she begged.

My fingernails now raked the tree that hid me, digging into the bark, repeatedly scraping. "Good idea," I said as I turned to her. "You go do that."

"What about you?"

I refocused on the dock. "I'm not letting that boat out of my sight. Contact the Coast Guard and the sheriff. Drag 'em back if you have to."

She tugged my sleeve. "Come with me, Slade."

I shoved her, knocking her from her squatted position onto her butt. "Go!"

She reluctantly obliged, darted off, fell and cursed.

I glanced toward the cars. Nobody looked our way. I snatched my gaze back to where I thought Savvy was. I heard a faint rustle as she hurried, her departure surprisingly covert.

I shifted my weight to the other knee. Katydids joined the frogs, rising in a crescendo, bouncing around the trees.

A breeze carried a tangy whiff of pluff mud and shellfish from the boat forty yards away. The Black Hulk disappeared into the hold with Wayne slumped motionless over his shoulder. Purdue's cigar's ash glowed in the young evening, and I caught sight of Wink on the bow.

Damn you, Wayne. How stupid to pair up with Purdue's guys. Like they gave a rat's ass about Jamie.

Someone hollered. The shrimp boat's engine coughed. Wink jumped onto the pier and slipped rope from two posts.

No, no, no.

I inched behind a smaller tree closer to the clearing. Wink walked to the stern, checked something, then hopped back aboard.

Bent low, I sprinted to the pier. I hid behind a huge fat piling, praying the boat wouldn't drift.

"What's going on down there?" Purdue said, addressing a scuffling noise in the boat's belly. He descended out of sight.

I hauled my ass straight for the boat now four feet off the dock . . . and leaped. My toe snagged the boat rail, my .38 fell into the water, and I fell headlong into a pile of netting. I kept my face buried in the vinegary rope, staying statue still. My neck wound stung with each hammering heartbeat. I peered up, expecting to find Wink hovering over me. Surely he heard the splash. But he remained at the bow.

Then he turned. I froze. The whites of his eyes reflected bright in the residual light on the shore. I swore he looked straight at me.

Blood pounded in my ears.

He reached into his shirt pocket and drew out a cigarette. The lighter's flame cast an orange, jack-o-lantern glow on his jagged features, black brows and greasy hair flapping over his collar in the breeze.

Afraid my snow-white bandage might act like a beacon, I gritted my teeth as I eased it off, the continual pull stretching skin and stitches. I finished, then balled the dressing and tossed it over the side.

I had no clue what to do now.

The engine fired with a cough and sputter, and the boat cut the dark-green water as it moved out to sea. Geez, I hated dark water.

Life forms bigger than people lived below the surface, and their images had terrorized me since Daddy carried me to an aquarium at age three. The hammerhead hugging the wall of the giant water tank sent me into shrieks. Giant turtles, eels hiding in rocks. All those huge creatures in the deep, below me, hidden, waiting.

The boat rolled and my gut churned. I swallowed hard, willing bile to go back down, praying I could keep a grip . . . and think of a miracle.

It would take Savvy a half hour or more to reach police. Even if by some wonder I freed Wayne, how would we overcome four men who dumped bodies for marsh bait? Was he even conscious? He hadn't exactly strolled on board.

My hopes rose when Purdue hollered, and thumps sounded from below. Was Wayne fighting back? He was resourceful, maybe hiding a weapon, smart about situations like this, right?

My insides flopped about like a beached catfish as I sneaked a peek over the side. The dock shrank into the night. The craft eased to the left, revealing only shadows of scrub vegetation on the bank. No lights meant no people. No help.

I slid back onto the rope, trying not to give up.

The engine noise covered my movement as I slouched in the stiff, foul-smelling netting, drawing some of it over me. A stray piece of what I hoped was dead crustacean dug into my midriff, but I remained cemented in place.

Purdue ascended the ladder. He flipped his cigar butt over the edge. My spirits rose when I heard Wayne swearing in a defiant, guttural tone I'd never heard before, using language he'd never released in my presence.

Dull thuds came up the stairs. "He just woke up, boss. Causing a damn fuss." The Hulk leaned against the railing. "Hit him again or what?"

"Nah," said Purdue. "We'll dump him in an hour. Weight his feet. Don't want the body showing up like that damn Haitian. I still ought to brand you for that, Darryl."

The name didn't fit the big beast.

"Tell 'em you don't know nothin'," the huge man replied. "That's what I told the government woman. Nothin' they can do about that. She ain't come back, either."

Purdue's head rocked back as if acknowledging a reminder. "That's another one we'll take care of. That's the damn nosiest woman I've ever run into." He scowled at his chief assistant. "You screwed the packing shed up, you know. The kid ain't dead."

Darryl slumped, not nearly the threat he appeared on the farm. "He burnt up bad. Might not make it."

Purdue slapped the side of the cabin. I jumped. "Your job is to eliminate threats quick, clean, and hard. You left goddamn loose ends all over the place."

"I didn't have nothin' to do with the cop snooping 'round," he said.

"Goddamn agent," Purdue scoffed. "Like I give a shit about tomatoes. When did they come up with farm police?" He hocked saliva, then spat into the night.

Purdue's hit man could've backhanded him over the side, but instead, the big guy acquiesced to the scolding. Purdue held unbelievable control over his men.

Water splashed the hull as the boat gained speed. Wind whipped hair in my face, and I tried to tuck it under my collar. My nose dripped from the salt air. We were headed way out to sea . . . where it got real deep.

Stars twinkled to life in the clear night sky. The moon hung bright but low. In another hour, it'd rise high enough to light up the place, giving everything a silvery glow. Just in time for dumping a body—maybe two. The thought sent a shiver through me.

Savvy should've reached the sheriff's office by now. How long would it take the Coast Guard to take this seriously, then arrive? How would they even find a lone shrimp boat?

"How many we pickin' up, Mr. Purdue?" Darryl asked.

"Guy said ten workers and as many kilos."

The Hulk whistled. "Pretty good haul."

Purdue nodded toward the floor. "Got those bags secured? Took me a lot of tomatoes to scrape up that kind of cash." He laughed, and Darryl tried to echo the sound, but his effort came out a nervous chuckle, in a deep base.

I'd gotten it all wrong. The gym bags were full of cash, not drugs. Money to purchase slaves and cocaine.

I needed to figure out some sort of plan, even if it was only to toss Wayne and me overboard with something to float on. The image of all that dark water underneath me sent a deep, paralyzing fear through my bones.

"Too many people flapping their damn mouths." Purdue lit another cigar. Smoke spiraled from his lips and dissipated in the breeze. "Martin bringing in the goddamn Gullah kid was a stupid fucking move. Water under the bridge though, huh?" He laughed.

Was Martin a cohort, or someone who crossed the line into dangerous territory in his zeal to help Kamba? I didn't expect the young man to be anything but an avid supporter of the St. Helena Just-Say-No program. Jumper had concerned me more.

Purdue blew out a tunnel of smoke. "That's what he gets for dealing on his own. Liability's gone now." He removed the cigar and picked a piece of tobacco off his tongue. He studied the stuff on his finger. "And nobody steals from me. Hank should've taken care of that insurance idiot by now."

Another jolt of fear coursed up my spine. They'd ordered Hank to kill Teddy. And he'd used his method of choice, fire. I could see the Haitians rising up seeing Hank burn yet another person, after losing Rene's sister just the day before. They murdered Hank for revenge. Of course. They wouldn't have taken the time to tie him up and build a fire.

The Hulk moved to my side of the boat. If he stared hard right, he'd see me.

Darryl continued to stare at the water. "But where we selling tomaters now?"

"Shut up with the questions," Purdue said.

They traded tomato crop and bought drugs and Haitians with the proceeds. Then they most likely distributed the dope amongst tomato boxes in cooled produce trucks for export, from what Doug Rabon said. Or at least that's what I figured, since he was banned from watching when Heyward's crew brought in a crop. Guess we'd stomped through their plans in our own cumbersome way because of Monroe's simple loan audit.

My stomach rumbled, and I pressed hard to mute it.

Purdue twisted back around.

I stiffened.

"Did you pack the cereal like I told you?" he said to Darryl. "Don't need this boat stinking from puking darkies. Last time it took a month to clean the smell."

The big *darkie* he spoke to straightened at the debasement and moved away from the railing.

Take him out, I thought. Purdue was the oldest and least fit aboard, but the most deviant. What I wouldn't give for Darryl to mutiny and toss his boss to the fish.

A hand smothered my mouth. Wink whispered in my ear. "What the hell you doin' here?"

My body quivered with fear. One of the Three Musketeers stared me down, the one I knew the least about.

"Hiding," I said with a whimper.

"Wink? What you doing?" the boss shouted.

"Kickin' this net outta my way. Almost tripped over the shit." He released me and walked toward the others. "Want me to check on that guy down below?" he hollered. "I'm bored outta my damn mind."

"Whatever," Purdue replied. "You won't feel bored when you're guarding a load of new pickers. Those bastards get ornery when they have to change boats."

Wink went below, his footfalls lazy and hard.

I blew out shallow pants; I couldn't draw enough oxygen.

What would Wink do now and why hadn't he already done it? Would he wait until time to chunk Wayne over the edge, then grab me in a flashy display of loyalty? Would he kill me first or let me bob as shark bait? It hit me that Wink didn't need to decide yet. There was no rush. He possessed all the time in the world to handle me.

I covered my mouth and pressed my head against the netting. Jesus, what would happen to Ivy and Zack?

"When we get back, we deal with the lady in the farm office," Purdue said.

"I ain't seen her lately," Darryl said. "Think I ran her off."

"Not the investigator, stupid. The office girl—the one who left. That piece of ass Dawson messed around with."

After Wayne and I sank to the bottom, Savannah would be next. These scum disposed of people like last week's casserole. Office cohorts like Harden Harris now ranked a lot lower on my crap scale. My calves cramped, the pain growing, throbbing into my hips.

"The current girl's not as bright as her sister was," he said. "All I gotta do is threaten doing something to the first one and this girl pisses her pants."

What? Savvy had no sister.

Darryl farted and it brought low snickers from the rest.

Purdue shook his head. "How'd you like to live in Alabama or Mississippi? How about Louisiana? We need to find another port. Too dangerous here now. They'll come looking for their agent."

Hulk pushed off the wood edge. "I kinda likes Alabama. Got a cousin in Mobile."

"Yeah," Purdue said. "I'll find us a place by next week." He pointed his cigar at the flunky. "I aim to run a tighter ship there, you hear?"

The realization struck me. They spoke about Melanie . . . Savvy's old clerk. My bet was on her handling the third signature in the loan file. With only two women in the office, that meant sweet, blonde Raye *with an e* was sister to the bitch who'd doctored the paperwork, put loan money into Purdue's pockets, and screwed Teddy.

Savvy would kick herself from here to Atlanta when she found out.

If I lived long enough to tell her.

Wink's clunky boots against stair tread heralded his appearance. "He was almost loose. Somebody did a half-assed job."

Darryl took a slow, measured step, then faked a lunge at Wink, like a kid on the playground daring another bully.

Wink jerked. "Wish you'd do your job, you lazy fuck."

The Hulk appeared taller and broader than before, as if the insult gave him permission to expand to his full height. Wink was an idiot to confront someone with fifty pounds on him. Was he showboating, planning to dispose of his competition? Then he'd tell Purdue about me and prove himself the prince of the hired help. They'd laugh. Have their way with me, or kill Wayne in front of me, or weight us down to the bottom of the sea.

Every cell in me retracted, trying to retreat where there was no place to go.

"I already beat your ass once, Spic," Darryl said. "Took you a week to lift a bucket of tomatoes."

"I ain't never done tomatoes. That's for darkies," Wink said, tossing his chin up like an exclamation mark on the slur.

Darryl leaped forward. Purdue hopped out of the way.

A shadow flew from the hold, shoving Darryl into Wink, then Purdue. A mass of writhing, grunting bodies rocked the boat. Boots and fists kicked wood, bone, and flesh amidst painful grunts and cries. Purdue leaned against a mast and grinned at the ensuing melee.

The scrap headed my way. I threw the rope camouflage off, stood, then backed to the bow.

No place to hide now. The moon hung high in the night sky and illuminated me. Purdue's eyes spread wide with recognition.

Someone landed on his back at Purdue's feet. Focused on Wink and Darryl, the fighter didn't see Purdue grab a fishing gaff. Moonlight shone on Wayne as he stood. Purdue raised both arms, lunar glow showing the hook poised like death's own scythe.

Chapter 33

I CHARGED Purdue, both hands clutching the gaff, and knocked him against the gunwale. He cursed and fought to wrench the pole free. I stomped on his foot and then shoved a knee toward his groin. He twisted left. Too late to adjust, my knee glanced off him and struck the boat, and an agonizing jolt shot through my thigh. Wink pulled me away. "Stay out of the way!"

Wayne and Darryl, locked together, collided with me. "Sla—" Wayne began to speak, but Darryl planted a right hook to his jaw and he fell back.

I lifted a chain with a large hook on the end and tried to swing it, and amazingly caught Darryl across the knees as I could lift it no higher. He stumbled, going down on one leg only to quickly rise. Wayne connected with a punch to the man's chin.

The boat's engine stopped. Louis rushed out of the steering house wielding a six-inch hunting blade. "Dis time I gut you for good, bitch."

I dodged the knife. Wink grasped Louis' arm and twisted until the weapon clattered to the floor. Louis spun back and kicked Wink into Darryl, who turned and connected a punch. Louis retrieved his knife. The knife glinted in the light as it sliced across my abdomen.

I staggered, holding the wound. The idiot laughed as he stepped in to finish the job. Wink crashed a wooden pole across Louis' head. The bastard collapsed and lay still.

Blood seeped moist under my fingers. Muffled anarchy rained around me as I stood dumbfounded, studying my injury in a surreal moment. Someone rammed into me, and I fell on my back inside the wheelhouse. A high-pitched whine filled my ears. Shit, was this how someone bled out?

Blood soaked my once light-blue shirt and oozed toward my jeans. The diameter spread. I splayed my fingers across it tighter and lay back on the floor. Oh God. I was dying. This wasn't fair.

Wayne's pain-filled grunt outside forced me to sit up. He couldn't fight them alone, and I sure wasn't coming to an end on a stinking fishing boat. I yanked open the cabinets around me, rummaging through life vests for a weapon. Then moonlight glinted off the radio set.

Wringing a dial and punching the handset's button with a bloodied finger, I shrieked, "Help! Federal agent in need of urgent assistance.

Someone. Anyone." After yelling across several channels, my wilted voice scared me. Was standing still or moving worse when one bled to death?

Purdue filled the doorway, his eyes burning with hate.

This catastrophe was all this bastard's fault. I dove, my shoulder aimed dead center of his belly. My weight carried him outside into the railing.

Darryl twisted around. My bout of aggression evaporated as his monster hands reached for me. I waited for my bones to snap in his grip. Instead, he heaved me over the side.

The fall took forever.

I flashed back to the day I was six, and my dad made me jump off the high dive at the community pool. Drop, drop, drop, then splash, sinking until I touched the bottom and pushed up to the surface. Except this time, the water was pitch-black. There was no bottom. Nothing to grab, touch, or swim to between me and an unseen land.

Water filled my nostrils. Salt burned my eyes, searing my fresh wound. Heart racing, I kicked against the invisible enemy, and finally broke the surface, coughing and sputtering. I fought to stay above the choppy waves, uncertain whether the metallic taste of the water was my own blood.

"Slade!" Wayne shouted.

I swam frantically for the boat. "Here," I yelled. "To your left!"

A muzzle flash blew away with the wind as a bullet zipped through water a mere foot from me. Another spat water to my left. Shit. I struggled to stay afloat, panicking where to go.

Wayne hollered my name again. As I opened my mouth to respond, water sloshed in and started to choke me.

Someone shouted, "Jump!"

After hearing a splash, I stroked frantic, away from the boat. I focused on moving, worried any second a bullet would find its mark in my back.

An explosion ripped the night air.

I screamed, jerking around as I groped, splashing. A wave pounded into me, sending me beneath the surface. Still trying to shout, disoriented which way was up, I fought, reaching for air. A second blast flashed while I was submerged, its force flushing water up my nose. My lungs burned for oxygen as I breaststroked away from where I'd seen the orange fireball.

I shot up to the night air, hitting a splintered plank.

Fiery pieces of wood and shrapnel fell with soft, delayed splashes. A chunk of boat bombed the sea's surface with a thud six feet from me. Gulping a huge breath, I dropped below the surface again, my eyes scrunched shut.

Floating suspended in the liquid darkness, arms and legs extended, I dared a look. Pitch-black. Something soft brushed my leg. My heart leaped, and I slammed my eyes shut again, more afraid to see a shark come at me than one catching me by surprise. How long before all the pieces of the *Magnolia Lady* fell? Who would I see when I surfaced? The pressure in my lungs blossomed to pain. How much longer could I hold it? I tried to think about fields, pastures, anything connected to dirt instead of water. I longed to taste air.

Chest burning, I broke the surface and sucked in the warm night. Twisting, I panted and gazed at burning lumber and debris. "Wayne!"

I swallowed a scream as I paddled toward the flames and wreckage, darting left, right, hunting. God, no, don't take him. Please let him be alive. Where the hell were the life vests?

Fuck, I was going to drown out here.

Struggling to gather my wits, I scouted for something to grab. Nothing remained large enough to climb onto that wasn't on fire. My shouts shifted to pleas, still screaming for Wayne.

A body drifted toward me—Louis. Without legs. I swam aside to let it bob past. I screamed louder for Wayne.

An ice chest drifted nearby. I grasped at it time after time, but it rolled under my grip. I punched it out of my space. Behind it floated a seat cushion with one strap intact. Tucking my arm through it, I leaned on my makeshift life preserver and wailed.

My throat hurt, but I bawled harder, calling for Ivy, then Zack. "I'm so sorry. So, so sorry." The damn waves kept choking—gagging me. "I don't want to die, God. Please don't do this." Head pounding, I dug deep and screeched, "I hope you're burning in hell, Purdue!"

I reached across my torso, cradling myself. Shivers and scary flutters of weakness dragged me to the edge of an anxiety attack as I faced the fact I would never see my children again.

And something might eat me.

A hand gripped my shoulder. I spun. Wink's welt-covered face stared back.

I belted him, relentless with my free fist. "You bastard—" Water sloshed in my mouth. He moved from my reach. The blazing sting in my side made me wonder if my gash ripped wider.

Another arm encircled my flailing one. Captured, I writhed, clutching my cushion, expecting to be yanked off it and held under.

"Settle down!" boomed the voice I never thought I'd hear again.

My senses caught up with my fear. "Oh God, I thought you were—" I froze. Adrenaline spiked through my body as I ensnared Wayne's neck.

Then I slung around, empowered. "You son-of-a-bitch!" I screamed at Wink.

Wayne jerked me, squeezing my upper arm like a vise. "Slade! Stop! He's not the enemy."

"Hang on." Wink swam off, retrieved a life vest, and swam back. He shoved the vest toward me. "Here, take it."

I punched it back. "I don't want anything from you."

Wayne grabbed the vest and forced my hand through one of the holes. I quivered with fright and pain. Wayne drifted around in front of me. "Are you all right?"

"Humph," I said, my pulse slowing. Wayne seemed fuzzy. "I thought they'd . . ."

"A few loose teeth. Haven't fought like that in years." He smiled. Wink did, too. Their grins didn't make sense. Not when we were marooned at sea.

Then I snapped alert as Wayne lightly slapped my face. "Open your eyes. Are you hurt?" he asked.

I blinked and tried to see without the blur. "Louis pulled out a hunting knife."

Shock flashed across his face. "What? Where?" He started searching, trying to hunt around the edges of the life vest, but most of me hid below the dark water.

I peered down to show him my spot, and my stomach's contents erupted into my throat. Alarms returned about the miles of water beneath me, behind me, all around me. "It's across my ribs."

He floated me horizontal in the water and lifted my shirt best he could with the vest. "Oh, babe, we've got to get you to a hospital. You're bleeding like mad."

"Don't try to make me feel better or anything," I said after a cough.

"Woman, you're damn lucky," Wink said, floating closer.

"I don't feel all that lucky." The shivering was constant now. Through the chatter of teeth, a groan escaped. "Don't trust him, Wayne. He's Purdue's man."

Wayne drew me closer. "He's an ICE agent, babe. He cut me loose. He also blew up the shrimp boat, which probably saved our asses."

Wink coughed as water hit him in the face. He tried to grin for my sake. "My bosses are gonna have a cow."

The mental shift from thinking him an asshole to believing him a good guy didn't compute. He'd terrified me that night on the shed roof.

My limbs felt heavy. My breathing turned shallower, but I still recalled the farm, the shed, those Haitians. "You let that girl die," I tried to say. "You let them burn those migrant workers. What kind of an agent—" Water sloshed in my face. I coughed out brine. Bile rose and fell in my throat again.

Wink bobbed effortlessly, waiting until I paused to rest. "I've seen no one die and hurt no innocents, and that's the truth. Heyward just started trusting me. Hell, I chased that kid and Teddy Dawson off the boat so

Heyward wouldn't catch 'em, or he'd have them trussed up to dump tonight with your man here."

"You tried to hunt me down at the farm," I said weakly, that evening still vivid enough to include Wink's search for me in the trees around the camp.

"Lady," he said, "I was doing my damnedest to find you and get you outta—"

Then Wink was gone, debris making a lazy spin in his wake.

I glanced at Wayne, scared, waiting for something to snag our legs. "Oh no," I whispered, scanning for what could be sharks after my blood. My wound had risked us all. Wayne swam to the spot where Wink disappeared, gyrating one way, then another, searching.

Wink popped up ten feet away sputtering and wrestling with the Black Hulk, face-to-face. They disappeared below the water again, in a splashing fury.

"Stay here!" Wayne ordered, like I had someplace else to go. He swam to where the two men went under and dove. The quiet chilled me to my core.

They emerged. Wink's fists pummeled Darryl's upper back as if beating a frozen side of beef. Wayne jumped into the frenzy and all three went under. Water churned like catfish spawning, swirling around without breaking the surface. Then it stopped.

For some stupid reason, I counted.

At fifteen, only two men surfaced.

"Thank God," I said.

"I think . . . I better count bodies while you stop her bleeding," Wink said, panting hard.

"Smart idea." Wayne swam toward me, then worked at readjusting the vest around me tighter.

As much as I didn't want to, I cried. Tears fell for Teddy, Savvy, my kids, and me, for the whole damn lot of us. I had found Wayne, but we were far from safe.

The lawman touched my cheek to hold my focus. "We're going to be okay. Think you can . . . Slade?"

His words didn't make sense, like they rang in a long tunnel. I asked him to repeat himself, but he didn't understand. Ringing rushed into my ears and my body lifted. No more worries about sinking. No more fear of dark water. None of it mattered anymore, and I was all right with that as a calm encircled me.

I came to once, the back of my head resting on Wayne's shoulder, my feet floating before me. The vest wrapped too tight around my midsection. I tried to complain, but the bright summer moon faded to black before I could.

Someone lifted me. When would the angels arrive? Surely they served hot chips and beer in heaven. The wet feeling left. No more worries about fish. Dying wasn't so bad. Just wish I could describe it to the kids.

I opened my eyes in a room that pulsed with lights and the hum of machines, the beeps of electronics. A strange man about my age held my wrist. A handsome dude. I smiled and moved my legs, then sensed my nakedness under the blanket.

He spoke over his shoulder. "Your girl's awake, y'all." He laid my arm back down. "Try not to move, ma'am. That's a healthy scratch you got there." He moved aside.

Wayne stepped next to the cot and leaned over me, his dark hair combed back slick, still wet. I liked him better with it swept across his forehead. "You scared the crap out of me, Butterbean."

"I'm not a damn vegetable." My voice squeezed out raspy, painful.

"We're on a Coast Guard boat, going back," he explained.

I swallowed, thirsty, dry as a cracker in a Saudi desert. "Did they pick up anyone else?"

"Not a damn one of 'em made it, Slade. Don't worry about it."

Remembering Louis' slice to my midsection, my hand wandered toward the wound, but Wayne stopped me. "Don't. It's not stitched, just bandaged. We're getting you to a hospital. You went into shock."

"I thought I died."

"Well, you didn't," he said with an exaggerated gruffness. "And shut up about it."

"Yeah," I said from behind closed lids. "Love you, too."

Chapter 34

IT WASN'T UNTIL dawn that the hospital staff let me doze more than a catnap. My ribs took twenty stitches, my neck a few fresh ones. They woke me for supper. I gave Monroe and his black-and-blue face my pineapple gelatin. Savvy slipped me a chocolate chip milkshake.

Evidently, Wayne had remained around like furniture in the pastel room and asked Monroe to bring him a change of clothes from the motel.

Various styles of cop came and went, with their lists of questions. My cadre of agricultural buddies covered most of the bases with them so I could rest.

Later Savvy and I talked. Tears in her eyes, she told me she hated the way Teddy'd died, but admitted he did it to himself. No doubt she'd have trust issues with men for a while.

I called the kids and my parents, informing them of some facts, but not much more than an accident had landed me in the hospital for a night. Mom wanted to come down from Charleston, but Wayne talked her out of it with personal assurances as to my safety. The Amicks demanded they continue to pamper Ivy. Ivy whispered she held a detailed history of Dolly and Beau, her sleuthing having paid off. Zack said he'd return home as soon as I did. I smiled for a solid hour. He sounded so much better.

The doc released me the next morning, and Wayne argued with me all the way outside.

"I'm carting your butt back home," he said, holding the car door open for me.

"No," I said, trying not to twist to see him. "The drive is two and a half hours."

"Not in my car." He shut the door and came around to slide behind the wheel.

My glower drew no reaction from him. "The kids don't need to see me like this. You need to finish this case, and Savvy is—"

"Savvy is fine," he said.

"Take me to your motel room. I have friends to help me here . . . close friends."

A briny marsh odor filtered through the AC vents, a pungent yet natural smell that reminded me of my old Charleston home and usually lifted my spirits. I donned sunglasses to avoid the glint off the water, and measured the impact of the last three days.

Ends still dangled, as Purdue would say. The government would now collect its loan through insurance and foreclosure with no more Heywards around to pay. Dan didn't die in a shrimp boat explosion, but since a now-dead Hank probably killed Dan at very dead Purdue's direction, it was a moot point. They never identified who shot at me, but I let Teddy's death serve as closure on that issue.

At the motel, equipped with antibiotics and painkillers, I propped up on the bed, bored I wasn't working, but sort of glad my stiff and battered body had some time to regroup. My knee had swollen larger than Monroe's. The air conditioner came on. The low drone soothed Wayne and me into much needed naps.

Later, Wayne called Wink, and practically joined at the hip, they went out to grab dinner. Monroe came over from his room, forehead still bandaged and still nursing a minor headache. Savvy came and played nursemaid to us both. I still moved like the Tin Man from Oz.

The guys returned with shrimp, fries, and coleslaw. Wink dressed spiffy in khakis, a button down shirt, and loafers. He would've walked right by me on the street, and I'd have never known him. "You clean up nice, Wink."

He laid out the food on a table against the window. "You can call me Mark now. Mark Sanderson."

"But you're—"

"My mother's Mexican and my father's from North Carolina."

We finished our meal. Monroe returned to his room. Wayne threw wrappers in the trash as he asked Wink questions about how ICE would close their end of the case, and I sat quietly, recuperating, thinking, almost dozing off at one point. Savvy excused herself, making an extra effort to exchange niceties with Wink. I thought I saw business cards exchanged.

Once she closed the door, Wink cleared his throat. "Have one more piece of info I feel you'll need before I head back to Atlanta."

"Can you nail Evan?" I asked snapping back to attention.

He gave me a crooked grin. "No, but your girl in the agriculture office is part of all this."

My hand rose to my mouth.

Wayne squinted. "Savannah Conroy? You sure?"

Wink quickly shook his head. "No, no. Not your friend. The clerk. Raye somebody, I believe. Saw her a couple of times at the farm. Once she hid when Evan showed up to check whatever it is you people check."

I almost rose off the bed. "You're just telling us now?"

His mouth curled to the right. "You were pretty beat up yesterday,

Slade, and this guy," he nodded toward Wayne, "was exhausted and only interested in your well-being. One day more didn't hurt."

I recalled Purdue's boat conversation, especially about Teddy getting a piece of some girl's ass. So Melanie and Raye were sisters. Reaching for the phone, I hit speed dial only for Wayne to take the phone away. "Let me take it from here, Butterbean. You're on leave. I'll tell you when it's okay to inform your girlfriend. If you want any chance of nailing the last two people involved in this case, let me tie up the loose ends right."

The word *right* didn't set well with me, but I'd promised to listen to more of his instruction as I coped in my new investigative role. I'd sort of paid a price for running renegade, even if we did solve the case.

"Today your cut-up, shot-up butt stays right here," he continued, but I didn't hear the rest. I awoke later to find Wink gone, and Wayne snuggled next to me, but I couldn't drift back to sleep. In the quiet, all I could think about was dark water and bodies.

"OH, GEEZ," I moaned the next morning, contemplating a strategy to roll out of bed.

Wayne came over and held out a hand. "Good morning, Butterbean. It's almost eleven. I've already been out and back."

Twinges of pain darted throughout my body as I hoisted myself upright, holding onto him for support. I was so glad the kids couldn't see me this way.

He enfolded me and lightly kissed my cheek. "Why don't you stay here today?"

"I need to see Kamba." I took a step. "A hot bath will limber me up."

"You can't get in the shower, remember? I offer a mighty fine sponge bath, though."

A snicker escaped through my grimace. "No. Give me a sec, though." I walked two steps. "Take that back. Give me a bunch of seconds."

The swelling in my knee had diminished, yet I still hobbled. I'd amassed more stitches in forty-eight hours than my whole family had seen in a lifetime. Wayne dug around his suitcase and laid one of his polo shirts on the bed next to my slacks. "What's that?" I asked.

"Your shirts are all messed up," he said. "Bloodied, cut, dirty . . ." He held the pastel shirt up. "This is better anyway. It's not so fitted. Come on, hold up your arm here—"

"I need a bra first."

"Right." He rummaged through my bag, then stopped. "Um, it's in a hospital bag. Covered with blood."

Great. "Then give me one of your T-shirts, too," I said.

When I came out of the bathroom, Wayne was hanging up the phone. "Anyika said we could come by, but she wasn't sure Kamba would see us."

I sat on the corner of the bed, the big polo puddling around me. The milk crate preacher was still mourning Martin. First his son and daughter-in-law and now his adopted son, gone due to drugs.

We grabbed breakfast at a drive-through and headed to St. Helena one last time, to see Kamba. En route, Wayne gave me the nod to divulge information to Savvy. She picked up on the first ring and asked quickly how I was, her impatience to know more about the case's final details almost palpable.

"Wayne finished interviewing Raye, Savvy. I take it Evan hasn't come in yet?"

"Nope, putting him on AWOL, the sorry piece of crap. And as soon as I can get the paperwork processed, he's fired. So did Wayne give you the green light to tell me anything?"

"Well, let me start that Teddy was screwing one of your clerks, hon. I heard Purdue talk about it on the boat."

She spit back a response. "Which one?"

"Not sure," I threw back, knowing the momentum helped her cope. "Melanie and Raye are sisters."

"Well, shit. I can only get my hands on Raye. What if it's not her?"

"Raye'll faint before you finish your first sentence. Purdue mentioned threats against Melanie when I was on the boat. Poor Raye probably fears for her sister. Let her be."

She stopped talking.

"Melanie's probably dead," I said.

"Yeah, I get that."

I thought a moment on how harshly to paint Savvy's assistant manager. "Evan was innocently conned on the loan signatures. His biggest fault, in my opinion anyway, was he let you take the rap, probably hoping I'd bail you out."

"Well, shit," she said. "Who says the state director won't think I orchestrated the whole staff?"

"Because there's no proof against you." I wished I could see the look on her face. "And by the way, speaking of proof, we found the file. Raye had it. Teddy destroyed the notes in the file about the crop inspections, by the way—the ones you wrote up and never did."

"He still covered my butt."

"He had a soft spot for you, Savvy," I added.

"I know how hard that is for you to say, hon."

"Yeah," I replied.

JUMPER GREETED us when we arrived at Kamba's. Huge, bright white bandages shined on both his dark arms, another on the side of his neck. Kamba led everyone into the house, in better spirits than I expected, probably due to Jamie's return. "Jumper saved Doug Rabon when that packing shed burned," Kamba said.

I winced as Wayne studied the man's wounds. "Looks painful."

"Beats the alternative," Jumper said. His stare hung on me a second too long. "Some people have been burned and not survived to talk about it."

I held his gaze. "You're so right."

"I can live with a few scars," he added, then he clapped once. "Well, enough of that." He held out his hands to make an announcement. "I'm working full-time for Mr. Mel Cribb now. At Sweetbriar."

Kamba's smile of admiration brightened my day.

An hour flew by too soon, and after the congratulations and lemonade, Wayne and I headed to the car. "When are you going back to your street corner in town?" I asked Kamba as he opened my door.

He shook his head. "I'm leaving that alone for now. Think I'll give talks about Gullah history. Maybe write a book. You nipped a lot of the drugs in the bud, Ms. Slade."

"Not sure I can take credit, but I'm relieved. Jamie learned a good lesson from this. Probably better than any of us could've accomplished preaching at him," I answered.

Anyika ran out and gave me a pale-blue conjure bag. "Take dis back wit you."

I hesitated.

"It be good luck, honey," she said, her belly rolling up and down with laughter. "Put it under your pillow."

"Don't forget what I taught you about haints, too, Ms. Slade," Kamba said as I sat in the car and buckled up. "Your dream ghost should rest easy if you follow my directions."

"Still wish I knew who gave me the bad conjure bags," I said, tucking the fresh one in my purse.

Kamba's wrinkles gave way to a knowing grin. "Suspect whoever is long gone. Not good to dwell on the bad of the past."

I gave the credit to Teddy just to give myself closure. He'd have pulled such a stunt. "Thanks, Kamba," I said. "Take care of those boys. And I'll buy the first copy of your book."

WAYNE AND MONROE were already leaving the state director's office when I rushed in. An empty seat awaited me across from Dubose, who waited behind her desk. I might as well have been given a lone chair under a light bulb.

Margaret Dubose had the answer back from the U.S. Attorney with recommendations on how to address the legalities of our investigation. Her manicured nails rubbed side to side on her desk blotter. "This investigation is inconceivably . . . what's the word?"

A string of adjectives pinged around in my head. Harebrained, ludicrous, stupid, irresponsible? The most absurd piece of bumbling lunacy she'd ever seen? I knew more than she did about the past two weeks, but I feared how much had trickled to her ears. The shed for one. Please, don't mention the night on the shed.

"Remarkable," she said, pursing her lips. "That's the word."

I exhaled. I could do remarkable.

"I thanked Mr. Prevatte for his work in Beaufort with a financial token of appreciation in his next paycheck," she said. "Mr. Largo will receive a letter of commendation for his file. You, however, my dear, are a different story."

Uh, oh.

"Raye Tankersley is to be terminated," she said. "The U.S. Attorney won't pursue criminal action against Evan Koon, and they aren't interested in Raye. The connection is too tenuous."

"Doesn't seem right," I said.

"Pardon?" Dubose asked.

Wayne would tell me my words were fruitless. But I'd go to my grave hating Evan's escape from accountability. "He shouldn't get off that easy," I said. Justice was blind in dealing with that man. Out of all the tainted, crooked, loathsome individuals in this madness, the one that got away belonged to Agriculture, under my jurisdiction.

"Out of our hands, Slade," Dubose said. "You'll live much longer accepting that. He's being terminated as well since he hasn't reported back to work. Move on."

I almost felt a cowboy boot nudge me under the table. That was it; the results of an investigation that left me scarred, literally and figuratively. Nothing in our bureaucracy stopped, changed, or took a break as we'd spent time on sinking boats, in a slave compound, and in the emergency room. I'd lost and regained a close friend. Lost and regained a lover. Seen enough people die to cast a Hollywood slasher flick.

"Slade." Dubose said my name without a period, like she held a lot more to say.

Here it came. The tongue-lashing. My heart fell into my still-recuperating gut. "Yes, ma'am?"

She leaned forward on her desk. "You have an overkill tendency, my dear. Often in spite of the good common sense God gave you."

I settled in, poised, waiting for her chastising shot.

"And it almost got you killed. It's a good thing I requested Mr. Largo to watch you. Assigning you to Monroe was an attempt to curb your zest and keep you out of trouble. Apparently you're hard to bridle. A big change from your Charleston days, I hear."

My face grew hot. Now I understood why Wayne kept trying to send me home from Beaufort.

"There's an art and a wisdom in selecting your battles, choosing when to throw yourself in harm's way. I'll bow to your determination and spirit this time, but we have Mr. Largo and his kind to take the bullets. Is that clear?"

"Yes, ma'am."

Then she smiled. "That said . . . I thank you. And I'm sure Savannah Conroy thanks you. Just function with a little less mayhem next time." She lowered her chin slightly. "I'd hate to lose you, Slade."

At the mention of Savvy, I opened my mouth to speak, but she held up a finger. "Ms. Conroy's getting a letter of reprimand. No discussion."

And on that final note, Dubose dismissed me.

Wayne stood in my office making calls. Monroe had returned to his divison. As I rounded the corner toward the restroom, my nemesis Harden Harris blocked my way.

"You're a damn liability, you know that? If that woman thinks she's going to reward you for playing a fool down there with your girlfriend, she's got another thing coming."

I tried to ease by him. He snared my upper arm. "You put the last state director in jail. He was a good friend of mine. I haven't forgotten that."

I lowered my voice. "I haven't either. It's been less than a year. The statute of limitations hasn't expired, so don't make threats." I looked toward my arm. "Hands off."

Instead he gripped harder. "Evan's a good boy. Savannah Conroy's head should've rolled for the shitload of crap down there. This is politics."

Wayne appeared and knocked the man's hand off me. "Care to deal with me, Harris?"

"She's a loose cannon," he said. "Especially with a damn skirt in the director's chair."

Wayne took a half step toward him. "I'll be a loose cannon if I see you touch her again."

"Evan broke the law," I said, now certain the communication taking place between Columbia and Beaufort had channeled betwixt Harden and Evan. "He deserved more than he got."

Harris shoved open the entrance to the ladies' room before he checked himself and turned right to the men's.

"He won't do anything," said Wayne, staring after him. "I won't let him."

I dared wrap him in a hug for anyone to see. "Of course you won't, lawman."

Over Wayne's shoulder I could see Monroe watching from down the hall, a smile on his face, as if he had all the time in the world.

Chapter 35

DOLLY WALKED the kids outside as I pulled into her drive after work. Daddy had hugged Zack hard before returning him to my oversight last night. According to my father, they enjoyed a fruitful two weeks. My little man seemed back to normal as he punched Ivy before climbing in the car, my daughter's returning fist whiffling empty air.

Dolly brought out Zack's backpack. "Your stomach healing okay, Slade?" She studied me. "You appear a bit tuckered, hon."

"I'm doing all right, ma'am. You busy?"

She tucked a curl behind her ear. "No. What you need?"

"You got a bottle of wine available? The cheapest brand you've got. I'll replace it."

"Let me get you a good bottle. Bourbon doesn't give you as bad a headache, though."

I grinned and shook my head. "It isn't for drinking. That's why it needs to be cheap."

She soon returned with a grocery store brand. Handing me the bottle, she showed puzzlement. "You cooking with it? That's all I'd ever use this stuff for."

"No, ma'am. Hop on in. Got an errand, and I think you'll appreciate it more than me."

"I love secrets," she said. Her apron still on, she slid into the backseat with Zack and fastened her belt. "This is exciting, isn't it?" she said, poking Zack in the ribs.

"Yes, ma'am," he replied. In the short time he'd been back, I'd never seen a happier child. Daddy's personal attention, the same kind I'd received at Zack's age, usually from behind a fishing pole, seemed to have tapped the sweeter side of my boy. He was the same Zack who'd curled up on a sofa with me before his father died.

Ivy crawled in the front, eyeing me with a wary look. "Where we going, Momma?"

"You'll see," I said.

Ivy had spent the last two weeks sleuthing for information on Dolly's relationship with Beau. My daughter evolved from her brush with danger last year with a keen sense of proactive curiosity. She craved answers to questions, deciding it more comfortable to snoop and intercept the solutions rather than just be told or wait to find out. Beau's supposed haunting of our home became her excuse to test those sleuthing skills. She would pester Dolly until she alienated the dear woman. I saw myself in my child, overdoing, charging ahead thinking she has the right without paying attention to what might be collateral damage in her wake. Time for Ivy to close her case, too.

We drove into a tiny cemetery outside the town of Chapin. I carried the bottle to the grave site of Beau Wessinger and motioned for Dolly to stand beside me. Top unscrewed, I poured splashes on the grass, about a foot in front of the tombstone. "Kamba said to give you what you needed, Beau. Here it is." Then I passed the half empty bottle to Dolly.

She grinned impishly at Ivy, who hung back a step, suspicious.

"Wish Buddy was out here with us," Dolly said.

"I thought Mr. Amick didn't like Beau?" my daughter asked, then covered her mouth.

Dolly drew Ivy to her. "Sugar baby, Beau was Buddy's best friend." She snickered. "They used to throw back a few, drinking stuff not much better than this."

Ivy's face still shined from embarrassment. "I thought Beau was a secret . . ."

"Lover?" Dolly asked slyly.

Ivy broke eye contact. "Yes, ma'am."

"I figured you thought that with all the questions you asked. Baby, I was more jealous of Buddy and Beau than the other way around. I often thought Beau dated me just to mess with Buddy. Turns out, that's why Buddy proposed. He won my hand, but it broke his heart to watch Beau drink himself to death." She brushed Ivy's hair out of her face. "He doesn't like to talk about those memories, dear."

Dolly tipped the bottle until it emptied. "Rest easy, Beau," she said. "Next time you get a powerful thirst, just let me know. I'll send Buddy to the store for you."

"Amen," I said. Now maybe he'd haunt her dreams instead of mine when he needed that refill.

After dropping Dolly off at her place and feeding the kids, I relaxed on the back porch with an iced tea, sifting through the accumulated mail.

Zack came out on the porch, our cat Madge in a hug. "Momma?"

"Come on out, kid. Have a seat. I missed you so much."

He settled in a rocker, his feet not touching the ground except when the chair tilted forward. "I'm proud of you," he said, stroking the cat.

I laid down the bills and kept rocking, both of us watching the lake. "How come?"

"We don't have a daddy anymore, and you do both jobs now."

"I love taking care of you."

"Yeah. Grandpa said I could've lost a momma, too."

"Really?" I marveled, seeing how close Daddy danced around the truth.

"Yes, ma'am. He said I was lucky to have Ivy, too, but I'm not telling her. She'd never let me forget it."

I suppressed a laugh and motioned my seven-year-old onto my lap, Madge and all. With no one else around, he let me snuggle. I kissed the side of his head. He pretended not to notice.

Two minutes later, he hopped off my lap and went inside to annoy Ivy. I kept the cat, each stroke across her downy coat taking me to a calm place. My eyes slid shut.

Savvy had cornered me once in the hospital. As we waited, spent, she rubbed my leg, concerned about my welfare, hunting for lighter topics to discuss. "So, you've got two men hungry for you. My, my. The Special Projects Representative has a social calendar."

"Oh, Savvy, not now," I'd said.

She straightened magazines on the table beside her. "What are you going to do?"

"Nothing to do. I like Wayne," I said, throwing her the only right answer in my book. "Monroe's a dear friend, and he's blurring the distinction."

"You sure?" she asked.

"Of course," I said, with the right amount of shock.

She analyzed me from under slanted lids.

I opened my eyes to stop the memory. A frog leaped on the sliding glass door next to me. Darkness had fallen. Nudging the concrete patio with my foot, I rocked back and forth as I listened to the soothing sounds of the lake, happy to at last be home.

Acknowledgements

As secluded as a writer is in her storytelling, she is not an island, and a book is not a one-woman production.

My family sings my praises to anyone who will listen. Bless you Gary, Nanu, Stephen and Tara. Also to my parents, Dave and Fran, and my new extended family, Phylis and Anthony, all who've worked hard to open the eyes of many new Carolina Slade fans.

My critique family ranges from Sussex to Australia, Tucson to Canada, France to Galveston, and of course, South Carolina. Barrie Kibble, Sidney Blake, Sharon Pennington, Jake Steele, Benjamin Hall and others in the Well. Bill Kaliher, Steve Vassey, Louis Grubb, Melinda Cotton and the rest of the crew with SCWW, not to mention the intensely gifted Betsy George. You made me recognize the darlings to discard, and the gems to polish. Thanks to Pat Van Wie for helping me see the obvious. Hugs to the ladies at Bell Bridge Books for their phenomenal hand-holding. Thanks to my FundsforWriters fan base who have defined me over the last decade. You've shaped my world.

Finally, to the citizens of rural South Carolina, and particularly Beaufort County. I express sincere appreciation for the use of your rich region as the backdrop for this novel. You are a hidden treasure in a state already steeped in fertile history. I pray I did you justice.

About C. Hope Clark

C. Hope Clark was born and reared in the South, from Mississippi to South Carolina with a few stints in Alabama and Georgia. The granddaughter of a Mississippi cotton farmer, Hope holds a B.S. in Agriculture with honors from Clemson University and 25 years' experience with the U. S. Department of Agriculture to include awards for her management, all of which enable her to talk the talk of Carolina Slade, the protagonist in most of her novels. Her love of writing, however, carried her up the ranks to the ability to retire young, and she left USDA to pen her stories and magazine features.

Hope is married to a 30-year veteran of federal law enforcement, a Senior Special Agent, now a private investigator. They met on a bribery investigation within the U.S. Department of Agriculture, the basis for the opening scene to A LOWCOUNTRY BRIBE. Hope and her special agent live on the rural banks of Lake Murray outside of Chapin, South Carolina, forever spinning tales on their back porch, bourbon and coke in hand, when not tending a loveable flock of Orpington and Dominiquer hens.

She also currently manages FundsforWriters.com, a weekly newsletter service she founded that reaches almost 50,000 writers to include university professors, professional journalists and published mystery authors. Writer's Digest has recognized the site in its annual 101 Best Web Sites for Writers for a dozen years.

She's published in The Writer Magazine, Writer's Digest, Chicken Soup, Next Step Magazine, College Bound Teen, Voices of Youth Advocates (VOYA), TURF Magazine, Landscape Management and other trade and online publications. She speaks at several writers' conferences a year. Hope is a member of Sisters in Crime, Mystery Writers of America, EPIC, and MENSA.

Website - www.chopeclark.com
Twitter - www.twitter.com/hopeclark
Facebook - www.facebook.com/chopeclark
About.me - http://about.me/hopeclark
Editor, FundsforWriters, www.fundsforwriters.com

CPSIA information can be obtained
at www.ICGtesting.com
Printed in the USA
LVHW031703020721
691402LV00002B/83